RIDERS ON THE STORM

From their hiding place, Jutta and Frida watched the men searching about the barrow with lanterns. Suddenly there came a rumble of hooves and a rush of wind.

Frida dragged Jutta to the ground. "Myrkriddir!" she cried. "Stay down! Don't look at them!"

The storm broke with thunder, explosions of lightning, and wild cries and laughter that chilled Jutta to the bone. Turning her head, she saw horses and riders capering in midair above her, each figure glowing with unearthly blue light. Manes, tails, hair, and cloaks flew about in the storm. Jutta clung to the bristly earth with her fingers, lest the wind peel her off the top of the barrow and toss her aloft like a leaf.

"Close your eyes and hang on!" Frida shouted.

Jutta saw the eerie figures descend to circle the barrow, their horrible hag faces livid. Flushed out like rabbits, the men began to run . . .

By Elizabeth H. Boyer
Published by Ballantine Books:

THE SWORD AND THE SATCHEL
THE ELVES AND THE OTTERSKIN
THE THRALL AND THE DRAGON'S HEART
THE WIZARD AND THE WARLORD

The Wizard's War
THE TROLL'S GRINDSTONE
THE CURSE OF SLAGFID
THE DRAGON'S CARBUNCLE
THE LORD OF CHAOS

THE CLAN OF THE WARLORD
THE BLACK LYNX

KEEPER OF CATS

KEEPER OF CATS

Elizabeth H. Boyer

A Del Rey Book

BALLANTINE BOOKS • NEW YORK

A Del Rey® Book
Published by Ballantine Books

Library of Congress Catalog Card Number: 94-94648

ISBN 0-345-38180-7

Manufactured in the United States of America

First Edition: January 1995

10   9   8   7   6   5   4   3   2   1

CHAPTER 1

The house of the five grandmothers stood on a rocky crest like an untidy suicide making up its mind to tumble down the mountain into the settlement below. Jutta groaned inwardly at the sight of it—its ancient stone walls were clotted with black and green moss, goats grazed on the sagging turf roof, and one wall stood precariously propped up with an assortment of poles and rocks. Flowers and moss sprouted on the roof and between the stones, frivolously bedizening the three gables that once had boasted three proud carven dragons' heads. The grinning dragons, now toothless and blackened, offered sanctuary to cheerful sparrows.

All the doors and windows stood gaily open to a parade of chickens, geese, and of course cats. A dozen of the lazy creatures lolled indolently on windowsills and doorsteps and dotted the sunny paddock walls like furry hummocks of multicolored moss. One enormous black cat crowned a fence post, glaring at Jutta and her mother as their cart rolled past, then it leapt down and scampered away toward the barn, tail waving aloft like a warning flag.

"Modir," Jutta said in a level, sensible voice, "you cannot leave me here. This place is a madhouse."

"How can you say that about your own dear grandmother and sweet great-grandmother?" Dalla demanded in high dudgeon. "This is your kin and clan, and you cannot speak that way of them."

"As if you cared much about the old clan ways," Jutta said. "If you did, you'd be living here with them, instead of in Ingsvik with a husband and children."

1

Dalla shook the reins impatiently as the pony leaned into his collar to drag the cart up the rocky hill. "I've told you, nothing is more dear to me than the traditions of our Hestur ancestors. The clan way has well served our female ancestors from practically the beginning of time and has made us the people we are today." She lifted her chin, surely a fine picture of a woman with her long russet hair drawn back in a fat braid, with her elegant chiseled profile haughtily poised. Her fine blue woolen cloak, red hood, and gown were liberally embroidered with many colors, and her fine leather boots bespoke an appreciation of life's nicer things or, rather, an insatiable demand for them, brought on by a life of pampered ease.

"I can't believe you ever enjoyed living here," Jutta grumbled as the cart lurched through the tumbledown gate and into the dooryard.

"Hush. Some of the happiest days of my life were spent right here. I told you this appearance of poverty is only a sham. They've got more money than ever you've dreamed of. I want you to do a bit of looking around while you're here. Dear Amma Margret can't live forever, and I'd like to know what I stand to inherit from her. She won't tell you a word, though, except how desperately poor she is, so you've got to be very clever. I know they are up to something here. You can see this rocky little farm isn't enough to keep alive on."

"And you're sending me here to starve?" Jutta demanded. "You sent Asta to learn to be a great lady with Pabbi's relatives, but I get sent to this heap of rocks to become a beggar with five old skeletons?"

"Hush! These are your kinswomen! I won't hear you speak of my mother and grandmother that way. Asta is your older sister besides, and Thorgestr's mother is going to find a great match for her. You'll get your turn one day, I promise."

"I hope so," Jutta muttered. "I don't intend to spend the rest of my life mucking around on a farm."

"Now, put on a good face and remember all I've told you. Be sweet and kind and a great help to your mother-kin, and you may find out something that will benefit you."

"I don't think they need any help," Jutta grumbled. "Amma

Margret is still as sound as a two-year-old colt, and the others are younger than she is. Why couldn't you have sent someone else to do this? I don't like thrall's work, and I don't like cats."

"Dottir, I chose you because your older sister has no idea of how to take care of herself. She has always demanded to be pampered, and she has never made up her mind for herself about anything since the day she was born. Your two younger sisters are still at the brainless stage. A few more years and there may be hope for them. I remember when you were at thirteen summers—I thought you'd drive me insane. Nothing I told you stuck in your brain for an instant, and there you were flitting about like a butterfly from one thing to the next, so happy and full of delight, but I would have rather asked a yearling filly to clean the house than ask you to do more than one thing at a time. But now you're nineteen and beginning to be sensible. I know I can trust you to do what must be done here, where Thura and Sissa can't think, and Asta refuses to. You're my only hope. You're like me—clever and sharp-eyed. Your older sister is like your father, Thorgestr: other people's problems and ideas are an inconvenience."

"I'm not sure what it is you want me to do," Jutta said, casting off her resentment with a sharp sigh. Her mother very seldom complimented her. She was not the sort of mother who petted and spoiled her daughters, knowing they would have to find a place of their own in a world where a woman either was kept like a coddled pet or had to work her land and make her own bargains in the market. Asta was pretty but too dull to take care of anything, not even a pet field mouse—she had let dozens of them starve in her care, forgetting about food and water until it was too late. She forgot about chores, forgot about helping, and so the burden of her laziness inevitably slid down to rest upon Jutta. Jutta was responsible, Jutta was strong. Jutta could ride a horse twenty miles to pay for some sheep, Jutta could load and drive a wagonload of feed to a neighbor. Jutta could ride the horse that was misbehaving so it would be gentle enough for her younger siblings to use, no matter how many times she was thrown off. Thorgestr— usually as he was leaving for hunting—often proudly said she was the best son he had. So she would be until her three younger brothers grew up, and then she would be shoved aside and ignored. At five, seven, and nine, they were now the most spoiled of babies, demanding all manner of things she had never had. How inconsiderate of her mother to bestow four daughters on the world first, then the three sons as an afterthought. They were going to be as helpless and selfish as Asta, and no one would think it strange, because that was the way they were expected to be.

"What I expect you to do," Dalla said, "is simply to find out how much wealth remains to the clan. We have a claim to it, you know, as the last remnant of the Hesturkonur. I want to buy old Thvari's land for you. A sack of gold will melt away, but prime land will keep you forever. Asta has her portion, and so shall your sisters by the time they are gifting age."

"Then why don't you just ask?" Jutta demanded. "Amma Margret is your grandmother, and Amma Thruda is your own mother."

"They're still angry at me for leaving the clan to marry your father. I've been kicked out of my place in line. You will take my place as the inheritor of all they have, and then we can buy you the land. Were I to ask, Amma Margret would stick her fists on her hips and say, 'Well, you can ask your husband to buy you what you want. He takes care of you now, not your clan.' "

Jutta had to smother a smile. Dalla's pinched up expression and tone of voice sounded exactly like her great-grandmother Margret.

Sigthrudr—Thruda to everyone who knew her—kept one eye on the road as she worked. It was dyeing day, and she was getting some truly wonderful colors. Never had the madder root made such a nice red, but the blue was her special secret, which she would never reveal to anyone, except possibly Dalla, her only living daughter. Once there had been three daughters, growing up tall and sunny around her, but disease and childbirth had carried off the first two and Thorgestr Sorenson had carried off the prize, Dalla, her youngest. For many years she had supposed that was that, the end of clan Hesturkonur. All the younger girls had left, wooed away to farms and steadings to live with husbands and their families. Some had married young chieftains of ancient clan renown, but after the end of the thousand years of wars with the Dokkalfar and their allies the land was subdued; no one cared much for the hereditary profession clans anymore.

Perhaps they weren't really needed anymore. Perhaps it was foolish to cling to the old ways, when mothers and daughters stayed together and the men for the most part stayed away. The men bought giftrights and arrived for giftings, returning to claim their young sons at age six; then they rode off to war to get themselves killed. It was a satisfactory system back then; there were no widowed wives and orphaned children left to starve. The clans always looked after their own. Peacetime, however, kept the restless warriors pinned down at home with domestic concerns. It was only natural that they wanted a wife around to relieve the burden of the numerous responsibilities of farm, field, and fold. Women were far more experienced at the humdrum responsibility of making a farm prosperous, what with the call to glory always tickling in the ears of the warrior-born.

Thruda wondered if Dalla wasn't often lonely, without the company of her mother, grandmother, great-aunts, and the numerous cousins and relations. The clan provided a warm and happy nest for Thruda; she couldn't imagine wanting to leave. Her arranged marriages had all been of short duration, and none of her six husbands had seemed particularly good company. They were interested in warfare; she was interested in her children, her weaving and dyeing, and her special sheep with the silky wool that lent itself so readily to carding and spinning and weaving. Menkind were mysterious, violent creatures, and she had wept to see her two small sons being taken away by their fathers to be made men of; she had never seen them again, only heard word that they had died. After their funeral pyres had burned to ash, their bones were later brought home and safely interred in the Hestur barrows with scant ceremony, but Thruda had felt no sorrow at the deaths of those strangers. She remembered her sons as fat sticky babies and young boys playing at horses and warriors, knowing even then by instinct the fate that awaited them.

Thruda's daughters had been much more comfort; then she had lost them, too. But still she had her mother, Margret, the senior survivor of the clan Hesturkona, and her aunts Ingi, Sigla, and Dora. The clan of women had been undisturbed by men for many years with the last of the young girls gone— undisturbed by men except for old Bjalfur, who had wanted to marry Dora for the past eleven years. His brain was failing, Dora was certain, and she was too old to attempt something as newfangled as permanent marriage.

Thruda surveyed her bright skeins of wool with satisfaction as they hung to dry on the branches of a dead plum tree growing in the wall. It had sprouted from a seed dropped there by Thruda's father when he was first gifted to Margret, so Thruda and the tree had been the same age. She had not been pleased when the tree had begun to die ten years ago, at a very young age of ninety. Trees and Alfar weren't living as long as they used to, Margret had observed by way of consoling her daughter.

Thruda hoped she could interest her granddaughter in the trade she had chosen. Jutta was a bright and restless child, much more suited to the typical Hesturkona life of breaking and training fine horses. The girl had a wonderful touch with a horse, a light, firm hand that never dragged a horse's jaw into unsightly gaping, legs and seat that naturally formed to a horse's back. Jutta could lift a horse into flight over a wall as gracefully as a bird, even if the horse had no idea that it was a jumper.

Muddling and picking about with sneezy wool would never appeal to Jutta. Thruda sighed, letting her uneasy forebodings brush her sunny expectations with wings of gloom. Young girls nowdays weren't suited to clan life. They knew what it was to become friends with boys; they became acquainted with their fathers and often admired them exceedingly and patterned their future husbands on the example their fathers set. It was so complicated. And no longer were marriages assembled by the clan genealogists and matchmakers. Mothers and fathers and assorted relatives intervened, and worse yet—Thruda knew from her own sad and confusing experience—the young people often considered themselves qualified to decide that they wished to be married to each other. Yet there was still something of the old independence of the women's clans in that, and the women reserved the right to abandon their husbands at their own discretion. If they parted on particularly acrimonious terms, the woman's brothers often arrived shortly to assassinate the former husband. Times, indeed, had changed, and possibly it was not an improvement, although a word of criticism would never escape Thruda's lips. She yearned too desperately to see Dalla and Jutta as often as she could. Thorgestrstead was twenty miles away, a good brisk half day's journey on horseback.

Dalla was proud like her grandmother Margret and sensitive as most proud, headstrong people tended to be, and the two of them had flared out at each other when Dalla had decided to leave. Margret had not willingly relinquished her last hope for the revival of clan Hesturkonur, nor had Dalla wished to surrender her notions of lifetime stability and wedded bliss to one man. Margret's sharp tongue had only served to defeat her, and Dalla had gone away with Thorgestr, bitter words ringing in her ears. Subsequent visits and twenty-odd years had soothed the differences between grandmother and granddaughter only somewhat.

Now it was scarcely to be comprehended that Dalla had herself offered her second daughter, the best of the four girls, to stay at Bardhol and continue the clan traditions when she was nineteen, old enough to marry.

"It will be like having another daughter to raise," Dora said, her matchmaking instincts rising to the surface.

"A peace offering," Ingi had said.

"Another mouth to feed," Margret had added.

"As if we didn't already have enough to worry about," Sigla added with an anxious frown as she mentally inventoried a host of menacing and unpredictable events that might accrue because of one minute change in her life.

The clatter of pony hooves and the rumble of wheels startled Thruda out of her thoughts. A hairy little horse of extreme durability and a great thatch of mane and forelock trotted into the dooryard, drawing a two-wheel tilt and snorting feistily at the cats gathering around to greet the visitors.

"Here she is!" came the happy cry as they rolled into the courtyard. "My little barnabarn! Jutta, how much you've grown! You're practically a lady now!"

Jutta cringed. It was what Amma Thruda always said, probably since Jutta had been two days old.

"Hello, Amma Thruda," she replied, dutifully stifling a sigh and casting a vengeful glare at her mother.

Amma Thruda left her kettle, wiped her hands, and came toward them with a radiant smile, the shortest, youngest, and plumpest of the five grandmothers. Her silvery hair was still streaked with strands of the russet inherited by both Dalla and Jutta, a great source of pride for Dalla and of endless humiliation for Jutta. There were a thousand insulting names for a red-haired person and none for blond or brown. Her red hair bristled like the coat of a wolf instead of lying smooth and sleek like her mother's.

"Modir, you could buy your skeins already dyed at the fair," Dalla said, embracing her mother and bestowing a kiss upon Thruda's soft withery cheek.

"They don't get the nice colors that I do," Thruda said. "And besides, they want your soul for their skeins, and why should I pay someone to do work I can do for nothing? I know where to find all the plants, and I shear the sheep myself, wash the wool, card it, spin it—"

"Modir, you work too hard," Dalla said. "That's exactly why I've brought you Jutta. She's a good stout girl and will help you with all your work."

"The clan will prosper," Amma Thruda said as she looked at Jutta. "All six of us. It's not like the old days, but there is hope."

"Now, then, I don't wish to talk about that. No sense in flogging a dead horse, is there? Speaking of horses, I see you still have your old mares. I thought you were going to get rid of them before another winter set in. And you've bred an-other?"

She twitched a shoulder toward an emerald pasture walled around with mossy stone, where six black mares grazed in pasture up to their knees. A young foal capered about, red-coated until its first year, when it would start to turn black, like all true Hestur horses.

"We were, but we got to thinking about Hesturkonur without horses and it was just too horrible. We'll keep them until either they or we die, I suppose. And Ingi did want to see another colt out of Elska."

"They eat enormous quantities of hay in the winter. You should get a little pony like my Badger. He can pull as much as a big horse, and you can ride him, too. He eats hardly anything in comparison."

"Perhaps I will someday," Amma Thruda said. "He looks like sensible transportation. I'm delighted with any horse who brings my daughter and grandchild back home to me. It seemed a long dark winter, didn't it? One of the longest and darkest I can remember, and I'm sure I heard wolves howling nearly every night."

"Wolves! Modir, I wish you'd come with me to Thorgestrstead for the winter. I don't want to come up here one spring and find nothing but your bones. We don't have wolves in the lowlands."

Thruda laughed, a merry infectious sound that made even Jutta smile. "I don't think Thorgestr would like having five grandmothers, even for the winter. I couldn't leave your grandmother and your aunts. They rely on me for so much. They're the ones with the old bones, not me. They need to go to the lowlands for the winter. But they won't, and we both know it."

"Then you must come this summer before the haying."

"Perhaps I shall," Amma Thruda said, but they both smiled, knowing she would never leave Bardhol. "You must be perishing for your dinner. What are we standing out here for when we could be eating some of Dora's blueberry skyr? Come in; the rest will be along in a moment. I saw Svartur racing toward the barn to tell Margret you're here."

Jutta smothered another sigh as they parted a multicolored sea of cats and went inside the house for something to eat. As usual, it was cluttered with cats and a few chickens and doves and geese. Her nose was already running and her eyes watering, and she hadn't even sat down yet.

"It doesn't look like much now, does it?" began Amma Thruda, which was how she always started a lengthy journey down the tangled paths of Amma Thruda's memories of the old days when the women's clans had ruled Skarpsey and determined the fate of most of the men and women on the island. It seemed terribly important to her, so Jutta listened politely. Most proud and famous of all was the Hestur clan, renowned for its fiery horses and warrior sons. The sons were all dead long ago, and the horse herds had dwindled to the six aging mares grazing in the pasture. Only five elderly women remained, besides Dalla and Jutta.

"Many things have changed now," Amma Thruda summed up her dissertation with a sigh and a shake of her head.

"Now, Modir, I hope you're not going to start in on me again," Dalla said pleasantly. "A great deal of water has gone under the bridge, and there's no sense in talking about it now, is there?"

"Still, it was so good then," Amma Thruda mused, "and we'd all be together now instead of you so far away at Thorgestrstead and living with that man instead of your Hestur mother-kin. Still, he is a very nice man, and the old ways have to move aside for the new order. I just never expected to be a part of it, somehow. It happened so suddenly."

The sunny doorway darkened, and a familiar if dreaded voice boomed out. "So. The little infidel has returned with her peace offering."

"Modir," Amma Thruda said with a hopeful smile. "Your granddaughter and great-granddaughter are here."

"Amma Margret," Dalla said, nodding to her grandmother. "How pleasant to see you once again."

"No, it's not," Amma Margret retorted, flinging off her rusty old cloak and snaffling it on its appropriate hook before it had a chance to stray for an instant. Still tall and straight, she was the eldest of the five grandmothers and Jutta's direct ancestor. Her relationship to Ammas Ingi, Sigla, and Halldora was a little distant, but they were certainly related to Amma Margret and therefore were kin. "And you know it. Guilt will do that to a person. Taints their whole life, especially in cases where a girl disappoints her grandmother so severely. Irreparable damage can be done. Now, what have you got to eat here, child?" She cast her beady eye over the table as if she didn't expect to find much beside the mudpies and ditch water of a children's picnic.

"Soup and fresh bread and butter?" Thruda said in a sudden flurry of doubt. "Pickled cabbage? Some cheese?"

Amma Margret settled for the soup and some bread.

"Margret!" someone called from outside. "Margret, where are you?"

"Halloa! Ingiborg! I'm inside here with the children!" Margret called. She slapped some butter on her bread with a sharp sigh. "She's losing her eyesight to an alarming extent. I hope she can find the house. One of these days she's going to miss it and end up in the middle of town with everyone staring at her."

Amma Ingiborg always moved with inadvisable haste. She plunged into the house, nearly tripping over the doorsill, bumped a chair, and almost knocked a plate and cup off the table when she took off her cloak and threw it at a peg. A gale-force wind always seemed to surround her; things were swept off the table or were falling over or getting lost, and cats were getting trodden on or tripped over when Amma Ingi was in the room.

She beamed at the sight of them, her cheeks still pink from the fresh wind outside, her eyes sparkling. Her hair had escaped from its braiding, framing her rosy countenance in an exuberant white halo.

"The children! How wonderful that you've come!" she exclaimed. "This old mountaintop is such a bleak place without any young faces to look at, only our sour old mugs."

"You could have a cozy little house in the settlement," Dalla said. "With room for a garden and a little pasture for a cow—"

"What would we do in Mikillborg?" Amma Margret demanded in horror. "Bardhol has always been the Hestur hall and home, and this is where we belong."

"But it's such a windy spot," Dalla said. "And so close to all those old barrows."

"The graves of our ancestors," Margret snapped. "Someone has to watch over them."

"Did you see the new lambs on your way past?" Amma Ingi inquired brightly. "The old black ewe has triplets for the fourth year in a row. I'm so glad it is spring again. It seems that the winters are getting longer and blacker every year. My, how you've grown up, Jutta. I can remember when you were just this high." She demonstrated a small height with one hand, knocking a loaf of bread off the table with her elbow. Before three hungry cats got a chance at it, Margret reached down, picked it up, and slammed it back down on the table with a martyred sigh.

"And you wore your hair in little braids. I used to fix it that way for you, just the way my mother fixed mine when I was a little girl."

Amma Sigla and Amma Dora came into the house and hung up their cloaks, also chirping and beaming at the welcome arrival of their guests.

"How nice to see you, my dears!" Amma Sigla exclaimed. "Did you have a pleasant drive from Thorgestrstead? Such a long distance, and I was so afraid it was going to rain. There was a flood not long ago, and the river crossing was washed right out. I wonder if anyone got carried away by it. I worried and worried about you getting caught in a flood."

"What nonsense," Margret said. "It didn't even rain. Sigla, you worry yourself into knots every day over the most foolish things. Dora, sit down and eat."

"Won't it be a treat to have a young girl at Bardhol again?" Amma Dora said. "Our own little Hestur kinswoman. All our hope in the future rests in you, my dear child."

Jutta could scarcely swallow, feeling the burden of all that hope settling on her shoulders and wondering exactly what it was she was supposed to do. The Hesturkonur in the old days had bred, raised, trained, and ridden the fiery Hestur horses, riding bareback with knives between their teeth in case they encountered someone who needed his throat slit for some insult real or imagined. So it seemed, to hear her mother tell it.

"You must be nearly gifting age," Amma Dora continued, her eyes alight with the prospect. "I suppose there are any number of fine young men in the settlements. The Hesturkonur bride-price was the highest price paid in the South Quarter. Hjallgrimr Botviksson paid two hundred marks in gold and fifty ells of red cloth for my first son."

"Oh, don't get started," Margret snorted with a flap of one hand. "We've heard all about your prize-broodmare days, Dora, but now you're out to pasture with the rest of us old nags, so don't give yourself airs. We were all there with you and we had our sons and our glory, and all that is gone now, buried in the barrow mounds."

"But wouldn't it be fun to have another gifting at Bardhol?" Dora demanded with a shiver of anticipation, turning to Dalla and Jutta. "I could begin looking out for a suitable match. I could spread the word in Mikillborg that another Hesturkona is available. We could have a grand three-day feast, just like we did in the old days."

The ammas all started talking at once.

"My dears," Amma Sigla said, "wouldn't it cost a lot of money? And people usually eat a lot of unsuitable food which disagrees with them, and to take the trouble of traveling all the way to Bardhol—"

"Oh, it would be such splendid fun! We'd wake up this dull old house again!" Amma Ingi scarcely noticed knocking the milk jug off the table in her excitement. The cats were delighted to clean up the milk. Reinforcements poured in through the open windows and doors while Amma Margret picked up the shards of pottery.

"We'll have to kill a calf," Amma Thruda ventured, "and roast it in a pit. I hope we have a good crop of turnips and potatoes. I think we ought to spread out a little more manure on the garden just to be certain."

"She'll have to have some new clothing, of course," Amma

Ingi said, "unless some of our old things in the trunks would fit her. I know there's some excellent stuff there, and she'll need plenty of extra clothing if she's going to be traveling." She leapt to her feet and stepped on a cat, ready to start tearing into the trunks at that instant.

"Let's not make it in the spring, then," Amma Sigla said, instantly anxious. "The floods, you know, and washed-out roads and crossings, and she could catch her death of cold in a downpour—"

"Halt!" Amma Margret declared. "Sit down, Ingi; and Sigla, there's not a cloud in the sky; and you, Dora, hush all this talk about giftings. You'll frighten the poor girl out of her wits, and she'll run away in the dark of night and marry some poor landholder and we'll never see her again."

All eyes unexpectedly came to rest upon Dalla, who hemmed softly and raised her chin.

"I assume you're speaking of me," she said with a dangerous glint in her eye. "Thorgestr was never a poor landholder, and I certainly didn't sneak off in the dark of the night to marry him."

"Of course not, my dear," her mother, Thruda, said with an anxious little smile. "It's just that you were the first Hesturkona in our direct line to abandon the old way of clan marriages. Staying with one man and all the children is not the old Hesturkonur way, and it just takes us a little while to get accustomed to new ideas."

"Modir, I have been married to Thorgestr for twenty-two years, and we've had seven children," Dalla said. "I should think you'd have gotten accustomed to the idea by now."

"It takes time, it takes time," Amma Margret said.

"It's never too late to go back to the clan way," Amma Ingi added hopefully. "Your little room and bed up in the loft are just the way you left them."

"I don't think a clan gifting is what Jutta has in mind," Dalla said. "After being raised in the new order of marriage, her ideas of family are not the same as yours. Instead of different fathers siring children and taking away the sons, she is used to one father and one mother staying in the same house and raising their children together."

Amma Margret coughed and cleared her throat. "Didn't we talk about this newfangled nonsense enough when Dalla was a child of gifting age? Can't we just eat our food in peace? This child is not our child, and we don't have to provide feasts and clothing and giftings for her. She is her mother's responsibility, not ours."

"But the clan used to make so much money from its giftings," Amma Ingi burst out. "This unfortunate notion of one man and one marriage is what has impoverished us!"

Dalla cleared her throat gently. The grandmothers all looked pained, and Amma Margret said, "Oh, Ingiborg! You're as clumsy with your words as you are with the rest of yourself."

"I'm sorry; I didn't mean Dalla specifically," Amma Ingi said in much distress. "All the young girls left to live with men. But it just seems that Dalla should have wanted to stay, coming from your line, and you being the leader of the clan, and her standing to inherit—"

"Inherit nothing," Amma Margret said snappishly. "We were impoverished long before Dalla decided to leave the old ways. She made her decision, and it seems to have been the right one. I can't imagine her wanting to live with us when she could have a lovely place like Thorgestrstead. Birthrights never sold well after women decided to leave the clans."

"It still seems strange to me that women are now so— available," Sigla said with a shudder. "So unprotected."

"We have our husbands," Dalla said. "And their brothers, and I would have had brothers if they hadn't all gotten themselves killed in noble and useless causes. When my sons are old enough, they will be all the protection I need."

"You will always have us," Amma Ingi said.

"As if five old women could be called protection," Amma Margret said, rising from the table. "I'd feel safer with the cats."

CHAPTER 2

Dalla departed early the next morning, exuding heartless cheer as she made her way back to the well-ordered world of Thorgestrstead after depositing her second oldest daughter in the ancient gloom and squalor of Bardhol.

"You'll be all right," she said briskly to Jutta, gathering up the reins of her pony. "Before long it will seem like home to you, and I shall come to visit as often as I can. You can become used to it, you know. Borrow one of the horses. It's not as if we're all that far away."

"Their horses are all so old, if I tried to ride one that far, it would probably die," Jutta said. And if she went home, there was a strong possibility they would have to force her to leave.

"You will be glad you did this one day," Dalla said.

Jutta made no reply, preferring to look as miserable as possible and as forlorn as a lost dog as her mother drove away. She hoped Dalla would forever carry the image of her poor abandoned daughter languishing against the gatepost, staring after her with eyes like desolate dark pools.

Margret watched her standing there a moment, shuddering mentally at the waves of misery she saw radiating from the perpetual anguish of youth. What was she going to do with this young creature? Fragile as a newly hatched moth, as stubborn and dense as a billy goat, shimmering with life's hopes and dazzling promises one moment, then cast down in the muddiest sloughs of despair the next.

"Well," she said with a wintery smile, "why don't you get a basket and we'll bring in the eggs."

Margret showed the girl all the hens' inventive hiding places

16

for their eggs. Six today. Thruda would boil them for their late breakfast. The girl made very little comment, too subdued by misery to notice even Svartur rubbing and purring around her ankles in an attempt to make her feel welcome. He looked up at Margret, his yellow eyes rounded in astonishment, kneading his paws up and down in a helpless gesture of friendship ignored.

"Yes, I know," she murmured at him. "Very unhappy."

"Well," Margret said gruffly when the eggs were all found, "we're very glad to have you here with us, but frankly, I don't know what your mother is thinking of. This is no place for a young girl these days. It was fine when we were young and women kept themselves sequestered away in their clans, but things are different now. Your mother can't seriously expect us to start up the old traditions of clan marriages again, can she? I don't think I'd have the least idea how to go about making the arrangements anymore. There has been a certain amount of opposition to the old ways. Permanent marriage has gained a tremendous amount of approval, and rightly so, I think. Your mother seems to have made a success out of it, at least. I can't think why she wants you to take such a step back in time. It's a very strange gesture for her to make after all these years. Well, I shan't worry you about it at this point. We must allow your mother to make her peace offering, and we must accept it as well as we can."

"I'm sorry to be such a nuisance," Jutta mumbled in misery.

"Nuisance? Don't be absurd. You're our own family, my own great-granddaughter. Listen to that—I must be getting awfully old. You will always be welcome here with us. We'll try to do our best for you, but you must remember how steeped in the old ways we are. Life has passed us by for many years, and we've been happy to let it, but you're going to find us very old-fashioned, I'm afraid. Such as those pantaloons you're wearing, and those tall boots, and that short tunic, instead of a gown coming down to your toes. Isn't it rather mannish attire, my dear?"

"I suppose it seems so," Jutta said, "but young girls nowdays reserve long gowns for special occasions or for stay-

ing at home. We like our breeches for working and traveling
and riding. It saves a lot of washing and mending of fine linens."

"I daresay it does," Margret murmured doubtfully. The boots
did look like a good idea, much easier to put on than her old
leggings and laces. It was a chore, bending down and wrapping
them on each morning, and several times a day she had to stop
and tighten them. But she would never give up her skirts for
men's pantaloons, although all her hems were frayed from
dragging over rocks and brambles.

Jutta's misery was unabating. Amma Margret started in on
Jutta at once, commencing the first day of a life of unrelenting
labor. At Thorgestrstead they had thralls to do the mundane
chores like gathering the eggs; carrying the water, firewood,
and peat; following the sheep up the fells; stirring kettles; and
washing up after the meals. At Bardhol it appeared that Jutta's
grandmothers did everything for themselves, and Jutta was expected to help. At home Jutta worked when asked specifically
and when there were no thralls about to do it; otherwise she
pursued her own interests—breaking colts, riding, a little hunting with her dogs, and quite a bit of traveling to and from the
weavers and tailors who made her clothing and the bootmaker
who made her boots, bridles, and saddles. Then, too, she spent
time visiting friends and relatives, anywhere from one week to
several months, depending on the occasion. It was the typical
busy life of a wealthy landholder's daughter. Work was not intended to interfere with her plans.

Here there was nothing but unrelenting drudgery. And everywhere the cats followed her, particularly the big black cat
who favored fencepost sitting. His name was Svartur, and not
a single white hair marred the midnight complexion of his
coat. His round yellow eyes surveyed her in mild astonishment
when she dropped eggs or kicked the wood basket. He
marched at her heels when she went to the spring for water,
detouring only long enough to sharpen his claws or stalk birds
or pounce after mice in last year's tall brown grass, with nothing visible but the tip of his tail. It was not the following that

Jutta minded so much, it was the running commentary on all she did. He yowled and muttered and nattered continually as if he had never seen such nonsense. As soon as Jutta returned to the farmstead, Svartur dashed away to find Margret, caterwauling about every dropped egg and how many times she had rested on the way back from the spring.

The other cats were just as bad. They had no respect for anyone or anything. She found them sleeping on her clean clothing; they caught birds and ate them on her bed, heedless of the feathers and bits of blood. When she tried to eat, there were cats trying to get into her lap, cats standing on their hind legs poking at her plate with inquisitive paws, cats ready to snatch the food right out of her teeth.

The ammas thought nothing of it when a cat sat in their laps and hooked morsels off their plates. Even Amma Margret, who seemed the most stern and sensible of the lot, cut up her dinner and fed half of it to the cats, crooning and talking to them, calling them her adorable babies and other nonsense.

At night Jutta's bed was not her own, either. Three or four large cats always joined her, taking baths, purring, walking around on her, and wanting to be petted before settling down in places most calculated to be in the way. In the morning she often awoke with cats on her head, around her neck, or weighing down her feet like boulders.

The cats ruled the house. The first rule was always to give the cats whatever they wanted. They were even allowed to sleep in the middle of the table as long as it wasn't being used for anything else. If a cat occupied a chair, Jutta wasn't allowed to wake it up and shoo it away merely because she wanted to sit there. Waking up any cat any time unnecessarily was considered the greatest breach of manners, although the sleepy creatures seemed to spend the majority of their lives curled up in the sun like loaves of rising bread dough or sprawled inside out with their paws clamped over their faces.

Instead of being grateful for all this preferential treatment, the cats seemed insufferably arrogant and spoiled. Amma Thruda's gregarious gray cat Mishka, rubbing and purring in an ecstasy of affection, demanding to be held and petted, could also become as aloof as a butterfly, disdaining the defilement of human touch. Amma Sigla's amiable orange cat Loki had to sit on her lap at every meal, graciously accepting the best tidbits, basking in all the worrying and fussing unjustly bestowed on him. Margret's Svartur ruled, insisting on his choice of whom to bother for handouts, seizing everything that landed on the floor, or else he soundly thrashed every other cat under the table. If Amma Dora dared to pick up another cat to pet it, her fussy white cat Asa flew into a jealous rage and bit her on the ankle. Amma Ingi's cat Rugla truly befitted her mistress—a haphazard, rumpled calico with a face half-orange and half-black, a comical cat that was always falling off or out of something or into something such as the butter churn, the water bucket, or the milk pail. "She just doesn't have any judgment," Amma Ingi sighed when Rugla fell down the chimney.

Worst of all was the visit of several women from Mikillborg. They came rattling into the dooryard behind a pair of sleek white ponies and offered a trilling "Halloa!" to announce their arrival.

"Here's those meddling long noses from Mikillborg," Amma Margret grunted, straightening from the backbreaking work of repairing a dry stone wall that had fallen down during the winter. "What a nuisance they are, always interrupting our work. I suppose we must go in and talk to them and offer them something to eat. I hope there's nothing but boiled prunes."

"We've got fresh bread and rhubarb soup," Thruda said. "Come along, Jutta. We'll go ahead and fix it."

Jutta liked her grandmother Thruda. She was the youngest of the lot, and there was always something youthful about her, perhaps because the other ammas persisted in calling her "the child" and treating her as if she were about ten years old. Now that Jutta had come to live with them, they had two children to worry over and push around.

The ladies from the settlement sat down amid a sea of curious cats to eat their bread and rhubarb soup.

"We heard that a young girl was here with you," commenced the well-upholstered Gunnhildr, bestowing a condescending smile on Jutta. "What a pretty little thing she is—to be hidden away on the top of a mountain this way when there's so much going on down in the settlements. When you come down to the markets, you must certainly stay awhile with my daughter Gudny. She has a great many friends you'd like to meet. The young people like to get together for dancing."

Jutta looked into Gudny's simpering countenance and felt her skin turning hot with embarrassment, or maybe it was a touch of windburn from the harsh spring wind that had lashed at her while she had worked on the wall. Casually Jutta slipped her work-roughened hands into the folds of her coarse gray gown, remembering when they had been as smooth and pale as Gudny's.

"Yes, of course," Amma Sigla said brightly. "That sounds delightful. When we bring our wool down to trade, we'd be delighted to stay with you. In our glory days we used to do some splendid dancing."

Jutta saw a faint shade of dismay flit over the worthy Gunnhildr's face.

"Indeed," Dora said. "At my gifting to Jokull Hodbrodir we danced for three days. Are you going to allow your daughter to pick her own husband, or do you still have some small degree of respect for your old clan ways?"

Gunnhildr glanced uneasily at her two companions, Asvor and Thorgerdr. Their smiles were becoming rather bright and nervous. Thruda's gluttonous Mishka had hooked down a slice of bread, and the finnicky white Asa sat in Thorgerdr's lap, casually drinking her soup. The cats always knew which people they could bully.

"Well, we've got several nice young men in mind," Gunnhildr replied, "but it does seem the style for girls to choose whomever they wish. It's still somewhat like the old days. My mother was a Hestur."

"Yes, I remember Brynhildr," Amma Margret said. "If she hadn't died, it would have broken her heart to see the Hestur clan so scattered and forgotten."

Asa was no longer content with stealing bread. She climbed out of Thorgerdr's lap onto the table and daintily nibbled at the jellied calf's foot.

"Goodness," Sigla said anxiously. "She's never eaten calf's foot before. I hope it doesn't make her sick."

"What a lovely cat," Asvor murmured faintly as Mishka hopped into her lap and peered brightly into her face as he kneaded his paws up and down on her plump legs as if he hadn't seen such a nice soft bed in quite a while. The women of Bardhol were unrelentingly skinny, except Thruda.

Mishka was indeed a handsome cat, silvery gray in color with an array of iron-gray spots and stripes and a very charming face sprigged with enormous white whiskers. In theory he belonged to Amma Thruda—or she belonged to him. It was abundantly clear to Jutta who worked for whom.

"Asa, do be sensible," Amma Sigla said anxiously. "She gets sick very quickly when she eats something that doesn't agree with her. I hope she doesn't start vomiting. I stayed up with her all night when she ate an entire plum pastry."

As nearly as Jutta could tell, the cats all had iron stomachs, capable of digesting bird bones and Ingi's haphazard attempts at cooking.

"Truly you have many excellent cats," Gunnhildr said with as much enthusiasm as she could muster when Mishka decided to join Asa in the middle of the table, demanding a share of the calf's foot. She uttered a horrible little growl and pinned the meat down with one clawed foot to establish her claim of ownership. Mishka withdrew from this primitive display of greed and began the obligatory washing that concluded every meal. Unfortunately, he was unaware that his tail had come to rest on Gudny's plate. It was a very long and handsome tail, ringed with elegant silver stripes, and he was terribly proud of it, judging by the way he waved it around when he walked and the amount of time he spent carefully grooming it. Anyone should have been honored to have such a lovely soft tail draped across her plate during mealtime, but Gudny's expression stiffened to one of intense dislike.

"They are lovely cats," Gunnhildr said firmly.

"Cats?" Amma Margret said. "They really aren't cats."

"No?" Thorgerdr murmured faintly.

"Cats are mere animals," Amma Margret said. "These creatures are a great deal more. Ordinary animals are content to live in barns and paddocks and pastures. Animals are men's servants, their currency, their livelihood."

"We call them kettir," Amma Ingi said with dignity, resting her elbow on Gudny's bread, oblivious of the honey. "It is an old word but much more descriptive than 'cat.' "

"Kettir?" Gunnhildr murmured in an odd tone.

"Yes," Ingi said. "You notice that they seem more intelligent and affectionate than your ordinary cat who lives in the barn and field. Also note their eyes, which are larger and rounder than typical cat eyes, and their large ears. These are not mere cats, my dear ladies. We like to think of them as little people wearing fur coats. They are better company than many people we know."

"Do be still, Ingi," Amma Margret said pleasantly. "Not everyone likes cats or kettir, and you shouldn't go on about them."

"Well, our kettir are special," Amma Ingi said.

"Yes, they certainly are," Gunnhildr said, venturing to reach out and touch Mishka, perhaps hoping to get him to move his tail off her daughter's plate. Mishka instantly withdrew, sniffing at her hand as suspiciously as if it were a dagger in the hand of an assassin. With an alarmed expression on his face, he hurriedly debarked from the table and headed for the door, darting one appalled glance back over his shoulder before slinking away in worried haste. Jutta wished fervently that she could escape half so conveniently.

"I think I would like to have one, whenever you've got kittens," Thorgerdr said staunchly.

"They're fearfully expensive," Amma Sigla said. "We don't just give them away to anyone. We have to be certain you are the right owner for a kettir and that the kettir is the right kettir for you. With the proper kettir at your side, a great deal of valuable information will come to you, and your kettir will protect you from the unseen harm that infests the world—"

Jutta's hand shot out seemingly of its own accord and knocked over the soup tureen, rendering the table awash with rhubarb soup. To her satisfaction, quite a bit of it slopped onto the lap of the simpering, sneering, snickering Gudny, whom Jutta was learning to hate with an inspired hatred. Almost as much as she hated the willful, wicked kettir that scuttled away from the deluge of soup.

When the Mikillborg women left, Jutta hoped she would never see them again, or they see her. For days the bitter humiliation of that hapless dinner haunted her and poisoned every moment that might have been pleasant. Visitors from the outside world ought to have been warned off from approaching Bardhol with a plague sign. Yet four days later another hapless outsider approached.

"There's another dratted fool wasting our time," Amma Margret observed, straightening her back and looking away down the fell. Jutta was glad to stop the backbreaking work of throwing rocks out of the field to take a moment to look. This time the visitor was not coming from the direction of Mikillborg down below the hill, and he was coming on horseback.

By the time Margret and Jutta reached the house, the stranger's horse had been turned out in a paddock, hungrily cropping the fresh green grass. It had the look of a horse that had traveled far, relieved at last to have reached his master's destination.

The stranger himself was also made comfortable by Amma Dora and Amma Thruda with a cup of ale and a nice meal of stew out of the kettle on the hearth. A ring of kettir surrounded him, their faces all turned toward him, whiskers pricking with adoration as he doled out to them most of the boiled fish from his plate.

"Margret, my sister," Amma Dora said by way of introduction when Margret had hung up her cloak.

The stranger would have risen, except that Mishka was ensconced on his lap, purring loudly and persuasively reaching out his silvery paw at every bite the stranger took. He was a tall and lean man with a bristly fringe of beard and hair burned reddish by the sun.

"And I am Gunnar of Threlkeld. I came because of your kettir."

"Threlkeld. That's near Murad, I believe," Margret said, seating herself at the table and nodding to Amma Thruda to bring her some of the stew.

"Yes, just a few miles inland. I was visiting at the house of Thord Holmsteinn."

"Ah, yes. That would be our little Perla. A lovely little white kettir with a long coat and green eyes."

"The darling of Holmsteinn, I assure you."

"And how has Thord prospered in this last year?"

"To an amazing extent, and he has solved the difficulties with his neighbors and distant kinsmen. He told me where he got Perla and what a blessing she is to his household. I knew I must come and see for myself where the kettir come from."

"They like you. That's a good sign. Tell me more about yourself and your situation, my friend Gunnar."

"I am a scholar," he replied, rubbing Mishka behind his ears and eliciting a loud purr. "I am studying under the tutelage of the great Meistari Asbrandr, who has devoted his life to the observation of nature. We were studying lightning and thunderstorms and the power they generate—rafmagn. We were compiling a great body of descriptions and conclusions, a most fascinating study of rafmagn and ways to harness it and its possible uses. Asbrandr spent twenty-two years studying the useful herbs, and thunderstorms are rather recreational work for him. We happened to be at Holmsteinn setting up a tower for the lightning to strike—there is a neck of land there which is almost always struck by lightning every time it storms—when the meistari and I became acquainted with the kettir. She came rubbing around our ankles, quite diverting us from the expected lightning strike. I became immediately fascinated with the little creature when I realized it was not merely a cat. We had studied cats for six years before giving it up as a lost cause. Cats are simply not predictable enough to make any definite conclusions about. And now we have discovered the existence of a new species. How was it you named them kettir?"

"I didn't name them, no more than you discovered them. It is a word from an old, old language," Margret said. "One kettir is a kettir, two kettir is kettir, and the little ones are kettling and kettlingur. And they are not a new species, as you say. Kettir have been among us for a very long time indeed. This master of yours sounds like a very learned man. I suppose he has studied all the sciences—astronomy, physics, medicine, mathematics, and all that sort of thing?"

"Yes, indeed. He is a wise and ancient man. He thought he had seen all there was to see and that everything had been recorded in books. I, too, believed in the learning of men—until I saw the kettir at Holmsteinn. Then I suddenly realized that in spite of my great intellect as a scientist, within me there was a vast unexplored continent where my overinflated knowledge was as weak and small as an infant child. I saw that along with the physical side of everything that stands upon the planet there is a strange and shadowy side as well, which ordinary men never see. What I wouldn't give to walk in that world of spirit and shadow, because I know there is knowledge there that scientific man does not suspect."

"And what does your great master Asbrandr think of your quest for this mysterious knowledge?" Margret asked.

"He sacked me at once. He thought I had a brain fever and lost my mind. He laments exceedingly at such a waste of talent. He says there is no inner journey, that all there is to see of life is before our eyes and measurable by our fingertips or at least our intelligence."

"And what do you say?" Margret asked.

"I don't know quite what to say, only that mortal intelligence is not limited by the physical boundaries around us. I'm beginning to think now, after all the knowledge of the world that I have obtained, that the old wizards were not such charlatans, after all. I have seen powers in the earth and sky that Asbrandr pretended not to see because he could find no explanation for them in all his books of wisdom and science. The ancients knew something we don't, and they knew how to use the powers of the old sacred sites. The hills and standing stones and rings and ley lines assisted them, guided them, and protected them. Now I daresay you think I'm insane and you're becoming quite frightened of my continued presence in your house. I apologize; I hadn't intended to wax so eloquent upon such a ridiculous topic. I assure you I'm quite harmless, and I'll depart if you command it. I'm sorry, but I think I've discovered something far more exciting even than studying lightning and rafmagn."

"Yes, I know you're a harmless fool," Margret said with her rare smile lighting up her craggy features, like a warm day in midwinter. "I assure you, your search will not be in vain."

"Then I was right. The kettir are not born creatures, are they?" Gunnar leaned forward eagerly.

"Oh, no, indeed," Amma Thruda said. "We make them ourselves, using certain—"

"*Hem!*" Margret said with a warning glint in her eye that silenced Thruda. "We shall teach you about caring for a kettir, and we shall send you away with one of your own if we deem you a worthy recipient."

"I will give you all I own," Gunnar said. "It isn't a fortune, and I hope it will be enough."

"I'm sure it will be adequate," Margret said. "All you own is a small price for what you will be given. Thruda, I'm thinking of that young kettir, the gray one with white paws. I think he will be a good guide for our friend Gunnar on his journey into the unknown country."

"Oh! The adventurous one—Hugur. Yes, I'll go out and find him. I'm sure he's up in a tree somewhere getting into trouble." Thruda emptied her lap of two cats and went outside.

Jutta stared at Gunnar as he pulled his purse from its hiding place in his clothes and emptied out twenty gold marks on the table.

"I wish it were more," he said.

"It will be enough," Margret said, and the coins disappeared into her worn leather pouch.

Jutta went outside to look for her grandmother. She found Thruda standing precariously on the crumbling roof of a pigsty to climb onto a high wall, where a young gray cat was crouching just out of reach, uttering soprano squeaks of pleasure and rubbing his jowls on the stones. Each time Thruda advanced toward him, he retreated just out of reach. He purred and rolled around on his back, keeping his evil yellow eyes on Thruda, each time slithering dangerously near the edge.

"Throw rocks at him," Jutta suggested.

"We mustn't frighten him," Thruda said, stepping on a loose rock and nearly losing her balance. "We wouldn't want to hurt him or he would forever lose his faith in humankind."

"Well, what about our faith in kettirkind?" Jutta demanded. "That little monster isn't going to come down. He's just playing games with you because he knows you want him. I can't believe that somebody would pay everything he has for one of these creatures. Nor can I believe that Amma Margret would take it. How in good conscience can she sell a cat for twenty marks in gold?"

"You don't understand," Amma Thruda said. "This is not a cat, it's a kettir. Owning a kettir is the greatest privilege a person can ever aspire to."

"You don't understand. It's not a privilege, it's tricking a crazy person," Jutta retorted. "Obviously, this Gunnar's got rafmagn on his brain and he's lost his wits."

"You have much to learn," Amma Thruda said, wedging her toes between the stones. Hugur, of course, rolled farther out of reach, then suddenly leapt up, distracted by the twitter of a nearby bird. Hoisting his tail aloft like a flag, he scampered down the wall and onto the roof of the barn. Jutta sighed impatiently.

"You aren't going to catch the little beast," she said. "He's too wild."

At that moment Amma Sigla put her head out the back door and uttered a piercing cry: "Kettirkettirkettirkettir!"

Hugur bounded down from the wall, bird forgotten, and galloped toward Amma Sigla, along with several other odd kettir that had missed out on the great occasion of the visit of a stranger. Hugur reached her first, rearing up on his hind legs and sinking his claws into her apron in a determined effort to climb into her arms. She scooped him up and bore him inside with his paws wrapped around her neck, purring and squeaking as if he hadn't seen her for six months.

When Jutta returned to the house, Gunnar and Hugur were

getting along famously, sharing the rest of Gunnar's dinner.
Sharing, according to a kettir, was when the human courte-
ously allowed the kettir to take whatever it wanted. Gunnar fed
him the rest of his fish stew bit by bit, while Hugur urged him
not to be so slow by reaching out his paw and singing a purring song of deepest affection and hungry entreaty. All the
while he kneaded his paws up and down in the sincerest form
of feline flattery.

"You must be certain that he gets plenty of sleep," Amma
Margret was saying. "He's still a baby until he's a year old,
and he needs his rest."

"Don't allow him much milk to speak of," Amma Ingi
added. "It gives them the runs, you know."

"Don't allow him to get a chill," Amma Sigla warned.

"And you must always speak to him with kindness," Amma
Dora said. "Kettir are very sensitive to disapproval, and their
feelings are easily hurt."

"Just give him whatever he wants and you'll both be
happy," Amma Thruda said.

Jutta eyed the gray cat with rising bile. It was all too sick-
ening. He was going to a far better home than she had when
her mother had palmed her off on her grandmothers. What an
astonishing scheme this kettir selling was, and it had probably
taken years to build it up. Her mother, Dalla, was not going to
be pleased, although the ammas had probably raked in quite a
bit of gold doing it.

Gunnar went away the next day with Hugur in a basket tied
to his saddle. Jutta decided that he deserved the fleecing he
had just gotten at the hands of her grandmothers if he was so
stupid to believe there was anything special about a cat. He
was so grateful and pleased that there were tears in his eyes.
And Hugur, peering out of the basket, looked intolerably smug,
yowling and singing as if he were gloating at leaving the home
farm. Cats being the sneaky characters they were, he would
probably show up at the door in a few days, grinning and begging.

"Well, I'm sure they'll be very happy," Amma Dora said.
The advent of the twenty marks in gold brought a festive at-

mosphere to the grim severity of Bardhol. On the very next market day the cart was hitched up to a couple of the aging Hestur mares, and the ammas put on their best clothes for a trip to Mikillborg. The best clothes of the grandmothers were nothing like anyone had seen for at least fifty years, hooded and tasseled and embroidered and black. They looked like five beaky blackbirds roosting on their rattly old cart.

And to make the horror complete, Amma Margret decided to take the kettir.

"We're taking the cats?" Jutta asked blankly. "But why?"

"They love going for rides," Amma Margret said, perhaps reading the astonishment in Jutta's face. "We always try to take them wherever we go. Traveling broadens the younger ones and prepares them for going out into the world as they must do someday."

"Mishka is broad enough," Amma Ingi said as the big cat settled his gray-barred backside in her lap, purring like a kettle boiling. The other four elder cats settled themselves in their favorite positions, in their traveling baskets tied to the side rails of the cart, or in laps or hogging the seats, made comfortable with fleeces.

The younger kettir, four of them now that Hugur was gone, leapt into the cart with waving tails and bristling whiskers, smelling every inch of it and yowling happily. The cart lurched away with her grandmothers roosting stiffly facing forward, with the nine cats staggering around with their tails in the air, goggling at the scenery passing by on both sides and offering a running commentary of yowls, chirps, and trills. Jutta sat on the tailboard with her feet dangling, her back turned to the cats and the grandmothers.

"I hope it doesn't rain," Amma Sigla called out. "I don't like the looks of that cloud. And we must return home before dark. You know how dangerous it is to travel after dark. There might be trolls—or worse. I remember when we were children, you couldn't go wandering around after dark, and even in the daytime, on cloudy days you could hear trolls growling around in the high crags. And they had a nasty habit of rolling rocks down on travelers, too."

"The last troll in these parts got made into boots fifty years ago," Amma Margret retorted. "Those people with their church bells have rid the country of more than the trolls, I fear."

"You never know for certain," Amma Sigla insisted. "Anything could happen. There could be one left, and that's enough to eat the lot of us or roll down a big rock."

"I don't see any trolls," Amma Ingi answered. "Halloa, you trolls up there in the cliffs! Stay up there and don't frighten poor Sigla, do you hear? Look, there's someone now. Is it a troll?" She pointed suddenly toward a ragged figure ahead of them on the road leading to the settlement. A tall thin fellow with a walking stick was coming toward them, laden with a huge bundle on his back.

"No, it's only old Bjalfur, and he must think we're insane, with you talking to the mountains," Margret snapped. "Do be still, Ingi; you're frightening the kettir."

"Not to mention embarrassing us in front of our neighbors," Dora added with a sniff.

"Good morning, neighbor," Margret greeted him when they were within speaking distance.

Bjalfur was a great tall scarecrow of a man, much reddened by wind and sun, wearing a long flapping gray cloak and huge hairy boots of some indistinguishable skins. To Jutta's critical eye he dressed like a wild man.

"Good morning, sisters," he replied, stepping aside to let the cart pass. "A good day to take in the market. I hope you are fine, and the cats as well."

"Simply superb," Margret replied. "Would you like a ride along with us to market?"

"No, I'm coming along much later," he answered, leaning one elbow on the side of the cart for a nice long natter. "You go on ahead and don't trouble yourselves with me. That's a fine batch of young catlings you've got there. I hope they enjoy the market. Should be plenty of fresh herrings to tempt them with."

Dora elevated her nose in disdain. "Our kettir never eat raw fish. It upsets their digestions."

Old Bjalfur offered Jutta a sly wink, almost indiscernible

among his wrinkles, and she was incensed. Either he was making fun of her grandmothers or he was flirting with her. Either idea was completely repugnant.

"They might like it if they only tried it," Bjalfur said. "Cats aren't so set in their ways as people are."

"Oh! It that so?" Amma Dora snapped, turning pink.

"It's never too late to change and try something new," Bjalfur replied with another wink at Jutta.

"Some things aren't worth trying," Amma Dora retorted huffily, averting her face. "Are we going to sit here all day, Sister, or are we going to the market? Everything will be gone by the time we get there, at this rate. No sense wasting our time in a lot of useless talk."

Old Bjalfur grinned and offered a creaky little salute as Margret shook the reins.

"Try again, Bjalfur; she'll come around," Amma Ingi said with a cackle, followed by a squawk as Amma Dora elbowed her. "What's the matter with you? You know he's in love with you. Just one more on your long list of admirers shouldn't be any offense to you, should it?"

"At his age?" Amma Dora cried. "It's ridiculous! What does he want with a wife?"

"Companionship beside his lonely fire," Amma Ingi said. "Someone in the house when he comes home."

"He can't have very many years left, though," Amma Sigla said. "Do you think he's got a funny color? I'm certain I heard him cough."

"None of us would be judged sound if we were horses," Amma Margret said. "He looks pretty good for his age. I think I'd take a chance."

"I think he's quite nice," Amma Thruda offered.

"Then you marry the old goat," Amma Dora snapped. "I never heard such nonsense! I couldn't imagine looking at that face for the rest of my life, or his life, either."

"Well, he'd have to look at yours," Amma Margret said, "so you'd be even. I say if he's willing to put up with you, there must be more to him than we suspect."

"Living with a man!" Amma Dora snorted witheringly. "It

simply isn't practical. It's against nature. Marriage is a foolish fad that won't last, mark my words. I bore twelve children in my time, and all but two of them had different fathers from different tribes, and that is the way for the race of Alfar to remain strong and healthy. And what a fine lot they are, too, the ones that are still alive. The clan way is the best way. Mark my words, the world will come to grief because of this falling away from the old and honorable tradition of clan giftings. People are going to become awfully mixed up."

They kept quarreling about it until they were well into the barrow mounds, when they gradually fell silent by mutual accord. Jutta gazed around at the grassy mounds encircled with stones, suddenly conscious of a great silence of earth and sky that soon amounted to a definite uneasiness. She glanced at her grandmothers. They were all gazing around intently, letting the horses follow the well-known road.

"Are these all the graves of our ancestors?" Jutta asked Amma Thruda over her shoulder. "What a lot of them there are."

"Many more are dead than are left alive," Amma Thruda said. "That's what comes of being from a warrior clan. Everyone is dead except the women. All the fine husbands and sons are in those mounds, while we go on at Bardhol, the same as ever, except that we are getting older. You are our last hope."

"Last hope for what?" Jutta asked, a trifle impatient. It was a line she had heard a dozen times since coming to Bardhol, and it made no sense to her. The glory times of the Hestur clan were gone forever, and nothing could bring those days back.

"It doesn't look like much, I know," Amma Thruda said. "Five grim old women, a few horses, and a scraggly bit of rocky land."

"I don't even feel like I'm much help to you at all," Jutta said. "I never milked a cow before. I certainly never sheared a sheep or birthed lambs."

"It wasn't always this way," Amma Thruda said. "At one time you could really hold your head up and feel proud to be a Hesturkona, no matter how poor you were. You could be proud of your blood and your ancestors. But now it's a ques-

tion of wealth and position, not mere quality. We would like to
have something to pass on as an inheritance, something that
will keep alive the memory of the glories of the Hestur clan.
And you are the one that will be our last heir, it seems. Everyone else is either dead or too far away from their clan roots to
care anymore."

"That's all right, Amma Thruda. Don't let it worry you. I
know it would be silly of me to expect a great fortune from the
clan merely because I'm the chosen heir. I shall just content
myself with being the last Hesturkona."

"Still, there are a few things we treasure," Amma Thruda
said in a lower voice. "And we want the right person to have
them."

Jutta's heart leapt with sudden hope. Perhaps her grandmothers had put something away for an inheritance, something valuable that they could pass down to her, something that would
enable her to raise the level of her current expectations. Her
grandmothers were certainly clever enough to put something
aside and feign dire poverty for the rest of the world to see.
Otherwise, every shirttail relative for hundreds of miles would
be prowling around hoping for a handout.

Amma Thruda reached out and smoothed Mishka's silvery
fur. "Here is our treasure," she said. "Our precious kettir.
Someone must continue their lineage and their care. One day
you'll understand what a treasure they are."

Jutta's high-soaring hopes plummeted like a rock. It was
only the cursed cats she meant. Amma Thruda went nattering
on a while longer, talking about this and that, but Jutta was too
furious and disappointed to pay much heed. A long lifetime of
wealth and power and position, and now all that was left for
her to inherit was a dozen ill-mannered, overweening cats.

When they reached the market, it was even worse than Jutta
had feared. Everyone seemed to know her grandmothers, calling out greetings to them and trying to hide their amusement
and pity. With mounting horror, Jutta realized she was part and
parcel of a spectacle, tainted by her grandmothers' eccentric
reputation.

"And how are the dear little kitties today?" burbled the

burly, red-armed old woman who sold fish when they stopped at her cart first. The cats all got out of the cart to rub around her ankles, purring in an uproar of insincere admiration. Anyone who smelled permanently of fish was bound to be popular with cats. No doubt they thought they could eat her in a pinch. "I've got some very nice haddock they'll enjoy. Not to mention the salmon, of course."

"Salmon gives Bensi the runs," Amma Sigla said. "So he can't have any of that if we get it. He loves mackerel and herring, though. But Ordig has got to have some smoked herring. I promised him some for being good last week when we had company. Aside from dragging a big vicious rat into the house still alive and scaring everyone to death, he was a very good boy."

As they left with their parcels and a cartload of waving cat tails, Jutta's ears burned, and she glanced back to see the fishmonger laughing after them.

"Halloo, Hesturkonur!" called a woman selling all manner of pickled pork and tripe and trotters. "I think your cats would like some lovely svid."

Every purchase required the utmost consideration and arguing among the ammas and determined haggling at the price, even when the amount was almost minuscule. Jutta remained seated in the cart, wishing she could disappear. The cats rubbed and purred around her companionably, ignoring her when she discreetly elbowed them away. Everybody who passed through the market stalls stared at her, grinned, and whispered.

To make matters worse, she saw Thorgerdr and Gunnhildr and her daughter Gudny approaching, well dressed, of course, and accompanied by a couple of Gudny's smirking friends.

"Oh! Here are our dear cat ladies!" Gunnhildr declared with a smile that was too broad and friendly. "And their dear little granddaughter. How do you like living at Bardhol so far?"

"Very well, thank you," Jutta said with all the freezing hauteur she could command.

"Do you like cats as much as they do?" Gudny inquired in an amused tone, looking down her long nose and stifling giggles. Her two friends were not so polite; they snorted and snickered with hilarity every time they looked at each other, which was often, with maliciously sparkling eyes.

"No, I fear I don't much care for them," Jutta said.

"What do they do with them?" Gudny asked.

"They find homes for them," Jutta answered. "And they spoil them outrageously."

"How long will you be staying with your grandmothers?" Gudny asked.

"I suppose indefinitely," Jutta replied.

"Then we must become friends," Gudny said. "We shall drive up and visit you often, and you must come and stay with us now and then."

"I don't know how often I can be spared," Jutta answered. "There is a great deal of work to be done, and sometimes people come for cats. But I would be pleased to see you as often as possible."

"Is it very difficult taking care of the cats?" Gudny asked, keeping her face serious and polite. The cats seemed to know when they were being discussed; they gazed at Gudny and the others with pleased expressions and fanning whiskers, purring with great sociability.

"No, not really," Jutta replied, wishing a large crack would open up and swallow her and the cart and the cats. "They have to be taken out for exercise each day so they won't get too fat."

"Exercise!" Gudny bugled, which was the signal for her friends to giggle. "You mean you take them for walks?"

"I take myself for a walk, and they follow," Jutta said, feeling a fiery blush commencing in the pit of her stomach and traveling slowly toward her face. "I don't really like the cats; they're my grandmothers' occupation. I wouldn't treat them for a moment the way they do. They act as if the cats are small people in furry clothing, but to me they're nothing more than animals. Spoiled and useless animals, at that."

The girls tittered again. "What a strange inheritance," Gudny said. "You must have been quite disappointed when you found out there was nothing more."

"Inheritance?" Jutta repeated.

"Oh, yes, your grandmothers have been talking for quite some time about the inheritance they're passing on to you," Gudny said. "Long before you arrived, they were telling everyone that clan Hestur was not dead yet and how you'd get everything they have. I daresay you expected something besides a bunch of cats."

Jutta shrugged her shoulders. "Appearances are not quite what they seem sometimes," she said frigidly. "My grandmothers have never cared for a lot of idle show."

"Oh, what a lovely cat!" one of Gudny's friends cooed, holding out a plump white hand so a cat could rub against it. "Their fur is like silk! So soft and pretty! Do you think I could have one?"

"Certainly," Jutta heard herself say. "Take two or three if you like."

CHAPTER 3

Kata took her time petting the kettir and cooing over them, which they all adored and for which they put on a great show of purring and stropping and slanty-eyed stupid looks of adoration.

"I'll take this one," Kata said, picking up a young cat with brilliant red-orange stripes trimmed with white feet and chest. Draping him across her shoulder, she started away, chattering happily. "Isn't he cute, Gudny? Thanks for the cat, Jutta. Won't you come with us and walk through the market? It's such fun to see who's here and what they're wearing."

"I can't. I have to stay here and watch the cats. Maybe I can give the rest of them away and join you."

"You'll have to come visit, truly you will." Laughing and chattering, Kata and Gudny and the others departed for a day of fun and frivolity among the market booths. Jutta sighed heavily and glared at the cats, which merely purred at her, if they were awake. One day, Jutta vowed, she would walk through the market in grand style, and all the merchants would bow and scrape to her, knowing that she was rich enough to buy everything they had and more besides. Poverty was not for her. She needed all the fine things that could be bought to comfort her and protect her from life's bruises. It was a very bruising thing to sit there with a bunch of cats while people smiled tolerantly at her and whispered behind their hands about her eccentric grandmothers.

After a good long while the grandmothers returned to the cart, and Jutta's pleasant feelings began to dissipate.

"Where is Bensi?" Amma Margret demanded, running her eye over the mass of cats the instant they returned to the cart.

"I gave him away," Jutta said with a sinking sensation in the pit of her stomach. "A friend of Gudny's liked him. Was that the wrong thing to do?"

"Gave him away?" Amma Margret repeated. "Gave him away?"

The other grandmothers stared at her in horror. Amma Thruda hastily placed her package in the cart. "We may be able to find him," she said briskly. "Come along, Jutta; we'll go after her."

"She really liked him," Jutta said lamely. "I thought you always wanted to find homes for the cats."

"Cats! They are not just cats!" Amma Margret exclaimed distractedly. "They are kettir, and they must go to certain people at certain times. We don't just give them away willy-nilly to anyone who thinks they want one. Where is this girl? We must have that kettling back!"

In a fog of misery Jutta led them through the market. They asked nearly everyone they met if they had seen Kata and Gudny and Thorgerdr and Ilsa—or, rather, Bensi in the company of Kata and Gudny and Thorgerdr and Ilsa. After alerting nearly every person who had come to Mikillborg that day, they finally discovered Kata and Bensi at a cloth maker's stall, looking at some very expensive goods.

"Oh, it's Jutta," Gudny said with a bright smile. "Did you decide to come to the market, after all?"

"I'm sorry," Jutta said in a sort of mumble, "but my grandmothers want the cat back. It seems they had him promised to someone else and I didn't know about it."

Kata commenced pouting. "But you said I could have him. I really like this cat, and he likes me. I want him. You promised."

"Well! This is a lot of fuss about a cat!" Thorgerdr declared. "Can't you just give him to her and give your other people a different cat?"

"This is not just a cat," Amma Margret said. "This is a

kettir. We cannot just hand them out to everyone. The last one sold for twenty marks in gold."

"Twenty marks! That's a fancy price for a cat," Thorgerdr said, hoisting one eyebrow skeptically. Her pinched nostrils flared as if she thought she scented a lie in the air. "I don't see why you have to make such a fuss about it when the world has a great deal too many cats in it as it is."

"Never mind," Kata said with an ominous little scowl darkening her smooth countenance. "I don't want your cat if you really insist on keeping it. I'm sure I can find a nicer cat when I want one. Come along, Gudny, we've got more important things to do."

She thrust Bensi into Jutta's arms and turned away with an arrogant little toss of her head. In a moment Kata and Gudny had linked arms and were laughing in that conspiratorial manner calculated to make Jutta feel like sinking into the earth and never rising.

"You mustn't feel badly," Amma Thruda said. "They're only foolish young girls who care for nothing but themselves. I think their mothers pamper them entirely too much. I daresay they've never even milked a cow or fixed a wall. They don't know what it is to work and appreciate life."

Those were two incompatible ideas as far as Jutta was concerned. Jutta turned and headed toward the cart with Bensi clasped in her arms.

"You found him!" exclaimed Amma Sigla, who had stayed behind to watch the cats. "I didn't think we'd ever see him again. Is he all right?"

She hugged him and examined him for gaping wounds, broken bones, or maybe a rampant disease. The other cats greeted him with delighted yowls, as if it had been years since they'd seen him. Jutta seated herself on the tailboard and stared grimly straight ahead. It was a pity how her life had come to an end just when she thought it was beginning. She had been born into a respectable family of adequate means, so she should have had a pretty decent life. All hope of that was snuffed out, however. She could see herself growing old, alone and cast out, abandoned by everyone except the cats. They were a curse, foreordained to find her and blight her young life while it was still forming in the bud.

Thanks to the delay searching out Bensi in the market, it was nearly sundown when they finally departed, their business concluded. The elderly mares knew when they were pointed homeward, so they moved at a gingery trot, snorting and tossing their heads.

The shortcut through the barrow field seemed ill advised to Jutta, who was looking at the slowly darkening sky with apprehension.

"Can't we go around?" she suggested to Amma Thruda.

"Go around? Whatever for?" Thruda replied. "These are the graves of all your relatives. Even if they were still haunting them, they'd do nothing to us. We're the last protectors of the Hestur clan. All these barrows belong to us—and all that's in them."

Jutta jounced along in silence a moment. "You mean there's valuables in them?" she asked.

"Of course. No proud Hestur clansman or woman would think of being buried without some worldly wealth to show his or her status in the next world."

"Is it still there?"

"Certainly, except for what has been stolen by barrow robbers."

"Then our ancestors didn't take it with them to the next life, if it's still there. Does that mean they didn't need it, after all?"

"There are some things we don't understand," Amma Thruda said with dignity. "We always included a burial treasure as a show of honor. If the dead person had no need of the gold itself, I'm sure they were pleased with the gesture. Maybe happy draugar won't come back to trouble their relatives. Maybe they stay around guarding the gold instead of searching out old grievances to avenge. I'm sure it's a good policy, except that it tends to encourage barrow robbers, who have no fear or respect for the dead. And very little for the living, either. For the most part barrow robbers are a vile and desperate lot who would cut your throat for an old gold ring. Then they sell our family treasures for a song to peculiar dealers in antiquities."

"Antiquities?"

"Yes. A cup is no longer a cup, a sword is no longer a sword. It's an antique and more valuable than it was when it was new. Even if it's too old to be useful, people still want them to look at. I don't understand it myself, unless the cup or sword belonged to someone you knew or were related to. What I wouldn't give for my grandfather Sigmund's two-handed gold drinking cup. I remember it as a child. But it's out there, buried somewhere. After a few years no one remembers who is buried where any longer."

"No one knows who is in these barrows?"

"I fear human memory is a fragile thing. And we are the only ones left to carry all the knowledge of the Hestur clan. Who could expect us to remember everything? Besides, they're all dead now, so what does it really matter, since they're all our kinfolk?"

Jutta scanned the dim humps of the barrows. Once indeed the Hestur clan had been exceedingly numerous, if one counted the barrows now, and it was customary to bury as many of the dead as possible in each mound before digging another.

"So many of them," Jutta mused. And each person was buried with as much gold to honor him or her as the nearest kin could possibly afford. "I expect you could fetch a fine price for some of the old things from one of those antiquities dealers."

"I wouldn't think of selling our family treasures. I want them where the barrow robbers can't ever get them. Times being what they are, the treasures our ancestors buried with their kin and loved ones are no longer safe, as they once were. This world no longer has any respect for a barrow, Jutta. There once was no greater dishonor than defiling the sacred honor of the dead. But now no one fears or honors anything. I just can't bear to think of Afi Sigmund's cup falling into the hands of strangers who never knew him."

"But the old things are worth lots of money," Jutta said. "If you had them, you could sell some of the unimportant pieces and live more comfortably."

"Comfort is not worth such a high price," Amma Thruda replied.

The full moon began to rise over the barrow fields, a gleaming slice at first, gradually increasing until it gleamed malevolently in its full splendor. Jutta could even see the details of its ancient and pitted face, which had given its cold impassive light to the nefarious and heinous acts of mankind from the earliest times since they had discovered its powers.

Amma Margret shook the lines, encouraging the horses to trot. "And here we are, crossing the barrow fields after dark under the full moon, just where I didn't want to be," she grumbled. "Barrow robbers are always out by the light of the full moon, digging away at what doesn't belong to them. I wouldn't be surprised if we found ourselves in the morning with our throats cut."

"Dear me," Amma Sigla said. "We left the house in a mess, too. People will come in to find our burial clothes and look around and think what a lot of messy housekeepers we are. I couldn't bear for that nosy Thorgerdr to sniff around criticizing everything in that snippy way of hers."

"I hope they'll know enough to bury me in my red wedding clothes," Amma Dora said anxiously. "It won't be half a treat to walk in on all my old husbands. Dead for fifty years, all the stupid fools. They should have listened to me, and they would've lived much longer. Didn't I tell each one of them to settle down to a quiet life? But no, every time there was a feud or a fight somewhere, they had to go charging off all wild-eyed to get mixed up in it and get themselves killed. Now look what's left of all their glory and fame. Just me and a lot of old barrows."

"We should have just given Bensi to that girl and been done with it," Amma Ingi said. "I don't expect an orange cat is worth dying for."

"Hush! Nobody is dying!" Amma Margret snapped.

"We're easy prey for barrow robbers," Amma Sigla said. "I knew something like this would happen."

In spite of all their fears, they arrived home safely, a circumstance that seemed to disappoint them considerably.

"Well. I told you we'd be fine," Amma Margret growled.

"It might just as well have happened as not," Amma Sigla said stubbornly.

The cats, ungrateful scoundrels, demanded to be fed. This task naturally fell to Jutta and Thruda.

"I don't see why they just can't go out and catch a mouse," Jutta grumbled as they mixed portions of boiled meat with milk and bread.

"These are kettir," Amma Thruda said. "They hunt for recreation, not survival. They know that people were created just to take care of them."

"They're lazy and useless creatures," Jutta muttered. "They won't do any work normal cats do because you spoil them so outrageously. If you'd just throw them out into the barn, they'd soon learn they have to hunt in order to survive. Either that or starve to death, which might be just as well."

"Making them into ordinary cats would not be hard," Amma Thruda said. "But then they would no longer be special cats. The world is full of barn cats, struggling and fighting for survival, just the same as the rest of us, and their attitudes are just as grim and self-centered. Do you think they care two sticks for any of us? Or we for them? Of course not. But take Mishka now, my darling." She picked up her gray cat, which glared indignantly and pedaled with his back feet to get down and eat until Thruda returned him to the floor. "He lives to be beautiful and companionable and adorable. There is no higher calling for a kettir than to be curled up asleep on his owner's lap or purring in your ear."

"Amma Thruda, I'm going to bed," Jutta said, too disgusted to listen any longer. "It's been a long day."

Those cats were simply taking advantage of five lonely old women. They were skilled deceivers, like a pack of lazy relatives moving in with their better-off kinfolk, eating them out of house and home.

In two days' time old Bjalfur put in one of his infrequent appearances. Jutta was hauling a heavy bucket of water from the well when she saw his ragtag scarecrow figure in his flapping gray cloak advancing up the road, pegging his way along with a tall walking staff. In vain Jutta peered around for her grandmothers: Margret and Ingi were in the fells with their small flock of sheep, Sigla was in the field, and Dora was off hunting dyeing herbs with Thruda.

"Well, come on, you rascals," Jutta growled to the three young kettir that had been assigned to her for the day: Hringur, a gray cat with rings around his tail; Hunang, a little female with long silky fur the color of honey; and the notorious Bensi she had tried to give away. Their sharp little faces peered at her over a stone scarp like a trio of nasty little weasels as she started away.

"I'm not coming back for you," she said over her shoulder, still walking.

The kettir climbed onto the rock and watched her. She called again when she was farther away, but they didn't move. Finally Jutta turned and stalked back to them and stuffed them into the firewood basket Amma Margret had provided for them to ride in, strapped to Jutta's back.

"I'm not your slave," she muttered to them. "You could walk as far as I'm concerned. You could even die and I wouldn't care."

Hringur and Hunang and Bensi clung to the top edge of the basket, peering around with their huge round eyes and purring as loudly as they could to show their appreciation for all her trouble in carrying them about.

Old Bjalfur waited in the yard, resting on a large flat rock outside the door of the house, where other ill-assorted things tended to collect: broken tools to be mended, a bundle of herbs drying in the sun, rags the kettir liked to sleep on, and other junk no one knew what to do with. Including Bjalfur. She hadn't noticed before that he had only one eye, the other covered with a patch. Jutta sighed impatiently and clucked her tongue. He had brought a posy of flowers to bestow upon the unamiable Dora—somewhat wilted now after the long slow trek up the mountain.

"I'll put them in a jug," Jutta said. "Maybe they'll perk up by the time Dora gets home. You shouldn't have walked so far just to give her flowers."

"I had to have some reason to come up here," Bjalfur said, his one faded blue eye twinkling like a jewel in a leather pouch. "I've protected your grandmothers for a good many years, whether they knew it or not. I get uneasy after a full moon rises, and I knew you were out the other night. I didn't hear your cart until much later than usual coming back from market."

"It was my fault. I gave away one of their precious cats, and we had to get it back. You shouldn't trouble yourself so much over them."

"Why not? Because I'm so old?"

"Well—"

"I haven't begun to crystallize yet." He held up his hands, large and gnarled, to show her they were still solid and substantial, not transparent with the white Alf-light that came to claim ancient Alfar who lived to the age of wisdom—not the fate of the Hestur clansmen, unfortunately, who had all perished violently while still in the prime of their youth and ignorance.

Jutta was embarrassed. She looked away from his piercing blue gaze and said "Well" again.

"I have other well-meaning friends and relations who think I should live with them and enter into a pampered and irresponsible dotage. I wouldn't last long if I gave up the struggle now. An arrow only falls when it becomes aimless and loses its direction. Why do you think I chose to sit upon this cold hard stone? Opposition, my dear child, creates strength."

"Won't you come inside and make yourself comfortable?" Jutta said. "You are allowed to be comfortable once in a while, aren't you?"

"Not very often," Bjalfur replied, rising to his feet with a regretful sigh to follow Jutta into the house. "It might get to be a bad habit. Has Dora made up her mind to marry me yet?"

"I'm afraid not," Jutta said. "But she is thinking about it, and I believe she's secretly pleased. At her advanced age, however, she doesn't see the advantage."

"She's very old-fashioned," Bjalfur said. "The clan way of marriage seems the only way for her, but I can change her mind. Her own little house and a husband to boss around would be pleasant for her if she only knew."

"Aren't you afraid a wife might make you too comfortable?" Jutta asked, setting out an ale horn and, after a moment's indecision, a small jug of her grandmothers' best company ale. She didn't know whether old Bjalfur qualified as an honored guest.

"A Hestur woman could never make any man very comfortable," Bjalfur said. "That's why I settled on Dora. Opposition, you know. I fear I'm getting too accustomed to my peace and solitude. I'm getting too satisfied with my life. It's time I stirred things up a bit. I thought I'd start by getting married again."

Jutta wanted to suggest that if he wanted to be truly miserable, he could marry Amma Margret, but she knew that wouldn't be respectful.

"Are you prepared to pay a very high bride-price?" Jutta asked. "Amma Dora, in her day, exacted the highest cost from her suitors, and I see no reason why it should be changed now just because she's older."

"That's of no matter," Bjalfur said. "I'm more concerned about what she brings with her to the marriage."

"Oh! If you think you're marrying a rich Hesturkona, you're sadly mistaken," said Jutta, suddenly perceiving the situation in an entirely different light. "You think you're marrying into wealth? I hate to disappoint you, but we're just barely surviving up here. You don't see a lot of gold and silver just lying around, do you? Well, that's because there isn't any. I think you'd better rethink your notions of getting married, because obviously all you had in mind was Hestur treasure, which is all buried out there in those cursed barrow mounds." She flung out a hand toward the open doorway, which afforded a view of the green barrows at the foot of the lane.

Bjalfur was trying to get his pipe going, which occupied

most of his attention until it was belching a row of little white puffs.

"And more's the pity, that," he said finally. "Barrow robbers will have it all within a few short years. Let them have it, I say. It wasn't worth dying for the first go-round, and it's still not worth dying for. Let Sigmund look after his own tomb if he's so keen on protecting his treasure."

"But it's Hestur treasure," Jutta said, feeling all cold and pinched in the jealous grip of the most needy sort of envy. "I think it's completely selfish of our ancestors to bury all their wealth with their dead kinfolk, when the tail end of the clan would certainly appreciate a bit of relief from unrelenting poverty and hard work. Besides, times are changing. We've all realized a barrowful of treasure does no one any good, least of all the dead person it was buried with. I wonder just how much treasure is buried in Afi Sigmund's grave."

"Enough to excite a great deal of unhealthy curiosity among certain greedy persons," Bjalfur replied with a crusty glowering from beneath his bristling eyebrows at her. "Best to let that treasure rot away rather than waste your life yearning after it."

"I'm not going to yearn after it," Jutta snapped. "But I don't think barrow robbers ought to have it, either. Can't your chieftain do something to protect our graves? Isn't Einarr Sorenson a distant relative of the Hestur clan?"

"Yes, I believe his mother was, at least. But it's not his way to get involved in private disputes. Margret would not look kindly upon his interference. And barrow robbers are a murderous and desperate lot. There could be a lot of bloodshed over that buried loot without it ever being found."

"If we knew which barrow was Afi Sigmund's, we could dig up the treasure and put it in a safe place," Jutta said. "That would prevent any further trouble."

Bjalfur chuckled rustily and warmed his throat with a slosh of ale. "Now, there's your chief problem. No one knows which barrow is his, and there are nearly a hundred mounds on that plain. Not even Margret knows who is buried in more than five or six of them."

"Is it a very great treasure buried with Afi Sigmund?" Jutta asked, trying not to sound too eager. "Or is it just a cup and a chain or two and an old sword?"

"No, it's truly a treasure trove, if legend is to be believed," Bjalfur said. "I was just a small child when he was killed, and I can remember somewhat of his funeral. I remember seeing the wagon he was buried in, with his carcass dressed in his finest clothes, propped up as if he were still alive. He was surrounded by gold and silver, enough to dazzle the eyes of a young boy. But I was most upset because of his horses and hounds being killed to go along with him. I thought that was a terrible waste of fine animals that had no idea of all this burial nonsense."

"Then surely you must know what barrow mound is his," Jutta said.

"Then surely I have forgotten," Bjalfur said. "I am the oldest Alfar in this settlement. I've forgotten a hundred years' worth of things I used to know. Besides, one barrow mound looks much like another after a very few years. My child, put all thoughts of that treasure out of your mind. It is bloodstained loot stolen by Sigmund from his enemies. I can't imagine that it would bring anyone any more luck than it did its past owners."

"Luck or no luck, it is still a Hestur responsibility," Jutta said.

Just then Dora and Thruda returned with their baskets full of roots and leaves and stems and things, followed by a procession of kettir, which realized that company had arrived. Company meant a fresh person to torment and steal food from, and the food for company was generally better than the everyday food at Bardhol.

Jutta excused herself a few moments after Thruda and Dora took over the preparations for their guest.

"Did you finish filling the water buckets?" Amma Dora asked. "And take a few kettir with you so they won't just sleep all day. We have to stir up their brains so they'll learn to use them. I wish I were coming with you. I know what this old fool came here for."

"Is he all that bad?" Jutta asked. "He seems rather a pleasant fellow."

"For a man, he is, I suppose," Dora said reluctantly. "I've had much stupider husbands. But I just can't imagine living with a man until the end of my days. It would be far too different from living with my sisters. And besides, what would Margret do without me? Ingi means well, but she's as clumsy as a cow and prone to peculiar enthusiasms. Sigla wakes up in the night with a new thing to worry about, and it takes the rest of us days to soothe her down again, and Thruda—well, she's your grandmother and I love her like my own child, but that's what she is—just a child. I fear she's flighty and irresponsible."

Jutta considered her grandmother Thruda a moment and how she planned the cooking and the washing and the thousand little details of her busy outdoor work, taking care of her precious sheep from birth to the stew pot to see that they provided her with the wool for her expert weaving. She sheared their wool, washed it, dyed it, carded and spun it into thread, strung it up on her loom, and commenced weaving finer cloth than could be had anywhere in the market, which was formed into clothing for them to wear as well as fine things for various people in the settlement. Jutta would have been proud to possess a cloak or gown made by Amma Thruda. She wondered how hard Amma Thruda would have to work before her mother and her mother's sisters considered her fully adult.

"Do go ahead with your walk," Amma Dora continued. "Watch out for some fresh watercress for us, and some of those tiny wild onions would flavor our soup wonderfully."

"Watch out for snakes," Amma Sigla said, suddenly inspired to a new worry. "I've never seen any, but I have a feeling they're out there waiting to bite someone's ankle."

"And stay out of the barrow field," Amma Margret added.

"Don't allow the kettir to overtire themselves playing, or they might sleep through supper tonight," Amma Ingi suggested. "We can't have their growth stunted from lack of proper nutrition."

Jutta hoisted the kettir basket onto her shoulders, wondering when a kettir had ever overexerted itself for any reason and how one could ever miss an opportunity for eating. Eating and sleeping were their chief activities, interspersed with bursts of creative play, such as attacking Thruda's freshly washed wool and scattering it hither and yon, or walking on the rising bread dough—or even taking a nap on it—or chasing Thruda's weaving sticks until they were lost, or biting holes in baskets and boxes just to see if they wanted what was inside. If they did, it was either eaten or played with.

She made her escape from the house before anyone else could give her any advice or instructions. Her objective was the barrow field, despite Amma Margret's warning. She passed the spring where she had filled the water jars and buckets, then followed an ancient crumbling wall to the end of the sheepfold and past the ruins of several huts where thralls had lived in the prosperous days of the clan. Now cows lodged there, rubbing against the sagging doorways, and goats nibbled on the collapsing turf roofs. The six black mares raised their heads from their grazing and watched her—the last of the numerous beautiful creatures her ancestors had trained and taken to battle. The spindly foal capered, her coat the golden color of willow bark, while her black nose promised that she, too, would one day be as dark as her dam.

Jutta reached the first of the barrows. It was a fairly large one, as high as a tall house and as long as three wagons. The stone lintels had collapsed years before, and the thick green turf was doing its best to obliterate any sign of human interference. In a few more years the barrow would be nothing more than an enormous hummock, unremarkable except that nearly a hundred more hummocks just like it made the plain look like a giant's boggy pasture.

As Jutta walked on to the next barrow, the three young kettir hung over the top edge of the basket, offering their opinions in squeaky chirps and purring trills, and one of them kept kneading the back of her neck with his needlelike claws in his joyous appreciation of the excursion. When she stopped and set the basket down and ventured to lift the kettir out, they gladly attacked her hand as if it were a new toy she had thoughtfully offered them. Anything that moved was the target of their sharp baby teeth and piercing claws. Jutta examined four new scratches added to the scratch marks she already had, not including the ones on her ankles where Bensi had ambushed her two days earlier. Mercilessly she dumped the kettir out of the basket and stalked away, leaving them to follow or be eaten by something, whichever they preferred. They preferred to follow, pouncing on the hem of her cloak and snatching at the tassels on her boots.

Jutta circled each barrow, studying them with a growing sense of discouragement. As she pressed on farther toward the center, she began to see how easy it would be to get turned around and disoriented unless one prudently selected a landmark on the hillside of Bardhol to keep one's bearings.

The sun was slipping down in the west when she espied a different sort of hill in the middle of the oblong barrows—a round hill with a jagged crown of upright stones set in a circle. By then her legs were tired from climbing barrows, so she paused, stooping to gather the kettir back into their basket. Then a dark figure in a long cloak stepped from the shelter of one stone to confront her.

CHAPTER 4

"Who goes there?" a woman's voice demanded.

Jutta slung the basket over her shoulder and advanced a few steps. "I'm from Bardhol, and I might ask you the same question, since these are the graves of my ancestors."

"My ancestors, too. Everyone in Mikillborg has Hestur blood somewhere. You don't look like any of the women at Bardhol to me."

"They're my grandmothers and great-aunts," Jutta said. "I've just come to live with them."

Something in her tone must have struck a dismal note. The woman inquired, "And you don't like it?"

"Well, it isn't what I expected to do with my life."

"I daresay not. You must have an older sister at home who is receiving all the suitors and the best dowry. One who is not as pretty as you, perhaps."

"It's not an unusual situation, I suppose. Asta threw a fit because one of her suitors happened to look at me once. It was no fault of mine, I assure you."

"Perhaps your grandmothers' inheritance will make up for it one day," the stranger said.

Jutta laughed. "Yes, I shall inherit a drafty old house on the mountainside and a dozen cats."

"This isn't the most friendly way of talking. Won't you climb on up? There's quite a good place for sitting."

The woman was of middle years, handsome now where once she had no doubt been beautiful. Her fair hair, braided around her head, was barely silvering. Tall and well dressed in a long blue cloak and booted for riding, she looked more as if

53

she should be on the way to market or to visit a friend instead of a lonely barrow field. Her tanned countenance bespoke plenty of outdoor experience. A white horse was hobbled to graze in the center of the circle of crooked stones.

"I came from Mikillborg," she said, perhaps noting Jutta's appraisal of the horse and her garb. "This is such a pleasant spot, in a lonely way. I am Frida—or Holmfridr—from Thorungard. And I know you're Jutta from Thorgestrstead. And these must be some of the famous Bardhol cats."

Jutta's face flushed as she reached the crest of the mound with her basketload of cats. She sat down on one of the great fallen stones and dumped the cats out unceremoniously. Unoffended, they gazed around for new adventures, their eyes round and bright with excitement.

"Yes, I fear so," Jutta said. "I don't particularly care for cats myself, especially spoiled-rotten ones like these. They have to be treated like people—better thàn most people, in fact," she added bitterly, thinking how the cats never had to do a moment's work, not even catching mice, while she had to work like six thralls from morning until dark.

The three young kettir sat down in a row and stared at Frida with all the rudeness they could possibly muster, with their round eyes nearly popping out of their empty heads. Jutta had never seen them concentrate on anything with such intensity. Young kettir usually flitted from one pounce to the next, interested only in the next moving object.

"They are pretty little creatures," Frida said, "but you can give me a dog any day for loyalty and intelligence. I suppose you're wondering what brings me to the barrow field and you're being too polite to ask questions."

"No one cares much who walks around here, I don't think," Jutta said, waving a hand toward the barrows, which had begun to cast long shadows, until only their tops were left in daylight.

"I'm here attempting to chart the old ley lines," Frida said. "I've got old writings and maps, but the land has changed considerably since those days, and a great many of the markers are missing, as well as the holy sites themselves. Only this one we're sitting on remains definitely Sol-knip—hill of the sun."

"Ley lines?" Jutta murmured with a frown. "I don't see any lines, unless you count sheep trails."

"Nor will you. These lines are invisible bands of power stretching from one place to another, covering many miles. Our ancestors used to travel along these lines for protection from their enemies. Places where several lines cross are places of great power, and these were the places where they tended to put their sacred sites for important rituals. If we only knew how to use that power these days, we could eliminate sickness and plague and guarantee the fertility of our livestock. No doubt we would have many more powers than we do today. Our ancestors knew how to use the influence of the stars and the earth and all the elements for their advantage. Now our powers have fallen sadly into disuse, and we are dwindling slowly into extinction, much like the Hestur clan, which was once so vast and powerful, now reduced to a handful of elderly women. There is a new race coming—the Sciplings, a barbaric race much inferior to the Alfar. They have no subtle powers, only brute force and destruction."

"How—how do you know all these things?" Jutta asked, feeling a chill settling around her heart as well as a growing glow of awe and admiration.

"I have studied the histories a great deal," Frida replied. "I have conversed with old people to learn all I could about the old days and the lost glories of the Alfar race. From what I have learned, I know the Alfar race is in decline. People like the Sciplings, who believe in nothing, have a peculiar way of draining the power from all they touch. One day we will have to go into hiding if we are to survive at all as a people."

"Into hiding? Where shall we go? This is our land, and we have been here since—since the first people took breath and the lofty gods fought to subdue the elementals of earth and sky to make the world a fit place to live. This is our land, and my ancestors' bones lie here in these mounds. I'm not going any- where because of these barbarians. When will they be here?"

Jutta's proud Hestur blood was stirring, and she was almost ready to take up arms and fight off the strangers herself.

"Perhaps you've seen them yourself and didn't know it. They have been and gone many times, but they will be back. They've learned somehow of Sigmund's treasure mound, and they want to find it. Gold has an extraordinary hold on Sciplings, and they'll do anything to get it, even at the cost of their own friends' and families' lives."

"They know about our gold? But it isn't theirs to covet. It still belongs to the Hestur clan, even if it is buried. They've got no right to it. The Hestur clan isn't extinct yet, and we'll fight to protect what's ours."

"There are smarter ways of protecting your treasure than to fight over it," Frida said. "The Sciplings are adept fighters, and you and I are not. But there are things that we can do, such as tracing the old ley lines. I am almost certain that Sigmund's barrow would be the most important burial site, so it must have at least two lines crossing it. If we could only find the lines, we could find the barrow and the gold before the barrow robbers do. I would far rather see the gold returned to Sigmund's direct descendants than fall into the hands of these thieves."

"Have you found any lines yet?" Jutta asked.

"Yes—at least I believe so. At least I have found the old track that runs all the way around the barrows, where our ancestors used to walk along beating the bounds. It was an ancient ritual for marking the division between order and chaos, ours from theirs, man from nature. In the old days life was far more uncertain. There were elemental forces opposed to the efforts of Alfar to subdue the land. The air was almost thick with magic, and powers were to be had just for the asking."

"But no more," Jutta said. "We have tamed the earth for our use."

"Yes, but not without consequences. Once tamed, all opposition ceases and the pursuit of knowledge therefore comes to a halt. Ofttimes what has been learned begins to be lost again as the need for those skills diminishes. At one time every Alfar was as powerful as the wisest wizards and sorcerers are today.

Every child was educated in the use of powers and elementals. Now only a few are true to their heritage and strive to retain their knowledge. If we don't keep seeking, we'll be as brutish and ignorant as the Sciplings, mere mortal men who deny the unseen forces and despise the magic we know governs the earth beneath our feet and guides the stars above our heads. I fancy myself as a student of the old magi, a self-taught student, with very minor ability, but at least I am awake to the possibilities surrounding me."

Jutta felt her heart beating in joyous flight. "I think that sounds so splendid," she said. "I've long known there was meaning in the things I saw, but no one would tell me what it meant. Like this circle of stones: someone dragged them here and stood them up, but how and for what purpose?"

"I can tell you that. It was an observatory for the motion of the stars and planets. At certain times as they swing by us overhead, the influence of certain planets is more pronounced on the earth and its inhabitants. It behooved our ancestors to know the propitious times and when they were coming so they could plant their crops or begin new enterprises." She rose to her feet and led Jutta on a tour around the circle of stones, touching each one lightly as if it were an old friend. "This is the stone the winter sun rises above at solstice. That is the central stone where you stand to look over the others. At one time there may have been a circle of holes around the larger circle for predicting eclipses of the sun and the moon. Eclipses were fearful things for our ancestors. It was an interruption of the normal powers."

"Eclipses! Fancy that! However on earth did the people haul these great stones up here and stand them upright?"

"It is something of a mystery. I don't believe it was done by ordinary means, myself."

"Then it was done by magic, wasn't it?"

"I believe so. You don't seem to have any trouble in recognizing the results of powers when you see them. You must be more sensitive than most young people. I fear I've seen far too many young women who think of nothing but their fine clothing and how they appear to others' eyes."

"I used to be that way," Jutta said rather wistfully, remembering her glorious days at the Ingsborg markets, wearing her utmost finery and sailing around in the company of her other friends, humiliating the plainly dressed girls of lesser means and flirting heartlessly with the young men. "But now I can see there's more to life than mere show. Do go on about the stones. I want to hear about their powers. Is there a way of telling what the future will be? Or for finding lost things, perhaps?"

"Most certainly there is, if only we knew the keys. As you can see, a great deal of power has passed through these stones. Their bases have almost turned to glass from the heat. One day we may know how to capture and use that power, but for now, alas, I know so little. This much I will show you, though."

She took a small wad of string and a weight from her sleeve pocket and dangled the string. The weight was an old gold ring, which twirled slowly, aimlessly for a moment, then commenced swinging until it was moving back and forth at a brisk rhythm. When Frida moved slightly to one side or the other, the swinging became a circling.

"You see, we are directly atop a site of much power," Frida said, moving along a line toward the eastern slope of the hill. "This line continues eastward, but I lose it about midway to that barrow. Another line comes in from the far north barrow and loses itself somewhere between here and there, and yet another comes in from the west."

"And they all meet at Sigmund's barrow," Jutta said.

"So I believe. Or they once did. Over the years the markers have been lost, and I suspect the sources are neglected. I have walked over every inch of these barrows with this string, and I find traces here and there. There is much I haven't found yet but so much that I could tell someone. If I had a fraction of the knowledge your grandmothers must have, I could probably identify the barrow where Sigmund lies."

"They say they don't remember. They were young when he died, and there are many barrows that look alike, so you won't get any help from them. I don't think they want it found, anyway. Could you show me more of your dowsing? I've hardly seen it done before, except for a new well once."

"Certainly. Most people nowadays don't believe dowsing is worth much except for well digging. It would be nice to have an apt pupil. Especially one so young. You could go far if you could find the right teachers."

"I would like to go as far from Bardhol and Mikillborg as possible," Jutta said.

"I believe I could help you with that," Frida said. "I would be delighted to have someone to teach my limited knowledge to, in the hopes that one day you could go much farther. I am bound here by family and landholdings, but you—or someone like you—could leave here and find a teacher and accomplish great things. Particularly if somehow we managed to find your ancestors' treasure. You have the greater right to it, you know. Better you than some barrow robber."

Jutta's heart flamed with ambition. It was as if she had been stumbling along in the dark tunnel of her despair and suddenly had come into view of light and promise. Fervently she thanked whatever lucky spark of intuition had led her to the barrows this day. Otherwise she might never have met Frida, her deliverer, her hope for the future.

"Here, why don't you try your luck with the pendulum?" Frida suggested, holding out the string to Jutta. "Perhaps you've got a touch that I don't have."

"Oh, I don't think—I have no talent—what do I do?" Jutta sputtered. "I believe in dowsing, but how much do you have to believe before it works?"

"Move this way. Don't worry about a lot of stuff that doesn't matter. Just let it swing freely wherever it wants. Hold your hand as steady as possible and it will do the work."

The pendulum began swinging briskly as Jutta slowly crept along. When she put her hand on one of the upright stones, the pendulum whipped violently. She gasped and took her hand off the stone hastily.

"Ah! Did you see that? Amazing!" Frida exclaimed. "You are a true channel for the ancient powers!"

"Am I indeed?" Jutta gasped.

"Of course. Now go ahead and see where it leads you. You are directly on the line when the pendulum swings in a circle."

Jutta followed the line step by step from one barrow to the next.

"Here is a marking stone," Frida said, pausing significantly with her foot on a low stone protruding from the earth. "These were placed along the line at intervals so the line could be found without dowsing it every time. You can see, if this line continues straight indefinitely, it crosses through a great many barrows."

"And one of them could be—" Before she could finish, a furry apparition rose up from the tall grass in a pouncing arc and snatched the dowsing string from her fingers as it twitched to and fro invitingly. Jutta caught a gleam of wicked yellow eyes and a flash of orange fur bounding through the grass and scrub.

"Bensi!" she shouted furiously, and plunged after him.

It was Bensi's favorite game, snatching up something and racing away with it, eluding his pursuer with great skill.

Finally she caught up with him, almost at the same instant he lost interest and flopped down on his side under a bush, breathing hard and giving her a look of fearless amusement. It was what she hated most about kettir, she decided at that instant: they had absolutely no proper fear of mankind anywhere in their wretched little bodies.

"You little monster, I'll wring your neck!" she cried, going down on her knees to make a grab for the string and pendulum. Bensi shot away, leaving her the string. As she drew it out of the entangling thicket, the gold ring came away with a handful of earth and sticks in her grasp. As she let the refuse fall away, she realized that the sticks were small human bones, still strung together with tendon and cartilage. For an instant she thought the ring had come to settle around an intact finger, but then she realized that what she was seeing was a second ring, one set with a small red stone. She gasped and dropped both rings and the bones and stood staring at them, telling herself it was the twilight deceiving her eyes.

"What a little thief," Frida said.

Jutta unaccountably said nothing about her grisly discovery. She bent down and snatched up the plain gold ring, setting her foot on the finger bones to hide them.

"The kettir!" Jutta gasped suddenly, feeling the blood drain out of her face. "It's getting dark, and I haven't seen the rest of them in quite a while. I've got to get home. If I've lost any of them, my head will be on the chopping block. Bensi! Hringur! Hunang! Come, you wretched little beasts!"

They searched and called to no avail until it was completely dark. Then a new voice joined in the calling, and Jutta recognized Amma Thruda's sweet call with a twinge of guilty remorse.

"Amma Thruda? Is that you?" she called out.

Amma Thruda came trudging up the side of the barrow with a lantern. The gray shadow of Mishka bounded at her heels, yowling an excited greeting. "I thought you were getting benighted, so I decided to come looking in case you were lost," she said, a little breathless from exertion.

"I've lost the kettir," Jutta said glumly. "I'm sorry. We got to looking at ley lines, and I forgot to watch them."

Amma Thruda turned to Jutta's companion.

"Oh, yes. Frida of Thorundsted. How do you do?" Amma Thruda inquired. "Looking for ley lines, were you?"

"Yes. It's a hobby of mine, and very educational if you're fond of history," Frida said.

"History is all around you buried in these mounds," Amma Thruda said. "Better to study living things and how to make them prosper instead of dead men's deeds and skeletons."

Jutta shivered, remembering the bones she had found. They weren't old bones, crumbling away to dust. They were fairly recent bones, within the past year, she guessed, and she dreaded to think they might be human. Surely some animal with long jointed toes—a badger, perhaps, or maybe a bear— something that large. But animals didn't wear rings.

"It is the history of our people," Frida said with a smile in the lamplight. "It is our duty to study them and learn from their triumphs and mistakes."

"Well, night isn't the time for it," Thruda said. Then she

raised her voice in her inimitable kettir call, filling the night with a war cry—"Kettirkettirkettirkettir!"—until she was out of breath.

Before she was through her second summons, the kettir came bouncing through the grass, uttering their soprano mews of delighted greeting. They swarmed up Amma Thruda's apron as if they hadn't seen her in a week, climbing into her arms and onto her shoulders, purring in three-part harmony.

"I knew they weren't lost," Amma Thruda said. "Only hiding, the little rascals. Well, come along, let's get home to supper. I expect they're almost famished. Growing kettir must be fed at regular intervals."

"Good night, then, Frida," Jutta said, handing her the string and the golden ring. "Thank you for showing me about ley lines. It was wonderful and interesting. Shall I see you about here again soon?"

"Good night, Jutta. Yes, you shall almost certainly see me here again, poking about in my scholarly way, picking over bits of forgotten and probably useless history. So we might all become one day, if no one is left to care."

She unhobbled her white horse, mounted, and disappeared confidently into the deepening gloom.

"I hope she is all right, it's so dark," Jutta said. She shouldered the kettir hamper, and Amma Thruda transferred the kettlingur into it, still purring and trilling. Mishka's deeper purr mingled with theirs as he bumped around their legs, trying to trip someone.

"The moon will be up soon," Amma Thruda said, "and I don't intend to be in the barrows when it happens."

"You're not afraid of some old stories about draugar, are you?" Jutta asked, her heart thumping warningly as she thought about the bones she had found.

"Stories, no," Amma Thruda said. "But there are other things about these barrows that aren't the least bit healthy. And they have nothing to do with draugar, I'm sorry to say, so you won't be hearing any good ghost stories from me."

"Then what kind of stories are they?" Jutta persisted, walking more quickly so she was beside her grandmother.

"Oh, just a lot of gossip and idle chat," Amma Thruda replied evasively with an airy, unconvincing manner.

"No, there must be something. Tell me; I'm not a little bit of a girl anymore, frightened by owls' voices."

"No, no, I cannot say another thing."

"Why not?"

"Amma Margret told me not to, and she's my mother, and a daughter should do as her mother tells her without asking questions. She said simply to tell you not to come here again."

"But why? Telling me to stay away isn't enough. I want reasons—the truth—and then I will know why I must obey Amma Margret. Or why I mustn't, if her reasons aren't good enough."

"My dear child, you must always obey Amma Margret, even when she is wrong."

"But why? Just because she's my great-grandmother and the oldest surviving member of a clan that almost doesn't exist anymore?"

"Well—yes," Amma Thruda said uncomfortably. "Isn't that reason enough? She is very wise and a good leader, is she not?"

"Of course she is. But I want to know for myself why I'm forbidden to come back to the barrows."

"Amma Margret feels that it would be unhealthy for you to keep coming back here." Mishka seconded her opinion with a loud meow.

"Unhealthy? But why?"

"Do you have to know exactly why about everything, child? Can't you just take the word of your elders?"

"No. How will I ever be as wise as you and Amma Margret if the only things I know are what people decide to tell me?"

Amma Thruda sighed deeply. "In my day the word of our elders was the law. It seems to me young people today don't care much for the law or their elders."

"Amma Thruda, I do care. But tell me the truth and I will care far more."

"Well—what you say does have a ring of truth to it. It's just that for the past couple of years there've been some disappearances in the barrows." Mishka commenced a serious of uneasy yowls, treading close to Jutta's heels, stopping and staring, then hurrying to catch up.

"Disappearances?"

"Well, more than that. Killings, as well as disappearances which are suspected of being killings. It may be the work of barrow robbers. There, I've told you. Now don't say a word to Amma Margret or she'll be upset with me for telling you."

"What kind of killings are they?"

"Oh, must we talk about it here? Now?"

"Why not? I don't see any barrow robbers or ghosts right now, do you?"

"Aren't you frightened of anything?"

"Have you seen anything suspicious in the barrow field, Amma Thruda? I know you always tell the truth."

"Thank you, and yes, I have. But this really isn't the place to be talking about such things. I promise I will tell you more when my flesh isn't crawling and I don't have the feeling we're being followed."

Jutta's mouth suddenly felt dry, and she heard her own heart knocking loudly in her ears. Mishka kept up his anxious twining and head butting, still uttering his demanding yowls. Carefully she glanced behind her, seeing nothing but the silvery tops of the barrow mounds touched by the light of the rising full moon. The image of finger bones scrabbling through her fingers refused to be banished from her thoughts. Right willingly she trod along at her grandmother's heels and made no further comment or delay.

As soon as the lights of Bardhol came into view and they started the rocky climb up to the house, however, her tongue was loosened. Mishka spurted ahead, looking back over his shoulder at them and yelling encouragement at his slow-plodding human companions.

"What kind of killings, Amma Thruda? You promised you'd tell me," she said.

"Oh, dear. You're going to hold me to that? I was afraid you would. Let's stop here and catch our wind a moment, but we must hurry or everyone will start to worry."

They halted at the lower gatepost, where a dark shadow leapt down to the ground with a grunt, followed by eager meowing. Svartur touched noses with Mishka, then rubbed around Thruda and Jutta, purring and trilling in delight.

"It always happens sometime near a night of full moon," Amma Thruda said. "The bodies they've found, at least, are discovered shortly after, so I suppose something goes on by moonlight. The poor creatures are badly beaten, their clothes torn by thorns and thickets. They look as if they'd run a hundred miles, and their faces are terrified."

"How many bodies have been found?"

"Four. But then there are four others who disappeared that no one can account for. And all of them women, too. I tell you, it's not a very nice thing. Now do you see why we're so worried?"

"Yes, and I'm glad to know the entire truth. I hadn't thought it would be anything so awful. More like Amma Sigla's snakes. But does anyone have any idea who killed these women or why?"

"No, no one knows. Plenty of guesses, but it's still a mystery. I hope I'm not the next victim when Amma Margret finds out I've told you."

"We'll be murdered together, since she told me herself to stay out of the barrows. Amma Thruda, I think I may have found another corpse today when I was searching for the kettir. Frida was showing me how to dowse, and Bensi snatched the string out of my hand and ran away. I found him under a bush, and when I grabbed the string, it had fingers tangled up with it. One of them was even still wearing a ring."

"How very unlucky!" Amma Thruda gasped. "We'll have to go back and find the place and see what you found. Then we'll tell Einarr Sorenson, the chieftain."

CHAPTER 5

"It would be Lina, the girl from Stein-hof," Amma Thruda said in a hushed tone, and Amma Margret nodded grimly.

The body rested at the bottom of a barrow, possibly where it had been rolled downhill into the bushes. After nearly a year of exposure not much remained to identify it except the clothing and the hair. Silently Jutta picked up the ring she had found before.

"We shall have to notify Einarr," Margret said. "There's no doubt about who she is. I remember that ring. I wonder what fool notion the girl must have had in her head to get involved with barrow robbers."

"Why was she even here?" Jutta asked. "Stein-hof is on the far side of Mikillborg. Maybe she was kidnapped and carried here."

"Makes no sense," Amma Margret replied. "Lina was a plain and decent person. She was too sensible to get herself kidnapped and old enough to be over youthful romantics." A piercing glower raked over Jutta, suggesting that present company possibly was not exempt from romantic flights of fancy.

"She never married, you know," Amma Thruda said.

"She was only around thirty," Amma Margret retorted. "I don't know what age has to do with anything, or marriage, either. She was in the wrong place at the wrong time, whatever her reasons were, and somebody killed her. I hope you take note of her example," she added, turning to Jutta. "I told you to stay out of the barrows, yet you came straight here in defiance of my orders. Maybe barrows hold some strange attraction for disobedient and foolhardy people. I certainly hope you don't end up like poor Lina because of your disposition to disobey."

"I'm sorry," Jutta said. "But I wasn't alone. Frida was here studying the ley lines."

"Wasting her time." Margret grunted. "I've seen her prowling around here. A fine lady with not enough to keep her busy, so she wants to fill her head with useless information. She'd better be careful or she'll be the next one that disappears."

"Are we going to tell Sigla about this?" Amma Thruda murmured.

"I don't see how we can keep it from her once Ingi finds out," Margret said with a sharp sigh. "And you know we don't keep secrets at Bardhol."

"Perhaps we can break it to her gently that another body has been found," Amma Thruda suggested. "So she won't be so frightened."

Amma Ingi pounced on them the moment they turned in at the gate. She was lurking there waiting for them, with an empty egg basket over one arm suggesting that she was busily going about her day's work instead of craning her neck looking for them. "Where have you been off to so early in the morning?" she demanded. "Sneaking away before breakfast without telling the rest of us? What if someone else had wanted to come with you? Don't you think you might have worried the rest of us?"

"Hush, Ingi," Margret snapped. "We've found Lina's body in the barrows."

"Lina's dead?" Amma Ingi whooped, clapping her hands to her face in distress.

"We shouldn't be talking in front of the child, should we?" Amma Thruda asked anxiously, preparing to bustle Jutta out of the conversation as if she were six years old.

"I'm not a child," Jutta said with a dangerous glare at her grandmother. "I'm the one who found her and led you to her, and I haven't swooned away and fallen apart yet."

"But you might get bad dreams," Amma Thruda said.

"What rot," Margret snapped. "Jutta is a Hesturkona. She doesn't have time to be a silly female."

"Poor Lina," Ingi went on. "I hoped she'd run away to marry someone her family didn't approve of. I never thought she'd be dead. How did it happen? I wonder where she's been all this time and how she came back only to get herself killed. Or was it natural causes?"

"Natural causes in the barrows?" Margret snorted. "And she's been dead a year, Ingi. We found her body where her killers left it."

"But it might have been something else," Amma Ingi said. "Maybe a snake bite, or lightning, or she just dropped dead. We can't be sure she was killed, can we?"

"Yes, we can, knowing the reputation of the barrows as well as we do," Amma Margret replied.

"Oh, this is too awful," Amma Ingi said. "We never knew those others they found. But poor Lina, she never meant any harm in her life—just a little sharp sometimes and certainly too critical when it came to husbands. And many times I thought she considered herself just a bit above us all, as if she deserved better. I'll bet those other three who disappeared are in there somewhere dead, just like poor Lina. For all her silly faults, she didn't deserve to die and be left out there in the barrows. None of them did. Such a miserable fate. Who could be doing this awful thing, Systur?"

"Let's only hope that they have quit," Amma Margret said. "So far nothing has happened this year, and we've had two full moons."

"Poor Lina," Amma Ingi grieved, taking out her handkerchief and a sifting of small disorderly objects. Then she suddenly caught sight of Amma Sigla coming out of the barn with a basket of eggs and halted her weeping in midsniffle. "Halloa! Sigla!" she trumpeted. "You'll never guess what! They found poor Lina in the barrows. Dead a year and eaten by foxes and ravens. Nothing left of her but bones and scraps and rags!"

Sigla gasped and dropped the egg basket. Even from a distance the others saw her face go white. "We'll be next, I just know it," she said flatly. "One night we'll all have our throats cut, and they'll find us in our beds. I'm going to get out my burial clothes and give them to Thorgerdr so someone will know what I want to wear. And I'm going to start keeping a cleaner house. You know how people like to talk when they come in and find the house of death in total disarray. Nobody is going to whisper behind their hands about our housekeeping abilities after we're dead. From now on we're going to be ready. I wonder what we should do about the kettir."

"Trade your brains for theirs!" Amma Margret snapped. "Sigla, we're not going to be murdered, and even if we were, I wouldn't waste my time cleaning house because of a lot of tongue-wagging gossips in Mikillborg!"

"But imagine them pawing through our stuff!" Amma Sigla exclaimed in outrage. "And Ingi has saved everything and patched her underthings a thousand times so she looks like the ragman underneath, and all of her skirts are frayed!"

"What's so upsetting about a bunch of worn-out smocks and petticoats?" Ingi demanded with a shrug. "Everybody's got some rags and tags and tatters somewhere, haven't they? And who's going to care after we're dead?"

"Well, I don't have a single loose thread anywhere!" Amma Sigla retorted. "You could take an example!"

"Ho, there's Dora," Amma Ingi said, her eyes lighting up again when she spied Dora far across the sheepfold. "Yoo hoo, Dora!"

"Hush, Ingi!" Margret commanded. "Don't you have any more respect for Lina than to bellow about her all over the mountainside? You're not a cow with a lost calf! And you know how Sigla worries about these things, so you go bawling it out in the worst possible way. You haven't got a scrap of consideration for the finer sensibilities, have you?"

"Well, I'm sorry I don't mince around hinting at things I mean to say," Amma Ingi retorted. "I just say what needs to be said and be done with it." Huffily she strode away, leaving a long thread from her underskirt snagged on a bush.

In short order Jutta was dispatched to the far side of Mikillborg to find the chieftain, Einarr of Sorengard. With doubt she eyed the tall black mare she was supposed to ride, wondering if the ancient creature would make it that far and how long it would take her. Elding was her name, but Jutta could see nothing about her that indicated anything so fiery and quick as the lightning she was named for. Once astride Elding's rather bony back, however, Jutta discovered that the horse moved out with a good will into a ground-eating trot of amazing smoothness. She stopped a few times to rest her horse and was at the chieftain's hall at midday.

A dozen dogs came barking out at her, followed by several thralls and the family of the chieftain. When they learned what news she carried, word spread through the farmstead in moments. Einarr and two guests were just returning from a hunting expedition, and Jutta was brought into his hall in haste.

Einarr struck an imposing figure, tall and stoutly built for an Alfar, with a bushy chestnut beard and hair worn long and tied back. His nose was rather long and sharp, and his eyes burned with the restless fire of a hunting hawk kept on a short tether.

"So you've found a carcass," he greeted her, his normal voice only somewhat less than a shout. "Why should that be of interest to me? Haven't I seen plenty of dead bodies in my day during the great wars?"

"I daresay you have, if you went to the great wars as a small infant," Jutta answered, wondering if she was going to be forced to dislike this man.

Einarr answered with a shout of laughter and turned to his two guests. "Hah, this girl is a treasure! She knows blustering rot when she hears it! Bless her, she's smarter than most."

"No, I wouldn't be so boastful," Jutta replied. "You and my father, Thorgestr, are about the same age, and I know my father missed the great wars and bitterly regretted it. I suppose if he'd gone, he'd never have had the opportunity to be my father, so I think it was a good thing. War is greatly overrated, I think, as a proof of one's manhood."

"Thorgestr is a lucky man indeed to have such a daughter," Einarr said, turning to his two guests with a chuckle. "In all your travels, have you ever seen the equal of Alfar women in brains and pluck?"

She looked at the two guests more attentively, feeling a sudden eerie prickling of her scalp and neck hairs.

These men were strangers—strangers to the place they were

in and strangers to anything Alfar, although nothing in their appearance seemed amiss. The only obvious difference was their stature, which was even greater than Einarr's. In bone and muscle, they made Einarr look very fine. It was a strange and heavy coarseness of features, extending even to their fingers, which were gross and clumsy-looking. Their clothing was much the same, although more drab and worn with much travel. Their boots were of strange manufacture, the like of which Jutta had never seen before, and their weapons had a heavy power about them that Jutta did not like. Like Alfar clansmen of the northern tribes, they were fair-skinned and light-haired, with pale eyes, but she felt no kinship with them. They had an atmosphere, she realized suddenly with a jolt of alarm—an atmosphere of destruction. These were Sciplings, creatures who were human but not Alfar.

"No, indeed, I've never seen the like," rumbled the burlier and redder of the two Sciplings, his hairy lips parting in a broad grin. "Delightful creatures of amazing beauty as well." He made her a rather fulsome bow to extend a small degree of grace to the brazen compliment, but Jutta's eyes narrowed with disdain.

"I'm sure you've admired a great many women in your travels and tried to deceive them all with your blandishments," she retorted. "Or is it merely the custom of Sciplings to slather praise upon strangers, hoping to impress them?"

Einarr's mouth opened in a roar of mirth, and he slapped the broad back of his guest. "Petrus, my friend, you are as transparent as glass! She's made a perfect fool of you!"

Petrus grinned, turning even redder. He rubbed the back of his neck and shrugged away his embarrassment. "All I can say is I'm sorry you're the friend of such an idiot as I am. She's too quick for me. Simon, see if you can say something without insulting her."

Simon appeared much younger than Petrus—his son, perhaps—not nearly so sunburned and craggy and somewhat finer in structure.

"How do you do?" Simon inquired rather nervously, blushing to the tips of his ears.

Jutta smiled, very much enjoying the upper hand. "How do I do what?" she replied.

"I meant—that is to say, I'm merely extending a friendly greeting to you, from me—not that you are doing anything or that I am asking how you do it," Simon answered, smiling suddenly with rare, shy sweetness. "Although I'm certain that whatever you turned your hand to, you would do it extremely well."

"Including making an ass out of you Sciplings," Einarr added, whacking his knee with a howl of mirth.

"I have no intention of making strangers to Mikillborg feel uncomfortable or unwelcome," Jutta said, darting him a warning look that silenced him. "Particularly Sciplings, who don't have a lot of the advantages of the Alfar. My mother always taught me never to make less of those who might be disadvantaged in any way, whether it be in their appearance or in their wits."

Einarr laughed again, throwing back his head in a whole-hearted bellow of sheer enjoyment. He dabbed at his eyes, his shoulders shaking. Then he offered Jutta his arm, saying, "It would be an honor if you'd come in to dinner. I hope you've got more insults for us." He drew his hand through the crook of his elbow and patted it affectionately, propelling her along.

"Actually I came to tell you about poor Lina of Stein-hof, and you're turning a sad occasion into a party," Jutta retorted sternly.

"I promise we won't enjoy our meal, then," Einarr said. "No more laughing, no more smiling, you two," he added severely, glowering at Petrus and Simon, who faces were fairly beaming with pleasure and anticipation. "She's here on a mission of utmost solemnity, and we must put on the appropriate sorry faces."

"No, truly, your manner is disgraceful," Jutta declared, withdrawing her hand from his not without difficulty and bracing her fists on her hips. "A woman is dead, and you're making jokes about it?"

"I knew she was dead a year ago," Einarr said, widening his eyes with great innocence, and a cloud of imagined hurt settled over his countentance. "I was very sad at the time and angry at whoever might have done such a thing. What is it you would like me to do now, so much later, when the killer is miles hence, Lina's property is divided up among her sisters, and her mother's tears are dried?"

"A mother's tears may be dried, but her heart is still aching," Jutta said. "She will want to know that a funeral pyre must be prepared, and you shall take Lina's poor bones to her to be buried. You shall give her a small bit of gold to comfort her, and you shall promise to find her killer if he ever returns to Mikillborg. You can waste whatever outrageous compliments upon her that you choose. Even insincere compliments have a way of cheering the heart."

"Don't be angry with me," Einarr said, taking her hand again and putting it through his arm. "I'm full of bluster and noise and wind and confusion, but don't hate me for it; it's only my way of hiding. Like an old dog who barks the loudest, it only means I'm the most frightened. Now, can we be friends and sit down to eat and drink?"

Jutta studied his twinkling eyes, surrounded by the wrinkles of care and diligence and no little sorrow. "I think we can be friends," she replied. "But I'm not so sure about your Sciplings. Where did you get them, and what are they good for?"

"They are extremely good for insulting," Einarr said with another cheery guffaw. "Come in to dine with us and you may insult them all you wish."

A pleasant meal at the long table awaited them. The rest of Einarr's family was assembled: his wife, various elderly people from both sides of the family, the odd aunt and uncle come to visit indefinitely, and a host of assorted children. After they had commenced, another youth slipped into his place at the far end of the table from Einarr, his every motion denoting extreme stealth and discretion.

Einarr, however involved in his discourse, was not to be deceived. He broke off in midsentence in the middle of a self-derogatory anecdote and glowered down the length of the table, inspiring a pall of silence to descend on the room.

"I see we are joined by my son Leckny," he declared, "who has finally seen fit to seek out our company."

Leckny slowly raised his eyes to contemplate his father, the guests, and the rest of his disapproving family staring back at him. He was a slender youth, just starting to grow tall, with a thick thatch of wheat-colored hair falling over one eye. His unconcealed eye, a startling deep blue, darted apprehensively toward Einarr.

"I'm sorry I'm late," he murmured. "I had some trouble with my horse. I had to walk home."

"I daresay your horse didn't feel like going hunting this morning any more than you did." Einarr snorted, sawing off a great hunk of oozing meat and thrusting it into one cheek so he could gnaw away at it with furious gnashes of his jaws. To his Scipling guests he grumbled, "I don't know why it is that a man's son so often takes after his mother's side of the family. I've given the boy everything he needs to be a hunter—hounds, horses, bows, arrows, hawks, and a hundred teachers to show him how to use them—but he says he has no taste for killing. No taste for killing, can you imagine that? Was there ever a true man who didn't know it was his duty to kill things—including his fellow man when necessary, when all other means of reasoning with him don't succeed? How is a man to feed and clothe his family if he doesn't hunt and kill something?"

Waving one plump hand, Einarr's wife, Mabil, shook her head and cast her eyes up to the rafters in virtuous martyrdom. "It isn't I who spoiled him," she declared. "He's been different from the start. His little brothers are as bloodthirsty a lot as any man can desire. Just yesterday they shot and killed a dozen songbirds with their little bows and arrows, and you can't get within a dozen yards of any barn cat on this place."

The three younger brothers grinned hideously like a trio of fox pups, bright-eyed, freckled, frowsy little engines of destruction who gnawed at their meat with grubby hands, snarling among themselves over the best bit.

Leckny kept his eyes on his plate, poking dispiritedly at

what was on it. His set shoulders and clenched jaws denoted that it was an old argument.

"We no longer dress in skins," Jutta said into the stillness of the family dispute. "Nor do we have to kill our own livestock if we have thralls and hired men to do it. I see nothing wrong with disliking the act of taking a life. I maybe get a squeamish feeling whenever I have to wring the neck of a chicken."

"It's just womanishness," Einarr grunted, shaking his head. "Women always dislike the blood and the kicking and thrashing, the last pitiful cries of the dying beast."

"Yes, and everyone knows that women are far more civilized than men," Jutta retorted, rising to the quarrel in a flash. "The day will come when killing is the exception rather than the rule. Then what shall we do with you old killers, who are always looking around red-eyed, thirsty for blood? I daresay we'll have to keep you all locked up, chained to a wall somewhere, so the rest of us can feel safe."

The Sciplings greeted her speech with a roar of acclaim, laughing in delight at the expense of their host. Einarr grinned amiably and shrugged his shoulders.

"Bested again," he said. "I think she's been taking lessons from my wife."

"If a woman has a good mind, she's not afraid to speak it," Mabil said with a good-natured grin. "Besides, we know she comes from Bardhol. I daresay Margret was just as outspoken in her younger days, since she doesn't hesitate to speak out now."

Jutta had never considered herself similar to Margret, but after a moment's consideration she decided the comparison was not unflattering. She smiled, glancing down the table at Leckny, who sat bolt upright with his face burning. He was about as handsome as anything she'd seen around Thorgestrstead and possibly more so.

Leckny suddenly stood up at his place, jolting back the bench so that his younger brothers were nearly unseated.

"I don't need anyone to stand up to defend me," he said, "let alone a mere girl!" So saying, he stalked away and slammed the door after himself with a crash.

"Well!" said Mabil.

"All the more for us," declared one of his younger fox-faced brothers, spearing the meat off Leckny's plate, which commenced a fresh squabble among the three of them.

Without much difficulty Jutta was persuaded to spend the rest of the day at Sorengard. She welcomed the opportunity of enjoying a normal farmstead similar to Thorgestrstead—where order and progress ruled—instead of the chaos and decay of Bardhol. After dinner, while the maidservants and thralls cleared away the leavings and washed up the mess, Mabil and Einarr and their guests settled down for a nice long afternoon natter on the grassy bank alongside the great hall. It naturally fell out that the older people talked together, leaving Jutta and Simon glancing at each other rather uncomfortably, while Simon pulled up handfuls of soft grass.

"I bid you welcome to Mikillborg," Jutta commenced in her best polite conversational voice. "I don't believe I've ever heard of Sciplings coming here before. Is it very difficult to find the way?"

"Thank you, and yes, it is difficult to find the way from our place to yours," Simon said. "In fact, that's why we've stayed as long as we have, waiting for the right things to line up so there is a gateway back."

"And has Mikillborg something to do with this gateway?" Jutta inquired.

"I don't understand it completely, but it has something to do with positions of stars, seasons, and certain places. My father consulted with a wizard, who guided us to Mikillborg and the barrow fields."

"The barrow fields? My ancestors are buried there."

"We don't plan to disturb them in the least. There is a place where all the ley lines meet, and at a certain time we can step through the barrier and be back in our own realm, in our own time—or so it is hoped. The wizard explained that we don't actually know how much time has passed in our realm. It could be nine hundred years, for all we know, or just a few moments."

"What a shocking thing, not to know what you'll find when you step through. Perhaps you'd better just stay."

Simon shook his head. "We were told that too many Sciplingur are already here, and our presence and our iron weapons cause grievous harm to the natural balance of your world. A couple of Einarr's ewes have birthed deformed lambs, and my father fears it is our fault."

"Ah, I see. That is unfortunate. I myself perceived that there was an atmosphere about you. Not that is it bad or anything unfavorable—you simply are not Alfar."

"We are lacking in magic," Simon said. "Tell me—if this isn't a rude question—do you have magical powers?"

Jutta looked away from his bright inquisitive gaze. When she was a child, her mother had struggled to suppress the latent powers that kept trying to erupt from her innocent child. A temper tantrum could set the house afire; a nightmare could conjure terrifying creatures. There were bonds, locks, bars, and doors that had to be taught in order to protect everyone from his or her own secret powers. People could not live together peaceably without agreeing to certain truces, including the usage of one's magical abilities. In modern times powers were somewhat frowned on as hoary old relics of grimmer days—dark, unpleasant attributes everyone possessed and feared and didn't discuss much.

"Most Alfar are not trained to do much with their powers," she said carefully, "so that makes us very little different from you Sciplingur."

"I wish I had powers," Simon said. "It would be wonderful to move things without touching them, to know things, to summon creatures to do my bidding."

"It's not as pleasant as you imagine. Sometimes your powers do the exact opposite of what you wish. And for every time you use them, something is taken away. A price is exacted, because often the enactment of what you wish is contrary to the natural law. So you may gain on one side and lose somewhere else. It's a dangerous gamble. Sometimes I wish I were like you, so I wouldn't have to worry about something unexplained happening."

"What do you mean, something unexplained?"

"It is difficult to describe to someone with no understanding of powers. We Alfar have abilities that you Sciplings cannot grasp, although I have heard that a few Sciplings are born with some powers and are looked upon as either madmen or freaks."

"If I had powers, I'd use them to get home," Simon said, averting his eyes, but his voice sounded wistful. "We've tried following the ley lines, but they're all broken and disrupted and lost. We may be trapped here forever."

"I wish I could be of help to you," Jutta said. "Perhaps I know someone who could be of assistance. I have a friend who is tracing the old ley lines. She mentioned a barrow where several lines meet."

"Sigmund's barrow? She knows where it is?"

"No, she hasn't found it yet, and there are a hundred barrows and they all look very similar. But she could find it, I think. I shall speak to her."

"I'm not certain you should. Those barrows are a dangerous place, I've heard. This woman's corpse you found is proof of that. Eight people have died mysteriously in the barrow fields, and I wouldn't want you to join them."

"How long have you been searching for Sigmund's barrow?"

"This will be the third summer. I was just a young lad when my father and I accidentally fell through one of the secret gates into your realm. I think I could live here quite happily, but Pabbi is anxious about my mother and sisters. And there is the question of our presence doing damage to the Alfar, so it is best that we leave. We need to find the barrow on a night called Brjaladur."

"The most unlucky night of the year," Jutta said with a shudder, remembering how her mother had hung up holly and evergreen and other salubrious herbs to ward off the evil that ran rampant at the time of the changing stars, when the good stars went into decline and the evil star Fantur the Red Rogue ascended. "It's at the end of summer—not far off. You don't have much time left this year to find Sigmund's barrow. I would be pleased to help you all I can. Sigmund was my direct ancestor. Perhaps he'll be more inclined to show me his resting place."

"It's dangerous in the barrows at night. I'd rather you didn't get involved with our plight."

"Dangerous? How might that be? I've heard there are barrow robbers, but you Sciplings are head and shoulders taller than most Alfar. Just the sight of you two giants ought to frighten a barrow robber to death."

"It's not the mortal barrow robbers we're concerned about," Simon said in a low voice. "There are other things, creatures of the dark that come to protect the secrets of the barrows. They call them Myrkriddir."

"Myrkriddir? That's an ancient legend. Someone has told you this to frighten you away. If there were Myrkriddir long ago, I doubt if they are still around, and even if there were, I can't imagine them choosing our barrow field to lurk in."

"Why not? It's a very out-of-the-way place for old legends to hide in. Few people are going to come poking their noses in."

"Have you seen any Myrkriddir?"

"No, but Einarr has, and all his thralls are terrified of them."

Jutta considered briefly, wondering if Einarr was telling stories just to keep the Sciplings out of the barrows. "Einarr is very kind to have taken you in all this time. He is truly an excellent man."

"Yes, truly. We insist on working to be of what use we can. Being stout fellows is a great help sometimes, when you don't have time to hitch up a draft horse."

Jutta laughed with him, and at that moment Leckny chose to appear, coming around the end of a wall as if he had been lurking there, watching them and perhaps eavesdropping. He stood a moment and glared at them, his eyes like blue fire, then to Jutta he said, "Come away from that Scipling lout. You don't know who you're talking to."

CHAPTER 6

"What do you mean?" Jutta inquired with freezing hauteur, feeling her hackles rising.

Leckny twitched one shoulder in Simon's direction. "You know very well what I mean. They're not our kind. They're Sciplings, we're Alfar. They're different. Not as . . . advanced as Alfar."

"Barbarians," Simon said with an appealing grin. "We hear this wherever we go."

"You're not a barbarian," Jutta told him firmly. "You're quite a nice fellow, I've discovered—unlike certain others I've encountered at Sorengard."

"Don't be deceived," Leckny said. "You just don't know these Sciplings very well yet."

"I think it's time I was leaving," Simon said, rising to his feet and towering over Leckny for a menacing moment before turning away. "We can talk later, perhaps, when certain problems aren't around."

Jutta turned on Leckny the moment he was gone. "How dare you? Who do you think you are, flouting our laws of guestright and common courtesy so flagrantly? Don't you know that Alfar have followed the rules of guestright for a thousand generations or more? And here you are insulting guests right beneath your own roof—your father's roof, I should say. Haven't you been taught there are penalties for insulting strangers that you might never have dreamed of?"

"These are Sciplings," Leckny explained with a pained expression crinkling his brow, as if Jutta were talking about welcoming pigs into the house. "And there are only two of them.

You don't know what they might be bringing among us—diseases that might kill us all or their strange ideas that could destroy everything we believe in or upset the delicate balance of natural powers. Chaos and natural elements could come crashing down on us and wipe us off the face of Skarpsey."

"Oh, faugh. I've heard about your supposed deformed lambs. It happens all the time, and immediately the ignorant and troublemakers start looking for someone to blame, someone who doesn't look quite right or act the proper way. It's too easy to blame the strangers in our midst for our troubles, you great fool."

"What makes you think you know anything at all about Sciplings?" Leckny demanded. "You've come here and clapped your eyes on them and promptly fallen in love with them, all in the space of time since dinner, and now you think you know more about them than I do? Let me tell you, my fine cat keeper, I could tell you things about Sciplings that would send you back to Bardhol at a dead run."

"I am not a cat keeper," Jutta snapped, feeling a blinding white rage stealing up on her. "At least I have the fortitude to wring a chicken's neck now and then. I'm not a squeaming, mincing coward."

"Excellent. If anything or anyone needs killing, we'll know who to call on when the day arrives when killing is the only measure of a person's worth. Strange how I'm quoting your own ideas, isn't it?"

Jutta's face burned with outrage and humiliation. She had been caught in her own trap. "This is totally different," she replied. "I can't abide your hypocrisy in maligning two homeless Sciplings who want nothing more from you than a resting place in the search for a passage back to their own realm."

"That's not all they want," Leckny retorted.

"Oh? Indeed, what else do they want?" Jutta demanded.

"Gold," he answered. "Alfar barrow gold. Why else did you think you were looking for Sigmund's barrow? Surely you didn't believe that story about ley lines. Everyone knows the ley lines are gone, broken down and destroyed. If they ever did work, they wouldn't work now for a pair of ignorant barbarian Sciplings."

"You don't know that," Jutta sputtered.

"I do know that Sigmund's barrow is full of gold, and Sciplings are famous for their lust for gold. It doesn't take a wizard to figure out why they really want that barrow. Gold is all Sciplings care about, and their lust for it overwhelms all bonds and loyalties."

"And your idiocy overwhelms all previous idiots. You're just prating all the nonsense you've heard other people say about Sciplings. Everyone says bad things about anything they don't understand."

"You'll find out the hard way, then. Has our friend Simon told you yet you ought to go to the Scipling realm so you could earn piles of money with your magical powers?"

Jutta opened her mouth, but no skillful rejoinder came out. She realized how deeply she hated this person when he grinned at her knowingly.

"They covet our gold and our powers in the most dreadful way," he continued. "Don't allow yourself to be deceived or to pity them for their supposed plight. I daresay they could get back to their own realm any time they wished."

"As if you knew anything!" Jutta sputtered at last, so furious that her tongue could scarcely speak straight.

"I know there've been eight women killed in the two years these Sciplings have lived with us," he answered in a low tone, darting a lowering glance toward Petrus and his father. "I just don't want you to be the next."

"Oh, so that's what you think? That's horrible! As if those women could have anything to do with the Sciplings finding that barrow! I've never heard anything more preposterous and lamebrained! Besides, you don't know they're all dead, do you?"

"I'm pretty certain they are. Your finding Lina's bones only reduces the possibility that some of them merely ran away."

"Why on earth would killing a bunch of women help two Sciplings get back to their own realm?" Jutta demanded.

"Sciplings worship death," Leckny said with a wry little

smile. "Don't think that because they're Sciplings they know nothing about power, especially the power of death."

Jutta felt an icy wave of gooseflesh ripple up her spine. "What utter nonsense," she muttered, shaking her head and hoping he hadn't seen her shiver.

"Go back to your grandmothers and your cats," Leckny whispered. "Forget about Sciplings and gold and barrows if you want to live to see your old age. I doubt that I shall. I fear I shall become the ultimate expert on death before this summer is out. Perhaps even by the next full moon."

With that, he turned and stalked away, leaving Jutta standing there staring after him. She shook off the peculiar feelings of dread he had inspired in her and joined the rest of the group relaxing in the cool breezes. Very soon it occurred to her that this was the life she had been born to, a life of comfort and ease, with other people to do the rough work and clean up the table after meals. Guiltily she thought of her little old grandmothers diligently hauling their water all these years in heavy buckets. At one time they must have had servants, but now they were their own servants.

Mabil and her female relatives were in the middle of making much of Jutta—young and pretty feminine society being limited at Sorengard—when one of the cousins suddenly broke off with a muffled moan, elbowing her neighbor.

"Oh, no. Here's that old madman again," she muttered.

Mabil rolled up her eyes. "Drat. I was hoping we could be spared his rantings and ravings for once and enjoy a nice occasion without having cold water dashed in our faces."

Jutta looked on with interest as a familiar raggle-taggle figure came tapping through the gate.

"Bjalfur!" Einarr shouted, as if he were in the throes of delight at seeing him. "Come over here and wet your dry and thirsty throat. It's a long way from Mikillborg you've come, and I expect you're parched as a pot of salt."

"That's Amma Dora's suitor," Jutta whispered, relishing the wave of giggles and arch looks her news created.

"Greetings," Bjalfur said, seating himself with a great sigh on the seat Einarr himself had just vacated. "This looks like a festive and idle party."

"As idle as we can be," Einarr said. "There's nothing good to be said for our enemies, since they seem to have ceased to exist, and this wretched prospect for peace seems to go on without hope of relief. I shall die an old man in my own straw bed, in bitter humiliation."

"I wouldn't be so certain," Bjalfur said. "You may yet have hopes of dying with a lance in your gizzard. You think that the evil tides of war have retreated, never to return, but like the tides of ocean, war will return one day."

"He's always going on about such things." Mabil sniffed. "I wish he'd just shut up. If we're going to have a war with someone, I don't want to be worried about it now."

That was the sort of talk the menfolk appreciated most. They gathered around Bjalfur to hear what else he had to say, with hungry expressions on their faces.

"I've seen longer periods of peace than this one suddenly turn dark and ugly," Bjalfur went on. "There's no telling about the Dokkalfar. You may think they've been beaten and gone into retreat, but they have worlds underground that you've never dreamed of. I daresay that legions of them are down below our very feet, forging swords by the wagonload and laying their plans. They will never rest until the dayfaring world is destroyed and their wizards have brought back the eternal ice and dark of the Fimbul Winter."

"I'd like to see them try it. We'll fix them," some of the younger men growled, almost pawing the ground in their eagerness.

"Well, it won't be easy, as lazy and soft as the Ljosalfar have become," Bjalfur said. "Dokkalfar wizards have not fallen into disrepute or retirement. They're still fulminating away at their vile spells, with their eyes set fast on the destruction of the Ljosalfar. Most of you will probably live to see the day they come up from their subterranean lairs like armies of ants searching for prey."

"I should be going home," Jutta announced, smiling to cover a deep and abiding uneasiness at all this disturbing talk.

"My grandmothers will be wondering if I don't get home before dark."

To her delight, they all clamored in protest, and Mabil seemed genuinely grieved that she wasn't going to stay for a week or two to visit with her. It was the Alfar way to keep guests as long as possible, weeks, months, or occasionally years, if the guests themselves didn't object, and usually they didn't if they had nothing to go home for. Much as she was tempted, Jutta knew she needed to be back at Bardhol.

"Then we shall ride with you and you can show us the last resting place of poor Lina," Einarr said when it was thoroughly established that Jutta's mind could not be changed. "I swear I shall catch the foul creature who is killing our women, and we'll hang him from his own roof timber, if he has one, or I'd be delighted to use my own."

Almost the entire household accompanied Jutta homeward— anyone who wanted a look, including Mabil, the three young fox-faced brothers, the Sciplings, sundry visiting relatives who had been under Einarr's roof for who knew how long, and five or six thralls in case they were needed for something. For a journey of such grim purpose, it was quite a festive procession trotting along over the green fells and through the shady glens. Notably absent was Leckny, which suited Jutta just fine. Bjalfur also chose to remain at Sorenguard, since he had just come from Mikillborg and his business of stirring up Einarr for warfare wasn't concluded yet.

"There—just there where I tied the scrap of her apron to the bush," Jutta said, pointing to the scrubby thicket where she had found the ring and the finger bones. The barrows and thickets, she knew, were all too similar for her to remember where she and Frida had been following the ley lines.

The chieftain took charge at once, and the menfolk moved into the thicket with a purposeful crackling of branches and a general trampling around.

"I don't see it," Einarr said, coming out after a moment, scratched and sporting a sprig of plum blossoms in his hood. "You'll have to show me where it is."

Jutta crept into the thicket, just as she had on the night

Bensi had been eluding her. To her astonishment, there was nothing to be found, not a rag, scrap, or bone. She sank down to her knees at the spot, staring as if her eyes were not to be believed. Then she heard a stealthy sound behind her, a footstep carefully placed with slow care, but the leaves and twigs of the thicket betrayed the intruder's presence. She whirled around, only to encounter Leckny creeping toward her with a repulsive grin on his face.

"What are you doing here?" she snapped, furious at the worried pounding of her heart and the intense burning of her blushing face. "I thought you had more important things to be doing."

"I do," he replied with a nonchalant shrug. "Did you find your skeleton yet?"

"No, but this is where I saw it. Someone has been here and taken it." She pointed to a few strands of long pale hair clinging to a branch and floating in the breeze. "Male or female, I can't tell which."

"Perhaps it was the Myrkriddir," Leckny said, widening his eyes and shivering his shoulders in an exaggerated shudder of supposed fear.

"You're hideous and stupid besides," Jutta said in disgust.

"Don't you believe in the Myrkriddir?" he demanded, placing one hand over his heart and striking a storyteller's pose. "Ghostly riders who gallop across the land in times of approaching evil, riding over rooftops to warn the people, clutching their reins in bony fingers, skull faces gleaming in the moonlight."

"It's nothing to joke about, you fool," Jutta snapped. "That's one of our ancestors' favorite tales."

"I'll bet you heard it from your grandmothers," he replied. "They're always trying to frighten people away from the barrows. They believe in Myrkriddir, don't they?"

"You can leave my grandmothers out of this, thank you."

"Halloa in there!" Einarr's voice boomed. "Did you find something?"

"She's gone," Jutta called, backing away. She snapped off the twig with the hairs floating from it. "All that's left are a few hairs on a branch. This is the place, though. I know she was here. And I had the feeling that she had died in this spot."

"You don't suppose she's walking, being disturbed by someone finding her, do you?" Mabil demanded in a hushed tone, her ruddy countenance blanching cold and pale.

Einarr shrugged his shoulders and plucked off the three long hairs from the twig. "I think not. It's been a long time indeed since I've heard any reports of the dead walking."

"She wasn't that sort of person when she was alive," Mabil said. "A very sensible girl, not the sort to be any trouble at all to anybody."

"But if she knew her murderer was nearby and unpunished—" Jutta said, then stopped lest her eyes and accusations drift unheedingly toward the Sciplings.

"Do the dead always walk in the Alfar realm?" Simon asked a trifle too eagerly. "Scipling dead are seldom as lively as the dead seem to be in the Alfar realm. A great many Sciplings have never even seen a ghost."

"Well, I assure you, we do have a problem with them from time to time," Einarr said, scowling in a preoccupied fashion. He darted a sharp glance at Jutta. "You're certain this was the spot?"

Jutta moved away from the thicket, her eyes on the ground. With a small cry of discovery she stooped, finding the finger bones and the ring where she had crushed them into the dirt. "Now do you believe me?" she asked, picking up the handful of evidence to place it in Einarr's palm.

"We shall ask Lina's mother about the ring," he said grimly. "But I'm satisfied. I'd take the word of a Hesturkona on nearly anything, even without this much proof."

"There was more," Jutta said. "An entire skeleton, but someone has taken it away."

"Who else could have known it was here?" Einarr asked.

"Only my grandmothers," Jutta said, "but I don't think they would do that." For a moment Amma Sigla's image bustled through her mind, clucking her tongue at finding an untidy old skeleton cluttering up the barrows of her ancestors. And Amma Dora would be horrified at the disgrace of her revered ancestors harboring a mere hired girl such as Lina, when all of them were of the noble clan Hestur.

Then, despite Jutta's indignant protestations, Leckny was assigned by Einarr to accompany her home to Bardhol.

"I shall go, too," Simon said with such an endearing lopsided grin that Jutta relented immediately.

"I don't really need anyone to guard me," she said as the three of them rode off together. "I've been here hundreds of times on this trail."

"But we now have a killer in our midst," Leckny said, darting a villainous glance at Simon plodding along behind on his heavy, lumbering Scipling steed. "Who knows who it might be? Everyone you look at might pursue a dark and murderous hobby every time the moon is full. It could even be me. Perhaps you'll never reach Bardhol alive." He favored her with another of his horrible grins, which made him look truly demented and dangerous.

"Maybe you'll be the next carcass they find if you don't silence yourself," Jutta said.

"Poor Lina," Leckny continued. "I wonder what she was up to. I wonder what she found out before she died. There must have been something that someone didn't want her to talk about."

"She was only a hired girl. What could she know?"

"Who knows what she could have known, except Lina? And her killers."

"Oh, so now there's more than one? More than just you, I should say?"

"Perhaps it was the Myrkriddir who killed her."

Jutta made a noise of utmost disgust and reined in her horse to ride beside Simon. They chatted pleasantly for a short while, until Elding's longer legs outdistanced Simon's horse. Leckny trotted his horse up beside her at once and continued.

"Maybe she was getting too close to finding Sigmund's barrow," he hissed. "You know she had ambitions of getting out of this quiet little place and going to one of the big settlements where ships and merchants from all over the world are always coming and going. Where you don't have to look at the same dull, stupid faces for the rest of your life." He sighed sharply and scowled involuntarily.

"Oh ho. You're tired of boring little Mikillborg, are you? The chieftain's eldest son and you've not got enough to satisfy you?"

"Maybe what I need is one of your grandmothers' cats," he retorted. "You at least have a wonderful career ahead of you, growing old on that mountaintop with a dozen yowling cats for company."

Instead of replying to his jibe, Jutta dug her heels into the ribs of her horse and sent the startled mare away at a flying gallop. Leckny's stout mountain pony gamely charged after her, uttering a worried whinny. Simon's horse fell into a determined, rolling gallop, very promptly outdistanced by the other two. Jutta's mare swiveled one ear back and cocked an eye at her rider, waiting for a signal. Jutta kicked the mare again, surging ahead at a glorious gallop, leaving the short-legged horses at an increasing distance behind and whinnying indignantly. It was only a few miles to Bardhol, and Jutta let the mare run to the bottom of the hill, where she halted to look back for Leckny and Simon. Leckny was visible in the barrows, pounding along bravely. Simon was nowhere in sight. She heard a faint whinny and smiled.

Knowing she would get a severe tongue-lashing for bringing a horse home wringing wet and winded, she turned and rode at a walk away from the barrows along a path she had not yet explored. It led southward around the edges of fields and a broad meadow where a flock of speckled sheep grazed. Across the meadow stood a hall of blackened turf, surrounded by numerous outbuildings and paddocks. It was a pretty picture, so she stopped to rest her horse and take a longer look at it. Exactly the kind of house and farm she wanted someday, with plenty of thralls to help her run it. She supposed her sister Asta would inherit Thorgestrstead one day and become mistress there. Jutta and her younger sisters could stay on with much reduced status if they wished, or perhaps they would marry and join their husbands' households.

Leckny's pony came pounding up behind her, lathered from head to hoof and puffing hard.

"I never thought that ancient nag of yours could run so fast," Leckny said, casting an eye over the mare, which was dry and calm, snatching up mouthfuls of grass. "It was pretty rude of you to run off and leave me like that."

"I thought you could keep up," Jutta said in feigned surprise. "I'm so sorry, but I suppose Elding still likes a little gallop now and then."

"No wonder she's called Lightning. But speed isn't everything when it comes to a practical horse. I daresay you wouldn't want to hitch her to a cart or have her pull a plow down a field."

"It would be an insult to harness a Hestur horse to a plow," Jutta said. "These horses are used to carrying warriors to battle, flying to the attack like the wings of death itself."

"Or for pulling a cartload of cats and old ladies to Mikillborg," Leckny added with a rude cackle.

Jutta elevated her chin and gazed at him with chilling disfavor. "Nor are they in any way compromised by it. If you want a cart pulled or a field plowed, you'll have to stick to short, fat hairy creatures such as you're riding. You may suppose it's riding, but truly you've never been on a horse unless you've ridden a Hestur steed. Of course, you'd have to learn to ride a real horse rather than a pony."

"You're the most haughty, arrogant creature I know," Leckny said.

"Wrong again. You don't know anything about me, and as far as I can see, you never shall."

"What pride you've got for a cat keeper. Where are you going?"

Jutta started away, turning her back to him squarely. "I think I'll just stop by to water my horse," she said.

"You can't. That's Thorungard."

"And why can't I?"

"They don't like strangers there. That Frida woman makes sure her ugly great thralls run everybody off."

"It so happens I'm not a stranger. I'm good friends with Frida."

"How is that possible? She's too good for almost everybody."

"We're going to study ley lines together. She has a vast amount of education when it comes to the ancient arts. She'll be glad that I stopped by."

Frida, however, was not at home, they were informed by a rather surly thrall who met them at the gate. They could water there horses down the hill at the back, but the mistress was not home, so nobody would be seeing her.

"Tell her that Jutta from Bardhol called and that I shall stop by again," she said in her most haughty tone. "Tell her that I immensely enjoyed our visit. And I see a watering trough just there beside your byre, so we shall be watering our horses there. I'm sure your mistress wouldn't like to hear of your rudeness to a friend of hers."

Thus defeated, the surly thrall suddenly remembered his manners. "If you'd like to light down, I shall water your horses myself while you rest in the shade of the tree. Stay as long as you like; that sun is hot and horrid today, ain't it? I'll send a woman out from the kitchen to fetch you a drink of ale. Mistress would have it so."

"Well," Leckny said when they were comfortably ensconced beneath an ancient tree, sipping horns of dark biting ale. "How did you come to such an acquaintance with this woman? No one knows much about her or her household. They were strangers when they came here."

"And we all know how strangers are regarded in Mikillborg," Jutta said. "Perhaps if anyone had made the effort, they would have become acquainted. Or do you always save your friendship for only the people whose ancestors first settled Mikillborg?"

Leckny shrugged. "We just don't ever get strangers in Mikillborg, except for these people at Thorungard, the Sciplings, and you. It's more than we should be expected to handle. And all within the space of two years."

"How did Frida come to own this place?"

"They say it was an inheritance. Old Thorun had no children of his own to pass it down to, and he hated all his brothers' sons, so he gave it to Frida. How they're related we have no idea. Old Thorun died soon after, still gleeful about disappointing his nephews."

"I think the people of this settlement are very unkind when it comes to strangers, if you are any example of how they are treated," Jutta said.

"Me? Why are you singling me out for your indictment? We were having a very civil conversation up until now."

"It's very obvious to me that you're placing the blame for these murders on the Sciplings for no other reason than that they are strangers. And it's also obvious that Frida is shunned for the same reason."

"Hmm. I'd never thought of her before as the killer, but she arrived about the time the killings started."

"You are full of the worst kind of rot," Jutta said.

"Yes, I know. I'd rather believe it's the Sciplings. They're barbarians, a much lower form of life than we Alfar. They have none of the finer sensibilities. I think they're little better than animals in human form, except that I like animals far better and hate to insult them with such a comparison."

"You see? You regard strangers as something less than yourself. These Sciplings are not so very different from us, except they don't have magical powers."

"Which makes them all the more dangerous. We have our powers to guide us when we make decisions. These Sciplings simply decide on whatever suits them at the moment. They're unpredictable creatures with very little regard for honor and family and tradition."

"How do you know all that? Have you seen them abandon their family and clan or violate their own traditions? What have you seen them do that is dishonorable? Nothing, right? I suspect they've been very pleasant company and good guests for as long as they've been at Sorengard."

Leckny scowled and threw out the last dregs of his ale. "I have good reason for feeling the way I do about them. Nothing has been the same in our house since they came. They are turning my own father against me."

"What do you mean?" Jutta demanded.

Leckny shook his head, clenching his jaws as if he wished he hadn't spoken out. "What has that wretched thrall done with our horses? It's time we were off instead of lolling here in the shade. My father must be wondering where I am."

In silence they rode back toward the barrows, where they found Simon waiting at the foot of Bardhol's hill.

"Where did you go in such a hurry?" he asked in mild reproof. "Everyone else is probably back at Sorengard by now and getting ready to eat supper."

Leckny bade Jutta a curt farewell and galloped away into the barrows without waiting for Simon to accompany him.

"Don't mind him," Jutta said. "He likes nothing more than being rude to people."

"I should know that well enough," Simon said with a wry grin. "But it's no matter. I've got broad shoulders. Can I ride home with you to your door?"

"I'm home already, and my door is just at the top of this hill. You're more interested in riding home to your supper, I suspect, although my grandmothers would be delighted to host a Scipling at their table."

"Another day, perhaps. We'll be out tonight hunting with the full moon."

"Hunting for your gateway back to your own realm? Then perhaps I won't see you tomorrow, or ever again, if you find it. A pity; I was looking forward to making a friend of a Scipling."

"Don't count on getting rid of me that fast," Simon said. "We've searched the barrows a hundred times and never found it yet. Perhaps I'll grow old here and never find it."

"Would that be so very terrible?"

"One hates to perish in a foreign land. Not enough mourners to sing songs and tell lies around your graveside."

"I'd be delighted to tell all manner of lies for you. But not too soon, if you don't mind."

"Yes, not too soon. I must first meet your grandmothers, at least. I've heard a great deal about them and their cats."

"Do you like cats?" Jutta asked.

"Yes, somewhat, if they're friendly. A man needs all the friends he can get sometimes." His glance in Leckny's direction betrayed his true thoughts.

"Pay no attention to him. I have a feeling he is jealous of you for some reason and that is why he is so hateful. Jealousy is a terrible fear of losing something important."

"It wasn't always so. We started out to be great friends two years ago. Then suddenly something changed, and he started to hate me. I don't even know why. It's too bad, because I liked him tremendously. You couldn't ask for a better friend than Leckny, but I've lost him. I guess I'm truly an ignorant barbarian, as he says. Good-bye," he said, turning his horse toward supper.

Jutta rode slowly up the hill, her heart sinking into its accustomed dull despair as she passed the fallen-in huts and barns and collapsed walls and sad decay of Bardhol's former glory. In the declining light of early evening everything looked older and more broken down.

And the cats were waiting for her. They came scuttling out of their hiding places, appearing on walls and posts and rooftops, yowling an excited greeting. Even fat old Mishka worked himself into an unusual enthusiastic display of energy by running up to a dead tree trunk and furiously sharpening his claws.

Jutta brushed the dried sweat off her horse before she came into the house, where she found her grandmothers ready to sit down to eat, with the cats already purring and twining around the table legs.

"Back so soon? I thought they'd offer to keep you for the night," Margret said. "It's no small journey there and back in one day."

"We came almost all the way back to search for the body, so I decided to come on home," Jutta said.

"Poor Lina," Amma Thruda said. "I expect her mother will be glad to know what happened to her, at least."

"We never found her," Jutta said. "Someone else got there before me and took away her skeleton. All I found today was a ring and a few finger bones. But Einarr said he would take the ring to Lina's mother to see if she recognized it. At least I had that much proof."

Amma Sigla sank back in her chair. "This is terrible!" she gasped. "Who could have done such a thing?"

"Who would want an old skeleton?" Ingi asked with a shudder of distaste that knocked her cup over into her plate.

"The graves of our revered ancestors are being desecrated by these barrow robbers and murderers," Amma Dora said. "How dare they disturb the final rest of some of Skarpsey's greatest heroes? Have they no respect for tradition?"

"Is there much power lingering in the old ley lines?" Jutta asked, nonchalantly buttering her bread. At once she detected a cool and wary change in her ancestors. Margret darted a wicked glare at Ingi, whose mouth was open to expound on the topic. Ingi shut her mouth with a snap.

"Who has been telling you there's power in the ley lines?" Margret asked. "No one knows better than we that there's very little left of the old tracks."

"Oh, the Sciplings at Sorengard are hoping to find a powerful enough site in the barrows so they can send themselves back to their own realm," Jutta replied. "Do you think they'll find it? Is tonight a good night for it?"

"I don't like the idea of Sciplings bungling around among our barrows," Margret said. "You say they're going to be searching tonight?"

"I fear so," Jutta said.

"A fool's errand," Margret snapped. "They'll never find what they're looking for. If it's powers they want, they ought to consult a wizard, if they can find a good one nowadays, which is about as difficult as finding a needle in a haystack. Maybe more so; you seldom see as many bad needles as you do bad wizards."

"Or haystacks," Amma Ingi added brightly. "There are plenty more haystacks than wizards, you know."

Margret continued to grumble around while the meal was

finished up and cleared away and the evening's sitting work commenced around the fire. Jutta worked on a huge pile of mending that she was sure none of them would ever see the end of. Her grandmothers seemed more constrained and less talkative, preferring to work in the silence of their own thoughts instead of their usual chatter. Amma Ingi, however, still nattered away about this and that, oblivious to the nonparticipation around her.

"Do have a cup of this warm milk," Thruda said when Jutta's yawns became too long and close together to ignore any longer. "It's just what you need to rest well tonight. It's been a long day for you, has it not?"

Jutta sipped at the warm fresh milk, suddenly feeling very sleepy. It had been a long day, she was forced to admit. "Bodies and barrow robbers and Sciplings," she said with a yawn. "It has been rather exciting. I'm more than ready for bed now."

"Finish your milk, then," Thruda said, "and I shall clean up the table. I can see how tired you are."

Jutta's eyes were scarcely staying open. Maybe her weariness made her clumsy, but she set down her cup of milk for a moment too near the edge of the table, and somehow Bensi got his head into it and commenced lapping away with great enthusiasm.

"Bensi!" Thruda said in horror, and Bensi jerked his head out of the cup, tipping it onto the floor. At once the tribe of kettir swooped in on the spilled milk and polished it off before Jutta could do more than move her skirt out of the way.

"Oh, well," Thruda said with a shrug. "It won't hurt if the kettir all sleep well tonight, too. Take as many of them with you as you wish."

Jutta didn't wish to take any of them, except maybe to the nearest well with a rock tied to their necks. Wearily she climbed up into the loft and fell into her bed, shoving aside Svartur and Mishka so she would have a pillow.

She slept like a stone for the greater part of the night, but something niggled at the edges of her consciousness, a familiar sound but something that shouldn't have been going on during the night. She awakened suddenly in the dark hours before dawn. The sound, whatever it was, had ceased. She knew it was early morning from the tentative crowing of the rooster whose beady eye never missed the first pale blush of dawn.

Then she heard a faint murmur of voices down below. Her grandmothers usually waited until good daylight to go out, not caring to risk their necks on unseen rocks in the dark.

Wondering if one of them was sick, Jutta knelt beside the loft opening to look down. Her grandmothers were standing around the table in their outdoor clothes. Jutta rubbed her eyes and pinched her cheek to make sure she was truly awake and not dreaming. She thought she was awake, but the scene was too bizarre. The table seemed to be covered with gold objects: chains, cups, rings, ornaments, and coins. Most were clotted with earth.

"There's that lot," one of them murmured softly. "Put it with the rest and make sure there's no sign."

"I think we frightened those Sciplings properly," said someone else in a loud whisper, probably Ingi. "They won't be back."

"Shh. They'll make their own misfortune if they do."

The gold disappeared into a sack, and Dora moved with it out of Jutta's vision, unless she cared to lean farther forward and poke her head into the room below. Jutta stayed still, scarcely breathing, wondering about the warm milk that had plunged her into such a stupor. The cats, she remembered, had retired to the hearth and collapsed with contented grins on their faces, which was nothing unusual for cats after a tasty meal.

"Now, then, to bed. I'm worn down to nothing."

They hung up their cloaks and gowns as neatly as ever and climbed into their paneled wall beds. The lamp was extinguished, and the room was plunged into darkness. Jutta crept back to her own bed and lay awake until dawn, listening to the muffled snores coming from the wall beds downstairs. There was no way past the realization, sticking up like an immovable rock in a plowed field, that her grandmothers were barrow robbers.

CHAPTER 7

Jutta kept her eyes on her grandmothers the next day, wondering if she had dreamed it all. It certainly made time pass more interestingly, imagining the spectacle of gentle Thruda and the fastidious Sigla and the haughty Dora digging into a barrow, throwing aside the bones and rags of supposedly revered ancestors to grub up the treasure buried so long before. Margret would grimly do whatever she set out to do, and Ingi would make a jolly occasion of almost anything.

Where they could have hidden the treasure was also open to much speculation. Jutta considered the linen chests and the wall beds, but people were into and out of them too frequently. The pure audacity of her grandmothers awakened her admiration and respect, particularly as they went about their usual pottery routines, fussing over ridiculous little details as if the magnitude of their deeds weren't weighing over their heads like a black cloud. They could be hanged for what they had done, yet Amma Sigla went nattering on about an egg basket that was missing, as if it were the most important thing in the world.

"You're very quiet today, my dear," Amma Thruda said that evening, after the meal had been eaten and they were all sitting comfortably about in the twilight, sewing and patching or holding kettir. "Are you still tired from your trip yesterday?"

Jutta had been wondering if her grandmothers were going barrow robbing again and whether to ask them if she could come. She snapped to with a guilty start when her grandmother questioned her.

"Oh, yes, maybe a little, I suppose," she said quickly to cover up her abstraction.

"I think it's something else," Thruda continued.

"Oh? What?" Jutta replied a little nervously.

"You're homesick. I think you need a special little gift to cheer you up."

A gold chain, perhaps, or a gold mug? Jutta wondered privately.

"A kettling of your very own is just what you need," Thruda continued with a beaming smile.

"A kettling?" Jutta eyed the current batch of young kettir—Bensi, Hringur, and Hunang—all curled up in a heap on the hearthstone, exhausted after a day of criminal activities. They were as desperate and villainous as any gang of common traveling thugs. Recently they had gotten one of Thruda's skeins of wool, washed and combed and spun with her infinite and loving care, and shredded it completely. When Jutta had gone to scold them and pick it up, they had included her as part of the game and commenced to shred her sleeves and skirt, also, even jumping up to take murderous swipes at her nose. They were fiendish little hellions unworthy of the least kindness. When Jutta attempted to shove them unceremoniously out of the way or even to give one of them a boot in his furry behind, they lacked the grace or common sense to realize she was angry with them. Horrid creatures, they were totally lacking in respect for any person.

"Yes, your very own kettling to take care of," Thruda said. "That's just what you need."

"But I don't want one of these little villains," Jutta protested, giving the bulging backside of Bensi a push with her toe, which caused him to roll over and start purring. In a moment they were all purring and grinning, trying to look appealing with their creamy bellies exposed, their paws curling and uncurling, and their eyes tightly shut with rapture. They were so insincere that Jutta wanted to shake them, but they would probably just purr harder or wake up and start biting her.

"I mean," she added quickly, lest she hurt her grandmother's feelings, "that I think they're destined to go to someone else. They only take advantage of me."

"No, you must have your own kettling," Thruda said. She poked Bensi with her toe, giving him a rub under his chin. "These fat, lazy fellows are destined for high places. What you need is a little kettling you can raise from an infant."

"Are there any prospects?" Jutta asked anxiously, eyeing Rugla and Asa, the ruling female cats. There were others, she knew, but she couldn't remember all their names. She hoped none of them were pregnant.

"Of course," Thruda said. "But we must do it exactly right. What I need from you is a handful of little personal objects you use all the time—a comb, perhaps, a few hairs of your head, a ring—things like that."

"But what for?" Jutta asked, wondering if her grandmother had gone wandering in her wits or had suddenly changed the topic of conversation without bothering to notify her fellow conversationalist.

"Oh, you'll see," Thruda said in her best grandmotherly tones, as if she were baking something delectable and keeping it a secret.

Jutta obligingly went up to her loft room and gathered the little things she had asked for. Thruda beamed at her approvingly, particularly over the comb with a hair or two stuck in it, then she dropped them into a blackened kettle. Jutta looked on in mystification.

"Tomorrow," Amma Thruda said. "I'll work on it tomorrow. It's too near bedtime for any kettir brewing."

Jutta eyed her grandmother and the kettle for a moment, then laughed uncertainly, wondering what on earth she could mean or if it was a joke.

In the morning Jutta went about her usual chores, with Svartur tagging at her heels or watching from a nearby vantage point. When no one was looking, Jutta did some covert snooping, hoping she could find her grandmothers' secret cache of barrow loot. She forgot all about Amma Thruda's kettir brewing until she came in at midday to eat.

Amma Thruda had her kettle in the yard, where it was

smoking furiously. When Jutta looked more closely, she realized there was no fire under it, as there would have been for wash day, yet clouds of white smoke roiled around, obscuring Thruda's form bent over the kettle.

"What is she doing?" Jutta demanded, feeling the hairs rising on the back of her neck.

"My dear," Amma Margret said, "come inside and sit down to eat and leave her to her work."

"What kind of work?" Jutta demanded after she had sat down to the table amid a sea of hopeful cats, whose tails were twining around her chair like a nest of sea serpents.

"Women's work," Margret said curtly.

"Spells, magic, summonings," Amma Ingi added. "Women in the old days were all passable sorceresses. The knowledge stayed with the women's clans much longer than it did with the men's clans. Why, we used to—"

"Hmm!" Amma Margret glared at her, silencing her just as she was drawing a long breath to expound on her topic.

Ingi let it out with a sigh. "Have some butter?"

"We don't talk about such things much anymore," Margret said. "It causes jealousy and fear among those who are lacking in such skills."

"Witchcraft is what they call it nowadays," Amma Dora said. "Besides, it's so frightfully old-fashioned."

"You mean Amma Thruda really is brewing up a batch of kettir?" Jutta asked. "You mean they don't mate and reproduce naturally, like real cats?"

"I've told you they're not cats," Amma Margret said.

"We cooked 'em up, every single one," Ingi announced with a jovial laugh.

"Ingi! Hush!" Amma Sigla cried. "Don't you know the talk this would cause in Mikillborg? Everyone would be calling us witches. We'd be blamed for every little thing that went wrong in the settlements. People nowadays have turned against magic to an alarming extent."

"Oh, pooh, everybody wants a good love spell," Ingi said. "We're Alfar. How could we totally turn our backs on the magic that made our ancestors great?"

"People's memories are very short," Margret said. "Now, that's enough said about magic. Let's discuss that roof that's falling down in the main barn. If we lose that barn, we're going to be completely without a barn for the horses and livestock this winter. We've got to hire someone to replace that timber for us."

"But Amma Thruda is really out there stirring up kettir?" Jutta demanded. "She really knows how to do that? Where did she learn? What other powers has she got?"

"Thruda has been making kettir for sixty, seventy years or so," Ingi said. "It's only a harmless little hobby with her, and the kettir are such good company for all of us, not to mention the people we sell them to. A few bits of gold here and there are always welcome."

"Ingi! We've heard enough about it," Margret said, dividing her scowl between Ingi and Jutta. "Suffice it to say that we are old women, the last of the Hestur clan, and with us dies a great deal of knowledge the world will be much sadder without. And I'm not just talking about the manufacturing of these fur-bearing freeloaders under the table. We, as well as our knowledge, are unwanted relics in this modern world, so we don't go cluttering ourselves or our skills in places where we're not understood or welcomed."

Jutta ate as hurriedly as possible so she could go back outside and have a look at Amma Thruda. Her grandmother gave her a small wave, totally wrapped up in what she was doing. Jutta sat down on the rock and watched until Amma Margret reminded her that she had work to do.

At sundown when Jutta returned, Amma Thruda was still at it. Finally, after dinner had been finished and cleared away, Amma Thruda came into the house, holding something in her two cupped hands.

"Oh! Let's have a look!" Ingi crowed delightedly, throwing down her haphazard mending and leaping up, treading on Rugla's poor disorderly tail.

Thruda came to Jutta and smiled wearily. She was sooty and dusty, but she still glowed with pleasure.

"Here he is," she said, holding out the tiny creature cradled in her hands.

It was the youngest kitten Jutta had ever seen, with the little triangles of its ears still folded flat against its round little head. Its eyes were tightly sealed shut, and its coat was as thin and delicate as silk. The color was an extraordinary shade of gray-blue, with four white paws. Its nose was a tiny scrap of pink with a white patch on one side.

Jutta held out her hands with an involuntary "Oh!" of sheer awe. She felt tiny soft claws and the silky softness of the warm little creature as it struggled helplessly to hold its head up. "You made this?" she gasped.

"No, no, I can't take the credit for making a kettir," Amma Thruda said, still smiling. "They are waiting to be let in, and all I know is how to open the door for them. Now you'll have to feed this little creature and carry him with you everywhere you go. I'll give you a kettling sack to wear around your neck. At night he'll sleep on your pillow, where you can hear him when he's hungry."

Jutta allowed herself to be saddled with the kettling sack and instructed in chewing up little bits of meat to make a paste for the kettling to eat. The helplessness of the little creature endeared him completely to her; she had never before been the sole means of survival for any being. He slept in his kettir sack most of the day, except when hunger awakened him to utter little demanding squeaks.

"I've never seen such a color," Thruda marveled each evening when he was curled in Jutta's lap, soundly sleeping. "Blue-gray is very unusual. But then, it's your personality that has colored him. It will be interesting to see what he's like when he wakes up a little. Then you must have a name ready for him so he'll learn it and come when you call."

When the kettling's eyes opened after seven days, his personality began to manifest itself, but by that time Jutta had already formed such an attachment to him that she viewed his budding aggression with amusement and tolerance. His ears were growing at an alarming rate, and his silky baby coat had grown into a fuzzy nimbus that stood out around him, including his stubby and always vertical tail. Once open, his eyes never seemed to blink, skinned wide open with a beady blue intensity that was almost frightening. Hunting and stalking were the ruling passions of his tiny life. Anything that moved was fair game, from beetles and dandelion fluff to Jutta's eyelashes or lips. The kettling sack was soon scorned with utmost indignation, and the minuscule scrap of catling followed at Jutta's heels wherever she went, bouncing along with his tail poking aloft, uttering a series of demanding mews. If he ever wandered too far away from her, he summoned her presence with astonishing shrieks until he was reassured of his safety.

When his energy supply was depleted, he fell into a deep stupor of sleep, usually on his back with his legs falling limply where they would. Nor would he awaken when Jutta picked him up, lying in her hands with his head dangling limply, like that of a strangled chicken.

"It's time he had his name," Amma Thruda said one day after Jutta's kettling had fallen into the bathing water, walked on the bread dough, jumped into two pans of rising cream, and eaten from a large joint of roasted mutton with ravenous little growls. When Jutta tried to pull him away, he sank his teeth and claws into it, screaming indignantly. "In the old language, of course. How about Ogn? It means 'terror.' Or Ofreskja— 'monster.' "

"No, he's not a monster," Jutta said, and the kettling took a slash at her nose. As she moved past Amma Thruda, he reached out with both sets of claws, hoping to snag her.

"He's not like any kettling I've seen," Thruda said. "I don't think he has a scrap of a conscience anywhere. He's a merciless little biter and scratcher."

Jutta's hands were mute testimony to that fact. "He's only playing," she said. "If he had another kettling to play with, he wouldn't attack us so industriously."

"I'll remember that. Never make kettlingur in batches of one. It's too dangerous."

"He can be very sweet and gentle. Sometimes he licks instead of biting, and he likes to cuddle when he's in the mood for it."

Truly, there was nothing like a sleepy kettling curled up on one's leg, or stretched out like a limp furry rag, or dozing in the warm hollow between one's neck and shoulder during the night. He trusted her absolutely not to stand up and drop him or to awaken him too abruptly from his slumbers.

"You're taking very good care of him," Thruda said. "He ought to grow up into a very nice kettir. He'll be a friend and protector to you for the rest of his life. And such an unusual color, too. We've never seen an almost-blue kettir before. It shows what an unusual person you are, you know. I think you are destined for great things."

"How can that be if I'm to live at Bardhol all my life?" Jutta asked in an astonishing little spate of bitterness that made her want to bite her tongue.

Amma Thruda only smiled gently. "You'd be surprised how fast things can change. We never dreamed clan Hestur would end up like this. And it happened all in the space of a couple of years. Well, never mind. If you're finished with that carding, you can take the kettir for a nice afternoon walk. Mishka is getting monstrously fat. But don't stay out too late. We've got the milking to do."

Jutta summoned the kettir, briefly hoping none would come, then set out on her walk along the old wall leading past the ruins of the once-renowned Hestur stables. By the time she got to the corner, she had about ten kettir following her, all yowling and nattering excitedly, which brought even more of them out to see what all the fuss was for. Some of them marched along soberly, scarcely looking right or left; others ran ahead and crouched in the grass, waiting for her. Then they launched themselves high into the air in mock attack and ran away with tails hooked and ears pinned back. Others wandered along, distracted by everything that moved, falling farther and farther behind, then racing to catch up or caterwauling in distress when they discovered themselves alone. Several others would turn back and go bounding after the lost one, and a game of race and chase would ensue until a different kettir was left behind and lost, caterwauling.

Jutta did not waste her breath calling to them. She turned

her back and walked resolutely to the edge of the first barrow, ignoring Svartur's increasingly agitated cries. He ran under her feet and bumped her legs with his head, purring and twining around until she could scarcely walk. Furiously she ordered him out of the way several times, but he ignored her words and continued to block her path, even throwing himself down on the ground and moaning piteously, as if he could go no farther. Looking ahead to the ring of standing stones, Jutta saw a familiar white horse cropping the lush grass of the barrow.

"Silence, you faker," she said to him, stepping over his prone body and striding toward the horse.

In a moment Frida saw her and waved.

"Jutta, how good to see you again," she called. "I was beginning to fear you'd given up on your studies of ancient lore and ley lines."

"No, I've been kept too busy," Jutta said.

"It seems you've brought your friends," Frida observed, nodding toward the herd of kettir taking various positions on the fallen stones. Some were washing their faces; others had flopped down on their sides, pretending to be exhausted.

"Ah, yes, I couldn't get away without being followed," Jutta said, feigning great nonchalance to cover her embarrassment. "And I think this one has made it his personal duty to spy on all my doings." She nudged Svartur with her foot. He looked up at her with round, astonished eyes, as if he were the most innocent and harmless thing in the world.

"They are cunning little creatures," Frida said. "And excellent company for your grandmothers. What a lot of unusual colors they are, and no two are just alike. Where do your grandmothers get these creatures?"

"Oh, strays, mostly," Jutta said, suddenly feeling evasive.

"And what a ravishing little creature in your basket," Frida went on as she noticed Jutta's kettling peering over the edge of his basket. "What a dear little thing. It almost makes me want to own a cat."

"This one is my own," Jutta said with a small, proud smile. "He's too small to find his own way, so I have to carry him around in this basket. He's every bit as loyal and intelligent as a dog."

"What lovely fur. I had a collar almost that same color once. Is he gentle?"

"Sometimes," Jutta said warningly, but it was too late. Frida reached her hand into the basket, and the kettling pounced on it with tooth and claw, delighted at the diversion, particularly since it was alive and prone to struggling and screeching when pierced.

"I'm very sorry," Jutta said when Frida managed to unfasten the kettling from her hand. "He thinks he's playing, but he can get very wild. Oh, you're bleeding."

"No matter," Frida said with a laugh. "I like an animal—or a person—with a little wildness to them. What a little ofsi he is."

"Ofsi. I like that for a name. He is a little bundle of violence, isn't he?" Jutta tried to stroke his head, but he growled savagely and tried to climb out of the basket.

"Most certainly. Look, he's gotten a taste of me and he wants more. What a little brute."

Ofsi glared at her, bristling up like a cockleburr. He rapidly switched his stumpy little tail back and forth and uttered a high-pitched kettir battle cry. Svartur answered with a sharp yowl and bumped Jutta's legs with his hard head.

"Well, have you discovered any new ley lines?" Jutta inquired, shutting the lid on Ofsi and hoping that would quiet him down.

"Perhaps," Frida said. "Let me show you. I never suspected it, but there seems to be a line coming in from the northeast, which would point us toward that big barrow over there. It might be worthwhile to do some dowsing around it."

"Do you think it could be Sigmund's barrow?" Jutta asked, her heart taking a nervous and hopeful leap.

"Possibly, possibly," Frida said. "Come along; we've got a few hours of daylight. Will your grandmothers miss you if you don't return immediately?"

"I'm supposed to be taking the kettir for a walk," Jutta said. "Are we not walking?"

"We are, but they aren't," Frida said. "It looks as if they intend to wait for you."

The kettir sat on the fallen stone, staring after her with large accusing eyes, huddling up on their briskets like furry hummocks of moss. Only Svartur was bold enough to follow at Jutta's heels as she accompanied Frida farther into the barrow field.

"It seems so peaceful," Jutta said when they stopped to rest a moment. "Who would dream that Lina was killed not far from here? And there are seven others."

"Yes. About three a year, it seems."

"And they're always women, and it happens at the full moon, according to my grandmothers."

"Women and the moon have an old and reliable association," Frida said. "You can bet these women were out in the barrows hoping to find a pot of gold with the aid of the powers of the full moon, and someone who didn't want them there killed them."

Jutta struggled to blank out the picture of her grandmothers with their cloaks still on, surrounding the table and their pile of loot. A great many people probably sneaked into the barrows from time to time, digging and stealing a bit of treasure from the dead. It could just as easily have been one of her grandmothers who had been murdered, she heard herself scolding; it was easier than imagining her grandmothers doing away with someone.

"It's horrible what greed can make people do," Frida said, shaking her head. "This poor woman—she was poor, no doubt, and desperate—probably thought she was going to become rich overnight. A great pity. But let's look at our prospects here. We could be sitting on Sigmund's treasure mound, chattering away like it was nothing."

They inspected the mound thoroughly, combing through the grass and bushes and small trees. Jutta found herself annoyed continually by Svartur, yowling and trying to rub on her and begging to be picked up and petted. He kept looking up at her and uttering hopeful little chirps and crooning calls, bumping against her shins with his bony head. Looking down at him in exasperation and knowing Frida was out of sight and earshot, she whispered fiercely, "Whatever is the matter with you? Are you trying to tell me something?"

Svartur answered with a loud yowl and dived into the thicket at the bottom of the hill, still uttering loud yells. When Jutta did not follow, he poked his head out and meowed questioningly. With a sigh, she got down on her knees and followed him, dreading to think that he might be leading her to another skeleton. What she found was the lintel from the doorway. It had fallen down long before, along with its two uprights, now buried in underbrush. Svartur sat on the blackened, pitted stone, washing his wide belly, with his rear end resting on ancient inscriptions carved in the blackened stone.

In an excited whisper Jutta called Frida to come and see what she had found. Svartur eyed Frida with misgiving a moment, then leapt down from the stone with a reproachful glare at Jutta.

"It hasn't been disturbed that I can see," Frida said in a voice vibrant with excitement. "This might be it. Your fortune may be lying here, just under your feet. Your key to escaping the doldrums of Mikillborg."

Jutta's heart began to race. "Why are you doing this for me? If the treasure is here, how can I ever repay you?"

"My satisfaction does not lie in gold alone," Frida replied with a smile. "My chief joy comes in helping people obtain what they really wish to have. Not to mention, I have an overwhelming respect for the honorable Hestur men and women in these mounds. I have no wish to see them dishonored by barrow robbers. Nor do I wish to see the last of the clan Hestur perish in poverty and obscurity. I want to see one last burst of glory for the clan, and that will be you."

"But it isn't fair that I should take it all," Jutta said earnestly. "I will see to it that you have a fair share for all you have done to find the barrow. You have done far more than I, after all."

"What a generous soul you are," Frida said. "How like a true descendant of the noble Hestur. No, I have no wish for personal enrichment from my studies. My quest has been one for knowledge as well as justice for the Hestur clan, both living and dead. It simply isn't right that common grubby thieves should break in and steal the treasure of centuries of battle and quest. Better that the living Hesturkonur should have it and restore the name and glory of clan Hestur once more."

"Still, you must be rewarded," Jutta insisted. "I, too, have the strong sense of justice and honor bestowed upon me by my Hestur ancestors. I swear to you by the bones of the ancestors lying beneath our feet that you will take your deserved share of whatever we find here."

"I shall bow to your wishes," Frida said. "After all, this is Hestur land we are standing on and you are the direct descendant of Sigmund."

"Well, when shall we start digging?" Jutta demanded.

"Not so loud," Frida said, holding up a warning hand. "We think we're alone here, but there may be listening ears hearing every word we say. And there are propitious times for such an undertaking which we must consider. After all, barrow robbing is a high crime."

"But we're not barrow robbing," Jutta said. "These are my ancestors; therefore, it is my gold. This is clan land; therefore, it is my land. I shall do whatever I wish with it. I am not a barrow robber for merely removing my clan treasures for safe-keeping."

"Indeed, you speak the truth. But certain people who have usurped the chieftancy are bound not to see it that way. Our dear friend Einarr Sorenson has a primitive way of looking at things. When your own intentions are rather low and scurrilous, you tend to believe everyone else is the same way you are. Einarr Sorenson would not be happy to know we are here right now. I suspect he spends quite a bit of time searching for Sigmund's barrow himself, and his dreams are full of what he would do with the Hestur treasure if he got his hands on it."

"Oh, I daresay," Jutta murmured, trying to hide her consternation. Einarr had seemed a jolly, honest fellow to her, and it was distressing to know that he had evil intentions hidden under all that mirth and bluster. "Then there's the matter of those Sciplings staying at his house. They say they're looking for a gateway back into their own realm, but all the searching seems to take place in the barrows, from what I hear. Sciplings are notorious for their love of gold, however they get it."

"These Sciplings cause me no end of concern," Frida said, her voice dropping to a low murmur. She glanced around warily. "Their very presence in our realm upsets the harmony of nature. Mark my words, there are consequences, and there will be worse ones. I've had my fears for almost two years now that these Sciplings have something to do with the deaths in these barrows."

"You don't think they are murderers?" Jutta whispered.

"Never let it be said I breathed the word 'murderer,'" Frida said, "but Sciplings do not have a good reputation when it comes to bloodshed. Short-tempered and unpredictable, I've heard, and not at all hesitant to spill blood. Life is not as dear to them as it is to us."

They started to climb to the top of the barrow, but Frida suddenly seized Jutta's arm, drawing her back around the side toward a clump of wild plum trees.

"Look there," she whispered. "No sooner did we speak of Einarr Sorenson than here is his son."

Jutta recognized Leckny's stout piebald horse. Leckny had halted on the top of a long flat barrow and was facing in the direction of Bardhol, as if he had intentions of going there. But after a few moments he turned back toward Sorengard and vanished behind a large shadowy barrow. Jutta experienced a short pang of disappointment mingled with a certain sense of pleasure.

"Goodness, it's getting late," Jutta said, suddenly remembering that she had to milk the cows. "Everyone will be wondering where I've gone to. We'll have to meet again tomorrow to discuss what we're going to do. Now I suppose I'll be milking a cow in the dark, and Amma Margret will be angry."

"Do be careful," Frida said. "Don't go out late at night when the moon is full. Particularly avoid the barrows. I no longer discount those old legends of the Myrkriddir, not after the things I've seen since coming to this settlement. The old ways may be waning, but nothing has happened to change the power of the old beliefs. Be cautious and speak to no one of what we may have found here."

"I fear my great-grandmother Margret will know exactly where I've been," Jutta said apprehensively. "She's got a nose for barrow dust."

Sure enough, Amma Margret was waiting at the cow byre when Jutta came hurrying home, trailing a crowd of yowling, hungry cats behind her.

"You've been to the barrows again," Margret said by way of greeting, one fist braced against her skinny hip. The menacing glint in her eye did not bode well for any argument in the matter.

CHAPTER 8

"Did I not specifically tell you to stay away from the barrows?" Amma Margret demanded. "There are dangerous people scavenging around those graves, looking for some supposed fabulous treasure. They wouldn't hesitate to cut your throat, as they did to poor Lina."

"Amma Margret, I saw no one today except Frida from Thorungard," Jutta protested. "And Leckny Einarrsson was there, too, so I was perfectly safe. Besides, it was broad daylight. Nothing is going to happen to me unless I go there during the full of the moon."

"You foolish child. You don't understand. Perhaps you have already set in motion the mechanism of your destruction without even knowing what you do."

"I am old enough to take care of myself," Jutta said, lifting up her chin haughtily. "I'm not a foolish child. In less than two years I shall be of gifting age, and I can marry whom I choose and move away from here."

"There are things about those barrows which nobody today understands," Margret said. "Old powers still lurk there. Strange things can happen. You young modern folks think we are old and superstitious, but one day you'll realize you don't know everything there is to know about this earth, nor will you ever. And you know nothing about this Frida person. In my opinion she does entirely too much snooping around in places where she is trespassing, so I would earnestly advise you not to have anything to do with her. She's another one who is going to get into trouble in those barrows one day, sniffing after that gold."

"She's not hunting for the gold," Jutta snapped. "She's a scholar of the old ways, and the only thing she is looking for is knowledge. She's found several of the old ley lines that used to be there."

"Ley lines are best left forgotten," Margret retorted. "Now, I have no wish to quarrel with you. I have said what I intended to say, and I hope you take it as a very strong warning lovingly given by one who is older and wiser than you. It is time we went and milked the cows." She turned and walked away, with Svartur bounding at her heels as if he were bursting to tell her everything he had seen. He darted Jutta one malicious look over his shoulder, and she would have sworn he had grinned at her with pure spite.

It was rather a silent, strained evening. Word of Jutta's misdeeds seemed to have spread among the grandmothers, and they all went about their evening work without their usual teasing and merriment. Guiltily Jutta regretted inflicting any pain on them. They were, after all, her kinfolk, and ancient besides, and their lives had been so peaceful before her advent. Sighing, she gazed into the fire and stroked Ofsi's fur. For once he was in a mood to be held and petted, purring noisily. A time was coming that Jutta both devoutly hoped for and dreaded, when she would have to choose between the life she wanted to live and the possibility that she would hurt or anger her grandmothers. If that gold were found and given to her, many people dear to her would be wounded by the course of action she would take.

"Have you named your kettling yet?" Thruda inquired pleasantly, glancing up from her sewing.

"Yes, I think so," said Jutta. "Ofsi."

"Ofsi. The impulsive. Yes, that's a good name for a kettir," Thruda said with a warm smile. "Especially yours."

"I hope it doesn't make him even more impulsive and wicked," Sigla said. "A name is a powerful thing."

"What's wrong with being impulsive?" Amma Ingi demanded, leaning forward suddenly and knocking over the small stool that held Thruda's balls of wool. "I've been called impulsive, but it's never been a hindrance in my life. In fact,

I think I've had an enjoyable life. When I have an idea, I act upon it before it gets cold."

"Cold enough for reason to set in," Dora said primly. "No one can ever accuse you of thinking too long before deciding to act."

"Is anyone else ready for bed?" Amma Margret asked, giving her stringy arms a stretch. "It's been a long day. Thruda, I believe some warm milk would help us all sleep better, don't you?"

"Oh, yes, indeed, it would," Thruda said.

As soon as anyone started fussing around with pots and pans and making cooking motions, the kettir all awakened instantly, whiskers pricking, eyes bright with anticipation. Thruda had to pour out a pan of milk for them, naturally, which kept them busy only a few moments and didn't distract them at all from the cups of warm milk Thruda poured out for everyone else. It was a ritual much enjoyed by her grandmothers, and Sigla insisted on adding a spoonful of honey to enhance the flavor. Jutta sipped at hers, not caring much for milk at any temperature whether or not it had honey in it. Warm milk had soporific effects she did not much care for. She drank less than a third of her generous cupful and poured the rest into the kettir pan when no one was looking. Amma Ingi provided a welcome distraction when she accidentally kicked a ball of wool into the hearth, where it commenced smoking and stinking.

Thanks to the milk, she fell asleep instantly, with Ofsi curled up against her cheek, his purring mechanism slowly running down as he dozed off. Yet once again her slumbers were disturbed by an incessant sound, and she awakened before dawn, her ears sensitive to surreptitious sounds downstairs. Creeping to the edge of the loft, she again saw her grandmothers returning in their outdoor cloaks.

"I don't know how much more of this I can tolerate," Amma Dora whispered, sinking into a chair with an exhausted sigh. "And here it is almost time to milk the cows."

Amma Margret heaved a small heavy bundle wrapped in cloth onto the table. "It may be killing us, but it is worth it," she grunted. Unwrapping the cloth, she revealed a tidy pile of gold jewelry, chains, and coins.

"I'm not so sure," Sigla whimpered. "What if we get caught? How can we explain ourselves?"

"Then we won't get caught," Margret said testily. "And just let anyone try to make me explain what I'm doing with the gold of my own ancestors."

"Well," Ingi said with a broadening smile, "if anyone catches us, we can scare the liver and lights out of them with Myrkriddir shrieking and flapping."

"As long as anyone believes in Myrkriddir," Thruda added. "It seems that people are getting much more skeptical. Their lust for gold is stronger than their fear of Myrkriddir."

"Especially those irreverent Sciplings," Margret growled. "One day something will happen to them, mark my words."

After that they readied themselves for bed. Jutta crept back into her bed, careful lest the floorboards squeak. When Jutta came downstairs considerably later, at her usual time, her grandmothers were going about their usual business of breakfast and dressing as if they hadn't just spent the night digging up a grave. Casually Jutta went outside to let Ofsi scratch five or six holes to choose among, and while he was deciding, she inspected their boots on the stoop. They had been cleaned pretty well, but the color of the dirt was that of the dark loamy soil of the lowlands, where the barrows lay, not the pale and sandy mountain soil of Bardhol.

She could not wait for an opportunity to slip away to the barrow field. When the milking was done, she was supposed to herd the cows away to some fresh grazing for the day, which gave her the chance she was seeking. She pointed the cows in the appropriate direction and threw a few rocks at them for encouragement, then she hastened down the mountain to the barrows.

Breathless, with Ofsi protesting at the rough ride, she arrived at the barrow she and Frida had chosen the previous day. On hands and knees she crept through the thicket surrounding the entrance. Even before she got there, she could tell the grave had been opened. Loose dirt had been scattered around carefully to avoid making noticeable piles. The hole had been filled in, but definitely someone had dug between the doorway stones and entered the mound.

"A pity, isn't it?" a voice behind her said, and she whirled around to confront Frida. "The moment we find a good prospect, someone beats us to it." Her eyes gleamed greenly, like Svartur's eyes, with an angry light.

"I told no one," Jutta said. "Someone must have watched us—ha! Remember? Someone did watch us!"

"The chieftain's son," Frida said with a sigh. "It doesn't surprise me in the least. No doubt he's in league with those Sciplings."

Jutta was on the point of saying there wasn't much in the barrow anyway, but luckily she realized she mustn't breathe a word of her grandmothers' nocturnal activities to anyone, not even Frida.

"I'm not sure he cares much for the Sciplings," Jutta said. "I think he wishes them gone."

"Well, it's of no importance now. They beat us to whatever was in this barrow. I just hope it wasn't Sigmund's treasure."

"Somehow, I don't think it is," Jutta said. "I don't see any wagon tracks. I would think that such a massive treasure as it is reputed to be couldn't be carried away in saddlebags. These thieves came on horseback. You can see there where the horses were tied."

Jutta pointed out a trampled area. Frida led the way to inspect the place, examining every discernible hoofprint.

"These horses are not shod," she said. "And I see small bootprints. Sciplings have extremely large feet. These were Alfar grave robbers—your friend Leckny, perhaps, and some of his father's thralls. I hope they didn't find much. I did have such high hopes for this barrow."

"We could spend the rest of our lives digging here," Jutta said rather bitterly, scanning the hundred or so green mounds rising up like giant hummocks. "And we still might discover that Sigmund's barrow was plundered years ago. I wish there was an easy way of finding the right grave so we could dig it up and be done with barrow robbing."

"I am trying," Frida said with a faint smile. "But I feel ever so much more hopeful now that I've got your help. I wonder if your grandmothers could spare you for a visit. It would be such a help if we could manage to come here every day to search out the lines."

"I shall ask," Jutta said, her heart leaping with excitement. Frida was a lady of no small consequence in Mikillborg, exactly the sort of person to help her escape from Bardhol. Frida would know other influential people, and people could be so useful sometimes. "Will you be here tomorrow so I can give you their answer?"

"I think I shall. If I am, I'll hang my scarf in that dead tree at the crossroads, just past old Bjalfur's house. You can see it from the gate of Bardhol."

Jutta spent the rest of the day deciding how she would approach the subject with Amma Margret. Then a masterful idea occurred to her while she was helping Amma Dora boil the laundry.

"Amma Dora, what do you think Amma Margret would say if I told her I was invited to stay at the house of one of the wealthiest people in Mikillborg? I've been afraid to mention it, knowing how much work is to be done around here before winter sets in."

"Wealthiest?" Amma Dora's eyes began to shine with enthusiasm. "And who might that be? Do they have a marriageable son your age?"

"I fear there's no son. But they might know someone else who does. It's the lady Frida of Thorungard."

"Frida of Thorungard! Well! She doesn't take to everybody, I've heard. How did you have the good fortune to meet someone of quality in such a short time?"

"We share a mutual interest in history and old lore," Jutta said. "I met her walking the ley lines in the barrows. She knows a great deal about the Hestur clan and the old ways. She has great respect for the old traditions."

"Well, I should think that Margret would be glad for you to have such an opportunity," Dora said.

"I don't know if I'll say anything. She might think I was just trying to get out of working."

"No, she ought to realize that our position in Mikillborg is not inconsiderable and that we must do a certain amount of socializing, as we did in the old days. I remember how we used to travel around, visiting all the grand houses and halls, showing off the beauties of the Hestur clan. It was so splendid, being paraded about in those days, in all our fine clothes. Now our pretty young girls of gifting age are being married off without a single gold coin going to the clan. Don't you think that's a dreadful shame? Now we shall have to present it to Margret in just the right manner or she'll get stubborn and refuse. She's very proud. Perhaps we can work on her there." Then she added wistfully, "If only we had the wealth we once had, you'd have suitors lined up to pay our bride-price."

"It doesn't matter how wealthy we are," Jutta said earnestly, suddenly haunted by the image of her little old grandmothers out digging up barrows so she would have an impressive dowry. Truly they were driven by some dire necessity to risk anything so dangerous. What if they were caught and hanged? The fault would all be hers. How could she accept a dowry obtained at such horrific risk? Yet if she did accept it, another voice reminded her, a prestigious marriage might be arranged for her and perhaps a more suitable place for her to stay would be found while she prepared her bride boxes containing the household items and apparel that she would need after her marriage.

"You mustn't think you have to provide for me," she said. "After all, my parents will have something to send with me when I marry."

"But it won't be Hestur riches," Dora said. "It will be mostly your father's wealth, and he's not of this clan. Let me speak with Margret. I think I can reason her into agreeing that you should spend some time with Frida."

"Perhaps tomorrow," Jutta suggested. "I fear Amma Margret is a little angry with me for going off into the barrows again."

"Yes, well, but it's only because she is concerned about your welfare," Dora said. "With the numbers of barrow robbers increasing and these frightful murders, the barrows are about the worst place you could go. I entreat you to stay away from them, or I fear the anxiety is going to make me quite as fussy as Sigla gets. Why ever do you want to go there, among all those rotting bones?"

"They are my kin," Jutta said. "I feel them drawing me to do something for them before it is too late. I believe they would want the ley lines found and charted."

"Yes, it is possible, though one doesn't like to think about it. The dead in their barrows ought to have the courtesy to leave the living in peace. I think it was a mistake to bury so much treasure with those corpses. It makes them almost as restless as if they were alive."

Jutta shivered suddenly, and Amma Dora caught herself up short with an airy little laugh.

"Listen to us talk! Did you ever hear such gloom and doom? How ridiculous we're being. My dear, go and start packing your things. This is proof enough for me that living within sight of those barrows is making you morbid. You need some gaiety and excitement. You're young and in need of entertainment, not the company of five old sour fossils like us. I shall speak to Margret at once. Your health and welfare are at stake here and mustn't be ignored."

Jutta felt immensely cheered for the rest of the day, infused with Dora's warm and effusive enthusiasm.

"Ho, Margret," Dora announced that evening after the meal was finished and cleared away and the most excitement anyone could expect from the evening was a pricked finger or a cat falling off one's lap. "Don't you think poor Jutta is looking pale and gloomy? Since she got here, her spirits have sunk in an appalling way. If we don't do something to cheer her up, I fear she's going to fade right away before our eyes, and then what shall we tell her mother? That we killed her daughter with hard work and boredom?"

Amma Margret looked up in astonishment at this business-like attack. "What do you suggest?"

"Jutta needs young people, singing, parties, bright conversation, and pretty gowns," Dora declared. "If she stays around us old crows much longer, she's going to forget how to smile and look pretty. She needs to go visiting to someone who will amuse her and make her happy. What's in Bardhol to make anyone happy, with all those graves always within our view, reminding us how short and fleeting are life and fortune?"

"Mercy," Amma Margret said. "I hadn't realized we were in such bad shape. I had the idea that we all rather enjoyed our peaceful little existence here, wrought out with our own hands. Is it really such a hard life?"

"For a young girl with some juice in her, it certainly is," Amma Dora said. "I can imagine myself at Jutta's age if I were sent to a prison such as this. Nothing but work and drudgery all day, early to bed, then up to start again. Young people shouldn't be worked so hard."

"Like young horses," Ingi chipped in. "We never over-worked our colts and fillies until they were mature enough to tolerate it. It makes them sour-tempered if too much is forced upon them too young."

"I don't mean to be sour-tempered," Jutta said quickly. "I appreciate what you're doing for me, and I don't mind the work at all."

"See there?" Dora said triumphantly. "She's only trying to spare our feelings. The dear little thing needs a holiday from Bardhol, Margret. If I were thirty years younger, I'd demand a holiday, too. Maybe I'm not too old to enjoy some gaiety."

"Hah." Margret grunted. "You've had enough gaiety in your life to last you a long time. I suppose Jutta could go back to her mother for a while."

"And bury herself in her mother's household?" Amma Dora exclaimed in horror. "She'd be right back up to her neck in work and boredom."

"Then what do you have in mind for her?" Margret asked with asperity.

"She's been invited to stay at Thorungard," Dora announced with no little pride in the lift of her chin and her satisfied smile.

"Well," Margret said. "That is a surprise. It seems you've

struck up quite an acquaintance with this lady. She's always been rather too good for most of the people around here."

"Jutta could meet some important people," Dora went on. "Perhaps it would even result in a nice marriage agreement. The young men around here are a hopeless lot of stag-hunting, ale-guzzling braggarts who lie about, doing nothing. We need to look farther afield, and I'm sure Frida has friends and relatives with plenty of influence. Thorungard was no small gift to bestow upon her by whoever gave it to her. I should like to know that sort of people."

"I daresay you've known enough of them for a lifetime," Amma Margret said. "Be grateful you don't need them any longer. So you think you could do with a holiday?" She turned sharply to Jutta.

"I believe it would do me good," Jutta said.

"At least it might keep her out of the barrows for a while," Amma Thruda said in a low voice, not looking up from her mending, underneath which a lapful of sleeping kettir sagged limply, as if their bones had been removed.

"I shall speak to this Frida person first," Margret said. "She must be of the highest character before we entrust our only heir to her. Tomorrow I shall send her a note, inviting her to Bardhol."

Jutta went to bed that night immensely encouraged. In the morning she saddled one of the mares and carried Margret's note to Thorungard, where she was met by the same surly thrall.

"Back again, are you?" he greeted her impudently, surveying her from head to foot with a mean and squinty eye. Jutta would have sold him off instantly at the next harvest fair rather than put up with his rudeness. "Well, the lady is indisposed this morning. She can't see you."

"I have a note for her from my grandmother," Jutta said, lighting down and dropping her reins in the thrall's hands. "I've been instructed to wait for an answer, so I shall, no matter how long it takes for the lady to become unindisposed. Put my horse in the barn and give her something to eat."

Jutta swept past the thrall and up to the main door of the

hall, where she was met by a maidservant who had been discreetly watching her scene with the thrall.

"Please take a note to the lady Frida," Jutta said in the tone of voice used by those accustomed to ordering thralls about. She pushed her way into the hall, breezing by right under the woman's nose despite her sputterings of protest. It was as elegant as Jutta had suspected. "I shall wait here by the fire."

"And who might you be?" the woman demanded haughtily, her face growing redder and her perpetual serving woman's scowl deepening menacingly. The only thing more ill tempered than a well-seasoned female servant was a suspicious mastiff trained to protect hearth and master.

"Tell Frida that Jutta is here, and that will be enough," Jutta said, seating herself in a comfortable chair padded with stitched tapestry, a welcome relief from the hard benches and chairs of Bardhol.

The woman went away, grumbling under her breath, leaving Jutta to reflect on the prevalent surly disposition of the servant class. With each passing year they seemed to have less respect for their owners and employers. Jutta tapped her foot and looked around with approval. The beams and joists were elaborately carved or painted in a bright and jolly design of twining dragons, snakes, and warriors fighting for their lives. The usual gloomy array of ancestral weapons and shields, which always lent such a grim atmosphere to a room, was gone from Frida's walls, replaced by elegant tapestries of the finest color and workmanship depicting pleasant scenes of mythical animals, flowers, and gardens.

After a short wait a young maidservant led the way to Frida's rooms, a modern stone addition that offered some privacy from the noise of the main hall. In the old days, everyone shared the hall and the only privacy was a bed with closable panels, like a big cupboard. Everyone lived together, lord and lady, warriors, retainers, thralls, and guests. Jutta was pleased with the idea of having a separate apartment with a bedroom, a sitting room, and a loft above for weaving. All was well furnished with tapestries, rugs, chairs, chests, and tables, all of the finest quality.

She found Frida dressed in a loose white gown, pink and damp from a morning steaming in the bathhouse.

"You must forgive me," Frida said. "I wish I'd known you were coming, and we'd have a pleasant little dinner. Can you stay for long?"

"I just came with a message," Jutta said, unable to stop herself from sinking into the luxury of Frida's rooms. "I believe she's going to let me come to stay. She wishes to speak to you first, to make sure you're of the highest character possible."

"Me? I shall have to be careful," Frida said. "I've been known to sing and dance and celebrate recklessly when the occasion permitted. What shall I wear?"

"Something very safe and boring," Jutta said.

When Frida came to Bardhol, she put on a drab gray dress and wrapped up her hair in a sensible braid. She chose a modest piece of Dora's excellent bread and exclaimed over its softness and fine texture.

"Well, it's all in the flour," Amma Dora said, flushing with pride. "It must be twice ground or you get those little hard bits of wheat. Some of us here don't have the teeth they once had," she added with a condescending glance toward Ingi.

Ingi snorted. "I can chew up my fodder as well as I could as a youngster," she said. "I've never had dainty teeth, and I've never lost a one. If I were a horse, you'd swear I was only fifteen or so."

"It's not common for a woman of your status to be interested in old barrows and ley lines," Margret said, putting an end to that line of talk. "I should think you'd be doing more visiting and traveling and celebrating."

"My father was a historian," Frida said. "There was nothing I enjoyed more than tramping at his heels, discovering the old straight tracks our ancestors made. Since then I've devoted my life to recording as much as I can find of the old ways, before the heedless present generation allows everything to slide into oblivion. The problems we've had with barrow robbers seriously cut into my fun, however. One scarcely dares set foot alone in the barrows anymore for fear of encountering these villains."

"But that doesn't seem to stop you," Amma Margret said. "You do a great deal of poking around among the barrows, don't you? Alone?"

"I have a couple of fearsome great thralls, very ugly fellows, who accompany me everywhere," Frida replied. "I assure you, Jutta will be perfectly safe with me. My mapping and charting is such boring work for a young person, however, I doubt if I can interest her in it for very long. There's really nothing much that I do except pace along the supposed lines and set up a few rocks to sight by and such things. Very dull."

"They why do it?" Amma Ingi asked, knitting up her great plain face in sincere puzzlement.

Frida laughed. "It gives me a sense of purpose in my useless life. I'm continuing my dear father's work, which gives me great satisfaction. Ley walking has become a popular sport for ladies who have too much leisure and not enough real work to do."

"And you wouldn't be doing it after dark, when the barrow robbers are lurking about?" Amma Thruda asked.

"Dear me, no," Frida said. "I like to be able to see what I'm doing. Nor do I have any intention of running into any barrow robbers. I've never seen any, and I don't intend to. Home is the place to be after it's dark outside."

"Well, it's a very strange hobby but a harmless one, I suppose," Amma Margret said, her tone still dubious. "It might also be a way of curing this dreadful fascination Jutta seems to have for the barrows. Many times I've told her there's nothing there for anybody to be interested in. Maybe now you'll convince her of that."

"I should think ley walking might get forgotten if you have sent out invitations for other company," Dora hinted with a sly little smile. "Dancing and whatnot, you know."

"Indeed, we might have a few small gatherings," Frida said, nodding her head. "Ley walking is a dry and dusty sport, after all."

"Then allow me to relieve your dusty throats somewhat," Sigla said. "I shall send home a cask of my humble brew with you for your company."

Jutta's arrangements were swiftly made. She packed her things into two saddlebags and threw them over the back of a horse.

"Elding is not accustomed to spending the night away from home," Amma Margret said firmly by way of farewell. "She would find the strangeness far too taxing on her digestion. I shall expect to see her returned before dark."

"I shall send a thrall," Frida said.

"I trust you will be home in four or five days' time?" Amma Margret suggested, her manner still very much put upon by the frivolity of Jutta's junketing about the countryside.

Jutta had been hoping for longer, but she nodded her head, making a sincere effort to appear agreeable. "Thank you, Amma Margret. This visit means a great deal to me. You won't be sorry when you see how much improved I am when I return."

Jutta rode away with her heart lighter than it had been during all the weeks she had lived at Bardhol. Ofsi enjoyed riding in his basket on her back, bouncing along with his head sticking out of a hole in the rushes, uttering fascinated trills and miniature yowls.

"I'm sure your little cat is welcome at my house, but I'm surprised you didn't leave him," Frida said. "To hear you talk, you needed a vacation from the cats as well."

"Yes, I'll be glad to be away from Svartur's piercing eyes," Jutta said. "I'm sure he spied on my every action and tattled on me to Amma Margret. But Ofsi is just an infant, and I really don't want to entrust him to anyone else. He won't be much trouble. I'm looking forward to this visit. I don't expect a great deal of entertainment and fussing over. What I would like most is to walk the barrows and see how you do your work."

"Good. That is what we shall do the most of, then. I'm sorry your grandmothers are so troubled about our safety. I assure you, we're perfectly safe with Thver and Thjodmar protecting us. I am so pleased that you were able to come. I feel certain that we are going to accomplish some very important work in the barrows in the next four days. It is, after all, the full moon—the best time for finding ley lines."

"By moonlight?" Jutta asked a little nervously.

"But of course by moonlight. We can see ever so much better. You scarcely need a lantern with a big full moon shining down on you, nearly as bright as the sun. I find it safer, actually, than carrying a lantern to announce your presence to any unsavory creatures who might be lurking among the graves."

At Thorungard Jutta was settled into a small room near Frida's, a room intended for Frida's lady's maid, who was thus relegated to the servants' quarters in the old scullery for the duration of Jutta's visit. A room of her own, other than a cramped loft, was an unknown luxury for Jutta. She had a panel bed, her own window looking down on the stables, a table and a couple of chairs, and a large cupboard with shelves for clothing and mending and shoes and other possessions. A small hearth and chimney served to heat the room in cold weather, and fragrant rush matting cushioned the flagstones underfoot. Tapestries warmed the walls; fresh new carving and painting brightened the beams and doorposts. Having a door to close against the rest of the household was a thrilling sensation; there was even a lock on it. How new and modern it all seemed to a girl who had grown up in a drafty old hall that had so well served her warlike, predaceous ancestors back in the warrior days, when twenty warriors and guests and boats and horses and livestock were all naturally welcomed beneath the same rooftree.

Jutta explored happily until suppertime, when a delectable meal was prepared and placed before her, then cleared away without the least expectation that she was to do any of the work. It was exactly the life for which Jutta was eminently suited. With utmost pleasure she allowed Frida's servants to attend to her every whim.

At sundown the first glowing rim of an enormous full moon commenced its luminous ascent into the sky. Jutta could feel a spirit of expectation rising in Frida, whose eyes began to sparkle as her manner became energetic.

"Well, it's time we were off on our expedition," she declared. "Put on some riding clothes—dark colors, so we won't endanger ourselves. Can't you feel the ley lines calling to you, begging you to come and discover the treasures of your ancestors?"

Jutta's heart beat faster at the thought of prowling the barrows by night.

"Yes, I'm ready," she declared.

"Good," Frida said. "I'll tell Thver and Thjodmar to saddle up our horses."

CHAPTER 9

The barrows by full moonlight glowed like a frosty hummock bog, mound after mound softened by shadow and moon.

"How will we ever find our way out again?" Jutta murmured to Frida riding beside her. The two surly thralls, alike enough to be brothers, rode behind them, not speaking a word.

"I'm well enough acquainted with the landmarks not to get lost," Frida said. "Don't you know where you are? Here's the crossroads, and that way is Bardhol, and that way is to old Bjalfur's."

"Then we're not too far from the place where I found Lina," Jutta said with an uneasy chuckle.

"Most unfortunate. Silly girl. So many people think they can just dig into a mound and find something. Most of these were robbed shortly after they were made. It takes special knowledge to find the good ones. And alas, but that knowledge is sadly lost and forgotten."

"But we shall find it again," Jutta said.

"Of course. Now, then, do you recognize this spot? This is where we found the doorway, the one that was robbed by the next day."

Jutta could not honestly say she recognized the spot, but she nodded her head anyway. Everything was pools of light and shadow and clumps of wild thickets of brush. They tied their horses and started up the side of the barrow. Jutta was glad to leave the sullen presence of the thralls behind. Frida reached the top of the barrow and stood still, listening with her head turned.

"What are we going to do now?" Jutta whispered.

"Hst! I thought I heard voices," Frida hissed, still straining to listen. After a long moment of hearing nothing stirring, not even the breeze, she sighed and shrugged. "Perhaps it was just my imagination."

For the first time Jutta was glad Thver and Thjodmar were waiting at the foot of the barrow. She shivered in spite of the warm cloak she was wearing.

"I would like you to hold this pendulum," Frida said, handing Jutta a gold chain with a weight on it. "Just hold it so, keeping your hand as still as possible."

"I don't think my grandmother would approve of this," Jutta murmured as the pendulum started swinging ever so slightly back and forth.

"We're on the line," Frida said. "Now let's walk to the north, down the side of the barrow, and see what it does. Stop to test it here."

The pendulum stopped swinging and hung motionless, so Frida directed Jutta slightly more to the west. Still nothing, so they worked their way around until suddenly the pendulum picked up a rapid swinging, almost straight west.

"Another line!" Frida whispered. "And look at the strength of it! I knew you'd be a tremendous help to me in finding these lines. You're the purest Hestur woman left, after your mother and Margret."

With the thralls lumbering behind at a safe distance, Jutta and Frida followed the ley line to the next barrow. The signal was still strong, so they continued to the next mound. Cresting its top, Frida suddenly seized Jutta's arm and sank down in the bristly grass.

Below them lanterns glowed rudely in the velvety dark, and the forms of men moved to and fro, blotting the light in irregular signals.

"The Sciplings!" Frida hissed furiously. "Blundering around in the barrows like blind oafs!"

Jutta watched a moment, unable to tell if they were digging.

"What are they doing?" she whispered.

"Looking for gold, of course! Idiots! And right in our way. What if that's Sigmund's barrow, with all his treasure inside it?

And besides the treasure, there are objects in that grave which ought never to fall into the hands of creatures like the Sciplings."

"What sort of objects?" Jutta asked.

"Things that would give them more powers than they could imagine, powers to do all sorts of evil deeds," Frida snapped. "They've heard tales about that barrow. Their evil hearts are lusting for gold and power. Many times I've seen the signs of their clumsy skrying and searching in these barrows."

"Simon told me that they are searching for a way back into their own realm," Jutta whispered. "Perhaps it's not the gold at all."

"We're speaking of Sciplings here," Frida said. "It wouldn't astonish me at all if they were the ones responsible for the deaths of these unfortunate foolish women. Lured them to their doom, no doubt, with promises of fame and fortune in the Scipling realm. Why are women such weak and silly creatures where men are concerned? The boldest woman will turn into jelly when she thinks some handsome male is interested in her, and always she is thrown aside when his admiration passes. And Sciplings are the worst. Has that odoriferous young lout Simon expressed any interest in you yet?"

"We talked awhile when I went to report finding Lina's skeleton," Jutta said, "but that's all. He was rather curious about my Alfar powers, however."

"Ah! You see!" Frida said. "Beware of him, or you may end up like Lina and the others. Well, I know what will discourage them. Stay here and I'll signal Thver and Thjodmar."

Frida moved down the barrow purposefully. Jutta watched as Petrus and Simon moved about the base of the barrow with their lanterns, as if they were searching for the lintel stones that framed its opening.

Suddenly she heard a thunder of hooves and a rushing sound like wind approaching. It was an astonishing racket for two riders. Jutta looked for the two thralls coming out of their hiding place, but what she saw was the two thralls fleeing at top speed in the direction of Thorungard, with two riderless horses racing behind them.

"Frida?" Jutta called into the torrent of icy wind now blasting around her.

Frida lunged toward her and seized her, dragging her down prone on the ground. "Myrkriddir!" she shouted. "Stay down! Don't look at them!"

The strange storm of wind seemed to break directly over their heads with a thunderclap and explosions of lightning. Over the bellow of wind came wild cries, shrieks, and laughter that chilled Jutta to the bone. Venturing to turn her head and glance upward, she saw the frightful apparition of horses and riders capering around in midair above her. Each figure glowed with unearthly blue phosphorescence. Manes, tails, hair, and cloaks flew about in the wild wind. She clung to the bristly earth with her fingers, feeling as if the wind wanted to peel her off the top of the barrow and toss her aloft like a leaf.

"Don't look at them!" Frida shouted. "Close your eyes and hang on!"

Jutta could not keep her eyes closed. She saw the five eerie figures circling over Petrus and Simon, their horrible cries piercing the roaring of the wind, their horrible hag faces livid with blue light. The Sciplings tried to mount their horses, but the horses broke away, bucking and squealing with terror, leaving their riders afoot. The Sciplings scuttled for cover in a thicket, but the Myrkriddir were not deceived a moment, plunging low into the tops of the thicket until it commenced glowing with the same eerie blue light. Flushed out like rabbits, the two Sciplings ran desperately, with the Myrkriddir howling after them.

Suddenly Simon stumbled and fell. The Myrkriddir circled around him with gleeful cries. He crouched, drawing his sword in a pitiful attempt to defend himself.

"Don't watch," Frida said swiftly, attempting to draw Jutta away down the side of the barrow.

"No, we've got to do something!" she exclaimed, resisting Frida's efforts to turn her away. "We can't just let them get him!"

"What can you do?" Frida demanded. "He is doomed!"

Jutta twisted away, scrambling almost to her feet, then she

flattened herself again as a wild and ragged figure rose up from the barrow lintels, as if a corpse had decided to come to life. Gripping a tall staff, the flapping apparition stood and confronted the swirling Myrkriddir. Raising his staff aloft, he uttered strange words in a shrill and reedy tone: *"Fara af stad!"*

The Myrkriddir suddenly swirled to a dead halt. Their horses sank to earth, as if their riders were too astonished to keep up their magical force, and the blue light faded almost to nothing. Then the leader of the Myrkriddir suddenly uttered a harsh command, and they all wheeled and thundered away, earthbound but nevertheless exceedingly swift, and vanished into the barrows. The ragged figure had also vanished by the time Jutta stopped gaping and turned her attention back to search for him.

"Will they be back?" Jutta gasped in the sudden silence. It was dark. The inky mist that accompanied the Myrkriddir had almost blotted out the moon; now it began to shred and dissipate. She was nearly frozen by the icy Myrkriddir wind, her cloak blown inside out, her hair tumbling in all directions. Frida crept back up the barrow and slowly got to her feet.

"I don't know," Frida said, shoving her hair out of her eyes. "Who—or what—was that flapping corpse figure?"

"I don't know," Jutta said, starting down the slope. "It was horrible, but it's gone now. Come, we must see if Simon is injured."

"Let him lie there! He mustn't know it is us! Don't you see that our lives could be in danger? They won't want anyone to know who they are!"

"It's only Simon! He's completely harmless! Come, we've got to help him."

Simon waved his sword rather feebly and snarled a challenge when he saw two more women approaching him.

"Be still, it's Jutta," Jutta retorted. "You've got no business threatening me, considering what you were doing here before you were so rudely interrupted."

"Jutta? What are you doing here?" Simon gasped.

"Never mind. I could ask the same of you, but I see you're

here with shovels, so enough said. I ought to have rejoiced to watch them have your barrow-robbing carcass, but I guess I have a soft heart. I'm glad you're safe now."

"I will always be the slave of your soft heart," Simon said with a faint chuckle as he sheathed his sword and a wince as he shifted his foot. "Please accept me as your loyal servant for the remainder of my life."

"Nonsense. Sciplings don't live long enough in this realm to make them worth bothering with," Jutta said. "Are you hurt in any way which would damage your value even further?"

"I think my ankle is only sprained and not broken, or I fear you'd put me out of my misery," Simon said, rising to his feet and tentatively putting some weight on his right ankle. Wincing, he sank back down on a rock. "Perhaps I'd better change my opinion. I don't think I'm worth saving."

"Ah. A pity, that," Jutta said. "It was pleasant knowing you. Shall we leave you here for the foxes and crows, or is there someplace else you wish to rot?"

"My own realm, if at all possible," Simon said ruefully. "That's why we're doing this. All we want is one token of power. And we'll leave it behind when we go."

"You're fools," Frida said, keeping her face shadowed. "What would Einarr do if he knew you were doing this? You're committing a high crime right beneath his nose, while you're in the shelter of his house."

"We are truly desperate," Simon said. "I hope you won't tell Einarr about this."

"Halloa!" Petrus shouted, huffing through the underbrush with his sword in one hand. "Simon! Are you all right? Are we saved, or are we still under attack by murderous women creatures?"

"You are still in grave peril," Frida said. "Those hags could come back at any moment. You are extremely fortunate to have escaped. By all I know of the Myrkriddir breed, they should have killed your son and the rest of us as well. That scarecrow creature turned them back. It was amazing."

"I'm so grateful," Petrus said. "I am your servant. Whatever you wish, I shall do it."

"I don't have much use for servants, unless you want to move to Bardhol and do my work there," Jutta said.

"I believe Simon has twisted his ankle," Frida said. "He's not going to be walking on it for a while. This will put a halt to your barrow-robbing activities, I fear."

Petrus glanced at Simon and drew a deep breath. "I can see it will be difficult to explain what we were doing here. But let me try. My son and I have been trapped in your realm for two of your years—who knows how many years have passed in the Scipling realm. We're only searching for a means of returning to the place and time where we belong. There is an object of power in Sigmund's barrow, a great golden cup which will grant the wishes of the one who owns it. If only we could find it, we could go home."

"I daresay you'd change your minds once you possessed the rest of the treasure," Frida said. "And the power that cup would give you would probably corrupt you thoroughly. You Sciplings remind me of children in many ways."

"We may never find the barrow or the cup," Simon said. "We may be here forever."

"Or until those Myrkriddir hags catch you," Frida said. "Let this be a warning to you of what might happen next time. Not to mention the penalties in this realm for barrow robbing. I believe you'd be hanged or burned alive. Then there is the small matter of the women who have been disappearing in these barrows. It is possible you would be suspected of those crimes."

"A Scipling would never do anything to harm a woman," Petrus said ferociously, giving himself a dramatic slap across the chest. "We are sworn to protect the finer and more defenseless sex with our lives and the last drops of blood in our bodies. As all the gods of this strange realm are my witness, I would never murder a hapless woman."

"You would rather suffer the consequences of being captured as a barrow robber?" Jutta asked.

"Sure and I would rather," Petrus professed as stoutly as before.

"Then Jutta and I are in no danger?"

"Most certainly not," Petrus declared. "But I am rather curious how you happened to come along at just such a peculiar moment, when most people are asleep in their beds."

"We were casting for ley lines by moonlight," Frida said. "And there was someone else here, who actually frightened away the hags with his words. Who was that?"

"A wizard," Petrus said. "Of great power and extreme modesty. I am bound not to reveal his identity."

"Ah, yes, I see," Frida said. "I hope you are not being taken in by a charlatan. Often they are exceedingly modest, also. We shan't mention him further if that is your wish and his. Now, how are we to transport this lame creature to Sorengard?"

"We are not. I shall escort you ladies home and then return for Simon."

"Indeed you shall not," Frida said. "We are capable of escorting ourselves home."

"No, no, it would grieve me to think of you alone in the barrows in the dark," Petrus said.

"And leave your injured son to the Myrkriddir?" Frida said. "We were capable of finding our way into the barrows, and I assure you we are capable of finding our way out. I left a couple of thralls back there a ways, and they will surely find us with our horses now that those hags have ceased their screeching and swooping. It is more within my power to help you than it is within yours to help us."

They quarreled about it until Jutta heard the hallooing of Thver and Thjodmar, returning with the horses. Then it became easier to insist on sending Thver home with Simon and Petrus, with Simon riding on one horse. Frida and Jutta climbed onto the other, leaving Thjodmar to walk behind them with his sword anxiously drawn.

"We shall forever be in your debt," Petrus said as they finally parted. "If ever there is anything I can do for you, just command me and I shall do it."

"There is one small thing," Frida said. "It is a foolish thing, as I am rather a proud and selfish creature. I don't wish it to be noised about that I was here tonight. I have a hobby of tracking the old ley lines in the barrows, and by moonlight it is particularly thrilling, although not usually so much as tonight. Everyone around here is bound to misunderstand. I might even be accused of barrow robbing myself."

"A lady of substance such as yourself?" Petrus snorted. "I doubt anyone would think you were the type who needs to rob barrows. One must be poor and desperate to attempt such a dangerous occupation, particularly where Myrkriddir are known to be protecting the graves. It is I who should beg your silence, or I may be the one hanging from someone's roof pole. It would grieve my host in particular to know he was sheltering someone who might be called a barrow robber." He bared his enormous teeth in an effort to be at once endearing and conspiratorial.

"No harm was done to any barrow tonight," Frida said with a musical laugh, "so neither of us can be called a barrow robber, can we? And we learned a very valuable lesson about Mrykriddir. They're not just a story made up to frighten would-be robbers away." She shivered and glanced around at the sky littered with stars. "What a horrible experience!"

They parted from Simon and Petrus and started homeward. Their horse was still spooked after the apparition of the Myrkriddir, snorting and shying at nothing in an anxious dance to get home to the safety of the barn.

"You are very silent," Frida said suddenly, startling Jutta out of her contemplations.

"I suppose I'm still terrified," Jutta said. "I've never seen anything so dreadful. They seemed so real, not like ghostly apparitions at all."

The details of the Mrykriddir and their costumes and horses still burned in Jutta's mind with absolute clarity, and the more she thought about it, the more detail she could remember, such as the design of their cloaks and hoods and the markings of their horses. Jutta would have recognized the familiar design of the Hestur cloaks and hoods anywhere: a voluminous hood with a long tasseled tail, with the cloak split and lapped in the back for riding comfortably on horseback. And one of the horses had a small white diamond on its forehead and a larger one on its nose, between its nostrils, connected by a narrow wavering trickle of white. It was Elding's face, Jutta's voice of reason whispered to her. And one of the other horses had two white stockings on the hind legs, like Thruda's horse Birki. Coincidence, she told herself. Jutta shook her head to rid herself of the nasty suspicions rising and clamoring like a flock of blackbirds. Her grandmothers being Mrykriddir was a ridiculous notion.

"You must be frightened, my dear," Frida said. "You are very silent. I'm sorry our jolly expedition took such a nasty turn tonight."

"I'm quite all right," Jutta said a bit curtly.

Yet the thoughts swirled around and around in her head like tiny Myrkriddir trapped inside her skull, shrieking and laughing.

"I can see our barrow searching is going to be a bit more dangerous than I'd thought," Frida was saying, as if at a great distance. "The two of us alone here is rather foolish. Of course we have Thver and Thjodmar, but two thralls isn't enough. I really don't put much weight behind Petrus' assurances. I think he would like to get rid of us so he can do his searching unbeknown to Einarr."

"You think he is the killer?" Jutta gasped. "If that were so, why didn't he just kill us and not risk Einarr finding out?"

"Two killings together would arouse a great deal of ire, particularly two women of status and substance," Frida said thoughtfully. "All the others who have died or disappeared have been simple common working sorts of people without much family to raise an uproar about their deaths. In some way, all of these women deserved to die, because of their grasping, greedy ambition to rise out of their natural-born stations. In other words, they took a chance and they lost. People understand that. But if you and I were callously murdered, it would be an outrage, and someone would have to do something about it."

"I see," Jutta said reluctantly. "It isn't very fair to those poor women, is it?"

"Fairness is not a concept which has been adequately described to the world, by and large," Frida said. "That is why you don't find much of it. Listen, I have a plan. Would it astonish you to know that there is quite a group of us who are all interested in tracing the ley lines? It's quite an occupation with us—usually a harmless one, or so I thought until tonight. I wonder if you would mind joining our expeditions when we go out tramping. There is a certain safety in numbers."

"Certainly, I'd be most happy to," Jutta said with a faint flutter of pleasure in the middle of her anxiety.

"Good. We've planned a meeting tomorrow night. I thought you'd like to come."

"Oh, indeed I shall." Perhaps the night had not been a total disaster if she would get acquainted with other people of wealth and substance, who might advance her worldly position with their friendship, as long as they did not know she was the granddaughter and great-granddaughter of the Myrkriddir.

Jutta must have groaned out loud at the thought. Frida swiftly inquired, "Are you all right, Jutta?"

"It's been a trying evening, and I'm very tried," Jutta replied. "I can't wait to get home and into bed."

Little Ofsi was waiting for her indignantly. She had never left him alone before, and he had vented his anger by climbing up the tapestries and racing around the room like a whirlwind. Jutta returned to find her clothing pulled down from the pegs, her combs and brushes scattered on the floor, and half her nightgown soaking in the water bowl. Ofsi greeted her by attacking her ankles and biting her soundly, as if she were a maurading giant. She picked him up to comfort him, and he bit her nose.

"Yes, I know, I've been evil to leave you," she murmured into his silky fur, and he commenced purring in hearty agreement. "But where I go, you can't always follow, little kettir." He peered intently into her face, as if understanding every word. "I must do great things so we can leave here. You don't want to spend all your life at Bardhol, do you?" Ofsi's round blue eyes never blinked, staring up into hers with fearful intensity. "I think that would be a great waste of both of us. So you must be patient and stop tearing up my things when you are displeased, or I shall get a dog."

He seemed to be hanging on her every word. Then he

lunged straight at her eyelashes, having detected some fascinating movements there. Eventually he forgave her and curled up for the rest of the night in the hollow of her neck, purring frantically and kneading with his little white paws.

On the following day guests began arriving at midday for dinner at sundown. Frida introduced Jutta to each one, and by the time they had all arrived, Jutta was floating happily in a sea of important names and faces and wealth. The dark mists of the barrows were forgotten in the good cheer and pleasant company she found herself in, as naturally as if she had been born for such things. She noted with pride that Frida, her friend, was the most beautiful of all the women who attended, the most animated in conversation, the one everyone wanted to talk to. Everywhere she heard learned chatter about the ley lines, the histories, the legends of the barrow mounds. One very pleasant plump lady named Britta cornered Jutta and talked avidly of the old writings of the heroic era, arguing forcefully that they were not mere stories concocted to entertain but true accounts of what had been done.

"You young people fail to appreciate your heritage," she declared. "What noble ancestors we all had! I fear our blood is watered down to almost nothing nowadays compared to what it once was. We were warriors and wizards and sorceresses, matching our wits with our enemies the Dokkalfar, fighting for our survival with trolls, giants, vargulfs, and dragons. Now we live in our snug little settlements and never venture forth to the wild inlands and mountains where the adventures lie. Whatever is wrong with us? What are we doing here, when we could all be making heroes of ourselves?"

"We are staying alive," remarked a woman in an embroidered gray gown, whom Frida had introduced as Ingudr. She was tall and thin, with her hair parted on either side of a narrow face like a bored horse's. "In case you hadn't noticed, our heroic ancestors had a way of getting themselves killed if the number of those barrows is any indication of what their warlike inclinations led them to. And these are only the ones the wolves and foxes didn't eat in some howling wilderness somewhere. Think of all those heroic bones lying forgotten, the only remaining evidence of some great heroic quest."

"But a little danger is the spice of life," said Britta, a stout little woman who did not appear likely to encounter anything more dangerous than a speck of dust or a raveled thread.

"Then life in Mikillborg is as bland as oatmeal gruel," Ingudr said languidly. "Many of us prefer it that way."

Jutta suddenly caught sight of the full moon commencing its slow ascent into the sky. Just a slice showed over the mountaintop in the direction of Bardhol, gleaming fiercely with incandescent orange light.

"I've got to go home," Jutta said suddenly, right in the middle of an intelligent conversation between Frida and two women who favored the idea of black witchcraft.

"What? But my dear, you've just got here," Frida protested. "Is something wrong?"

"I don't know," Jutta said. "Perhaps there is, at Bardhol. All I know for certain is that I need to see my grandmothers."

"They'll think it strange your holiday lasted only for one night," Frida said. "But if you must go, we shall ride to Bardhol in the morning. You mustn't miss tonight."

"No, I must go immediately," Jutta said anxiously. "I'm very sorry, but I feel most strongly that I should go to Bardhol at once."

"Trust to your feelings," Britta advised. "If your heart says go, then you must go."

"Waiting until morning would be more sensible," Ingudr said in a mournful tone.

"Then we shall go," Frida said. "It must be some emergency, or you wouldn't feel so strongly."

"No, I refuse to take you away from your guests," Jutta said hastily. "It isn't far. I shall ride alone if you'll loan me a horse. I know the way, and it's hardly dark yet."

"I shall not permit you to ride alone if you insist on going," Frida said. "I shall accompany you myself. I'll send word to the stable for horses and a thrall to go with us."

"I'm very sorry," Jutta said in a small voice. "I hate to take you away from your guests."

"They are all old friends. I expect them to stay a day or two and tramp ley lines and tell old stories, so we'll have a good visit. They'll scarcely notice I'm gone, and I shall be back in no time at all."

The road to Bardhol was broad and well traveled, so they trotted along at a good rate by the light of the moon. Jutta never supposed she would be glad to see the lights of Bardhol perched on the mountainside, but the sight of those lights soothed her anxieties and reassured her somewhat that all was well with her grandmothers.

"Will you come to the house and light down to rest and take refreshment?" she said politely when they halted at the cross-roads.

"I would like to do that, but if I turn and go back now, my guests won't have missed me," Frida said. "Useless, wealthy old women, all of them, and nobody is sorry to see them gone from home. I don't blame you for not wanting to stay with such boring company."

"I didn't find them boring at all," Jutta said. "They all seem so very intelligent, with ideas and learning. Actually, I felt like quite the dunce."

"I assure you no one considers you a dunce."

"I hope you'll invite me to visit again," Jutta said. "I hope you'll forget my ill manners."

"Your manners are beautiful. It pleases me to see a young girl who cares about her elder family members. I hope you don't discover anything seriously wrong when you get home. Please allow me to be of assistance if there is some sort of sickness or emergency."

"Thank you for your kindness."

With that, Jutta rode the short distance up the mountain to Bardhol. She dismounted at the door, to find her grandmothers all at the usual evening pursuits, although somewhat discomfited at her sudden nighttime appearance. Margret dropped her tapestry and Ingi knocked over her chair in her enthusiasm, which startled Dora out of her pleasant dozing beside the fire with three cats on her lap and bosom.

"Whatever is wrong?" Sigla cried out, instantly in a state of nervous panic at such an unexpected occurrence. "Why are you home so soon? Are you sick? Is somebody dead?"

"I had a strange feeling," Jutta said, "that I ought to come home and make certain you were all right."

"My dear!" Thruda said, putting down her wool and shuttles and coming forward with open arms. "Of course we're all right. Whatever has frightened you?"

Jutta nestled in her grandmother's warm embrace. "Oh, I don't know. I think I had some wild and feverish notion in my head that you were in danger of some sort."

The grandmothers all clucked in sympathy, especially the fussy Sigla, who was experienced at sudden and fearful flights of fantasy.

"It must have been something you ate," Ingi suggested. "I can remember eating some very old and potent plumabrot one time. It made me feel terribly strange. I kept running into the wall, I recall."

"I had a feeling that Frida woman didn't keep a good and healthful kitchen," Sigla said darkly. "Imagine, poisoning her guests with dreadful rich food!"

"No one has been poisoned," Margret snapped. "The only thing that has happened is that we've stayed up past our usual bedtime, and now it's time we went to sleep. We are pleased that you are back, Jutta, and I hope you are reassured that we are all in the finest fettle possible."

"Warm milk, anyone?" Dora invited cozily.

Jutta escaped without her cup of the noxious stuff, fleeing into her attic room with a feeling that she had been incredibly stupid to think that her grandmothers could not take care of themselves no matter what emergency arose. She thought of Frida's house and guests and hated herself. But that sense of danger had been so real.

Svartur and the other cats came up to visit her before she blew her lamp out, marching across her bed and purring a great welcome and kneading their paws up and down as if they were marching in place. Ofsi leapt up, eyes glaring, to defend his property, wrapping his little forearms around Svartur's massive neck and trying to bite him. Svartur ignored him, trying to maintain his dignity with a small kettling capering around him like an evil imp.

"You needn't look so smug," she said to them. "It wasn't you I came home to see. Besides, it's your job to see that nothing happens to them, isn't it?"

Looking up straight into her face, Svartur bobbed his head once in an affirmative. Jutta glared at him a moment, then blew out her little lamp.

She slept lightly that night, her senses turned sharply to any sound from down below. Several times she awakened, listening for indelicate snorting from Ingi's cupboard bed. Amma Dora frequently talked in her sleep—always about one of her paramours from the past—and Amma Margret flopped about frequently, muttering and sputtering. By morning Jutta was certain that they had passed a restful night, while she herself felt as if she had merely catnapped, with all her nerves on edge. She also felt more than a little silly for thinking that her grandmothers had been Myrkriddir. It was an irrational trick of her imagination, brought on by the panic of the situation. It was bad enough to know they were robbing barrows, but even that might have a reasonable explanation. They had hidden a few old pieces in a cellar, perhaps. Her mother had told her that Amma Margret had some wealth hidden somewhere.

Myrkriddir, she was quite certain, would not be concerned about hemming up an endless supply of table and bed linens, as Amma Dora was, nor would they get angry when Ingi heedlessly tracked mud into the house on her boots. All her grandmothers seemed far too engrossed in ridiculously mundane pursuits.

Jutta flamed with inner shame when she considered how she had suspected them. In broad daylight she could see that they possessed no magic capable of rendering themselves horrible. Each in her own way made it clear to Jutta that she was pleased to have her back so soon; even Amma Margret crustily offered her a sincere compliment on her horsemanship. Never had Jutta felt like such an ungrateful and hysterical idiot.

Still, she was relieved as the days passed and the full moon waned to its third quarter and there was no sign that her grandmothers were doing any more barrow robbing. She had not seen Frida for three days, since the day of her guest hosting.

Then, on the morning of the fourth day, a great hallooing and clattering came from the dooryard, summoning everyone out of the house.

CHAPTER 10

Einarr Sorenson in a huge red cloak was capering about the dooryard on the back of a great, snorting, cart horse–looking steed, accompanied by half a dozen of his thralls and relatives. Among the bunch were Petrus and Simon on their tall heavy horses, which still looked as if they would be more at home pulling wagons than under a saddle. Leckny was also there, keeping at a slight distance and wearing his perpetual scowl, not bothering to discard it when Jutta caught his eye. In fact, he scowled even more deeply and looked away.

"Halloa, halloa!" Einarr bellowed, red-faced and grinning as the grandmothers put in an appearance to greet him. "We've come on sad business, I fear, but we're still dreadfully thirsty, in case you've got anything to drink in the house."

The men all grinned hopefully and turned their eyes upon Sigla, whose renown as a brewer of ale was widely celebrated.

"If you can possibly behave yourselves like decent folk, we might have a bit of Sigla's dark ale," Margret said, feigning great doubt and reluctance as she swept her gimlet eye over the motley herd.

"We shall be as mild as mice," Einarr said. "As meek as sheep, as biddable as dogs, as gentle as—as—dead ducks." His twinkling eye lit on a brace of ducks Ingi was about to pluck for dinner.

"And as hungry as wolves," Margret added. "Light down and come inside to sit down like civilized beings or you'll get nothing at all from our cellar."

Her stiff manner softened somewhat as Petrus handed her a bulging sack that contained a white goose, drawn and ready for roasting. After everyone's boots were off and cloaks were hung on the wall, she ushered them inside and pointed out benches to be sat on.

"Guest!" Amma Dora whispered to Jutta, her cheeks pink with flustering and fluttering as horn cups and a keg were brought out. "This is like the old days! We always had company coming and going. Bardhol has become far too quiet for my taste."

"You shall of course be staying for something to eat," Amma Margret invited portentously.

Einarr shook his head with genuine regret. "No, I fear not, for today, at least. We're on direly important business, and besides that, we just stuffed this lot before we started and they've got to at least make it until noon before another feeding." He fixed a stern glare on the two Sciplings, who grinned back at him amiably, wiping their lips with their knuckles after sipping at Sigla's ale. "Now, then, it seems another woman has been killed in the barrows."

"No! Not another!" Sigla gasped, turning deathly white. "We'll all be murdered one of these days. I can't see any way out of it!"

"A respectable woman with a husband and children this time," Einarr said grimly. "Her husband came to us early this morning, saying she had been taken in the night. We're looking all about for traces of her or someone who might have an idea of what happened to her."

"Who was it?" Sigla asked, her worry-pinched countenance blanching with fright.

"Betla of Green-knip farm," Einarr said. "Her husband is Hrokr, who has been tending my sheep for years. Good steady people, not at all the kind to run away sudden like for no good reason."

"Oh, poor Betla," Thruda whispered. "I saw her at the last market, selling her turnips."

"These are strange times," Amma Margret said, shaking her head. "We've seen nothing of her, nor heard anything, either. We do what we can to warn people away from those barrows, but nobody listens. There is scant respect for the dead these days."

"Perhaps she only went away on a trip," Ingi said hopefully. "And forgot to tell anyone. I have a frightful memory myself sometimes. Perhaps she'll return, safe and unharmed."

"We can hope for such a thing," Einarr said, shaking his head dubiously, "but it's my suspicion she's dead."

"Was she red-haired?" Jutta asked suddenly, thinking she remembered the woman selling her turnips at the market.

"Aye, beautiful red hair, like a warlord's red gold," Einarr said.

"Ah, yes," Jutta said with a disquieting lurch. Betla, she knew, had also been visiting with Frida. Although she had not done more than nod to her during Frida's introduction, she remembered Betla's masses of pale red-gold hair hanging in neat plaits. She was a pleasant if common-looking sort, rather reddened and toughened from years of battling the elements for an existence, and even more out of place in Frida's knowledgeable company than Jutta had been. And now she had disappeared, perhaps on her way home from Frida's.

Jutta slipped outside, not seeing Leckny in their ale-guzzling number. He was sitting on the clutter of rocks and throwing small sticks at Mishka, who was curled up in a bugling heap on the wall.

"You ought to taste Sigla's ale," Jutta said. "She's really quite famous for it."

"You mean, if I were a true man, I'd be in there gulping and belching with the rest of them?" he retorted.

"No, that's not what I said at all," Jutta snapped. "Nor did I come out here to pick a fight. Why do you always have to go against everybody's grain? If everyone is eating meat, you don't want it. If everyone is drinking ale, you want water. If you fell in the river, you'd float upstream. Would it hurt you to be at least polite?"

"Yes, I'm sure it would," he said. "It would pain me terribly to be polite to stupid people."

"Like who?" Jutta inquired coldly.

"You."

"Oh? Indeed? And how am I stupid?"

"You know as well as I do—better, actually, because you're the one who is getting trapped by Frida Thorungard, not me. Long after you're dead, I shall be alive and telling everyone, 'Yes, I knew her, and I tried to warn her about Frida, but she was stupid and wouldn't listen. And now she is dead.' "

"What a rude and ignorant creature you are," Jutta cried. Never before had she encountered a person who could so instantly offend her every sensibility. "How dare you come here and insult me to my face!"

"It's not a bad face, but I've seen much better," he answered. "As well as much worse," he added hastily when Jutta picked up a stick and advanced on him. His belated and left-handed compliment didn't save him, however; she broke the stick over his head and moved in to deal him another good whack across the shoulders as he turned to flee.

At that moment Einarr opened the door and stepped out, emitting a bellow of laughter at the sight of his son hopping away with Jutta swinging at him with her stick and belaboring him with unladylike epithets she had heard in the barns and fields.

Leckny fled around the corner of the barn, and Jutta followed, giving him one last whack before throwing her stick at him.

"And don't you ever spy on me again!" she finished.

"Someone's got to," he returned, bolder now that she was disarmed. "Someone's got to know where to look for the body."

"Are you trying to hint that Frida might be at fault somehow?" Jutta demanded. "If you think you know something, why aren't you talking to her?"

"Sometimes the most guilty are the ones who appear the least sullied," he said with a smug and taunting smile.

"Oh, you are insufferable!" Jutta sputtered. "I don't know why I waste my time thinking about you!"

"I'm very good-looking, they say, and I stand to inherit the chieftain's seat one day, and my father is a wealthy man. Many girls think I'm worth wasting a thought on now and then."

"Let them," Jutta retorted. "I certainly shan't include myself in their number. Is there something you truly know about Frida, or are you just making it up?"

"Would you believe me if I told you anything bad about her?"

"No, I don't think so. How could you possibly know her as well as I do? I've stayed in her home as a guest. We've done a great deal of walking and talking together. And you've only looked at her from afar."

"True. I can't argue with anything you say. So go on your merry way and see what happens to you. I think it's time for me to leave." He smiled, bowed slightly, and turned around in his tracks to go back to the horses. Jutta glared after him a moment, then strode purposefully into the barn for her bridle.

Upon Einarr's return to the courtyard, his black horse awoke from a lazy doze with a guilty snort and went into fits of caracoling and fiery pawing. Around anyone else except his master he was a great lump of contentment who enjoyed having his head scratched above his eyes and between his ears. Little children could perch on his back and pilot him around at an amiable shambling gait. He reserved all his antics and showing off for his master, and today he commenced showing off in particular because Jutta rode up to join them on her grandmother's mare Elding. He pranced and snorted and lunged forward before Einarr was fairly in his seat, nearly spilling him off into the dyeing vat.

"We are going to search the barrows!" Einarr called over one shoulder when he had settled himself in the saddle somewhat, considerably ahead of all the others. "We'll ride all abreast and see if we can see something!"

"We shall ride to Thorungard first," Jutta added. "That is where I saw Betla last."

The farther she led them from Bardhol the more easily she could breathe. The riders spread out in a long line, riding abreast, and scoured the moor in their passage without finding a trace of Betla. As they neared Thorungard, the two surly thralls, Thver and Thjodmar, came forward to accost the search party with their weapons worn casually in full sight.

"Halloo!" Einarr greeted them at full lung capacity when they were still quite a distance down the road. "We wish to speak to your mistress! Is the lady Holmfridr in the house?"

The thralls conferred a moment while the riders approached to a normal speaking distance.

"The mistress is at home," Thver said. "But she isn't available for speaking."

"Go and tell her that Jutta is here," Jutta said. "Tell her that it is of utmost importance that we speak to her, a matter of life and death. Also let her know that the chieftain Einarr is standing in the road with fifteen armed men and wondering at her scant hospitality."

"You must come up and light down," Thver said a little more hospitably. "I shall tell the mistress you are here. She is probably dressing even now."

The search party gladly dismounted in the dooryard of the kitchen and accepted cups of ale brought out in a keg by a serving woman.

"A pretty house," Leckny observed, looking around with a smirk on his face. "What a pleasant and useless life, living in ease with a flock of people to do your work for you. I would like such a life."

"At least you've got the useless part down right," Jutta said, turning away from him and seeking out the company of Simon.

"What do you know of this disappearance?" Jutta hissed. "You were in the barrows the night Betla vanished, weren't you? I know you were there at least once."

"You saw us," Simon said. "We were attacked by the Myrkriddir on our first attempt. On the following night we were nearly overtaken by an apparition of another sort. It was a mighty group of horsemen flying along like death itself, chasing a deer or something. We got out of there and decided to wait until the next full moon. All the signs were against us."

"The full moon lasted five nights," Jutta said. "You made your two attempts and gave up?"

"Since my ankle was paining me, my father came out alone for three more nights to see if it was safe, but he didn't stay long. The Myrkiriddir were waiting for him each time at the crossroads. We never saw anything of that woman. I hope you'll continue to honor our pact of silence in this matter."

"I shall, unless I one day prove that you are the killers of all these women."

"Then we are safe," Simon said with his gentle smile to reassure her. "If we were not Sciplings and strangers to your realm, would you still think we were such vile creatures that would kill lone women?"

Jutta expelled a long sigh and shook her head. "I cannot truly believe that you would do something so evil. I just can't see any murder in you anywhere. But we must discover who the killer is. Nine women have been killed or have vanished without a trace. You would do as well to suspect me of the crime. We will all be looking strangely at one another before this is finished. I fear a great many friendships may be broken."

"Not ours," Simon said. "I am very hard to offend when it comes to my friends. I owe you my life for helping us out of the barrows that night. I will do all I can to help you find this killer—even though you continue to suspect me and my father."

Jutta sighed. "I don't know who to suspect. I hope it's someone I never heard of. But I have a certain involvement to protect, so I'm not going to ignore this matter and tell myself it doesn't concern me."

"I admire you for your courage and resolve," Simon declared, turning a little pink at his own boldness, which made Jutta smile.

Petrus had been watching their conversation from afar, but now he drifted closer to Jutta. Still maintaining an easy and smiling countenance, he said in a low voice, "I'm glad to see you smiling at last. I hope that it means our pact of silence is still safe. I do not wish to find myself swinging from Einarr's roof beam."

"Nor shall you have cause to worry if Simon is truthful," Jutta said.

"I have raised him to always tell the truth, no matter what

the cost," Petrus said, hoisting up his chin defiantly. "Eventually we must tell Einarr about our digging. Perhaps you can be our intermediary when the time comes."

"And when will that be?" Jutta asked. "I've discovered that the weight of this pact is getting heavier day by day, most especially now that another woman has been killed."

"Einarr is a good man," Petrus said. "But I fear his temper sometimes. In the old days it was a good thing to whack someone's head off first and ask questions about it later. It was the only way to stay alive. Einarr would have done well and lived long. But these aren't the old days, and I don't want my head whacked off. When I find Sigmund's cup and I am ready to leave this realm, we shall carefully explain to him what I have done—when I have the means of escaping back to my own realm. Then he can have that cursed cup." His voice dropped to a whisper when he noticed Leckny glaring at him suspiciously. "Now, there's a pair of eyes that I wish were clouded once in a while. He spies on us for his father, I think."

The Sciplings moved away and sat down on a fence at a distance from the others to await Frida's appearance. Jutta noticed that the Ljosalfar kept a polite distance from the Sciplings as well.

Jutta looked at Einarr, who was sprawling genially on a comfortable seat built into the wall, laughing uproariously at his companion's dog, which had just gotten a thrashing from the Thorungard dogs and was cringing behind his master's legs. Jutta had never suspected that he might be anything but a rather loud and jovial lovable lout. It was something she had seen before, however, among the men who worked for her father. Those who were the quickest to laugh and joke often were the ones with the quickest tempers and the blackest moods when they were feeling out of sorts. Her own father was a man of a mild and even disposition, without any boisterous guffawings or any deep pits of despair or fits of bad temper.

Most interesting of all was Leckny's apparent dislike of his own father. For all his supercilious sneering, Leckny was a keen and observant individual. Even now he was perched on a wall by himself, pretending to be terribly bored, but his eyes never left her for a moment. He had seen her conversations with the Sciplings and her considering perusal of Einarr. He nodded to her with a twisted little smile, narrowing his piercing blue eyes down to knowing slits, as if he knew exactly what she was thinking.

He looked rather surprised when she deliberately approached him and sat down on the wall nearby.

"I see you're finally ready for some intelligent company," he said with a fulsome grin. "It's such a strain trying to communicate with Sciplings. They're rather like large, amiable children, aren't they?"

"Be still, you toad," Jutta said. "I've been put onto a trail, and the scent is very strong and fresh."

"Dear me, you can track things, too? You're truly a young woman of amazing ability."

"You're trying to put me off, aren't you? Well, it won't work. I've wondered for a while why it is you work so hard to keep people away, but I'm starting to figure it out. I always thought you were just being stupid and obnoxious, which is what you want everyone to think. You're really hiding something, aren't you?"

"Who, me? What have I got worth hiding?"

"Something you fear. Something you don't want known."

"And what might that be?"

"Not exactly what. More of a who, I think."

"I fear I'm getting confused. You've made a great mistake if you think I know something. Just listen to my father and you'll find out how stupid I am."

"I've listened, but I don't think you're as stupid as you pretend. I think you know a great deal. Or at least one great thing you wish you didn't."

"Oh, what rot. Can't you just say what you're getting at? I don't enjoy playing cat and mouse."

"Except when you're the cat, you mean. You dislike your father to an amazing extent, even for an eldest son who wishes himself away and on his own somewhere."

"Well, just look at him. He's a monstrous loud bully with the manners of an ox."

"But everyone loves him in spite of his uncouth behavior, except you."

"There are only two ways of doing anything at Sorengard, and by that I mean the wrong way or Einarr's way. I seem to persist in doing everything the wrong way, myself, and so we lock horns over almost every detail of my life. What do you find so significant about that? It's a bit troublesome for me, but some of us are bound for trouble one way or another, so we manufacture our own to carry around with us when we can't arrange for lightning to strike us or some such misfortune."

"You're very clever, and witty, too, but I think you're still hiding something behind all your chatter. Something the Scipling said to me made me think that all may not be well at Sorengard, or at least as pleasant as it seems."

"What would the Sciplings know about anything?"

"They are more clever than you think. Why do you suppose it is that they are rather afraid of your father and suspicious that they might come to harm in your house?"

"Because they are robbing barrows," Leckny said with a glance around. "I've got no real proof of it yet, but when I find one gold coin upon them, I'm going to noise it about and they will be hanged or they will become outlaws. At any rate, I'm going to get them out of Sorengard. Now, is that enough for you, or is there something else? I thought I made that point quite clear before."

"Certainly you did, but tell me this. What is your father looking for in the barrows?"

Leckny lost his expression of bored arrogance and looked at her intently. "Who told you he was looking for anything? The Sciplings?"

"It doesn't matter who. I just don't believe your father is as innocent in this matter of grave robbing as he tries to appear. A great deal can be hidden behind a loud and blustering front. Is it Sigmund's cup he wishes to find? That would give him as much power as one of the warlords of old. Wasn't your grandfather a warlord? Wouldn't your father like to reawaken the old days of plunder and conquest? Think how rich some of these neighboring steadings have become during all these years of peace and prosperity. A man like Einarr would welcome the return of the old ways, would he not? You, on the other hand, have become much too civilized and squeamish to descend on your neighbors and plunder them."

"It is nothing but talk," Leckny said, cold and white, his eyes flashing like blue crystals of ice. "He may talk, but the grand days of magic and power are over. Even if he laid his hands on that cursed cup, it probably would not work for him. Something has gone out of the world, especially since the Sciplings have polluted our realm with their iron and weapons and greed. If Petrus had never shown up searching for that cup, my father would never have known of its existence."

"Then he knows about Petrus digging in the barrows."

"I've told him numerous times, since I have followed Petrus and Simon and watched them with my own two eyes. He pretends not to believe me, and Petrus puts on a show of innocence. It's a great scheme between them, pretending that nothing is happening. I believe my father is waiting for them to find it and hoping that they do, and when they do, he's going to take it away from them. This is not a quarrel you wish to be involved in, so I advise you to stay away from the Sciplings and don't get sympathetic with them. My father has no conscience when it comes to taking what he wants. I fear you could be mown down if you're standing in his way."

Jutta turned to look at Einarr, who was surrounded by his men and thralls and dogs, with a horn of ale in his hand and laughing jovially. Petrus sat beside him and had just said something very funny. Einarr gave him a friendly wallop on the back, spilling his horn of ale, and they roared with mirth, shoulder to shoulder, like the best of friends. It was hard to believe that they could enjoy each other's company so thoroughly while in their bottommost hearts they were bitter rivals for Sigmund's cup.

Jutta shook her head slightly. "I'm not sure I can believe it," she murmured.

"Believe it," Leckny said. "Friendship between two dogs lasts only until there is a bone or a bitch to fight over."

Offended, Jutta turned her back on him and walked away. At that moment Frida appeared at the kitchen door, stepping into the dooryard with an air that silenced all the laughing and joking. The scowling Thver and Thjodmar stood up, one on either side of her, at a reserved distance, but their protective attitude was unmistakable.

"What have I done to deserve the arrival of a mob of armed men at my house?" she asked in a light and bantering tone, but there was an edge to her soft voice.

"Nothing to speak of at all," Einarr said, hastily wiping his lips and rising to his feet. "It was most gracious of you to share a cask of your ale with this desperate and thirsty crew. We've been riding since dawn on a search of utmost importance, and we've come to you for your assistance."

Jutta had to hide a smile. They were only an hour from Bardhol and Sigla's fine brew, and he was making it sound as if they were nearly dead of thirst.

"I shall be glad to aid you in whatever way I can," Frida said. "I have two stout thralls to lend you and ten fresh horses."

"Thank you. We need all the pairs of eyes we can possibly get. Another woman is missing in the barrows."

"Who is it?"

Another man stepped forward, red-bearded, wearing a common cloak of homespun wool. "It's my wife, Betla, and she was seen here last when she was alive. I told her not to go, that she should stay home with her husband and children where she belongs, but she wasn't about to listen. No, she had to go off with these women who were above her in life, trying to show herself off to them. I told her they've got no use for a woman who has to work for her living; I told her they were a soft and useless bunch, doing nothing to earn their keep. Then there's this business of prowling about the old barrows, digging up old stones and pathways. It isn't healthy to get so interested in the old ways. I told her it was dangerous to mess with things we know nothing about, such as ladies of quality and old magic. What were they doing here, messing about with that stuff? It looks like a bunch of sorcery to me, and they've stolen away my wife from her home and her children!"

"Hrokr! Hush now!" Einarr chided as the rest of the men rumbled an uneasy affirmative. Thver and Thjordmar glowered ferociously, keeping their hands close to their weapons. "Mind what you're saying! In the old days that would've been taken as an accusation. Now I fear you've offended this lady mightily."

Frida stepped back to lean against the door frame. "I am not offended. I am severely grieved to think that harm has come to poor Betla. It is true she was here last in my house for three days, and then she went away, safe and whole from my doorstep, assuring me that it was no matter for her to walk back to Mikillborg, and perhaps she would catch a ride from someone. I saw her last just two days ago, in the morning."

"I don't know why she had to come here," Hrokr burst out. "She had no business with all the fine ladies. She had work enough to do without thinking about ley lines and magic. She had these ideas put into her head, and from then on nothing was good enough for her anymore."

"I assure you, Betla was most sensible about her station in life," Frida retorted. "She knew there was more to think about than slopping food to man and beast and mucking up afterward. All I offered her was a time to think of the mysteries and beauties of the world before going back to her drudgery. Is that too frightening an idea? You men can go and drink and tell lies without the hindrance of women's company, so let the women enjoy the company of each other without having men around. That's all we do here."

"That and mess about with powers that ought to be left alone," Hrokr snapped. "Betla often told me that if we knew how to work these lines and circles, we'd have better crops and the animals would be protected and none of us would have to sicken and die. She said there were powers beyond belief in those old standing stones in the barrows. She also said there were cartloads of gold there, just under our feet, if only we had the means of finding it."

"As if a group of soft and useless ladies such as we are could dig up a barrow looking for gold," Frida said, and the men all chuckled appreciatively. "Even Betla, as stout as she is, could not dig up a barrow single-handedly, and you can see from my hands that they've never touched a spade in all their days." She held up the palms of her hands, which were white and soft as silk. "But it is true that we have sought out the powers of the mind, since we have hardly any powers of the body, and there are those who would entirely disallow us any volition of our own. So it is that we seek to escape by the power of our own thoughts and knowledge. It would probably astonish you to know that we spend a great deal of our time doing nothing more than reading to one another."

"Reading! A fine pastime, poking your nose between dusty old pages." Hrokr snorted. "What use has my wife got for books? You see how they've tolled her senses away? And now she is most likely dead because of it!"

"Better to be dead because of a little knowledge than to die in utter ignorance," Frida said. Then she turned to Einarr. "Now, then, am I to expect a formal accusation and a trial for murdering poor Betla? Do you think I have nine neighbors who will stand up and say that I have killed her? If so, then I suppose I should ready myself to be hanged."

"No, no," Einarr said hastily, commencing to arrange his features into a pleasing and earnest expression. "We only came to see if she had stayed on here, perhaps, or to find out at least if you had seen her. I am satisfied that no wrong has been committed here, so we shall continue with our search. We thank you most graciously for your ale and your hospitality. We certainly intended no offense by any of the words which we have spoken."

"No offense taken," Frida said. "I shall do everything in my power to help you find Betla. I shall lend you all my thralls and serving help, and I will ride with you myself to help scour the fells. Let me pour you all another horn of ale while Thver and Thjodmar saddle the horses."

She carried the cask into the dooryard amid rumbles of approval, and the cups were all filled again. Even Hrokr was persuaded to have another horn of ale, which mellowed his combative attitude and brought tears to his eyes.

"She was such a good creature," he confided to one of his friends. "Never one to harangue a fellow or throw things in a fit of temper. You can't imagine how I'll miss her. Plenty of wives a man would be glad to get rid of, but not her."

Frida produced ten riders from her house. They spent the day riding over the fells between Thorungard and the barrows. Near the end of the day, when the shadows were getting long, they came at last to the edge of the barrows, where they halted to debate.

"It's nearly dark," some of the men grumbled, and it had been a long day, with only an hour's rest at noontime for a saddlebag meal.

"We've just gotten to the place where we may find her," Einarr said with a glint in his eye that said that nobody had better disagree with him. "We'll press on as far as we can, and when it gets too dark, we'll go home. Take your positions. Keep your eyes open and ride a bit closer together so you don't miss anything."

They had not been in the barrows half an hour when the dogs found the body of Betla in a thicket. They raised a lugubrious howl that brought the gooseflesh to Jutta's arms.

CHAPTER 11

"She looks as if she's been hagridden," Einarr said grimly once they had removed the body from the thicket. For a moment they all looked at the poor victim in silence, not comprehending the hundreds of scratches and bruises, the clothing shredded by branches and thorns, and the one decisive wound in the throat. To Jutta it looked as if she had been bled out like a sheep, but there was no blood on the ground.

"It used to happen in the old days," Einarr continued. "My grandmother told me how sorceresses used to change people to horses and then ride them on long journeys for the entire night. After five or six nights of hard riding, they died of exhaustion."

"That sort of thing doesn't happen anymore," Frida said. "Wrap her in a cloak. We'll have to tie her over a horse to get her home."

"Use mine," Hrokr said in a strangled voice, leading his horse forward. He didn't seem to be able to stop once he got started speaking. "This horse she raised from a colt. The mare died, and she fed it by hand. She had a soft heart for helpless things, she did, and it was such a hard life she lived. Other people might have become hard, but she always hoped that things would get better. Now I guess they never will. There weren't any good times for Betla."

When the job was done, Hrokr led the horse homeward, accompanied by a few Mikillborg men. "There's no sense in all of you going out of your way for me," he said gruffly. "I thank you for your help. You'd best be getting home to your food and fire. It's getting dark."

When he was gone, Jutta turned to Frida. She had been stronger and less squeamish than some of the men when it had come to removing Betla from the thicket and wrapping her up. Almost haughtily she had directed how the job was to be done, as if she were working in a state of cold fury. Jutta admired her more than ever at that moment.

"This killer must be caught," Jutta said in a low voice. "Every woman in this settlement is in danger. He must be a madman."

"Indeed," Frida said. "What pitiful and sorry creatures we all are, preying upon one another as if we were animals. Life is a short and brutal experience for some of us, filled with misery and pain. Perhaps Betla is better off where she is than where we are, still struggling against an inexorable foe. One day we all must die, too. I, for one, intend to live all I can and thus cheat death out of some of its inevitable victory."

"What's done is done," Einarr said with a sigh. "There's no sense to it and no sense in trying to make something of it, which is why I spend a great deal of my time drinking and sleeping. It keeps me from having to think. Well, then, there's nothing for us to do except go home now. I'm grateful to all of you for your willingness to help. Of course, you had no choice in the matter, since I'm your chieftain and you're sworn to uphold what I tell you to do. You're all good men—and women—and you worked hard. Now it's time for home and hearth, and tomorrow will be a good day. Leckny, you ride with the lass to her door and see her home safe to her grandmothers."

Jutta opened her mouth to protest but thought better of it. Sometimes a wise woman kept her demands to a minimum when men were tired and tempers were short.

"Come along, then," she said to him shortly. "See if you can keep up." Turning her horse around smartly, she thumped Elding in the ribs and departed at a canter, leaving Leckny rattling along in the rear.

"Halloa! Can't you wait up?" he demanded furiously, almost invisible in the descending twilight.

Jutta halted and waited with a supercilious smile for him to catch up.

"I just wanted to say I was sorry," he said when he reached her. "Sorry about Betla. It isn't fair that a man wants to kill only women. He must be a monster to prey upon only weaker creatures."

"Perhaps it is not a man," Jutta said. "Have you not seen the Myrkriddir flying through these barrows?"

"This is not the work of mystical creatures," Leckny said. "Myrkriddir don't exist any longer, if they ever did. Someone might like for us to believe that it was Myrkriddir that did this, but it was the work of one of our friends, relatives, or neighbors, for his own personal gain."

Jutta had never heard him speak with such earnest sincerity. "Surely it won't prove to be anybody we know," she said. "I don't think I could bear it."

"I don't want you to be the next one," Leckny said. "It seems that it's always a woman who is somehow on her own, who becomes too interested in those barrows. They've got a curse on them, a curse of death."

"I thought you didn't believe in magic," Jutta chided.

"I never said I didn't believe in curses. And if the lure of that gold in those barrows isn't a curse, I can't imagine a better one."

They rode in silence through the gathering mists, and no one spoke again until they were out of the barrows and safely at the crossroad, where a comfortable wide road led toward Mikillborg and the prosperous settlements beyond. A crooked, rutted little track led toward Bardhol.

"I suppose nothing can keep you from your maps and ley lines through the barrows," he said when they stopped to let the horses catch their wind.

"It's a harmless pastime," Jutta said. "Done in the daytime— for the most part."

"You've been to the barrows in the dark?" Leckny demanded with an incredulous glare.

"Yes, I have," Jutta said airily, enjoying her advantage. "And I'll tell you this: it's by no means a lonely place sometimes. You may doubt the existence of Myrkriddir, but I've seen them, and certain other people you know have seen them, too, although I know if you asked, they'd deny everything." Now she had said more than she ought to have and she became nervous. "Come on, I don't want to spend all night getting home. Elding is tired, and so am I."

She kept Elding enough ahead of him so that he couldn't talk or ask her any questions. He seemed to have descended into a thoughtful mood anyway and said nothing until they reached Bardhol and Elding was unsaddled and turned into her paddock. Five of six kettir followed Jutta from the paddock to the barn, purring and yipping a glad welcome.

"It's been an interesting day," Leckny said, stepping over several kettir that were caressing his ankles with their jowls. "You've given me a great deal to think about."

"Should I be impressed or worried?" Jutta asked as she put her saddle away and hung her bridle on its peg. "I'd hate to be responsible for your hurting yourself."

"And so would I," he added. "These women who have disappeared are all quite similar in their circumstances and station. All were dissatisfied in one way or another and always looking out for some way to better themselves. And you are dissatisfied, too, living here with these old women and their cats."

"So I may be the next?" Jutta inquired. "Just because I'm dissatisfied? Lots of women are dissatisfied with their lot, but they don't end up murdered in the barrows. I believe some of them have simply run away, looking for something better. So far we know of two dead and seven missing."

"No. We've found four dead, and five are missing. The ones we've found have been hidden in the barrows, and I think the missing ones are there, also, eaten up by foxes and ravens by now, as the murderer intended. It is convenient to noise it about that it was curses or Myrkriddir who killed them."

"Or even Sciplings," Jutta added, attempting to sound as if she were joking. "You've got little love for them, so mightn't they be the killers?"

"I plan to find out if they are or not," Leckny said. "I shall follow them the next time they sneak out during the full moon."

"I think that would be dangerous and foolhardy," Jutta said. "If they were the killers, they would make certain you didn't live to tell about it."

"You don't like to think about dear Simon being a killer, do you?"

"No, I don't. He doesn't seem to be the type."

"Any person can be a killer if they are determined enough to get someone out of their way so they can have what they want."

"How would these harmless women be in Simon and Petrus' way if they are robbing barrows?"

"They don't want anybody to know. They could be taking advantage of these foolish women who want to better their lot in the Scipling realm."

"Betla was not a foolish woman. She was clever and sensible, and like the rest of us, she believed that finding the ley lines would bring good luck and prosperity. There used to be ways to manipulate nature's powers, and we used to be able to do it and now we can't. It's a reasonable thing to want to reawaken those talents, isn't it? What harm could there possibly be in trying to increase the fertility of our crops and livestock?"

"Plenty of harm has befallen nine women," Leckny said. "I suppose they were all after the same thing, and it has turned out very badly for them."

"Perhaps there is no connection. Perhaps some of them truly disappeared, perhaps some of their deaths were accidental—"

At that moment an imperious little shriek emanated from the direction of the house.

"Oh! There's Ofsi! He knows I'm home," Jutta said hastily. "He hates it when I leave him. I hope he hasn't destroyed anything while I was gone. You must come in for something to eat and drink before you go home, and you can see Ofsi."

"What is Ofsi?" Leckny inquired dubiously, hearing the demanding "Mew!" approaching the barn.

"A kettir," Jutta answered, shoving aside the purring, furry mob twining around her shins. "Ofsi, my barbarian! Here I am, little darling!"

Ofsi came marching across the barnyard, still uttering his imperious falsetto yell. He wasn't much more than a handful of fur, stubby tail, huge ears, and round eyes glaring from a little round face. He strode purposefully toward Jutta, ignoring the big kettir, and climbed up her breeches, still yelling.

Jutta unfastened his sets of climbing hooks and held him to her cheek. "Isn't he a beautiful creature?"

Leckny extended one forefinger dubiously to Ofsi, who promptly grabbed it with all of his foreclaws and bit it, his eyes wide open and fixed on his victim's face.

"Yes, lovely," Leckny muttered as Ofsi made a lunge for his nose, which Jutta barely averted by holding on to his hindquarters. "What is the matter with that cat? Hasn't he got any conscience at all? He tried to tear my face off!"

"It's nothing personal," Jutta said. "He's fascinated by anything that moves—bugs, grass, lips, eyelashes—and whatever he sees moving, he pounces on it. And you must remember, he's not a cat, he's a kettir."

"He looks like a cat to me, and he acts like one, too." Leckny sucked on his perforated finger, scowling blackly. "He's a bloodthirsty little savage."

"Don't speak of him that way. Kettir know what you're saying about them."

"You're getting as odd as your grandmothers about their cats—kettir, or whatever you call them."

Jutta flushed, glad that the dim barn concealed it. "If you want some supper, you'd better stop all this chatter and come into the house," she snapped, stalking away with a procession of kettir bounding at her heels.

Her grandmothers were waiting to receive the news, and it seemed to strike them with particular force.

"Dead, is she?" Margret said. "The poor creature." She clenched her jaws angrily and scowled, even though Svartur was rubbing around her ankles affectionately and purring. He even stood on his hind legs and poked at her with his outstretched paw, begging to be picked up and cradled in her arms.

"Oh dear, oh dear," Sigla murmured faintly, sinking down in a chair, heedlessly sitting on poor Rugla, who was trying to take a bath. Rugla was still rather encrusted from upsetting a pan of cream on her head.

"Now Sigla, don't you go fainthearted on us," Dora said, nervously stroking the lovely green-eyed Asa. "Poor Betla was, after all, a woman of the working class, and she expected her life to be hard. I daresay she died with utmost courage."

"Where's Loki? He's the only one who can make me stop worrying." Sigla had scarcely mentioned his name before he leapt into her lap, peering into her face anxiously, his fur blazing as orange as flame.

"She looked as if she'd been hagridden," Jutta said, "as if she'd run for hours." She clasped Ofsi to her cheek, feeling the comfort of his soft and silky fur. Fortunately he was in a cuddlesome mood and commenced a friendly purring and kneading of his white paws. He even closed his perpetually staring eyes and drew up the corners of his mouth in a contented smile. Looking at him, she knew she would eventually shake off the cold horror that pervaded her now, but she would never forget the crime that had inspired it.

"Well, I wish you hadn't gone with Einarr," Amma Thruda said with a sigh as she dished out the evening meal in bowls: a fragrant soup flavored with wild onions, the small potatoes from the previous year, cabbage, and a lone hare she had snared. "It wasn't women's work, searching the fells for a dead body, and then to find her in such a state. Leckny, you may sit there beside Jutta. We'll put all the youth and beauty on one side of the table."

Leckny gladly sat down, fondly eyeing the fresh hot bread, a wedge of aromatic cheese, and skyr and the earliest of the tiny wild strawberries. The kettir also sat down gladly, in laps, on benches, and for once they did not choose to occupy the table, for which Jutta was grateful. They didn't much care for just soup. What they craved was a joint of roasted meat or some nice fresh fish fried up crisp with meal and plenty of grease.

"She looked terrible," Jutta said, trying to close her mind's eye on the pitiful sight of Betla's remains. Ofsi smiled up at her and kneaded his little white paws gently on her arm. "She looked nearly torn to shreds, then something dragged her into the thicket. We never would have found her except for the dogs. And the look on her face was absolute terror, as if she had seen something so horrible that it left a mark on her, even in death."

"The last thing she saw was her killer," Margret said grimly. "No wonder she was terrified. I know I would be. The poor, foolish woman, she should have stayed at home where she belonged, where she was safe, and in her station in life. But she did not deserve to die, no matter what her other shortcomings were." Margret looked around the table at the others, her eyes flashing.

"There's no crime in trying to better one's position in life," Jutta said. "I'm sure that's all she was trying to do, to make things a bit easier and more comfortable."

"No, no one can blame her," Ingi said, wiping a tear on a bit of tattered sleeve. "But she had a hard life. I'll miss her so on market days. She always sold me the best turnips and things. Now I'll have to go to someone else, who will probably try to sell me something not so nice. Who would've wanted to kill her? I'd like to know. There was no harm in her."

"No harm at all," Margret agreed, still looking tight and grim around the lips. "But there is someone around here lurking in those barrows who means harm to every one of the rest of us."

"It was so strange," Jutta said. "She didn't look as if she'd been beaten to death, with big heavy blows. It was more like she'd died of exhaustion."

"Don't go on about it," poor fearful Sigla whimpered, clutching her handkerchief. "It's too awful to talk about." Loki yowled in agreement and stood up to put his front legs around her neck so he could purr in her ear.

"But it wasn't like a normal killing," Jutta persisted. "The strangeness is a clue to the killer. Why did Betla run and run until she was dying? Her clothes were torn apart by the thorns and thickets, and her feet were a bloody mess. Why was she running like that? Who or what was she running away from in such terror?"

Part of her brain whispered "Myrkriddir!" but she refused to listen to it, refused to picture the Myrkriddir hounding Betla from the barrows.

"It's best not to brood on Betla's death too deeply," Margret said, "or by some strange mischance you may bring the same fate upon yourself."

Never one for wasting time with talk when he was hungry, Leckny now was fed enough that he was encouraged to say something. "I for one refuse to allow this killer to continue to prey upon the women of the Mikillborg settlements. I've taken a vow that I'm going to find him and turn him over to my father for justice. I'm going to watch very closely the people who go into the barrow fields."

"That's very commendable of you, young man," Amma Margret said. "Unfortunately, the barrow field is a vast place with thousands of places to hide. You don't have enough eyes in your head to see it all, nor time enough in one lifetime to be there at every moment. If you make yourself too trouble-some, you may find yourself the next corpse."

"No men have been killed yet," Leckny said.

"Well, you're not quite a man yet, either, in my opinion," Amma Margret retorted, surveying him with snapping eyes. "You're still a trifle green. Wet behind the ears. I myself have no intention of contributing to your early demise, so I'm order-ing you to spend the night here. You can sleep on that shelf closest to the fire if you're chilly or take the one by the door. Ingi will fetch you an eider, and I suspect you'll have plenty of kettir to keep you warm if the fire dies down."

Thoroughly chilled, Jutta helped clear away the meal when they were done and sat down beside the hearth with Ofsi sleeping in her lap. He had gone limp as a string, dangling his head over upside down, his jaw slightly ajar.

"That's the best he's been all day," Ingi grumbled. "I was

trying to do some mending, but he kept attacking me until I had to give it up. Then he went and jumped in the flour for the bread making. Nobody could touch him unless they wanted to be shredded up."

"He hates it when I leave him," Jutta said. "But it's difficult taking a kettir along when you go riding. The basket is so awkward and stiff."

"I shall make you a kettir backpack," Dora said. "A comfortable pack for riding or walking. I've often thought about these people who carry away our kettir and how tired of that basket they're going to become. It should be large and loose enough that a kettir could curl up in it and take a nap, and it must have plenty of airholes. A flap, perhaps, so the kettir could stick his head out and see where he is. Nor would he feel confined, if he could get his head out whenever he felt like it. I have some lovely big scraps of that bright blue I was making short tunics out of last year."

Dora commenced rummaging in her trunks of sewing. She was a gifted seamstress, and when she took her cloaks, tunics, and vests to the market after a long dark winter of nothing to do but sew, she sold them all before midday.

"Many of our kettir are far travelers," she continued, surveying her scraps. "They should have a means of comfortable and attractive accommodation. It should be colorful. Kettir adore bright colors. This way, the owner of a kettir can carry his beloved companion anywhere without fear of him getting out of a basket."

Jutta eyed the huge furry lumps that were Mishka and Svartur, wondering who on earth would want to carry such a load on their backs for very long. Much more sensible to make the fat creatures walk—if they would. Kettir were notoriously lazy and loved to be carried around.

"I'm going to bed," Jutta said with a yawn, gathering up her limp kettling. He stretched once until all his toes spread out and his tongue protruded, trusting Jutta not to drop him on his wee little impervious head, then went back to sleep in her hands.

"Remember, we're taking the dry cows up to the top shieling tomorrow to put in with Throm Fiddlasson's herd," Margret said.

"I think I'll stay home," Jutta said. "I'm going to be tired from today's searching."

"You're sure?" Thruda said. "It's great fun. We hitch up a cart and pack a lunch and take all the kettir, and they think it's the most wonderful lark. They jump around all day, playing and chasing birds and things."

"I don't think I'll mind having some time alone," Jutta said. "Go ahead and I'll take care of the eggs and the milking and the fires, so you won't have to get up so early."

In the morning Leckny helped harness the horses and hitched them to the cart, with eight or ten kettir yowling around him in high excitement. They rubbed against his shins and waved their tails and stared up at him, yelling instructions, or perhaps they were cursing him for his slowness. Some of them got into the cart, climbing on the seat and yowling as if they intended to drive.

"They act as if they know they're going on a trip," Leckny said, stumbling over Svartur, who glared at him reproachfully. Intelligent people did not stumble over kettir or cats. They had some idea of where to put their feet when small floor-dwelling creatures lived in the same abode. One was expected to walk with small steps, at a considerate shuffle, so some great heavy boot would not come down on a delicate tail or paw.

"Oh, they know, all right," Jutta said. "They know what you're thinking."

"Come now. Do you really believe that?"

Jutta flushed indignantly. "Of course. Ordinary cats might not always know, but kettir think better than plenty of people. Here, I'll prove it to you with Svartur. I'll think of something he likes—cheese and tender young rabbits."

Svartur's head turned around suddenly to look straight at Jutta with an adoring expression in his slanting eyes. He walked over to her and stood full length on his hind legs, reaching up with both paws toward her face. She picked him up, and he locked his arms around her neck, giving her a smeary rub with the corners of his mouth, which was as near as a kettir could come to giving a dear human a possessive kiss.

"Now I shall think of big barking dogs and doors that slam on tails," Jutta said.

Svartur's eyes opened and grew round with alarm. He climbed up on Jutta's shoulder and perched there with his paws all bunched up, and his tail fattened into a bristling club as he peered around worriedly.

Jutta soothed him until he was a purring blob in her arms again and Ofsi was getting jealous. He left his enjoyable sport of trying to fall out of the cart in fifty different ways and jumped on Svartur's back without ceremony to bite him on the neck as hard as his small jaws could bite. Svartur gave Jutta a mildly annoyed look, enduring Ofsi's attack as long as his patience would last instead of merely slaughtering the kettling as a normal male cat would have. When Svartur had finally had enough, he grabbed Ofsi around the neck and pinned him to the ground to give him a bath, a maneuver that usually sent Ofsi scuttling the instant he could get away. This time, however, Ofsi decided to stick up for himself. He scrambled away and glared at Svartur. Bristling up his fur, he stood on his tiptoes, tail lashing, ears flattened, and dived in for an ill-advised second pounce. Svartur rolled over and grabbed him in both arms and washed Ofsi even harder, kicking him with his hind feet all the while. Ofsi broke away and ran in a circle around Jutta, making indignant peeping sounds until she scooped him up in her arms.

The grandmothers emerged from the house, carrying enough cloaks, robes, blankets, bundles, and baskets for a weeklong stay on a polar ice cap. Arguing, they put everything and themselves into the cart, not without dashing back for a few more things someone had forgotten.

"How could you have forgotten the dipper, Thruda?" Amma Sigla deplored, hitting her full stride as clan worrier. "What's going to become of you when we're gone and can't look after you anymore?"

"I don't know," Amma Thruda snapped with rare spite. "I

suppose I'll have to die of thirst. Either that or dip my cup in the spring when I want a drink."

"And what about my darning egg?" Sigla called. "Did anyone see me put it in?"

"If you don't get a stocking darned today, the world isn't going to come to an end," Amma Margret grumbled. "Did anyone put in a rug for the kettir to ride on?"

"Wait!" Amma Ingi exclaimed in a voice of panic. "I've forgotten my underskirt!"

"Since when has that bothered you?" Dora asked. "You went to market without it twice last year."

"Yes, but I don't care for the drafty sensation around my legs," Ingi said, climbing out of the cart.

"Don't get that one with the threads hanging off all around," Dora warned. "I fixed you the gray one, remember?"

"Yes, but you turned it up too short. I feel like a little girl in braids, with my skirts half up to my knees."

"It's a good idea for someone who always drags her skirts over the rocks and thistles," Dora retorted, stroking Asa's ears as the kettir settled in her lap.

"Dora, you can't sit there," Margret declared in great exasperation. "I've told you a thousand times I don't want that much weight in the front."

"Well, I can't face backward. It makes me giddy."

"Do move this basket," Sigla said. "It's going to slide right into my feet."

"It needs to be there. Put your feet someplace else."

"Where's that cheese for old Fiddlasson? I don't want kettir gnawing on it or sun melting it. Last time, Ingi put her feet on it."

"Well, I didn't mean to. I couldn't see what it was."

"Jutta, my dear," Thruda said, "are you certain you don't want to come?"

"I'm certain," Jutta said rather too swiftly. Her grandmothers would go on like this the entire way, fussing about minor things and exercising all their worrying apparatus until they returned home exhausted. When they finally rolled away, they were still squabbling like seagulls, and the kettir clung to the sides of the cart trying to fall out as they gawked around, eyes round as saucers and huge ears pricking earnestly.

"You're sure you don't want to go?" Leckny asked.

"Do I look like an insane person? They'll go on like that all day, fussing and fuming because Amma Ingi forgot to bring a thimble, or whether Amma Sigla brought enough ale, or if the milk will be cold or warm for lunch, or if the kettir are too hot or thirsty or need to get out to dig a hole. I'm going to have a peaceful day here by myself instead of worrying about somebody's underskirts or who sat where in the cart last time."

"You're not staying just to enjoy my company?" He added a rather smirky grin, preening himself like a rooster in the hen yard.

"I'm not staying just on your account," Jutta said. "That would make me grasping at straws. You already think far too well of yourself."

Leckny devoured a huge breakfast and set out for Sorengard.

"Tell your grandmothers and the kettir that I had a splendid time," Leckny said earnestly. "I've never shared my supper with so many cats before. I didn't mind them eating every last scrap of meat in my soup, nor did I mind sharing my cheese with Mishka. And it was a most interesting experience sharing my eider with six enormous boulders that kept purring and shifting around and crowding me out. I could've done without the fight that broke out just before dawn this morning, though. I can't wait to tell everyone about my thrilling evening with the cat keepers."

"If we'd known you were so full of complaints," Jutta said, "we would've sent you home last night and let the barrow robbers get you. But Amma Margret had pity on such a poor little boy, knowing the killers wouldn't mistake you for a man."

"Laugh all you wish," Leckny said, swinging into his saddle. "You'll be forced to admire me when I've captured the barrow field killer."

"What a ghastly prospect," Jutta said. "Who will do the forcing? Perhaps if I were paid enough, I might admire you just a little."

"I knew your loyalty could be bought. I don't see how you could tolerate that Frida woman otherwise."

"Tolerate? I admire her greatly."

"I don't see why. She's so arrogant and domineering. She lives without a husband in that great house, and she's got a flock of servants and thralls to do all her work for her. If anyone could be killed next, she'd be the one I'd choose. She's giving the wives around Mikillborg lofty ideas with this ley line stuff she's trying to uncover—ideas that lead to women poking around in barrows instead of tending to their work. Ideas that even lead to their deaths. If these women had just kept to their own places, they'd still be alive today."

"And what do you mean by that?"

"Oh, you know. Women shouldn't worry about anything except their cooking and cleaning and whatever else they do. When they start having spare time and looking around for entertainment is when we start having trouble."

"Oh, indeed? Where did you come by this bit of amazing wisdom? Something you men invented while you were gabbling over half-gnawed bones and half-pickled with ale? It may surprise you to know that women are capable of a great many things besides looking after a bunch of ignorant men. I know I'm certainly tired of looking after you, so be off and take care how you trouble my presence again."

Jutta turned to stalk away, but Leckny was not inclined to leave. He dropped his reins and followed her, taking hold of her arm. She whirled around to glare at him. For a startled moment she thought he was about to kiss her, and perhaps he thought so, too. She met his eyes with a furious and surprised expression, and he swiftly lost his intention.

"What a nice arm you've got," he said, kneading the muscle consideringly. "Plenty of muscle for milking cows and making bread. When I decide to get married, I shall definitely keep you in mind."

CHAPTER 12

"Thank you very much. I hope I shall have migrated a thousand miles from here by that time."

"I would find you sooner or later and send for you."

"What did I ever do to deserve such a curse? First I'm sent to live with my old grandmothers and their cats, and now I'm burdened with your admiration. It's enough to make me want to murder someone." She gave Leckny a slanty and sinister scowl intended to send him on his way, quaking in his boots. It was a look she copied from the kettir, when they were contemplating a bird almost within pouncing range.

"I know you're not the barrow field killer," Leckny said, "so you can't frighten me. We had killings and disappearings long before you arrived. I can't think of any that happened before Frida moved in. People were content to ignore those barrows before she arrived with nothing better to do than dig up old secrets."

"It's not Frida's fault Betla was searching for gold," Jutta retorted.

"How do we know that's what she was really doing?"

"Don't be absurd. Why would anyone be in the barrows at night?"

"Why were you and Frida in the barrows at night?"

"We were looking for ley lines. The powers of nature are different by moonlight."

"Why does Frida want to find ley lines, anyway?"

"For health, prosperity, protection, power—anything to help the farmers and the fishermen have better luck. We used to have more power over fate and nature, and when the ley lines

176

fell into disuse, we lost it. We've lost our true contact with the powers of the earth. The lines channel the power, and if we channel it, we can use it."

"But to a working woman like Betla, power means gold," Leckny said. "I think all this lofty talk went right over her head and she thought of nothing but the wealth buried in those barrows. I believe she went looking for it, one way or another, and fell in with the barrow robbers somehow. Can't you see that Frida isn't doing these common women any favors by filling their heads with her strange notions? Notions which aren't going to work, by the way."

"And why not? Who says we can't find the lines and make them work?"

"There's bound to be more to it than just finding the lines. Wizards and sorcerers studied their entire lives to make nature work for them, to harness the forces of chaos. You and a bunch of women can't just blunder onto it and expect to change anything."

"Well, I know that. But we can discover the lines first and find out how to work them later. There's old books around that might tell about them. Frida's got a few she's studying."

"How can she ever know more than enough just to cause a lot of trouble?"

"I don't think it's fair to blame all these killings on Frida. She's got nothing to do with these murders. These women were the ones who made the mistakes somewhere and ran afoul of barrow robbers."

"Someone had to sow the seeds of discontent," Leckny pointed out. "And Frida is the one doing it. She doesn't even know the effects of her mystical gatherings."

"Oh, what a lot of rot!" Jutta said. "Go home! And try not to think. Like your father, it only gets you confused."

With her grandmothers out of the way, Jutta contemplated heading for the barrows for the day. But it seemed that an opportunity of another sort had presented itself, with her grandmothers all gone, so she searched for the gold she had seen them bring in from the barrows. She dowsed for it, using a string and a weight made from a gold button she stole from

Dora's sewing basket. A button that might have come from the barrows itself, she thought.

Ofsi thought it was a great lark. To him, a string was meant for one thing only—pouncing on. Fortunately, Amma Dora had finished the kettir backpack, a marvelous invention with shoulder straps and a strap around the waist. The top had a flap as well as a drawstring, which Jutta cinched up tight. Ofsi put his head out the small flap at the bottom and seemed perfectly content to be carried about.

Alone and unobserved even by nosy kettir, Jutta dowsed around in the house. Finding nothing, she explored the barns and outbuildings without any luck until she came to the old granary. It was a round building, instead of rectangular or square, where grain had been stored in more prosperous days. Now the roof was too leaky, and the grain was stored in the house. As Jutta dowsed and snooped, she thought how Bardhol had declined in living quality. Soon it would be down to very primitive status, as in the old days, when people and animals shared the same roof and fire. Fervently she hoped she would not be there then.

To her surprise, the old granary sent the dowsing pendulum into excited gyrations. Slowly she worked her way across the interior to the far wall, where firewood was stored in the shelter of the remaining roof. With her heart pounding, Jutta moved the kindling aside and saw where the paving stones were freshly loosened. Prying them up easily, she discovered an old box buried in the earth. Slowly she raised the lid and was rewarded with the stunning discovery of a box of old clothes. After sitting on her heels and staring at them in shock for a moment, she grabbed the old clothes and started hauling them out of the box. Ancient cloaks, long and dyed a shade of black that was turning slightly greenish; long heavy gowns of the same dismal hue; and long old-fashioned hoods without a particle of style to them. They were of excellent workmanship, evidently constructed to last nearly forever, which looked like Dora's work, and the cloth was heavy and tightly woven, as Thruda would have done, even as long ago as those cloaks had been made.

Jutta burrowed down farther, finally dragging out the last heavy cloak before she was rewarded with the soft tinkle of something metallic. There was the treasure at last, buried beneath the old black clothes. It was a tidy little hoard: some arm rings, sword hilts, plates, bowls, cups, various knives, coins, chains, and scraps that looked like the corner and clasp ornamentation of a little box, rotted away except for a few blackened shreds of wood.

The sight of the gold was enough for Jutta. It still had lumps of earth clinging to it, proving where it had come from. She folded up the old clothes and put them back into the box with the bundles of herbs that kept away the bugs and vermin: six gowns, six hoods, and six cloaks. The sixth had probably belonged to one of the old Hesturkonur who had perished years ago.

Jutta went about the rest of her chores hastily, lest her grandmothers return and discover she had done nothing while they were gone. As she thought about the gold under the woodpile, her uneasiness increased, picturing her grandmothers out digging around in the barrows. She couldn't begin to imagine how horrified her mother, Dalla, would be to learn that her ancient female relatives were barrow robbers. But Dalla had suspected that Amma Margret had some secret stash of wealth somewhere, and Jutta now knew it wasn't solely from selling kettir at outrageous prices.

Jutta trembled to think of them getting caught at robbing a barrow. Worse yet, the killer who lurked in the barrows could find them, and all five of them could be murdered. Not to mention the Myrkriddir flapping and screaming about. Her grandmothers certainly could not outrun them, not at their ages of eighty or ninety years, and their old horses could not outrun Myrkriddir horses.

It was the horses that brought Jutta up short, staring at them as she was feeding them their daily portion of grain and thinking what a waste of grain it was to feed six old mares that were never ridden or used much. Elding had been ridden the previous day and still bore the sweat marks of the saddle, but none of the others had been saddled in years, since the cart was a more sensible means of transportation for five old ladies going to market. Yet she could see girth marks on two of the mares and a small saddle sore on another, healing nicely under a blob of Ingi's redolent black salve. Ingi loved these last Hestur mares and always attended to them herself, even down to trimming their rock-hard hooves and filing the sharp points off their teeth. But Ingi said she never rode anymore, complaining that her bones wouldn't take the jouncing and someone of her age didn't need to risk falling off and breaking her neck. Many times Dalla had complained that they ought to sell the mares so they wouldn't have to store hay for them for the winter, but Ingi had looked hurt and demanded to know what was a Hesturkona without her horses.

And now she had a small orange filly romping about, kicking her heels in the air and rolling her eyes in a particularly wicked manner, showing what a handful she was going to be under the saddle. It was not a chore for someone with old brittle bones.

Jutta traced the lightning bolt on Elding's face. The filly suddenly perceived that her dam was ambling away across the pasture, heading for the stream, and uttered a piercing whinny. She thundered away with her shaggy little tail held straight up in the air, still whinnying in her shrill little voice. Suddenly Jutta's mind placed that sound. It was a moonlit night; she was in bed and strangely unable to wake up completely. Outside, the filly was whinnying desperately, the sound echoing with the thunder of her hooves as she pawed at the door of the stall where she was confined. Then Jutta's mind was filled with another picture, of the Myrkriddir swirling around her and Frida on that bristly barrow top, with Simon crouching below, unable to fend them off. Clearly, through the murk and grue, she saw the flashing of horse eyes ringed with white, the red flare of snorting nostrils, and the lightning bolt streaking down Elding's face, from the large diamond on her forehead to the small one on her nose, and another horse with two white hind stockings—like Birki, now peacefully grazing in the pasture like a sedate retired broodmare.

Jutta sat down on a piece of fallen wall, gasping. Ofsi struggled to climb out of his pack, wanting to be played with. When she released him, he attacked her hand, then leapt at the hem of her cloak trailing on the turf, then bucked around in an excess of high spirits, trying to catch his own tail.

The black cloaks hidden in the wood room, the mares so well fed and cared for. Jutta stood up and went to stroke them, feeling the hardness of their muscles, which meant that they had had plenty of exercise instead of standing about most of the time eating their heads off in the pasture. These were active saddle horses, not retired broodmares. They were the mounts of the Myrkriddir, thundering through the barrows, protecting the graves of the Hestur dead, and her grandmothers were the Myrkriddir, owners of the black cloaks carefully hidden away in the old granary.

She watched the little golden filly racing across the soft turf, bouncing and leaping as if she considered herself a two-hundred-pound butterfly. They had locked her in a stall, of course, not wishing to be burdened with a filly on their midnight ride. The filly had raised a desperate ruckus, wanting her mother, which was what Jutta had half heard, drugged as she was by the warm milk and something else that had been put into it.

It was no wonder her grandmothers did not want her awake to know what they were doing. They had not seen her and Frida that night, or surely they would have done something to see to it that she never went into the barrows again—sent her home to her mother, perhaps.

The cold chill of the stone Jutta was sitting on seemed to creep into her very marrow. What else were her grandmothers willing to do to protect their gold and their secret? Were they willing to kill?

Jutta's first thought was to get to Frida as quickly as she could and tell her what she had discovered. It was nearly noon-time and she was feeling hungry, so she stopped long enough to tear off an untidy hunk of black bread and a slab of cheese, which she would eat as she walked to Frida's house. There was enough to split with Ofsi, who was aggressively demand-ing his more than fair share, which was all of what Jutta was eating, and she could have what was left, if anything. With a determined glint in his round golden eyes, he started climbing up her breeches and overskirt. She picked him off like a leech as he screeched in protest and stuffed him and some bread hastily into his pack. He fastened his claws and teeth into the food with falsetto growlings and sputterings, as if it were something he had to kill before he could eat it. Jutta tied the drawstrings and struck out across the pasture, heading toward the barrows.

Coming to the crossroads, she looked first toward the barrows, wondering if Frida had come to do some mapping this day. She hadn't considered the question long before a shaggy form suddenly reared up from behind the cairn that marked the way.

"Halloa," a hoarse voice rumbled, and Jutta recognized Hrokr, the husband of poor Betla—a more unkempt Hrokr, with sticks and dirt in his hair, as if he had spent the night curled up on the ground beside the marker. He squinted at her with cold pale eyes, and she drew back a step. "Well. It's the lass from Bardhol, isn't it?"

"Yes, and I know who you are," Jutta said, suppressing a wave of sudden, uneasy fear. He had a wild look to him, like that of an animal on a chain, and obviously he hadn't washed himself or combed his hair and beard for quite some time. "Betla's husband. I was there when she was found." She nodded slightly toward the barrows.

"Aye, you were," Hrokr said. "Were you thinking of going into the barrow field today?"

"I was on my way to Frida's house."

"It's a long walk. But I'll save you the journey. She's not home."

"Did you see her pass this way?"

"Aye. She went into the barrow field. She didn't see me, sleeping as I was under a bush."

"Then I'll go after her and speak to her. Will you stay here and keep watching?"

"Aye, that I will. I want to know everyone who comes this way and takes the turning into the barrow fields. One of them will be the killer, one day, and then I will have him. Then I'll have my revenge for Betla." He smiled gently and sadly, and Jutta felt ashamed of being afraid of him and his mighty grief.

"Hrokr, I'm sorry she was killed. She didn't deserve such a hard fate."

He drew up his thick shoulders in a shrug, shoulders that had lifted and carried and strained all his life. "Maybe something good will come of it. None of those other women had me for their husband. I won't rest until I've caught the beast that did it and spilled his blood on the ground for her. Then she'll rest easy, and so will I."

"Is there anything I can do to help? I live close by at Bardhol. I can watch, too."

"Watch, then, and tell me who you see. But don't you fall into this monster's foul snare, my lass. Be always wise and mindful of your own health. No one can hurt Betla anymore, and no one had better try it with me."

"Come up to Bardhol when you're hungry and my grandmothers will feed you. How are your children standing up to this terrible loss?"

"Grieving, of course, and missing their mother. My sister is looking after them. I think of the look in their eyes when I'm weary, and then I think of that killer's eyes watching my Betla perish, and I know nothing is going to stop me from finding that evil creature and watching him die."

"Good luck to you, Hrokr. I'm going to find Frida now."

To her disappointment, Frida was not alone when she found her. Three other women were with her. One of them Jutta recognized from their last gathering; the other two were strangers and not particularly well dressed. Frida beamed at Jutta in delight.

"Jutta! I had a feeling I'd see you today! You remember Hallgrima, and we've also got Gunna and Tova. Our leywalking occupation is becoming so terribly popular, pretty soon we'll have nearly everyone in Mikillborg doing it. Gunna, my pet, would you fetch us the basket and the jug? We've all earned a rest and a bit of dinner."

Gunna, Tova, and Hallgrima kept a respectful distance when

Frida and Jutta sat down. They were dressed in working clothes and had the hard-bitten and silent look of women who were accustomed to working outdoors. Gunna, however, wore a rather nicer cloak of serviceable gray, only slightly frayed around the hem, and Tova was possessed of a pair of good sturdy boots, well worn but well made by a bootmaker, which Jutta suspected had been a gift from Frida. Hallgrima also wore a good cloak, russet in color and quite new.

"Frida, I suspect you of giving your things rather freely to these women," Jutta said in a low voice when the three women had moved away to watch old Bjalfur making his careful way along the road below, pegging each step firmly with his walking staff.

"Jutta, my dear, they had virtually nothing to their names," Frida said. "I notice these things when I travel about. I told them I would give them work or help them find better positions. I have too many cloaks and boots and gowns, so I gave them away. I can always have something new made, but women in such circumstances will never have the chance for a nice warm cloak. I would rather buy myself a new one than find some poor creature frozen to death come winter."

"I wish I were able to help others the way you can," Jutta said, warmed with admiration.

"You mustn't tell anyone, though," Frida said. "I don't want my patronage broadcast about and made to look more wonderful than it is. I merely try to do my part to relieve some of the suffering among the working poor. All Hallgrima needs is some experience at sewing and cleaning and serving and she can get a house job instead of working outdoors. Gunna and Tova are not much older than you are, but one would swear they were middle-aged women to look at them. I plan to teach them all to read a bit, to sew and cook, and some of the finer skills so they aren't mere laborers. And of course I shall teach them about ley lines and their history. I hope to awaken some pride in them and remind them of what Alfar used to be and could be again. I blame it all on the curse of ignorance and complacency. As a race we were far better when we had to fight the Dokkalfar for our very existence."

"I shall see if I can find you some Dokkalfar to fight," Jutta said.

Frida laughed, but she added, "Perhaps they are more of a threat than we think. Do you truly believe they are all destroyed or driven underground?"

At that moment Ofsi wriggled out of his pack and leapt atop a fallen stone to glare at Jutta defiantly.

"Speaking of Dokkalfar," Frida said, "there's a little hairy one now. My, he's growing, isn't he?"

"I'm afraid so," Jutta said. "It just means bigger teeth and claws. I'll be glad when he's out of the destructive stage. Amma Sigla says it's something they all go through, then they're gentle and affectionate."

While she was saying this, Ofsi hurled himself on her foot and commenced biting and scratching her boot as if it were a monster he was sworn to kill. When Frida reached out a hand to him, he leapt away with a great startled spring and hissed at her, every hair standing on end. His tail arched in a fuzzy loop like a handle behind him.

Jutta laughed. "You startled him. Ofsi, don't be so brainless. Come here, you little idiot."

Ofsi replied with several spits and sputters and a couple of stiff-legged bounces. He also added a high-pitched wail, astonishingly loud for such a small morsel of kettirdom.

"He probably smells my dogs on my clothing," Frida said. "Dear me, do you think he'll attack us?" she added in mock alarm.

"Perhaps it was the cheese he had for lunch," Jutta said. "Amma Thruda says not to give them very much cheese. Ofsi, do run away and play. You're being a nuisance." She tossed a small lump of moss at him, eliciting another flurry of spitting, sputtering, and bouncing. Clearly he blamed Frida for this untimely attack. He never took his eyes off her for a moment.

"There was something I wanted to tell you most urgently," Jutta continued in a lower tone, glancing toward the other three women, who were seated on a long flat stone, talking among themselves. "I've found something which leads me to believe my grandmothers are the Myrkriddir."

"What? You're joking!" Frida burst out with a peal of laughter, but Jutta did not follow suit. Astonished, Frida stared at her a moment. "You're really serious, aren't you? My dear, you must be mistaken. I don't think it's possible. For one thing, the Myrkriddir of legend are always dead spirits, trapped in a never-ending cycle of night riding because of some curse or misdeed. They aren't supposed to be living, breathing human creatures."

"But I found old black cloaks," Jutta said, "hidden away where nobody could ever find them. And that night the Myrkriddir caught Simon and Petrus, I swear I recognized their horses. Elding has a unique lightning bolt down her face."

"I think perhaps we were both a little overexcited and frightened," Frida said. "We really can't be responsible for what we see or do when we're frightened half to death."

"I wasn't frightened when I found those black cloaks," Jutta said.

"I'm sure there's a logical explanation," Frida said.

"Yes. My grandmothers are Myrkriddir."

"But Myrkriddir are magical creations. I don't think your grandmothers know the first thing about power and magic and summoning powers, do they?"

Jutta looked at Ofsi, who was now crouching behind a rock with flattened ears, glaring at Frida over the top. He was still fuzzed up from ears to stubby tail. There was no way to explain where he had come from, not without sounding like a perfect fool. Jutta quickly decided not to mention Thruda's kettir brewing or the gold her grandmothers had harvested from the barrows.

"You don't know a great deal about power yet," Frida continued. "Your curiosity is admirable and refreshing but perhaps a little too enthusiastic, which is understandable. You tend to see more than truly is. Indeed, I wish the Myrkriddir were your grandmothers. It would make them so much easier to deal with than the real Myrkriddir."

"I see. I was just hoping in some strange way that magic was a bit more real, perhaps."

"Yes, I think that's it exactly."

Jutta willingly allowed the conversation to turn to other things for a while, ashamed at her own gullibility.

"I think I'd better go now," Jutta said, rising to her feet and looking around for Ofsi. "My grandmothers went to the high shieling today with the cows and sheep, and I don't know for certain when they'll return. They've come to the conclusion that the barrows are a very dangerous place, and they don't want me coming here after what happened to Betla. Where's Ofsi?"

She found him doing his utmost to charm Gunna and Tova out of their lunch. Jutta had never seen him put on such a cute and adorable act. He let them cuddle him, purring and kneading his paws in ecstasy, politely reaching out one paw to poke gently at their bread and cheese.

"What a lovely kitten," Tova said, stroking his short and silky coat. "I've never seen a cat like this. He seems almost human."

"He's not a cat, he's a kettir," Jutta said. "It's a very rare and special strain of cat. Rather an improvement on your standard farm or house cat. If you asked him, he'd tell you he's better than most humans, too."

"Where did you get him?" Tova asked. "I'd give anything to have one. Does he like being carried around in that sack?"

"He's livid if I dare to leave him home. It's almost as if he was created especially for me and he wants to be everywhere I go, even if it means being carried in a sack. An ordinary cat wouldn't like that, you know. They prefer to stay home and wait if you go away."

"Where did you get him?" Tova persisted.

"My grandmothers raise them," Jutta said. "If you wish, I could speak to them about getting you one."

"I would like to have such a friend as you've got," Tova said wistfully, reluctantly surrendering a purring and totally deceitful Ofsi to Jutta. He was giving her an entirely false impression of himself. He narrowed one slitted eye at Jutta, as if he were winking.

"You may have your choice of the kittens in my barn," Frida said. "There are some lovely striped ones, gray or red, and even a nice black-and-white spotted one. I'm getting used to Jutta's cat, so I don't mind if you bring it into the house. They are usually clean and quiet creatures, I've discovered."

"Thank you, I'm most grateful," Tova said, dropping her eyes shyly. "But this little creature is not like an ordinary cat. He's different somehow, as if he's got a human spirit."

Ofsi basked in all this admiration, squeezing shut his eyes—with difficulty, Jutta thought. He was always wide-eyed and staring, alert for something that needed attacking.

"The poor girl," Frida said aside to Jutta. "No wonder she feels the need for a friend and a bit of comfort. Her parents are both dead, and there's no kin to take her in."

"She's a very pleasant person," Jutta said. "I think it's very admirable of you to help her."

"Tova, my pet, you must walk home with Jutta and see her grandmother's marvelous cats," Frida said.

"May I?" Tova asked quickly, her face lighting up with a radiance that transformed her weary and plain features with girlish enthusiasm.

"Certainly," Frida said with a smile in return. "Come home in the morning, and I'm hoping you can bring Jutta with you for a visit—if your grandmothers are inclined to spare you for a while."

Jutta experienced an odd and unexpected stab of jealousy to see Ofsi so willing to let Tova carry him and hold him and stroke his fur. Since they both seemed to be enjoying each other's company so much, she allowed Tova to carry Ofsi to Bardhol, answering the girl's questions all the way.

"He eats chewed meat, like you would do for a baby," Jutta said. "A tiny bit of milk—too much gives him a digestive upset—bread if he wants it, curds, some cheese. Those are the healthy things he eats, but I've also seen him catch grasshoppers and devour them with the legs kicking, beetles and flies and bugs, and once he caught a baby snake and was playing with it. One day he might be able to catch mice and birds, but at present he thinks mice are fine toys, when he can steal one from the big kettir."

"Why do you have to chew his meat for him? Doesn't he have a mother he is nursing from?"

"No," Jutta said, reluctant to explain how her grandmother had put a bunch of hair and stuff into a kettle and cooked it all day to produce a small kettir.

"I see. An orphan, like me."

"I'm sorry to hear that. Frida says you are alone in the world."

"Yes. I don't know where I'd be if she hadn't found me. I couldn't stay where I was because the farmer didn't want to pay me or even feed me any longer. Frida says she has plenty of work I can do for my keep, and she'll educate me so I can hope for something better."

"I'm glad I know Frida, too. Living with my grandmothers would be almost unendurable if I couldn't get away once in a while to talk to Frida. It is so pleasant to talk about something besides gathering eggs or darning stockings. My grandmothers are interesting in their own way, but I have no desire to be like them."

Thinking of the Myrkriddir, she shivered suddenly. Frida had not believed her. It would have been reassuring to have a friend under her circumstances, since she might be sharing the same roof with five Myrkriddir. Perhaps Frida was right. There could be another explanation for the cloaks and the barrow gold, a reasonable and good explanation that had nothing to do with Myrkriddir.

Since her grandmothers and the cartload of kettir had not returned yet, Jutta and Tova pitched in to do Jutta's chores for the day and were just finished with the evening milking when they heard the cart coming down the rough track from the mountains.

"Oh, look at the cats!" Tova exclaimed softly as the cart heaved into view with kettir swinging from the sides, craning their necks to see home approaching.

"Kettir," Jutta corrected her automatically, wishing that Ingi wouldn't stand up and wave and shout "Yoo-hoo!" as she invariably did on arriving home, as if she needed to announce herself to all and sundry.

"Yoo-hoo!" Ingi caroled, lurching out of her seat as the cart bumped to a stop and about a dozen kettir leapt to the ground. Ingi fell over backward into the cart, showing off her ragged underskirt to fine advantage as Dora and Sigla shoved her off their laps and set her upright again.

"Who's that with you, Jutta?" Ingi called, undaunted. "My eyes aren't what they used to be. It's not that Leckny creature from Sorengard, is it?"

"If it were, I'd flog him to Sorengard and back," Amma Margret growled. "I think he plans to carry off Jutta one of these fine days. He's got that funny glint in his eye."

"Him! A chieftain's son?" Amma Dora exclaimed, brightening up at the mention of her favorite topic. "Well, that would be a good match. We'll have to send his mother a little friendship gift—some of Sigla's best raspberry cordial, and one of Thruda's tablecloths, and I could sew up a nice jacket or something."

"No," Jutta said emphatically. "I refuse to allow you even to contemplate my marriage to Leckny. He reminds me too much of my younger brothers, always teasing me and finding great joy in making me lose my temper. If we were married, I'd be hanged as a murderess the first week. I'd simply throttle him, and then where would the family name be? I hope you'll spare us all the infamy of being the clan of the Mikillborg murderess."

"Strong feelings," Amma Thruda said. "I've seen loathing turn to loving more than once. Who is your friend, Jutta? Ofsi obviously thinks well of her."

Ofsi was curled around Tova's neck like a warm fur collar, kneading his paws in great appreciation.

"This is Tova," Jutta said, lifting her chin with pride. "Frida found that she had fallen into very miserable circumstances, so she took her in and gave her work. Tova came home with me and helped me with my chores in hopes of seeing the kettir."

"I'm so pleased to meet you," Tova said, clearly distracted by the host of kettir that had come to acquaint themselves with her boots and the hem of her skirt and to peer up into her face with approval. "They're such lovely creatures. What amazing faces they have, so intelligent. If they had words, they would speak to us."

"They do, all the time," Amma Thruda said with a smile. "You just have to learn to listen for their voices. Of course, we humans are sad and clumsy creatures and don't understand most of the time."

Tova sat down in the middle of the kettir so they could climb into her lap and rub their chins on her ear or jaw or nose, purring in delight. Ofsi was willing to share his new human acquisition, suddenly deciding he had to be fed. He stared at Jutta intently and uttered his piercing "MEW!" to command her obedience. When she ignored him for a moment, he sank his claws into her breeches and came hiking up her clothing as if she were a tree, to bellow his orders into her face.

When they were all on the utmost friendly terms, the kettir followed Jutta and Tova as they unharnessed the horses and trooped into the house, where Sigla was just ladling out bowls of aromatic soup.

"You'll never guess what!" Ingi blurted out, rubbing her hands joyfully. "We've decided that Tova must have a kettir for her very own!"

CHAPTER 13

"But aren't kettir very costly?" Jutta demanded before thinking.

"I couldn't afford to buy one," Tova said. "But if there's work for me to do, I'm very strong and used to all manner of heavy jobs. You've got a lot of fallen walls."

"That is exactly what I wish to propose," Amma Margret said with a ghost of her wintry smile. "If Frida won't mind us keeping you."

"I don't think she will," Jutta said, scarcely able to hide her delight. "Frida's goal was to find Tova a position and a better life, so she'll be pleased that we want her here."

Amma Thruda added, "Perhaps it will make Jutta's life here a bit more pleasant to have someone nearer her own age than we five old sticks."

Tova's eyes were on the kettir, which were posing before the hearth in all manner of adorable postures, washing their faces sitting, bathing their belly fur reclining, stretched out asleep, curled up asleep, alone or in pairs. The firelight gleamed on their radiant fur, giving each of them a rosy halo.

"I shall work for the rest of my life for the privilege of owning such a beautiful friend," Tova said, still shy, but the radiance of her features again transformed her from a work-worn drudge to a youthful beauty.

"You won't have to work the rest of your life," Margret said. "And remember that you do not own a kettir. It owns you. You must always keep him with you and think of his needs for food and sleep and entertainment. They are naturally rather sleepy creatures, so your most difficult job will be keeping him awake so he can be of use to you."

"Which one shall we give her?" Ingi knocked a loaf of bread on the floor in her excitement. "Hunang is like her name, as sweet as honey. Bensi is an adorable rascal, but he has a very brave heart. Ordig is an adventurer. He's definitely a man's kettir."

"Bensi it shall be," Amma Thruda said in her quiet voice, and no one offered any argument. She was, after all, the one who had brewed up Bensi, and she knew what had gone into his making.

Bensi heard his name spoken and looked up from a heap of siblings with an adoring expression on his face. The corners of his mouth were drawn up in a sleepy smile. He had been bathing his immaculate white chest and paws, of which he always took the utmost care. Of all the kettir except the elegant white Asa, he was the most diligent washer. When he was satisfied that his white chest and underbelly were spotless, he worked on his red-striped parts until he was too exhausted and content to wash any longer.

"Call him by his name and he is yours forever," Thruda said to Tova.

"Bensi! Come to me!" Tova said in a voice that trembled slightly.

Bensi opened his eyes all the way and stood up, arched his back in a luxuriant stretch, and opened his mouth in a huge yawn that nearly tore his jaws asunder. Then he crossed the room to Tova, waving the tip of his tail in a friendly manner, and leapt into her lap. Treading up and down and purring inordinately, he rubbed the corner of his lips across her chin, marking her for his own property.

"That means he likes you," Jutta said. "Sometimes kettir ways are a little hard to get used to. Bensi is not a terribly manly cat, but he's very affectionate. Ordig doesn't care for a lot of petting and cuddling and will walk behind you like a dog, but Bensi dreads nothing more than getting his white paws muddy, so you'll be carrying him around a lot. Which will only make him fatter and lazier. Ordig has muscles, and nothing frightens him. Bensi will run straight to you and climb onto your shoulders if he sees something alarming."

"Bensi is still a very brave young kettir," Amma Thruda said firmly. "He may seem like a dandy and a sissy, but one day he will prove himself in a way that will astonish everyone—including himself."

Tova stroked Bensi's glowing red fur and rubbed behind his ears in the special spot known only to the admirers of cats. Bensi shut his eyes and smiled, kneading his lovely white paws.

The next morning Jutta and Tova went about the milking, with Bensi and Ofsi frolicking at their heels. Ofsi considered Bensi a great personal favor, so he would have someone to jump on for biting and kicking, and Bensi's long ringed tail with the white tip at the end was nothing short of a red flag inviting constant attack.

"You're lucky not to have to go through this stage with Bensi," Jutta said a bit enviously when they sat down for a midmorning snack. Ofsi climbed onto her shoulder for a better vantage point for attempting to steal the food right out of her mouth, yelling demandingly all the while.

Bensi, on the other hand, had some manners. He sat down beside Tova and curled his tail around his toes and proceeded to charm her out of her lunch. He gazed at her with his eyes worshipfully squeezed half-shut, encouraging her with little bobs of his head. All the while he purred his loudest, completely confident that she would have no power to resist such a pretty picture of admiration. When Tova did offer him a portion, he sniffed at it daintily until she put it down at his feet, whereupon Ofsi fell on it with a warning snarl. He also growled while he was chewing, making a revolting yammering sound.

Ofsi admired nothing but food, and if it was out of reach, it only made him the more determined to get it. Once he got his teeth into something, he growled and sputtered and shrilled siren warnings to anyone who dared come near.

"He's a horrible little savage," Jutta said, trying to separate Ofsi from a large lump of cheese by pulling on Ofsi with one hand and the cheese with the other. She finally got Ofsi's teeth and claws out of it and stuffed him into her kettir sack. "There. Now we can eat in peace."

"Why did you choose such a violent little cat?" Tova asked. "Bensi is so gentle and well mannered."

"My grandmother chose him for me," Jutta said. "He was made up special just to torment me and teach me patience and love in spite of his bad behavior. If he lives to grow up, I'm sure he'll be a wonderful kettir, loyal and strong, but there are times when I'd like to wring his neck. This morning I was awakened by Ofsi throwing himself straight into my face. He must've seen my eyelashes quivering."

"What do you mean when you say he was made up special?" Tova asked.

Jutta sighed and looked away. Having a friend to talk and laugh with was just what she had missed since coming to Bardhol, and she didn't want to lose her. "These creatures may look like cats," she began, "but they aren't just cats."

"I know that," Tova said quietly. "I knew there was something more to Ofsi the moment I first saw him. He looked at me, and he spoke."

"What did he say? Feed me?"

"No, he said that he was my friend. I know it sounds ridiculous, a talking cat. But my mother still practiced the old ways before she died. People thought she was a witch. She said I had a gift, too. It's like having extra ears to hear with and hidden eyes that see. So when Bensi spoke to me, I heard what he was saying. Now you probably think I'm a fool, don't you?" She stroked Bensi's soft coat with her rough hand, still marveling at the texture.

"No, not at all," Jutta said. "When I first came here I was angry and clumsy, and Svartur used to scold me sometimes. I've been afraid to mention it to anyone. My grandmothers practice the old ways, too. I didn't want to tell you where the kettir came from for fear of you thinking I was absolutely insane. But you mustn't tell anyone—not even Frida."

"I won't tell anyone."

"The kettir are not born creatures. They are created."

"By your grandmothers?"

"By Amma Thruda. She takes scraps of things and hair and nail parings and just general trash and cooks it up all day long in a big old pot, and at sundown she's got kettlingur."

"Oh, how splendid!" Tova whispered. "I would give anything to know how she does it. There may not be anyone else who can make kettir in the Ljosalfar realm. The knowledge should pass down the family line. Perhaps you are the intended one to receive it."

"I don't know. I can't imagine myself doing something like that. My mother has always been very modern, and so have I. I don't even know if I could learn it."

"Of course you can. The eyes and ears are still there, even if you don't use them much."

"Perhaps you can teach me," Jutta said.

"I'm so glad I met you yesterday," Tova said earnestly. "I didn't care much for mapping ley lines until you came along. I'd been at a house south of here until the sheep went up into the fells. Frida found me the position. When it was done, she told me to come back and she'd find me another. She'll be pleased that I found my own. I feel that it was more than luck that brought us together. I believe we were fated to meet. Now I have two friends, where I was all alone before." Bensi bobbed his head at her again, and she added with a laugh, "Yes, and I have a new protector."

"I'm glad I found you, too," Jutta said. "I was feeling so terrible about what happened to Betla. You've cheered me up tremendously, and I'm so glad you're going to stay. I didn't plan to remain here long with my grandmothers, until you arrived," she added in a more private tone of voice.

"Oh? Where were you going?"

"I don't know. Anywhere but Mikillborg. It's such a boring little place. I'd like to see ships and foreign lands and foreign people and strange and amazing things from faraway places."

"So would I," Tova said eagerly. "Since my family all died, I have thought many times that I'd like to be a traveler, going here and there and working awhile for my keep and then moving on. But not forever. When I find a good place, I'd like to marry someone and settle down. Not some poky little farmer, though, who never gets his nose out of his rut long enough to look around."

"I would like to marry someone who . . ." Jutta thoughtfully puckered her brow. "Someone who makes me laugh but isn't a buffoon. I can't abide a clown. He also must be quite a bit taller than I am. With this thatch of red hair, I don't want to tower above my husband. And he'd better not be vain about his looks. I can't abide boasting and preening in a man. Our chieftain's son is a perfect example of everything I despise. There's no room in his thoughts for anyone else but himself."

"I know what you mean. Isn't it a shame there are no truly noble men left anymore? I think they were all killed in the great wars."

"I fear you are right."

Jutta found that she and Tova thought much the same on almost every issue. Even her own sisters were not nearly so similar to Jutta as Tova was in nearly every taste and opinion. They worked side by side, talking from dawn until dark, when they climbed into the loft and pulled up their eiders and continued talking in whispers far into the night. When Amma Margret heard them, and her ears were exceedingly acute for a fossil of her age, she called up the ladder, "I think I hear mice squeaking in the walls up there. Do we have a couple of mouse holes that need plugging?"

After ten days it seemed that Jutta had known Tova all their lives. She knew how Tova had been born into a farmer's family with five brothers and sisters and what a happy and peaceful life they had enjoyed until two years earlier. A sickness was carried into the community, and a great many people sickened and died, including Tova's parents. Anyone who wanted to survive had to pack up and leave, and Tova had taken her younger brothers and sisters to the east to leave them with her father's brother and his wife. However, her young siblings soon became too ill to travel, and one by one they died. When Jutta got to her uncle's house, she found no one there, and the yard had grown up in weeds. Neighbors told her that the plague had taken half the settlement, including everyone who was related to her. So Tova began traveling, and that was how she had come to meet Frida, as she was traveling and looking for another position.

"Frida is truly a noble person," Jutta said, taking a rest from the endless chore of repairing the fallen stone walls. Something that wanted to keep falling down ought to have been left down rather than fight the natural forces of chaos and decay. Tova gladly sat down and wiped her brow. Jutta was always amazed at Tova's strength when it came to lifting the big heavy stones; many of them Jutta would have just let lie. "If only there were more men like her. If not for her, we would never have met and become such friends."

"Her preoccupation with old barrows is not healthy, though," Tova said. "Especially with someone waylaying lone women and murdering them. I wish she would stay out of the barrow fields entirely. Since I've known her, I've had the unpleasant feeling that her hobby is going to lead to her death."

"No! Are you sure? We should warn her!"

"I've tried to tell her, but I've discovered that you can't really tell ladies of quality anything. She doesn't know how much I truly know. She thinks I'm just a simpleminded farm drudge." Tova smiled wryly, which gave her a mischievous expression. "It's good to stay silent and sort of stare and shuffle your feet a little. People begin to let down their guard. You find out what their secrets are."

"What do you mean? Frida has secrets?"

"Of course. You don't really think all she cares about are those ridiculous ley lines, do you?"

"No, of course not," Jutta said promptly, at a loss for words. "Frida is very clever about what she's up to. So clever, in fact, that I have no idea what she's doing. I thought she was interested in history."

"Oh, she's very interested in history. Especially the history of your ancestor Sigmund, who lies in one of those barrows with a great golden cup in his hand—a cup of great and ancient powers."

"Oh, that. I don't believe she thinks it works anymore. She's promised that if we should happen to find any of my ancestors' gold, it will be mine. I've told her about my dream of getting away from Mikillborg."

"She doesn't believe the cup would work anymore? If she truly thinks so, then she is mistaken," Tova said with another impish smile. "Or perhaps she isn't telling you all of the truth."

"I can't believe that Frida would lie to me," Jutta said, elevating her chin in her old haughty way as if to imply that equals had no need of deceit among themselves.

"One thing that I have learned in my two years of being a homeless wanderer is that everyone will lie to save his own skin or to line his own pocket. It simply can't be helped. Now, don't be angry at me. I still admire Frida at least as much as you do. And I admire you too much to tell you any lies. I would like to find that cup of Sigmund's. All I wish is for one drink from it, and then you may do with it as you wish, since it is rightfully yours if you are his direct descendant."

"What would a drink from it do to you?" Jutta asked.

"It would give me powers," Tova said. "The old powers of summoning spirits and elementals, knowledge of the future, the ability to go traveling in different realms, in different forms. In other words, it would make me a sorceress."

"I don't think it would be prudent to be a sorceress nowdays, not in Mikillborg," Jutta said, drawing back a little from the spark in Tova's eye.

"I wouldn't stay here. I'd go where I'd be appreciated. What would you do if you had the unlimited power to do anything you wished with your life?"

"I don't know, but I wouldn't work at repairing old walls that are just going to fall down again next winter. I've always pictured myself with a big house and lots of land and fine horses and plenty of servants to do the work. And gold and silver, of course, and lots of well-armed and loyal friends living nearby in case these times of peace and plenty don't last forever."

"That's all well and good, but if you knew the future, you could defend yourself. A traveler on the webs of time knows what lies ahead and can go backward to undo the seeds of destruction unwittingly sown in the past. You are like far too many Alfar these days, my dear Jutta. You are too content with your riches and safety and comfort."

"What's wrong with being comfortable? It's everyone's goal, isn't it?"

"It is, but there's more to this world than comfort. Besides, I have the feeling that it is all temporary, that the dark days of war and bloodshed will return, and it will be even more horrible than any wars we've ever known before."

"My, you're being rather grim today, aren't you?"

"I know how fast one's circumstances can change. I've traveled about a little in the past two years, and I've heard certain talk that I didn't like."

"Such as?"

"Oh, certain things that some people would call prophecies, from ragged and strange people that most folks wouldn't want lingering about their cozy settlements. When all is well and easy, no one wants to hear that we ought to be preparing for war again."

"No. I don't want to hear it, either." Jutta thought uneasily of the tattered scarecrow Bjalfur spouting his gruesome nonsense at Sorengard and what a chill wind it had blown into the jolly company. "I think I have a better answer for what I would do with Afi Sigmund's cup. I think I would see to it that Einarr Sorensen has all the preparation and forewarning that he would need to protect our safe and comfortable settlement from what you are talking about."

"Well spoken. Einarr is a good-hearted man. I worked there awhile last year. I didn't like his oldest son, either, that haughty and worthless Leckny. I won't like to see the day when he sits in the chieftain's seat for Mikillborg."

"Leckny is hiding his true self behind a show of vanity and shallow occupations," Jutta said, startling even herself with her assessment. "I don't know why I said that. I don't like him, either."

"Wouldn't it be splendid if we could find that cup?" Tova said, her eyes sparkling. "We know how to search for it. We've seen Frida with her dowsing pendulum."

"She knows ever so much more than we do," Jutta said. "If it was that easy to find, wouldn't she have found it by now?"

"Perhaps not. Maybe it's waiting for you to find it. You're the direct heir—except for your sister Asta, and she doesn't sound like she'd be interested in much of anything but clothes."

Jutta turned to look down into the valley, where the barrow mounds waited in a faint haze of warm rising mist as the air cooled toward twilight. Hill upon hill, like hummocks in a giant bog, they waited with their long-buried secrets, patient for centuries, yet now she could feel something urgent tugging at her.

Since it was such a pleasant day, the grandmothers brought the midday meal out to the pasture and sat down on the velvety sward to eat with Jutta and Tova. The sunshine invited basking and napping, and presently the rattling snores of Amma Ingi commenced scaring the blackbirds away.

"The wall is looking splendid," Amma Thruda said, rising to her feet and looking at the fallen stones in a businesslike way. "It was a job I never minded too much when I was a bit younger."

"You're too old now," Amma Margret said with her usual acerbity. "I stacked wall all my life, from the time I was big enough to pick up a pebble. I never lost my muscle for it. I expect I can still outwork these two young girls, who are mostly as soft as fresh cheese curds."

"Cheese curds?" Tova repeated, her eyes lighting up with the challenge. "With all due respect, Amma Margret, I am taller, younger, and stronger than you. I have done almost nothing but repair walls for the past ten years, since I, too, was big enough to pick up a pebble. I do not believe you could outwork me. Look at me; I'm as strong as a horse."

It was true. Tova was as tall and stout as some Alfar men. Her arms and legs were not at all willowy; she was built more like a nice strong tree, and her tanned skin was as brown as bark.

Amma Margret scowled, and her lips twitched as she braced one fist on her hip. Her eye scanned the next stretch of fallen wall. "All right, you young and arrogant creature, we'll work to that plum tree growing out of the wall, you on this side, me on the other. We'll see who gets there first."

"Margret, you're too old," Amma Sigla said with a worried pucker to her brow. "You'll hurt yourself showing off. Leave the heavy work to the young girls. That's why we wanted to hire them, remember? So they can work themselves half to death and get old like we are."

"I know it, I know it full well," Margret snapped, taking off her cloak. "I did say just to the plum tree, didn't I? Isn't that enough of a concession to the bitter outrage of old age and decrepitude for you?"

They set to work, Margret and Tova, replacing the stones on their sides as they encountered them. For a long time they worked evenly, not hurriedly, one getting ahead and the other gradually catching up. The kettir positioned themselves on the wall to watch and offer chirps of encouragement, with the younger ones trying to wrestle each other into a fall.

"This is nothing but arrogance on Margret's part," Dora declared with a sniff. "What's so great about being able to work like a man? I don't care to break my back just to prove I'm strong enough to do it and stupid enough to boast about it."

"Margret's going to hurt herself," Sigla fretted. "She's going to be terribly sore tomorrow, and we won't be able to go to the market."

"Look at her go!" Ingi said. "She's pulling ahead! Faster, Margret! Show that healthy young lass what an old dried stick can do!"

"Shut your mouth, Ingi," Margret replied testily, wiping the sweat off her brow.

Margret reached the plum tree ahead of Tova, amid the jovial cheers of everyone watching. Smiling rather smugly, Margret sat down on the stepping-stones that crossed the wall by the tree as Tova placed her last stones on the wall.

"I've got a little ale left for the victor," Sigla said. "I hope you haven't killed yourself, Margret. This will restore your blood and bile."

"What else is left to eat?" Ingi inquired. "Watching all this work has made me hungry."

"I am completely humbled." Tova laughed as she sat down on the stile. "Never again will I boast of my abilities around here. You've all had too much practice."

"Experience does have the advantage over youth," Margret admitted with a prim little smile.

Svartur suddenly uttered a loud cry, peering up into her face. A shadow crossed Margret's face, and she frowned, drawing a deep breath.

"Where's that ale for the victor, Sigla?" she asked. When she reached out for the cup, her hand trembled.

"Mother, what's the matter?" Thruda demanded. "You've gone awfully pale."

"It's nothing," Margret snapped. "I just sat down on this cold rock in the shade too soon when I was hot. If I get up and walk around, I'll be fine."

She rose to her feet to prove it, but she swayed shakily and would have fallen if Tova hadn't caught her. Sigla shrieked, and Dora began fluttering.

"Get her cloak! Lie her down! Get more water! No, maybe we'd better let her cool off first."

"She needs to walk around," Ingi declared. "That's what you'd do for a horse."

"I'm only a little winded," Margret wheezed, her eyes tightly closed. "Stop being so foolish! I may just have a touch of indigestion. That wasn't the best lunch we've ever had."

"Oh dear, oh dear!" Sigla moaned. "This is how poor sweet Eydis went. Have you got a pain in your chest?"

"Yes, but it's from the pickles!" Margret snapped. "If I just lie down awhile, it will go away. Where's Svartur? What's he crying for?"

All the kettir paced and wailed, and Svartur crouched in a compact ball beside Margret's head, uttering plaintive yowls with his eyes wide and staring.

"Let's get her to the house," Tova said, smearing a handful of dingy tears across her face. "I'll fetch the little cart, and we can pull her quite comfortably. This is all my fault. I shouldn't have raced her. It was nothing but pure pride and foolishness."

"Yes, Margret should have known better," Sigla said between sobs.

"You always were too full of pride," Dora said.

"What do you mean?" Margret demanded. "I'm not dead yet, am I? Now, go get that stupid cart. I suppose I shall humor you by riding in it. I certainly don't trust you to carry me. I think I could walk if you'll just give me a little time."

"No, we're taking you straight to your bed, where you'll be comfortable," Jutta said, her throat almost swollen shut with unshed tears.

"Take me to the bathhouse," Margret said rather weakly. "Heat up the stove and the water. I think the steam would do me good. Besides, I don't want to be buried dirty. Where's Svartur? I want him near."

Svartur curled up under her arm. His eyes were still wide, black with fear. He stayed at her side in the bathhouse, although kettir did not care for the hissing and steaming of the water being poured over the hot rocks.

Silently, miserably, Jutta and Tova took care of the outside chores while the grandmothers attended to Margret. Poor Ingi wasn't much use in doctoring anything but horses, so she and her helpful suggestions were soon banished from the bathhouse for fear of enraging Margret into a complete apoplectic rupture. So she and the unfortunate Rugla followed Jutta and Tova, distractedly breaking eggs, spilling the milk pail, and nearly chopping off her foot with the peat cutter.

"I don't know what we'll do without Margret," Ingi said after absentmindedly letting the calf in to its mother before the cow was milked. "She keeps us all together. She's a little sharp sometimes, but that's all my fault for being such a clumsy goose. I always have been, there's the pity, always such a trial to poor Margret."

"It's my fault if it's anyone's," said Tova, whose eyes were very red and swollen. "I shouldn't have let her challenge me. It didn't occur to me that she might not be as strong as she thought she was."

"None of us are; that's the secret," Ingi said with her warm and humorous smile. She put her arms around Tova and hugged her tightly. "It's not your fault. Margret might have bent down to tie her laces and the same thing would have happened—sooner or later. Blaming someone for the misfortune is not going to help you or Margret. As the person around here who is almost always guilty of the stupidest things, I've come to realize that assigning the blame to some poor unfortunate clumsy person who probably meant well is a serious character flaw among the human race. The world will end, and people will be standing around trying to figure out whose fault it was and saying, 'It's all your fault. If you just hadn't sneezed at the wrong moment, we'd all still be here.' Things happen, and sometimes they're bad. I don't necessarily like being the instrument so much of the time, but somebody has to be the instigator. I just try to compensate by being as cheerful and loving as I can be, so maybe the others won't hate me."

Tova laughed in spite of her tears. "As if anybody could hate you, Amma Ingi. Even if you managed to pour the milk in the sheep trough and the sheep water in the cream pans."

"Rats. Do you mean I've done that again?"

In the morning, Margret was somewhat better and the pain in her chest had subsided. Now came the truly dangerous phase, when Margret still felt bad enough to stay in bed but good enough to be grouchy about having to. Jutta went in to see her before breakfast and went away with her ears blistered, but she was smiling.

"I think she'll survive," she greeted Tova when she returned to the house.

Tova stared at her with the same frightened glare in her eyes as Svartur had, almost as if she hadn't heard.

"Jutta, come with me," she whispered. "I went out early this morning, before anyone came out of the house, and I found something. I hid it before your grandmothers could see it. I don't think we should tell them, either."

"What are you talking about?" Jutta gasped, scared to think of anything that could frighten Tova.

Tova led her to a small ravine not far from the house. From

behind a clump of gorse she dragged a stick, and on the end of the stick was a freshly killed goat's head, gruesomely ornamented with hair and bits of feathers and sticks and daubs of clay. With a bristling ridge from his shoulders to the tip of his tail, Bensi kept his distance, offering an angry hiss when Jutta took a step in his direction. Even Ofsi had the intelligence to swell up to four times his size and sound a shrill howling challenge at the thing on the stick.

CHAPTER 14

"What is it?" Jutta wailed, feeling her knees go weak with an inexplicable wave of fear.

"It's an insulting pole," Tova said grimly. "I've seen this sort of thing among people who still use and believe in magic. This was put here yesterday, and we didn't see it. And look what happened to Amma Margret."

"But what does it do?" Jutta whispered. "It's just a dead head on a stick."

"It's got powers," Tova said. "Someone wishes your grandmothers ill. A lot of spells and incantations went into the making of this thing, and blood was shed in an unclean ritual. The whole performance is symbolic of what the person would like to do to the person he hates. Or persons. I believe if I hadn't found this thing and taken it down, Amma Margret might have died."

"Who would do such a thing?" Jutta cried in fury. "No one hates my grandmothers. Everyone thinks they are a little strange, but nobody could hate them."

"Jealousy can take a host of forms," Tova said. "Isn't there someone you can think of who might be angry at your grandmothers for some wrong he imagines they might have committed against him?"

Jutta tore her eyes away from the pitiful goat's head to think. Ofsi was now advancing on it in a low stalking pose, one paw at a time, eyes bulging in morbid fascination. Or perhaps it had a smell of food about it mingling with the sorcery.

Jutta suddenly chuckled and shook her head. "I was just

thinking of the little gifts old Bjalfur likes to leave for Dora to find. If she'd found this, she'd still be screaming."

"Gifts? Why?"

"He wants to marry her, and she'll have nothing to do with him."

"How long has this been going on?"

"I think about thirty years."

"He might be getting impatient. Maybe he's angry."

"Bjalfur? I don't think so."

"Let's take this pole and show it to him. If he's the one who did it, he won't deny it. That's part of the power of these things. The victims must know who's working magic against them."

Tova carried the goat's head out of the ravine concealed under her cloak so no one would see it. As soon as the morning chores were finished, they grabbed a walking breakfast and set out.

Bjalfur's hut looked like the home of a large pack rat. The hut itself was wattle and daub and might not have looked too bad except for the skins of all kinds fastened to it in various stages of processing. Odd bits of strangely shaped driftwood formed whimsical guardian heads around the roof edges. Bjalfur liked whittling, so the yard was full of chips and several half-finished things he was carving from tree stumps, aided by the natural contortions of the wood. He had a heap of bones and skulls, a stack of gnarled walking sticks he was carving knobs and faces for, and a row of little sinister grinning figures that looked like trolls.

Tova shivered. "If this isn't the place for an insulting pole to be made, I've never seen anything more likely. Look at those trolls he's carving. Have you ever seen anything so evil?"

"He sells them at the market. Everyone has got to have one. He says they're lucky trolls and they'll frighten away the real trolls, who will think you know how to turn trolls into wood."

"Is that what he says?" Tova sniffed. "I daresay he could turn live trolls into wood with just the smell of this place. What is that stench?"

"Nettles. He's rotting off the stalk part to separate out the fibers for weaving. It's called retting, actually. Nettles make the finest cloth you can imagine. He rets them and sells them to weavers."

The door, reinforced with a shedding deer hide, bumped open, and a voice shouted out. "Halloa! Come inside for some breakfast!" A tuffet of wild white hair and a virulent eye peered around the corner of the door. Then the door was snatched open, and Bjalfur in his entirety heaved into the yard, eyes alight.

"Say, now, that's a mighty fine insulting pole you've got there, my ladies," he rumbled with a snaggling grin. "Is that intended for me?"

"Perhaps," Tova said, striking a belligerent pose. "If you are the one who planted it at Bardhol, we shall force you to eat it for breakfast."

Rather wildly Bjalfur looked down at her for a moment from his great tottery height. Then he clutched his sides, stooped over, and began laughing until the tears rolled down his seamy, hairy face. Bensi decided to assist by stropping around his shinbones, adding an even greater precariousness to his shaky stance. Ofsi sallied forth with his tail bristling, bouncing and bucking around Bjalfur's bootlaces. Bjalfur was enough of a rattletrap without the weakening effects of laughter and two kettir skilled in the art of tripping up people.

"My darlings!" he whispered, sinking into a chair constructed of a stump and strips of hide and sticks. "I fear you're going to half kill me!"

A look of extreme consternation flashed over Tova's face. "Then I will have half killed two old people since just yesterday," she said. "We found this in our yard this morning, and since you are known for bringing gifts to Bardhol, we thought we'd see if it was yours."

"Nay, nay, I wouldn't wish misfortune on anyone at Bardhol, especially the lovely little lass who has stolen my heart, the dear and beautiful Dora. A thing like this could harm her greatly."

"It already brought terrible misfortune to Amma Margret,"

Jutta said. "Yesterday her heart failed while she was mending wall. Today she is better, though, and growling like a wounded bear."

"That's good to hear," Bjalfur rumbled, his brows drawing down like thunderclouds over the blue lightning of his one good eye, "but such a thing as this enrages me to think that someone intends your grandmothers ill. You were wise to come to me, although thinking I would do such a thing is a lamentable breach of friendship on your part."

"We're sorry," Jutta said. "We thought you might have gone out of your mind with passion for Dora."

Bjalfur clutched his midriff, leaned his head back, and howled with mirth. When he could speak again, he mopped at his eyes and gasped. "No more, no more. I haven't laughed so hard in years. Almost as many years since I had a fit of serious passion. I fear you're going to kill me, and then I won't be able to help you figure out who stuck this miserable pole in your yard. That would be a great pity. I'm almost as ancient as the magic that went into the making of this thing, so I understand it well." He reached for the goat's head, the mirth suddenly deserting his features, leaving him with the cold and deadly expression of a snake. "This is a serious business," he rumbled, darting Jutta and Tova one of his lightning glances. "I never suspected something like this would bring me out of retirement. Go on home now and leave me to figure this out and I shall tell you when I know who has done this. Look well to yourselves and your grandmothers. Someone has declared war."

"Well," Tova said when they were well away from Bjalfur's hut, "you never told me how frightful he was. He's truly a masterpiece, isn't he? I can't imagine Amma Dora living in that horrible hut as his wife. The dirt and clutter would send her into a state of shock. Do you really think he can help us any? He can hardly stand up."

They returned home to resume the daily chores, received from Margret through Thruda.

"She says you're to continue working on the wall," Thruda said, "and someone must go up and check on the sheep. She doesn't trust that shepherd at the shieling, although he has been watching the settlement's sheep for at least twenty years. The new cheese has got to be started, there's a new hole in the barn roof we need some turf for, and unless we get some peat laid in for winter, we're all going to freeze to death. The garden needs weeding, it's time for a bread baking, we need some water in the house, and no one has taken the kettir for a good walk for a long time. They're starting to get mischievous."

Amma Margret continued to improve over the next seven days, advancing from the bed to a chair, where she could give everyone directions for the dozens of chores she was itching to do herself. Nothing pained her worse than the curse of inactivity, so she relegated herself to piles of sewing as long as her strength and patience held up.

Jutta and Tova worked briskly to finish their chores by dark and ended by taking the milk to the dairy house to cool and separate for the night. By that time a huge orange full moon was slowly rising over the barrows, gleaming with eerie malevolence until it was fully risen and apparently a bit farther from earth. At least it had always seemed so to Jutta, since she was a little girl watching that cold fiery crescent rising up, skybound and inexorable.

The grandmothers were also watching it, although they continued to fuss over the usual inconsequential things, such as mending and carding.

"A full moon," Amma Margret groused. "Who knows what is going to happen in the barrows tonight. That full moon brings out barrow robbers, murderers, thieves, and all manner of evil creatures. The only thing we haven't seen yet is walking draugar, but they're probably afraid of what they'll find if they do get out."

"Hush," Dora said. "You're exciting yourself needlessly. Hrokr is there at the crossroads."

Ingi looked up from her hopeless attempts to mend a skirt. At best she would have been inexpert; with her failing eyesight, her efforts were almost comical. She said with a grin, "Bjalfur is also standing guard. That should make us all feel safer."

"Oh, no, it doesn't," Dora snapped. "I don't want that old skeleton prowling around out there. I don't know what he thinks he's up to. I saw him yesterday at dusk perched on the rocks where he can keep an eye on the house. I could scarcely sleep, thinking about him up there spying."

"I believe I could ride a horse," Margret said. "One needn't do much more than sit and balance."

"No, you're not going to even think about it, Modir," Thruda said firmly. "Wait until you're strong again."

"Maybe I'll never be strong," Margret retorted stubbornly. "I could start going downhill and become an old lady sitting in the sun with a robe over her knees."

"I'm sure there'll be nothing wrong with your tongue, even if you're bound to a chair," Thruda answered. "The four of us will go ahead as usual."

"I daresay you will, and you'll enjoy yourselves, too," Margret grumbled.

"We shall do all that must be done," Sigla said, "although I don't see how we can enjoy ourselves, knowing you are here weak and ill and alone."

"I shall not be alone as long as Svartur is here." The kettir looked up at the mention of his name, his round eyes gleaming golden like crescent moons. He offered a chirp of affirmation and settled down again at Margret's feet, somehow knowing that she was too weak to deal with a heavy, sagging kettir on her lap.

"Well, then, we must carry on," Ingi said with an air of conclusion, and the others nodded in agreement. "Just as we always have."

"I believe I'd like some warm milk before I go to bed," Sigla said. "It will do us all good to soothe us to sleep. Fetch your cups, everyone."

Jutta elbowed Tova behind Ingi's broad backside during the temporary distraction of Ingi knocking over a half-filled pot of drippings onto the table, where it spilled onto the floor to the delight of all the kettir.

"Don't drink the milk," Jutta whispered.

Following Jutta's lead, Tova managed to pour her cup of

warm milk into the kettir pan. Then she yawned and stretched out her arms in a great parody of sudden exhaustion. "My, I'm tired," she said. "Bed is certainly going to feel welcome tonight."

"You've done a wonderful job on that wall," Amma Thruda said. "And such heavy work, too."

They climbed up into the loft and waited until they heard Ingi's amiable snores tickling the rafters below. Although she would never admit it, Amma Dora also contributed a ladylike accompaniment, always mindful of her noble position even when she was asleep.

"There will be a full moon tonight," Jutta said. "I've been keeping track of the days since Betla was killed. I'm sure that murdering creature who killed her is counting, too. Are you afraid to go into the barrows by moonlight? It's the only way not to be seen by my grandmothers or Hrokr."

"I'm willing, if not wise. But first tell me what you think you can do even if you see the killer—if he doesn't see us first."

"I think Frida will be there tonight," Jutta said. "I must tell her about the insulting pole and Amma Margret falling ill. I think she can help us more than Bjalfur in finding out who is warring against Bardhol. There's no other way I can meet with her now that we must do Amma Margret's work besides our own."

"It will be good to see Frida again. Perhaps we can help her look for the barrow tonight. But just remember that I've spoken for a drink from Sigmund's cup when we find it."

"I swear to remember."

Tova drew her belt knife and pricked a small hole in her thumb. "Let me see your finger a moment. This will help us never to forget what we have sworn today."

Jutta tried not to wince as Tova pricked her finger and encouraged a large drop of blood to well up. They mingled their blood in clasped hands, and Tova said, "Blood will always be the most true and honest way for two friends to swear loyalty to each other forever. There is nothing more pure than blood.

Now we shall always be like sisters, one in intention, united in our plan. We must be brave; we must be determined."

Then they wiped off the extra blood on the hems of their nightgowns, where it wouldn't show. Jutta and Tova crept down the ladder and slipped outside without interrupting the cadence of snores. If anyone had awakened to question them, they had rehearsed a plea to the undeniable call of nature.

It was almost as bright as day with the moonlight. Tova carried Bensi, ready to smother any excited yowls. Ofsi was silent in his sack on Jutta's back, rather sleepy from diving into the kettir pan to guzzle what he could before Jutta snatched him up in alarm. The other kettir lay like stones beside the hearth, drugged with whatever harmless powder Sigla had added to their milk. Once outside, Tova set Bensi down and led the way, straight down the hillside toward the barrow fields.

"Jutta, my dear blood sister," Tova began when they were well away, "would you please tell me why your grandmothers put sleeping powder into our milk. Or did they also add it to their own?"

"Their intentions are honorable," Jutta said. "They wish to keep us out of the barrows at night. Before you came, I made a nuisance of myself, I'm afraid." She halted, considering if she should say more, but Frida had laughed at her fears that her grandmothers were Myrkriddir, and she really didn't want Tova to laugh at her, too. She could almost smile at her own childish imagination now.

They avoided by a wide margin the cairn where Hrokr continued to lurk like a surly watchdog. It meant climbing through some nasty scratchy thickets and crossing an icy stream with their shoes in their hands, but they finally came across into an area of barrows where Jutta hadn't explored. The standing stones and circles where Frida did her daytime mapping were much more curious and thrilling to prowl around, and they marveled at the ancient powers that slumbered forgotten in those mossy mounds. For a long time they waited in the shadows of the standing stones, but the silence was unbroken.

"Frida's not coming," Jutta said, biting her lip with disappointment. "I thought for certain she would."

"The night isn't finished yet," Tova said. "Let's do some looking around. We'll hear her horse if she comes, and she'll probably have Hallgrima and Gunna with her. We can always find them when we hear them."

As she talked, Tova unwound a dowsing pendulum weighted with a small pierced stone Jutta recognized as amber. "The last thing I have from my mother," Tova said. "And I shall never part with it."

The pendulum commenced a brisk movement when Tova faced north. Tova set off northward, stopping occasionally to make slight alterations in her course.

The kettir romped at their heels, scuttling ahead to pause with lashing tails, following the flight of bats and skimming night birds. Worried lest an owl snatch Ofsi up in its talons, Jutta stuffed him, protesting, into her sack.

"There's nothing much here, according to Frida," Jutta said, a little breathless from keeping up with Tova's longer strides.

"Then why is there a little path?" Tova asked, pointing out a faint track through the grass and rocks.

"Rabbits, maybe," Jutta said. "They make trails sometimes."

Tova laughed and hurried after Bensi, who was racing ahead with his tail waving aloft, glancing back over his shoulder several times to urge them on with excited yowls and trills.

He finally came to a halt, treading his paws up and down, peering up into their faces, and yelling in a long nonstop cry usually reserved for demanding something especially tasty, such as an entire joint of roast meat. Jutta looked around for something significant. All she saw was an ordinary-looking rock sticking up out of the moss and grass, blackened by many years and honed by harsh winds.

"Look. The pendulum says there is something here."

They tracked the course of the swinging pendulum, with many halts and turnings back or aside.

"Hist!" Jutta pulled Tova down behind a bush to listen. "I thought I heard something!"

They lay silently, straining their ears.

"Were you there when they found that dead woman?" Tova whispered with a nervous gulping sound.

"It was terrible. You should've seen poor Betla. She was covered with scratches, and it didn't look like there was a drop of blood in her. It was a small wound in her neck, but she was drained as clean as a slaughter carcass at market. I've heard that draugar have a dread fascination for fresh blood, as if it could bring them back to life again. I don't want to end up dead, with all my blood sucked out by a draug."

"Neither do I. And we shan't, with our kettir to protect us."

"Kettir won't be any help," Jutta said in exasperation. "If someone came after us, all they would do is climb up a tree. I don't hear anything now. Let's go on."

"Where's Bensi?" Tova asked, glancing around. Bensi had been following closely, diverted only occasionally by the irresistible squeaking of a mouse or the twitter of a roosting bird.

As if he had understood, Bensi replied with an animated trill from somewhere ahead.

"He's found something," Tova said excitedly.

"What? How do you know?"

"Be still and listen," Tova said, pulling her along impatiently.

They crossed the rocky ridge of a barrow, plunging immediately into the gloom of the shadowy dark side away from the moonlight. The brush rose almost to their waists, and scraggly plum thickets reached out to claw at them. Bensi called eagerly, mimicked by piping squeaks from Ofsi in his kettir sack.

Tova struggled along ahead, still clasping Jutta's hand in a relentless grip. Suddenly, without warning, Tova dropped straight out of sight with a snapping of branches and a scattering of small rocks. She didn't have time to let go, so Jutta was jerked down into a gaping hole headfirst, sliding to a halt on her stomach, tangled up with plenty of rocks and a softer heap that was Tova, gasping and spitting out dirt.

Bensi capered around, meowing joyfully. Ofsi wriggled out of the sack, jumped on Jutta's face while she lay there wheezing, and bit her on the nose.

"I think we've found something," Tova said. A small shaft of moonlight showed her face, smeared with dirt and certainly scratched. She rubbed her nose on her sleeve, a most regrettable and unladylike habit she had, and helped Jutta to her feet.

"A broken leg, perhaps?" Jutta took a couple of limping steps, but she didn't think it was truly broken. Merely a bloody gash and full of sand, perhaps.

"Someone has been digging here," Tova whispered. "Look what a hole they've made. They covered it up with branches to hide it, and we fell through. Come on, help me."

She began pushing the dead brush aside, and Jutta reluctantly joined in. Someone had indeed excavated a considerable pit in the side of the barrow. Tova gasped when she uncovered a stone lintel etched with runes. Quickly she extracted her tinderbox from her belt pouch and lit a short stump of candle.

"I can't read it," Jutta whispered, realizing she had been holding her breath. "Can you?"

"No. I never learned anything about runes. I expect it says who is buried here and warns off anybody who would think to break in. I've heard of barrow robbers who broke into a mound and were struck dead by poison air."

"I've heard more about barrow robbers being attacked by angry draugar," Jutta answered. "Don't go in there, Tova!"

Tova stooped and disappeared under the lintel stone. In a moment she backed out again.

"It's full of dirt. Caved in over the years. It's going to take a lot of digging to get in."

"Do you think it's Sigmund's barrow?" Jutta whispered.

"I don't know. Someone else does; I think."

"How dare they? These barrows belong to the Hesturkona clan! No one's got any business touching them! And especially they've got no business digging up property that belongs to the Hesturkonur! They mustn't get that cup before we do!"

"No, indeed," Tova said. "Perhaps the thing to do is to tell Einarr, the chieftain, and have him capture whoever is doing this."

"Unless it's Einarr himself," Jutta said in a whisper. "I've heard from sources who know him well that he'd give a great deal for that cup. I think we'd better get out of here. I have no intention of becoming the next body found in the barrows."

"And give up the cup?" Tova asked. "We can't. We mustn't. The future of the Alfar realm might depend on it. Imagine the power you would have if you held that cup. Wealthy chieftains would pay dearly for just one sip."

"What a pity I didn't think to bring a shovel," Jutta declared. "We could just dig all night—and hope whoever started this hole doesn't appear and kill us. Maybe we'd find the cup. Maybe we'd find some distant relative of Sigmund's who has nothing but a box of gold coins or nothing at all."

"You mustn't always think about the bad things that might happen," Tova said.

"Hist! Listen!"

This time it was unmistakable. Voices were approaching. Jutta and Tova crouched down in the shadows of the excavation, unable to do anything but wait and listen to the ominous crackling of the cut brush being pushed away. In a moment a dark figure came sliding down straight toward them, trailing a shovel behind. Clearly he did not expect to find anyone awaiting him in his pit. His eyes must have been on the opening to the barrow, for he did not see Tova and Jutta. Nor did he see Tova poised with a rock the size of an egg. She had an arm as stout as a man's, and she heaved the rock straight at his head. A deadly shot with a stone, she had brought down at least one hare a day during her stay at Bardhol—and hares were a far more elusive target than was a totally unsuspecting full-sized man scarcely an arm's length away. He went down like a polled ox, groaning and twitching.

"Quick! Tie him up and get ready for the next one!" Tova whispered, whipping off her belt, which was a long sash of coarse weaving, ideal for tying up barrow robbers.

Before they were finished they could hear the next barrow robber picking his way through the dry twigs. Tova took up another rock, and Jutta laid hold of the spade and waited, each girl holding her breath. The first barrow robber was struggling around, grunting and moaning, so Tova knelt on his head with one knee to muffle the sounds in the dirt.

Something must have warned the other robber. He hesitated in his advance, listening and peering down into the excavation.

Then, after an interminable pause, he uttered a soft but blood-chilling chuckle.

"What have we here? A trap, I suppose," he said. His words were followed by the scything sound of a sword being drawn from its sheath. The dark bulk of his image was joined by a silvery narrow one that flashed in the moonlight. "Stand forth and identify yourself if you are a true and honorable man. Only trolls and wolves do their fighting in the shadows."

Jutta and Tova, of course, stayed still in the shadows, not being true men and therefore under no obligation to fight honorably by the rules men had set up regarding the best way to die in combat. Tova weighed her rock in her hand, considering the best moment to throw it.

"So you are not honorable? It's a thing I might have expected in a barrow robber of low status, who sneaks in by night to steal what others have found. So you lie in wait like a coward, a back stabber and throat cutter, instead of a true fighter, instead of standing up like a man and meeting me with men's weapons."

He brandished his sword in a heroic gesture. Tova selected a smaller rock, as her target did not seem inclined to come any closer. Gauging her distance, she stood up and flung the rock with all her might. If the barrow robber had thought to wear a helmet, the rock would have bounced off his head with little effect, but since he wasn't properly equipped for full combat, the rock bounced off his head and sent him staggering. Forward, backward, then he lost his balance and tumbled straight into the pit, snarling and thrashing around with his sword.

Tova and Jutta prudently retired to the barrow opening.

Their opponent rose to his feet, swaying slightly, looking around for his attackers. He took a few steps and nearly fell over the trussed carcass of his companion.

"My son! Have they killed you?" he rumbled, dropping down to one knee to untie the untidy package he had found.

The other groaned and struggled faintly, muttering thickly, "Pabbi, I've got a terrible pain in my head and I can't move my arms and legs."

"They hit you in the head with a rock and tied you up. Beware, I think they're still lurking about, waiting to brain us again."

"Who? I didn't see anyone."

"Simon, you are such a fool sometimes. These Alfar are far more wily than we've given them credit for. I've long thought Einarr must be wise to us and just waiting to take away what we've found."

"The Alfar realm is no place for Sciplings," the other added with a groan.

"Sciplings!" Jutta whispered indignantly, rising to her feet. "I know who this is! Simon! Petrus! How dare you dig up the grave of my ancestor Sigmund without at least offering me a share?" She crawled out of the barrow opening and stood up with her fists on her hips. "Maybe Tova's rocks have knocked some sense into your heads now. Yes, it is I, Jutta Thorgestrss-dottir."

"Jutta?" Petrus repeated, rubbing his skull in wonder. "Who is with you? Some great thrall with an arm like a catapult?"

"No, it's my friend Tova," Jutta said. "She has an excellent arm when it comes to small prey—and large Sciplings. If you think you're going to murder us, you'll get a lot more head-aches, because the ground here is filled with rocks."

"You were very foolish girls to come into these barrows during a full moon," Petrus said, "knowing as you do that someone here is killing people."

"We're not afraid of your threats," Tova declared in her clear voice. "Better that you should worry what we Alfar women can do to you if you attempt to do us any harm."

"What shall we do with them, Pabbi?" Simon asked, still rubbing his scalp. "We can't let them tell anyone, not when we're this close to finding the cup. You promised that we'd be home by the first hay mowing."

"And so we shall. I don't believe Jutta and Tova will stand in our way in the least."

CHAPTER 15

"We're not afraid of you," Jutta declared, trying to keep the quaver out of her voice. "You must have the hearts of craven dogs to kill poor women by night in the barrows."

"We have killed no one," Simon protested while Petrus sheathed his sword. "We only came here to search for the thing that will help us go home to our own realm. We don't even want to keep it, just to use it once and then we'll be gone."

"Indeed," Jutta said loftily. "And we are supposed to take the word of men who sneak out by moonlight from the house of their host to dig up the bones of our own ancestors? I daresay Einarr would be enraged to know what you do here. So enraged that he would hang you up from his own roof timber as thieves and barrow robbers."

At that moment something came crashing through the dry brush with a sudden cursing bellow, a large form that came rolling down into the pit, tumbling to a halt nearly at their feet.

"Halloa! Who's this?" bellowed the voice of Einarr as he hoisted himself onto his feet and glared around, knocking the dirt off his clothes and untangling himself from his cloak and the shovel he grasped in one hand.

"Einarr, is that you?" Petrus roared.

"Petrus! What are you doing here?" Einarr demanded in a voice filled with surprise.

"We came to rob this barrow, same as you," Petrus declared. "Isn't that a fine joke?"

Einarr uttered a mirthful roar and slapped his thigh. "You

mean to tell me you've been the one digging all these great holes these past two years?"

"Aye, one and the same, and we haven't found a thing in any of them except a few bones and a piece or two of gold that better barrow robbers than we had missed hundreds of years ago."

"Well, I never found even that much. You hogged it all." Einarr and Petrus laughed again, slapping each other around and raising a terrific cloud of dust.

"Well, I don't think it's anything to joke about," Jutta snapped. "I think you both ought to be hanged."

"What's the crime?" Einarr asked, wiping the corners of his eyes and still cackling. "There's no law against a man who wants to go out by moonlight and dig huge holes for nothing but his own amusement. There's certainly been no profit to the enterprise."

"The only crime is missing a night's rest," Petrus said, which sent them off again in fits of laughter.

"This isn't a joking matter!" Jutta shouted furiously. "What about nine women who have disappeared or were found dead? Is that something you're going to laugh off and joke about? Or is that just the way murderers regard their crimes? I believe one of us in this hole tonight is responsible for all those killings."

"I don't," Petrus said indignantly. "I know it's not me, and I've known Einarr for two years now, and while he may be a bit of an idiot and a loudmouth and occasionally he drinks himself into a stupor—but no more than every week or so—I know there's not a grain of evil anywhere to be found in his fat and worthless carcass. I would stand up beside him with my sword in my hand any day and gladly die to defend his honor, which may be a thing unsuspected, but underneath it all Einarr Sorenson is truly a great and noble Alfar."

"Hem, hem!" Einarr replied, swelling his chest with modest pride. "I don't know what I have done to deserve such friendship. All I know for certain is that anything this honorable Scipling utters is most certainly the truth. If all Sciplings were like Petrus of Borksstead in the Scipling realm, then the two realms could be indeed united in the bonds of greatest trust and friendship. In all the years that I have known Petrus and his son Simon I have never witnessed any dishonorable deed or meanness of character. Indeed, these Sciplings have both exhibited the most noble fortitude in the face of their dire plight. In fact—"

He would have gone on spouting his nonsense forever, and probably Petrus would have felt obligated to make another speech returning his outrageous compliments and lies, if Jutta had not interrupted with an abrupt "Come now, this isn't an ale hall for making your speeches, nor do we have all night. For the moment I shall be content with your protestations of innocence in the murders, and I confess I would be astonished if either of you were killers of women. I'd always assumed that the person robbing the barrows was going to be the same one doing the killings, and now I'm seeing that perhaps it isn't so."

"Particularly when you consider that neither of us has actually robbed a barrow," Einarr said. "We've done a great deal of useless digging, but that's no crime."

"If you actually found something, though, you'd take it," Tova said.

"Only the cup," Petrus said. "I wouldn't dare steal anything else from the dead. My hope is that the draug of Sigmund would understand my need and be glad to lend his powers once again."

"This is the cup of my ancestor Sigmund," Jutta said. "I consider myself the guardian of this clan, and that cup is not going to fall into the hands of buffoons. It's mine by birthright, since I am the last of the true living Hesturkonur!"

"And that's why you're here?" Einarr said, squinting in Jutta's direction. "You want the cup for yourself? Ha, I thought you were rather too fine and fancy a creature to spend the rest of your life with those fusty old cat women in that wretched place where they live." He grinned toothily in the moonlight in loathsome camaraderie. "My dear, it's not a job for ladies, I assure you. There's hours of digging and moving rocks to get inside that barrow. And of what use will you be to us? When we find the cup, we'll all share in its powers. There's no need for any of us to be greedy now."

Petrus coughed and hemmed. "I've been digging hither and yon for it for three years, and many's the blister it's earned me. Without that cup, I'll be trapped here until my son and I die. It's a desperate man I am, friends though we may be. I must have that cup ahead of all you others."

"There are worse things than my company," Einarr said rather testily. "I wouldn't think you'd be so uncomfortable at Sorengard if wars were to break out with the Dokkalfar. With the powers of that cup, Mikillborg and all the surrounding settlements would be safe. That seems to me a more noble purpose than just to rid the realm of a pair of obnoxious Sciplings."

"Neither of you have the right to it that I do," Jutta declared hotly.

"Right? By what right? Birthright?" Einarr demanded. "I'm as much a Hestur as you are. All the women from my mother on back were the finest Hesturkonur that a birthright could ask for."

"But you're not a woman," Jutta said, "and therefore you're not a Hesturkonur. You belong to the clan of your father, Soren."

"But Sigmund himself wasn't a woman," Einarr said. "He was the finest fighting man known in the realm. What use would a woman have for a warrior's cup? By rights it should fall to a male heir who wields the sword for the protection of the Hesturkonur. What protection could your scrawny little grandmothers offer Mikillborg?"

"Oh, you might be surprised one day," Jutta retorted.

"I think we should all go home until our tempers are mended somewhat," Petrus said. "Then we shall agree to meet together and arbitrate this dispute."

"What are we disputing?" Simon asked. "We haven't found a thing in this barrow yet to fight over. We don't even know if there's anything in it at all."

"We should dig and then arbitrate," Einarr said.

"No, we should have an agreement before we find the cup,"

Petrus said. "Otherwise we may not long be friends once it is found."

"Surely there's enough power in that cup to satisfy everyone," Tova said.

"Perhaps not," Petrus said. "Perhaps there is only one more use left in it. Who is going to have it, if it is?"

"Surely not a woman," Einarr grunted, half to himself.

Jutta was about to make a fiery retort when Petrus suddenly cocked his head, listening.

"Someone's spying on us," he whispered, casting his eyes up toward a dark thicket of scrubby plum trees.

Einarr snatched his knife out of its sheath. By unspoken consent, the three men separated like a pack of well-trained hunting hounds, swarming up out of the pit and surrounding the thicket. Einar plunged into its depths with a shout of discovery and promptly came crashing out with a captive in tow.

"I've got him!" he cried, delighted, as he led squad and prisoner back to where Jutta and Tova were waiting. "Shall we slit his weasand here and now? Or should we just break his bones and leave him for dead?"

"Neither, I hope," said a familiar voice, somewhat strangled. "Unless it's some sort of infanticide you wish to be committing. Please let go of my throat, Pabbi."

"What! Leckny! You followed me?" Einarr thundered. "What sort of nasty, suspicious act is this?"

Leckny shook himself to rearrange his habiliment and get the kinks out of his neck from being nearly throttled. "I knew something was going on. I saw Petrus and Simon sneaking out, then I saw you sneaking out after them. So I followed, not wishing to miss out on all the fun. I knew for certain something was afoot when you turned in the direction of the barrows."

"Well, I can't be letting barrows get robbed right under my very nose," Einarr huffed.

"Especially when you want a share of the proceeds," Leckny said. "Such as Sigmund's enchanted cup."

"Silence!" Einarr snapped. "It's only for the good of all

Mikillborg that I'm here. You, on the other hand, were merely snooping and spying."

"However it may be, he's here now," Jutta said, "and he must know what's afoot. So like it or not, he's one of our company. He'd better keep his mouth shut, though, or the rest of us will shut it for him."

"You needn't fear," Leckny said. "It's not to my credit that my father, the chieftain, is a barrow robber. It's not a thing I'm inclined to boast about in public places."

Einarr drew in a mighty breath to fuel his impending argument and defense, but he was silenced by an approaching thunder of hooves. The sound burst over the top of the barrow suddenly in a spray of pebbles and dirt and a blast of icy wind. The horses vaulted over the pit where they all stood, sailing far beyond what a normal horse could ever hope to leap across. Eerie cries filled the night with chilling terror as the ghostly riders turned and swept over the barrow again.

"Myrkriddir!" Petrus gasped, flattening himself in the dirt. "Get down, you fools! Don't look at them!"

Jutta looked up intently until Simon grabbed her by the knees and dropped her in the dirt.

"You'll go blind!" he cried. "Or at least lose your wits!"

Jutta pretended to hide her face, but she turned her head, searching the sky for the Myrkriddir. When they came roaring back, glowing and crackling like lightning, she counted them as they vaulted over the pit. Four. She sat up, mouth agape, thinking of Amma Margret at home with her heart ailment yet yearning to get back on her horse. Simon grabbed her by the neck and pressed her face into the dirt again.

"You fool!" Simon sputtered. "Do you want to become a witling, wandering around and babbling nonsense, like old Bjalfur?"

"Cursed hags!" Einarr growled, earnestly pressing his hands over his eyes. "Every time I think I get near to Sigmund's barrow, the Myrkriddir come flocking like the evil blackbirds they are! We'll have to run for it or they'll never leave us alone!"

"Now they know we're here, they'll be waiting for us next

time," Petrus groaned. "And this was the likeliest spot of all I've seen!"

"Then we'll have to come by day," Einarr said grimly. "They won't bother us then."

"We can't come by day," Leckny protested. "Everyone will see us, and then everyone will be digging into these barrows."

"Not if I frighten them out of it good and proper," Einarr huffed, blinking his eyes worriedly as he scanned the sky.

"No," Petrus said. "No one else must know. We're already far too numerous as it is. No daytime digging."

"There won't be any digging at all with these blasted hags," Einarr growled. "Listen; here they come again!"

"What are we to do?" Tova asked. "Are we trapped here until dawn?"

"So it seems," Petrus said. "We'd be fools to leave the cover of this hole. They could swoop down and carry us away, or kill us, or whatever ghastly thing they do."

So they waited, quarreling intermittently about who was to have the first use of Sigmund's cup.

"We should draw lots," Simon said. "That would be most fair."

"And leave the disposition of Sigmund's vast power entirely to mere chance?" Einarr snorted. "We have an opportunity here for saving several hundred people and their possessions."

"The Hesturkonur have always controlled the defense of this country," Jutta protested. "You should let us decide how it is to be done."

"What would a bunch of cat keepers know about warfare and defending a place?" Einarr snorted yet again.

"We don't even know that we're going to be attacked," Jutta said.

"There has been talk," Tova said. "I've heard a great deal in my travels. And old Bjalfur isn't as potty as everyone seems to think."

"I've got some sort of prior claim," Petrus said. "I've been searching the longest and digging the most."

"Wisdom should rule," Jutta said. "And who is older and wiser than my grandmothers?"

"Listen," Simon said. "The Myrkriddir have been gone quite some time. Do you think they've given up on us? They've seen that we're not coming out where they can get us, so maybe they've gone home, or back to their graves, or wherever it is Myrkriddir spend their spare time."

"I must get back to Bardhol," Jutta said uneasily. "If my grandmothers discover I'm gone, they'll be at their wit's end. Very alarmed, I'm sure."

"Go ahead, but be careful," Einarr said.

"Oho, you'd like for us to leave, wouldn't you?" Tova demanded. "That way the two of you can dig all night and find the cup and take command of it, without any regard to our rights to it. No indeed, we're staying here until dawn if we have to, so we can see all of you departing."

"I'm going nowhere until it's full daylight," Petrus said, sitting back against the wall of earth and folding his arms over his chest.

"And I'm going nowhere as long as you're sitting there with a shovel in your hands," Einarr said.

"But my grandmothers—" Jutta began. "You're right, though; we're not leaving. Well, they'll have to manage somehow and do to me what they will for punishment. We'll stay right here, too, until the sun comes up. And rest assured, I have a perfect view of this barrow from Bardhol, and no one had better show up here to dig while I can see them. My grandmothers would not take kindly to being robbed of their ancestral treasures in broad daylight."

"You won't be the only one watching," Einarr said with a genial grin. "No one had better come to this barrow alone, thinking to do a little private digging. I would look upon that very unkindly, I'm afraid."

"Then we'll all meet here tomorrow night," Petrus said. "Good. We'll have plenty of hands for the digging—at least until those cursed Myrkriddir appear."

"It's not those flying hags you fear," Tova said. "What you're afraid of is that one of us will find the cup before you do."

Shortly before dawn the Myrkriddir made a final harrying

pass over the pit and did not return. The sky lightened to dawn in the east, and the disgruntled barrow robbers cautiously emerged from their prison. Their farewells were not particularly cordial as they hurried away in various directions to avoid raising suspicion if they were seen. A flock of sheep and their herder dotted the sides of the green barrows with mottled white and brown, accompanied by the tune of muffled sheep bells and the querulous cry of lambs. Hrokr sat in an untidy heap beside the crossroads cairn, and down the road toward Mikillborg a merchant's cart had made an early departure for the eastern settlements, the two shaggy horses jogging along with a soft jingle of bells and harness.

Jutta and Tova came up the path with the cows, which were plodding moodily toward the milk house for their morning milking.

"Well! You're up early!" Amma Thruda greeted them cheerily from the doorway of the house, where she was putting her boots on. Her cheeks were rosy and her eyes were as bright as usual, not at all as if she, too, had been up all night guarding what she thought needed to be guarded.

Twice Jutta nearly fell asleep as she milked, with her head leaning against the soft warm gurgling flank of the cow, half hypnotized by the steady rhythm of the milk squirting into the pail. While Tova was in the spring house pouring the milk into pans to separate, Jutta walked down to the horse paddock. All the horses except Elding and the golden filly bore the marks of sweat and girth and bridle. Jutta made note of her observations and took a short detour past the old granary where the wood was stored. The woodpile above the box with the cloaks had been moved and rearranged.

Fortunately, Jutta and Tova were able to catnap throughout the day to make up for their wakeful night; they were sent into the fells to keep an eye on Thruda's precious white sheep, which she kept specifically for their fine wool. When they dozed overlong and the sheep began to scatter, Bensi awakened them with his anxious yowling and Ofsi pounced on Jutta's face in pursuit of her eyelashes. She was pleased to note that he was learning to considerately retract his needlelike little claws most of the time.

When they came down from the fell at sundown, they saw Amma Ingi from a distance, walking toward the crossroads on an intersecting path. She walked in haste, with a great deal of elbow action, looking up to see them above her only when Tova shouted a greeting at her.

"I can't stop," she gasped. "I've got to get Bjalfur to come up to look at the horses. Something has happened to them. They're all sick except little Faelinn. I don't know what it is. Bjalfur can save them. He must if he can, anyway."

Jutta had never imagined the jolly face of Amma Ingi streaked with tears and grief. "Shall we come with you?" she asked, her heart stricken to the core.

"No, no, go home and get your supper. I'll fetch Bjalfur. He used to be a good hand with a cure for man or beast. He can save them if anyone can."

Jutta and Tova penned the sheep and ran to look at the horses. Thruda and Dora were with them in the barn, while the little filly raced back and forth and squealed desperately in a small stone pen, unable to understand why she had been taken away from her mother.

The six mares stood with their heads despondently low, their spines hunched in misery. Already their hips looked bony and hollow, and their dull eyes made no note of Jutta's arrival.

"What happened?" Jutta gasped.

Thruda's glance was filled with weariness and the cold shadow of impending loss. "We don't know. They were fine this morning. I think they must have eaten something they shouldn't. It's spring, and everything green looks good to eat."

"But these horses know what to eat and what not," Jutta said. "I can't imagine them all getting poisoned on the same plant, either."

Dora stood stroking the neck of her mare, crooning softly to her. "At least we'll still have Faelinn," she said. "The proud breed of Hestur is not quite destroyed."

"Amma Dora, they aren't going to die," Jutta said.

"Horses die from pain," Dora said. "Even when the injury

is something they could recover from, the pain will kill them. It's nature's way of preventing them from suffering for long. They've eaten something bad for them, and they're very miserable. None of Ingi's usual cures have done them a bit of good."

"But they were fine last night," Jutta said. "And this morning."

"Yes. Whatever they ate was very fast."

Bjalfur returned with Ingi, carrying a ragged old satchel with a frayed rope for a shoulder strap. Dora stepped back into the shadows of the barn, drawing herself up in a huffy way, as if she expected to be insulted, but Bjalfur only greeted her politely and turned to the horses. Jutta expected him to examine them and look in their eyes and mouths and listen to their breathing, but all he did was stand and look at them for a long moment. Ingi watched him expectantly, dabbing away a few stray tears and giving her nose a good blow on a shred of her underskirt. Slowly he raised his hand, palm downward, fanning his hand gently back and forth, like a strand of weed in a flowing current. He walked around each horse, not even looking at them but gazing off toward the roof somewhere with a haphazard expression on his face. His hair and beard were more disorderly than usual, bristling in tuffets around his face. When he was finished wandering around the barn, ignoring his patients, he ended up near the doorway, gazing out toward the south with a deepening scowl.

"I think we're in for some stormy weather," he observed, gesturing toward a black and thunderous bank of cloud swelling up from the southern rocky prow of Blundscarp, which jutted out into the distant ocean like a pointing black finger.

"I don't care about the weather," Ingi snapped. "I just want my horses to survive. These are the last six Hestur mares that we know of. There may be others who were sold off and taken away years ago, but who knows where they are now or if they are still living."

"I am old, and most of my skills are forgotten," Bjalfur said. "Not so much by me but by the world that now surrounds me.

I don't know if the forces now here will respond if I attempt to command them."

One of the mares swayed weakly in her haunches and went down suddenly, her legs splaying out untidily. With a groan she made a feeble effort to gather her legs beneath her, but she was too weak to rise again. Dora surged forward, oblivious of old Bjalfur, nearly shoving him aside in her rush to kneel beside her horse.

"Oh, Elska, don't die!" she sobbed, burying her face in the horse's long black mane. Many times Jutta had seen Dora combing Elska's mane, removing every wind tangle and knot.

A great sorrowing knot rose in Jutta's throat, and tears burned her eyes. Nothing tore at the heart so much as the sight of a great, powerful thing of beauty like a horse suddenly reduced to a strangely small bundle of misery, lying stretched out on the ground, nearly lifeless. Even Elska's glistening coat was now dull, and her sleek muscles, once tight and hard beneath her glossy skin, were flaccid.

"Oh, Bjalfur," Ingi whispered, her face gray with despair. "Surely there's something you can do for them."

Bjalfur's black brows knotted up like the storm clouds as he watched Dora weeping over her dying horse. He clenched his fists and drew up his skinny shoulders into two sharp points beneath his ragged old shirt. His figure might have looked ridiculous except for the fiery glint of his cold pale eye.

"Aye, there's something I can do," he said in a gruff voice, turning suddenly away and snatching up his walking staff. "Just don't give up on me quite yet, not until you see the life drained out of my body and my vitals scattered on the ground. As long as there's fire in this old carcass, there's something that I can do."

Then he strode out of the barn and disappeared. Jutta waited a moment, thinking he would be back. Wonderingly she exchanged a glance with Tova, who looked just as puzzled as she was. Then Jutta went to the barn door and looked for Bjalfur. His raggedy figure was just visible, pegging along furiously toward his own hut in the ravine below Bardhol.

"I thought he was going to help," Jutta said with a flicker of indignation replacing her confusion. "But he's leaving. He's going home. What about the horses? Did he just go off leaving us with six dying horses?"

Ingi and Thruda said nothing, only looking at each other in one of those disquieting moments of subtle communication shared only by those who knew something that other people did not. In the silence the shrill cries of Faelinn came faintly to the ears of her dam, which flicked her ears and raised her head for a moment from the straw.

"Oh, Elska, it's your baby," Dora pleaded. "Please get well so you can take care of her."

Jutta turned away to hide the flood of silent tears that coursed down her cheeks. If Elska died, it would be questionable if they could raise Faelinn on cow's milk. She was only two months old and needed her mother's milk for another four months to grow perfectly healthy and strong. Foals could be weaned at two or three months, but the poor little creatures lost weight and struggled miserably.

Angrily she went about finishing the chores around the house for the night. No one felt much like eating, so there wasn't a supper. Sigla stayed with the horses instead of worrying Margret, since the horses paid no heed to her helpless spew of nonsensical fussing. Pale and silent, Dora attended to Margret and sat beside her, trying to distract herself with some mending. Fortunately, it wasn't a very important article; Jutta observed her picking out her stitches repeatedly until she finally put it down, complaining that her eyes were aching.

"I think it's more likely your heart is aching," Margret said, reaching out her hand from her bed and clasping Dora's to comfort her.

"Elska is going to die," Dora whimpered.

"But not unloved," Margret said in a whisper. "It would be worse for her if there was no one who had ever cared about the life of a mere horse. And worse for you if you had so little pity and kindness in your heart that the death of an animal didn't grieve it. Only the best hearts are broken, Dora."

Dora nodded her head, silently acknowledging that Margret, too, must be sorrowing for Elding.

Asa stood up to pat at Dora's face with her incredibly soft and fluffy white paw. All she could do was purr and rub and sit in Dora's lap to be petted, but Dora was comforted enough to smile at her.

Jutta returned to the barn, finding no change except that Birki had gone down, too; she was still breathing, but her gaze was unresponsive. The kettir clung to their owners as if they understood the tragedy taking place at Bardhol. Poor Rugla got stepped on at every turn, which might have been her way of momentarily distracting Ingi long enough to pick her up and smooth her rumpled fur and apologize for treading on her.

When the sun finally slipped down behind the horizon, Jutta could stand it no longer.

"Isn't there someone else who can help sick horses?" she asked Amma Thruda, standing vigil over Bjartur.

"In Mikillborg," she replied, "but that is a long way, and I don't think he would come until tomorrow. And I don't think there will be any sense in looking at them tomorrow, except that we will have to find someone to drag them away." She saw Jutta flinch and bite her lips. "I do like the idea that they will all be going together. I'm sure Borgunn would not want to live without her sisters, and none of them would know what to do without Elding bossing them around all day."

"I'll go to Mikillborg," Jutta said. "I'll get the healer and I'll bring him back here tonight if I have to tie him up and throw him over his horse."

"No, it's late and the moon is full," Thruda said with surprising firmness in her gentle tone. "I will not permit you to put yourself at such risk. Besides, my dear, the horses are dying. They've been poisoned. Even if we had the healer here right now, he could not save them."

"How can you be so sure?" Jutta demanded resentfully. "How can you just give up like this, Amma Thruda?"

"I've lived a long time, and I've seen poisoned horses and livestock all my life. They either die rather quickly or struggle along and come out of it and seldom are ever as strong and healthy again. A few are ill and make a good recovery, and maybe one or two of our horses will be lucky. I don't want our mares to survive if they are going to be weak and sick and no longer beautiful. They are old horses, but they could still hold their heads up and fly with the wind sometimes. How they could fly, the lovely creatures."

Jutta left the barn and attempted to comfort Faelinn. The filly was hungry and didn't want the crushed grain Jutta had to offer her. She wanted the warmth and comfort of her mother's bulk and generous bag of milk.

Suddenly resolved, Jutta searched out Tova and Bensi.

"Come on, we're going to get the animal healer," she said. "We'll be traveling most of the night, but we'll get a ride on the way home, perhaps."

"Oh, I think I can get used to staying up at night and sleeping when I can during the day. It's no problem at all."

They set out without telling anyone, naturally, to avoid time lost arguing and figuring out a way to sneak out of the house. Hrokr at the crossroads offered them a gruff greeting and a warning.

"The moon is full tonight. You'd better turn around and go home. You know what can happen here on a night like this."

"I must fetch the healer," Jutta said. "All the horses at Bardhol have been poisoned. I have no choice."

"Then go down the ravine, at least," Hrokr said. "It's the long way around the barrows, past Bjalfur's hut, but no one has been killed that way, as far as we know."

"We won't do the horses any good if we get killed," Tova said.

"That's true," Jutta said, feeling the foreboding of the barrows already upon her.

"You should turn back," Hrokr said. "All the horses in Mikillborg aren't worth dying for."

"No, because I don't care about them so much," Jutta said. "But the ones at Bardhol are killing me now if I just stand by and let them die without trying something."

"Yes, it keeps your mind off it," Hrokr said. "If only we had a way of stopping thinking sometimes, eh?"

Jutta and Tova took the dark path down the ravine toward Bjalfur's house. Somehow inconsequential talk sputtered out and died every time they tried it, so finally they fell into an agreeable silence.

"This is the place where Amma Sigla feared there were trolls," Jutta said with a nervous giggle, breaking the silence when they came to the place where the road hugged the side of a steep scarp, with the ravine falling away like a pit of darkness on the other side. Far below an unseen stream chattered away to itself in the dark.

"She's rather silly sometimes," Tova said, "but I like her very well. And Loki is such an affectionate and elegant kettir—fiery orange like the flames he was named for. It seems to me that kettir sometimes reveal the best and most hidden traits of their owners. Svartur is a protector, like Margret. Asa is a comfortor, and Loki lifts your spirits."

"Mishka is a joyous kettir, also."

"Like Bensi. He's such a friend to me, as if I'm the most wonderful person on earth. I can do no wrong as far as Bensi knows. If I can be such a friend to someone, then I will truly have lived well indeed."

"But what can you say for poor Rugla?" Jutta asked after a small pause, and they both burst out laughing. Poor Rugla was never called anything else.

"I think she's got a little too much of Amma Ingi in her," Tova said with a sigh and a giggle. "They both have far too many accidents."

"But you never see them complaining about it," Jutta said. "Ingi just picks up her mess as cheerfully as can be, and Rugla takes a bath to get rid of whatever she's fallen into or washes her poor paws, bruised from being stepped on, and in a moment she's back again."

"I think that's it. She never gives up. How many times has she fallen down the chimney hole?"

Jutta laughed. "Four times since I've been here. It's a regular thing with her. When the smoke doesn't draw out of the house properly, somebody looks up there and says, 'Is Rugla blocking the chimney again?' "

Their laughter sent Bensi capering playfully from one side of the road to the other, showing off his skills as a mighty hunter and pouncer and sharpener of claws. Ofsi struggled indignantly to get out, but Jutta kept him tightly cinched so an owl wouldn't make a meal of him.

"Hush, you little fiend; do you want to get eaten?" she reprimanded him, and he retorted indignantly with a piercing "MEW!" and a fierce ripping of claws.

"Whatever can you say of Ofsi that's pleasant?" she inquired with a rueful grimace. "If he's the best part of me, then I think I'm rather a horrible little creature."

"I think Ofsi is a little young and impulsive to judge," Tova said, "and maybe you are, too."

"Oh?" Jutta said, a little nettled at being reminded that Tova was older, more experienced, and smarter than she was, however gently it was suggested.

"Of course. You're young, and that entitles you to some mistakes."

"I haven't made too many mistakes," Jutta said. "Other people have, such as my mother for sending me here instead of someplace more suited to my tastes and background, but at least we got to become friends, and I did get Ofsi. I don't really believe I've made too many mistakes. Not even sneaking out and going to the barrow mounds or becoming friends with Frida when my grandmothers were so certain it wasn't wise. I'm probably fairly wise for my years, I think."

"Shh! What was that? Did you hear something?" Tova hissed, grabbing her arm and stopping her to listen.

They stood and strained their ears against the silence.

"No, I don't think—" Jutta began, but Tova raised her hand.

Something rustled in the scrubby brush among the rocks overhead—only the wind, maybe. Then Bensi arched his back and hooked his bristling tail, pointing downward in a definite warning of danger as he turned his head slowly from side to side, sniffing audibly. From his backpack, Ofsi raised a chilling wail.

"Run!" Jutta cried, and Tova needed no second warning. Calling to Bensi, she started down the road, and Bensi loped after her, taking the lead in a blinding rush of speed.

CHAPTER 16

They ran amid a growing babel of shouts, calls, and chanting, accompanied by the drumming of horses' hooves and the cracking of whips. A wave of cold wind raised the gooseflesh on Jutta's arms and made her scalp crawl with an eerie sensation of fear and repugnance.

"It's the wild hunt!" Tova cried, reaching back to pull Jutta along with her as she abandoned the roadway. They dived into the dark cover of an overhanging thicket just as the riders appeared, a dark clot swirling against the moonlit white of the road. Instead of coming along the road, however, they turned and plunged again into the dark tangle of brush and thicket and outcroppings of stone, heading northward in the direction of the barrows. In a moment the sounds of snapping whips and ghostly calls had diminished into silence.

"What was that?" Jutta gasped, her heart still pounding in her throat.

"The wild hunt," Tova said. "My grandmother told me about it. Ghostly riders under some sort of curse, doomed to ride the fells forever, hunting the prey that cannot be caught. If they ever try to dismount, they will instantly turn to dust and crumble away."

"I think I'd rather crumble away than endlessly ride and hunt," Jutta said. "And they were heading right for the barrows."

"Come on, let's put some distance between them and us," Tova said. "They could come back this way, and I don't want to get caught up with them. They capture innocent mortals and compel them to join the hunt, forever doomed."

238

"We'll be all right once we're away from these barrows," Jutta said. "Why does everything evil have to dwell right on our doorstep? The barrows are a cursed and blighted place. I wish we'd never decided to look for that cup."

"We were supposed to meet Einarr and Petrus and Simon tonight," Tova said. "I hope they don't find it and decide to split it two ways instead of four."

"Four? I thought we would be together on one wish from it. I didn't know you wanted to go your own way."

"Maybe I don't even want anything at all from that cup. The whole matter is beginning to taste like sour milk in my mouth."

Jutta wished she had the honesty to make the same confession, but she tightened her lips and said nothing.

"In fact, I'm beginning to regret this journey tonight," Tova continued. "It's a wild and restless night, with all manner of unseen things stirring. Can't you feel them in that chilly wind and hear bits of voices snatched away, like running water?"

"It is running water," Jutta said. "There's a stream in the bottom of the gill."

She could not deny her uneasiness, however. The errant wind seemed to carry snatches of voices to her ears and a sound almost like the baying of hounds, only there was something more dreadful and beastly about it than the clear voices of hounds. She felt the urge to run and run until that elusive sound no longer pursued her.

Worse yet, Jutta realized she had lost her bearings and had no idea how far they were along the road to Mikillborg. It seemed they had been walking forever, and none of the landmarks were familiar to her. But it was a straight road, with only a few joinings and no major crossroads after the barrows, so if they kept going, they should get to the first houses in Mikillborg.

A sudden shift in the wind, however, carried the chilling sounds of the wild hunt straight down the ravine, as if the riders were coming toward them. Bensi bristled up his fur and scuttled away as fast as he could go, looking back over his shoulder to offer some encouraging yowls.

"Run!" Tova exclaimed. "They're coming straight down on us! We can't hide! They'll see us even in the dark!"

"There's a light!" Jutta pointed suddenly. "I think it must be Bjalfur's hut! I thought we should have passed it by now, but there it is!"

In a moment they found the tidy little path leading to the jumble surrounding Bjalfur's hut. Stumbling through bones, hides, and heaps of rocks and wood, they at last pounced upon his raggle-taggle door, heaved it open with scarcely a knock to announce themselves, and tumbled inside breathlessly, slapping shut the door and tying it closed.

"Halloa!" they said, beginning to look around. A great fire burned on the hearth, which had shone out through the half-open door as a beacon to them. Bjalfur's table was cluttered with the remains of several mealtimes as well as snares and traps and tools, bits of string, bundles of dried plants, odd-shaped rocks, and scraps of bone. There were other things, unidentifiable in the leaping light of the fire, which Jutta did not care to inspect too closely lest she feel obliged to shriek in horror. One of them certainly looked like a dead rat, flattened somewhat, with what fur was still on it clinging in ragged tufts. After a glimpse of dried paws folded up under its long teeth, she'd had enough and backed away from the table.

"Well, he's not here," Tova said. "Maybe he went for the animal healer, after all. Let's sit down and wait."

"Do you think maybe we shouldn't go on?" Jutta asked reluctantly. "It seemed like a noble thing to do at the time, but Mikillborg is a long way. I wish I were at home with my grandmothers instead of stuck here with Bjalfur's old bones and things."

"Let's sit down and rest a bit and make up our minds," Tova said, starting to turn Bjalfur's chair around from facing the fire. Then she uttered a muffled shriek. "It's him! He's not gone!" she squeaked, pointing into the chair. Hidden by the high back of the seat, Bjalfur sat there stiffly with his eye open, not moving.

Jutta peered at him a moment in horror. "I think he's dead!" she whispered. "Well, we can't stay here."

"We don't want to go outside very much either, though, do we?" Tova said. "If he's dead, there's no harm in him. Unless he's going to turn into a draug and walk the face of the land, getting revenge on those who injured him while he was alive. Or maybe he's got a big pot of gold hidden someplace that he's got to protect."

Jutta giggled nervously. "I don't think he's got a big pot of gold somewhere. Why would he live like this if he did? Wouldn't he at least have some new clothes?"

"You never know," Tova said. "Maybe he enjoys looking poor so nobody will try to rob him."

Bensi tiptoed around Bjalfur's hut warily, stretching out his neck to sniff at things with a repulsed sniff and a disdainful shake of his paw.

Jutta ventured a closer look at old Bjalfur, who was sitting there bolt upright with his one-eyed glower, looking as if he were as alive as anything. In one hand he clutched an amulet attached to a blackened and greasy string. In the other he held out a dazzling crystal in the palm of his hand, a beautiful dark red stone the size of an egg, catching fire in its murky depths from the dancing blaze on the hearth. Jutta stared at the crystal, wondering what it was worth. The longer she stared, the more fascinated she became with it, imagining shapes of animals and people moving in its flickering depths. Quite helpless, she knelt down to get nearer to it, drawn by the scenes she saw inside it and quite oblivious to Tova nattering about clearing off a space on the table and looking for something to eat.

Jutta felt as if she were looking down a long dark tunnel into a world of light. She saw a tall man with golden hair and a blue cloak carrying a tall staff with a dragon's head on it, snorting smoke. He was surrounded by horses, Jutta realized, and he turned around to look at her in surprise.

"Get out of here!" he commanded with a gesture of one arm. *"Fara af stad!"* Jutta felt herself rebuffed, tumbling backward, rushing back to the hut.

"Jutta! Jutta! What are you doing?" Tova's voice tore at her suddenly, her hands snatching Jutta back roughly from the tantalizing world inside the crystal.

Jutta blinked and shook her head, almost startled to find herself back in Bjalfur's smelly old hut, sprawling at the feet of his smelly old carcass propped up in his chair. Looking up at him in sudden alarm, Jutta scuttled away from him and dropped herself into a rickety chair. Ofsi promptly climbed into her lap to scream into her face with his hungriest, most demanding voice.

"Tova!" she gasped, not knowing how to explain her experience. Then she said "Bjalfur!" and eyed him accusingly a moment, careful not to let her eyes rest on the red stone in his hand.

"You were entranced," Tova said, reaching out to take the stone. "I wonder what this is worth."

"No! Don't touch it!" Jutta shrilled. She pulled Ofsi off her shoulder and deposited him on the floor. "It's dangerous. You saw what it did to me."

Tova drew back, making signs in the air, runes for protection. "Well, it seems our ragged old friend had some secrets," she said. "Or has, in case he isn't dead."

"What do you mean? Of course he's dead. Dead and stiff. Does he look like he's alive to you?"

"It's hard to tell," Tova said. "In the old days wizards and sorcerers could leave their bodies behind and go adventuring in different forms on different strands of life. They did not believe that everything was confined to this one level of being. They could travel to places the rest of us can scarcely imagine. But it's a lost art now. Wizards have fallen into disfavor with most people."

"Wizards? Do you think old Bjalfur was a wizard?"

Tova pursed up her lips and looked at Bjalfur consideringly. "He's older than anyone I've ever seen, so I'd say there's a pretty good chance he at least lived during the great days of wizardry and magic. What I'd give to have lived then, when powers were everywhere just for the harnessing and taking. The powers are still here, but we have no one that knows how to manipulate them. People are such cowards now, content to sit in their little houses and grow fat and rich."

"Where do you suppose Bjalfur has gone?" Jutta asked, her voice quavering. "I thought I saw someone just then, when I was looking into the stone. A younger man, and he was with a bunch of horses."

"I almost wish we hadn't stopped here," Tova said, rubbing her arms with a sudden shiver. "This is almost as bad as walking on the road in the moonlight. But I don't want to go out there again. Let's just stay here until morning. It won't be much longer, with the sun coming up as early as it does now."

Jutta sighed and nodded. "Just so I'm a good distance away from him. I don't like the idea of him being dead, but I really hate the idea that he's not dead. He might be out there wandering around, like a draug."

"A draug always carries its dead and rotting carcass around with it, forever trapped by its own decaying flesh," Tova said, not without a certain degree of relish. "A fylgja walker, on the other hand, can take whatever form it likes. Usually they choose an animal form."

"Stop it," Jutta said. She addressed Ofsi, also, who was determinedly climbing up her pantaloons. "I wish your grandmother hadn't been so free with her terrible stories. I've got to find this little beast something to eat before he tears my eyes out. Is there anything at all edible in this wretched house?"

"There's a loaf of bread and some pretty fair milk," Tova said. "And a dead rat, but it's too dried up for Ofsi's little teeth."

Even as she spoke, Ofsi leapt onto the table and discovered the rat. With a savage little yell he grabbed it and dived off the table, heading for the cover of the woodpile to devour his prize.

"Oh, no! He can't have that! Get him!" Jutta dived after Ofsi, catching him by his tail just as he was nearly gone. That made him even more furious. Mouthing the rat, he screamed at her like a banshee in the middle of eating its lunch. He didn't stop his yammering until Jutta had forcibly separated him from the rat and put it up on a high beam where he couldn't reach it. He continued yelling for it and tried to climb up Jutta's leg, as if she were a convenient tree. The only thing that distracted him was some bread crumbled up with a little milk on it.

"You're lucky Bensi doesn't act like this," Jutta grumbled, watching Ofsi gobbling his food with single-minded intensity. If anyone came near him, he gobbled faster and growled at the same time. "I don't even know why I put up with this little beast. I never even liked cats before."

"One day you'll be rewarded," Tova said, stroking Bensi's elegant head. He beamed up into her face, smiling his kettir smile and slowly closing his eyes in adoration. "Now, do sit down and eat some of that bread. It's really quite a nice loaf. Do you suppose old Bjalfur baked it himself? I thought I saw an oven in the yard."

Jutta stole another glance at Bjalfur, who was still staring with his one eye into nothingness.

"I wish his eye wasn't open," Jutta said. "Here, I know. We'll put something over him. There's his cloak. Let's just cover him up so we don't have to look at him."

They draped the cloak over his head and felt considerably more comfortable about examining their host's quarters.

"This is truly a loathsome place," Tova said. "You can tell no woman ever sets foot across that threshold."

"Let alone a fussy old thing like Amma Dora. It puts her out of sorts when she finds the knives crooked. She even straightens up the rocks in the pastures, I believe. What a job she'd have straightening up Bjalfur."

"If he isn't dead, that is. We can't really tell for certain unless he wakes up or starts smelling."

Jutta looked at Ofsi wolfing his food in the middle of the table, surrounded by Bjalfur's unappetizing clutter. One had just as well be eating in a barnyard, surrounded by sheep and their droppings. Some of the dried objects on the table, in fact, had that suspicious appearance.

"Well, I can't eat in the middle of such a mess," Jutta said.

"I'm going to clear off this table and give it a good scrubbing. I don't think we should leave just yet, anyway." She glanced toward the door, hearing more of the eerie calling and the moan of the wind around the eaves of the hut.

Tova cocked her head and listened, too. Both of Bensi's eyes opened, and his ears stood up more attentively. The membranes of his eyes cleared and his pupils darkened in alarm when the wind rattled at the door.

"Is that door securely shut?" Tova asked.

"As securely as possible," Jutta answered. "Ugh, what do you suppose this is?" She held up a small bundle of little bones and sticks and dried herbs. "I'm just going to dump everything in this old satchel. If he wants it, he'll know where to find it, or somebody can take it out and burn it. I declare, some of the things that men just won't throw away are enough to gag a maggot."

Jutta cleared off the table, picking up most of the objects gingerly and hastily dropping them into the satchel. Then she scrubbed the table as best she could—certainly not up to Amma Dora's standards, but she was satisfied enough with the results that she could sit down to it and have some of the bread and milk. By that time Ofsi was ready to curl up on her lap, and she was expected to hold still so she wouldn't disturb him.

"Listen to that wind," Tova said. "If Einarr and Petrus and Simon are out there in the barrows tonight, they're a lot more miserable than we are. Look, it's even beginning to snow."

A sifting swirl of white pellets puffed in through the cracks of the door.

"It serves them right," Jutta said. "I hope they really freeze to death. I hope those wild huntsmen scare them to pieces. I wish we were home. The door at Bardhol is a lot stouter than that one."

"At least if it's snowing, the full moon is covered up," Tova said. "Perhaps the wild hunt will disappear once the moon is gone."

"At least it's going to be too dark to dig in the barrow," Jutta said with a nasty and satisfied laugh. "Of course, it also makes it too dark for us to try getting home unless we want to carry a lantern and risk getting hopelessly confused."

"I fear we're stuck here until morning," Tova said with a sigh, glancing toward the towering heap that was Bjalfur.

Jutta sighed impatiently. "I wish I'd listened to my grandmothers. I'd be home with them now, trying to be of some assistance, instead of being uselessly stuck here with something that we aren't sure is dead or alive. If I'm going to sleep here, I'm going to have to clean it up. He's got so much junk piled on the sleeping shelf that he'd have to sleep on the floor. Where do you suppose his bed is?"

"Maybe this is the way he sleeps," Tova said. "In his chair, since there's no bed cleared off."

They looked around in vain for a cupboard bed or at least a space on the sleeping shelf. It looked more like the nest of a giant rat, surrounded by all the sticks and rags and shiny things that rats were wont to collect. So they commenced heaping up the stuff to clear a space to sleep near the fire, where it was warm.

When they were done and the dust had settled, they curled up with their cloaks for covers, thoroughly wearied and ready for sleep. Napping and sleeping were the favorite human activities of kettir. They purred and kneaded their paws and selected for their sleeping post the most uncomfortable and inconvenient spot for their human bedfellows. Once that point of maximum annoyance was chosen, they went instantly to sleep, either curled up like a boulder in one's bed or stretched out at full length so as to maximize human discomfort. Once asleep, they pretended they could not be awakened to be situated elsewhere. A half-asleep person who only wanted to be fully asleep did not wish to thrash around and sit up in bed to remove a limp, heavy weight from his legs or, in some cases, from around his throat. Ofsi preferred to sleep as close to Jutta's face as possible, curled up in the hollow of her neck and shoulder or draped around her head. In the winter, she thought, a warm fur headpiece would be pleasant as long as it didn't wake up and decide to jump in her face for no apparent reason except its own amusement.

It took awhile before the kettir settled down. First Ofsi decided to play with Bensi. His idea of playing was to wrap his front legs around Bensi's throat and bite him as hard as he could or to bite his legs or tail until Bensi was so annoyed that he tried to get away. Run and chase was Ofsi's favorite game, and he went after Bensi as a sheepdog would go nipping after a sheep.

"I don't know why Bensi doesn't just thrash the daylights out of him," Jutta said with a sigh after the fifth revolution around the hut.

"He knows Ofsi is young and means no harm," Tova said. "I think kettir are more civilized than people."

Jutta doubted that. Ofsi had climbed up Bjalfur's cloak and was perching atop his head, swishing his stumpy tail furiously back and forth and defying Bensi to come up after him. Kettir had no respect for anything. Bensi ignored Ofsi and sat down in the middle of the table to take a thorough bath, beginning with his hinder parts. Just when he was well into it, Ofsi launched himself off Bjalfur's head, aiming for the table, but owing to a miscalculation in trajectory caused by his inexperience at aerobatics, he landed on the edge of the table and fell off into a basket of dried cow manure used for banking the fire. The basket, of course, was upset, making a further mess, and the experience was so exhilarating for Ofsi that he had to race around the hut four more times, knocking things over on each revolution. Exhausted, he jumped on Jutta and curled up on her head, purring breathlessly. In a few moments he was asleep like a stone.

Relieved, Bensi continued his bathing in the middle of the table, illuminated by the little rush lamp. Suddenly he froze in midlick, with his pink tongue still protruding a bit, swiveling his big translucent ears around to listen.

Jutta heard it, too, and elbowed Tova sharply to wake her up. "Listen!" she hissed.

"I don't hear anything," Tova grumbled.

Then the door shook slightly, as if someone were testing it from the outside. After a long moment they heard something sniffing loudly in the crack. They froze, scarcely breathing, and

Bensi rose to his tiptoes, every hair standing on end, his tail swollen to three times its normal size.

Claws raked the door harshly, and something whined. Bensi hissed and spit explosively, staring at the door.

"It's a troll!" Jutta whispered, clutching Tova in terror.

"I thought all the trolls were cleared out of here long ago," Tova replied.

"Well, there's one left, and it's trying to get in here. I never thought I'd live to be killed and eaten by something! Like a chicken or a goose!"

"You aren't dead and cooked yet. Look, let's grab a couple of those walking staffs and at least try to defend ourselves."

They armed themselves with the staffs, quietly taking positions on opposite sides of the door. The next time the claws raked the door, a hideous black snout poked through the crack, sniffing hungrily. Without any ado, Tova whacked the snout as hard as she could. With a startled yelp, the snout vanished and something went yelping away into the darkness.

"Take that, you wretched troll!" Jutta shouted. "We really showed him a thing or two, didn't we, Tova? He won't be back in a good long while!"

"I gave him a pretty good whack," Tova said with a satisfied little smile. "I can't promise it will keep him away forever, though."

Something dropped down out of the rafters practically onto Jutta's head. She screamed piercingly and leapt away, almost simultaneously realizing it was only Ofsi dropping off an overhead beam to the next safest point he could think of. What was worse, he had Bjalfur's rat in his mouth, which Jutta had to take away from him quite forcibly.

After a long interval of listening to the silence, Bensi gradually subsided once more into normal kettir size and shape and sat down again and licked his snowy belly fur, feigning nonchalance. No one would remember how he had leapt around spitting and hissing and growling, ignominiously taking refuge under a basket, if now he assiduously pretended not to care.

For Jutta, the remaining fragment of the night was so small

as to be hardly memorable as far as sleeping went. It seemed only a few moments before it was nearly dawn and Tova was thumping on her brutally.

"Get your stick! Our troll friend is back again!"

This time there was enough dim morning light to get a look through the crack at their dread tormentor. Jutta threw down her stick in disgust.

"That's no troll. It's nothing but a sad old dog, wanting to get in. He's probably Bjalfur's."

The old hound hung his head apologetically and licked his droopy chops, wagging his ridiculous curling tail all the while. Jutta had never seen such an ugly dog. His curly, mottled coat was wiry and rough, as if he had been dead a year or two, and his legs were astonishingly long. His spine seemed to have a peculiar arch to it, and his head was a great lump of a thing, rendered even more ugly by dozens of scars and old rips that had healed in grotesque patterns. One of his eyes was missing entirely, no doubt extracted at the same time he had acquired a huge wound across that side of his wretched face. Grinning and puffing and showing his yellowed old fangs did nothing to enhance his appearance, either.

"Oh, horrors!" Tova shuddered. "He must be Bjalfur's. Nobody else would own such a horrible object."

"He wants in," Jutta said nervously.

"Then let him in. He lives here."

The old hound trotted in gladly when Jutta held open the door. One or more legs were limping, she noticed, and a few patches of fur were falling out for unknown reasons.

"Never in all my days have I seen such a disgusting creature," Jutta said, shaking her head.

Bensi and Ofsi swelled up, rising to their toes when the hound took a disinterested sniff in the direction of the table where the cats were roosting. Ofsi flattened his ears and sounded a shrill siren call, his eyes bulging dangerously, and Bensi offered a virulent hiss.

The hound went at once to Bjalfur's rigid form and sniffed around under the cloak as if he were puzzled indeed at his owner's peculiar behavior. After a few snorts and sneezes, he shook himself with a leathery clapping sound from his flapping ears and rubbery chops and general loose skin, as if someone were vigorously shaking an old saddle. Then he curled up at Bjalfur's feet with a long gusty sigh.

"He stinks," Tova said, pinching her nose.

"Which one?" Jutta asked, and Tova pointed to the dog.

"It's time we were going," Tova said. "We'll be home in time to do the milking. I dread even thinking about what we will find when we get there. I expect all six of those horses are going to be dead, or nearly so."

Jutta sighed, nodding her head, bitterly regretting her impulsive decision to go charging off heroically in the night to fetch the healer. It had seemed like such a noble and splendid, self-sacrificing thing to do at the time, but now, in the gathering light of day, she realized it had been nothing but the desire to stop feeling so helpless in the face of the inevitable death of the mares.

"What should we do about Bjalfur?" Jutta asked as they were going out the door. "We can't just leave him here if he's truly dead. Or do you think he needs some kind of help to get out of this state he's gotten into? Maybe he's just sort of sputtered out for a little while, like a candle, but somebody can restart him again if they know how. Do you think he needs a healing physician?"

The old hound flopped his disreputable tail on the floor and blinked his saggy red-rimmed eye at them as they took one last look at the heap that was Bjalfur.

"I don't know," Tova said. "We'll come back and check on him after we see to your grandmothers. He's a little strange, but I think I like him."

They were well down the path into the ravine when Jutta suddenly clapped her hand to her side. "Wait, I left my belt pouch on the table."

"Run back and get it," Tova said. "I'll wait here."

Jutta ran lightly back to the hut and snatched open the door. Her eyes immediately rested on the interesting scene of Bjalfur fighting his way out from under his own cloak, muttering curses all the while. Jutta saw no trace of the old ratty hound.

"Well! Someone's made a fine mess of my house!" Bjalfur declared the moment he was clear enough to look around, his one eye glaring with astonishment.

"Tova and I spent the night here," Jutta said. "We were on our way to Mikillborg to fetch the animal healer and we were hearing funny sounds from the barrows, so we stayed here. You weren't much company. Do you often go off like that? You were just sitting there like a rock, staring away into nothing. We thought you were dead."

Bjalfur snorted. "Dead? I suppose one of these days I'll come back to myself and find that some well-meaning fool has buried me or burned me to ashes. In the old days people had more respect for other folks."

"I'm sorry. I guess it was wrong to come into your house when you weren't here. But you sort of were, and if you were dead, we didn't think you'd mind."

"You didn't have to clean it up. It's going to take me a week to get everything back where I can find it. Well, no harm done. I'm glad to be of service, even though I wasn't the most genial of hosts, I'm sure."

"No, you didn't say much. Your old dog was far better company. Where is he? Does he have a name?" Jutta looked around, but the hound was not in the hut.

"He's a wretched old thing which people like to kick around," Bjalfur said. "He's better left out of the way."

"I'd best be going," Jutta said, edging away. "We're most grateful for your shelter last night. There really was something stirring in the barrows. The wild hunt, we thought at the time, but I suppose that sounds foolish now, in broad daylight."

"So it may seem," Bjalfur said, "to people who don't listen to their own inner voices. If you thought last night it was the wild hunt, then it might be more foolish to discount it today merely because the sun is shining and you're feeling much braver now. Run home and help your grandmothers, child. I expect they're wondering where on earth you've gotten to."

Jutta sighed. "I know they'll need my help. I expect I'll have to get some thralls from Frida to help with those horses."

Bjalfur hoisted one eyebrow dubiously. "And why would you want to do that? Isn't my help enough?"

Jutta made no reply to that, recalling to herself that he had done exactly nothing to help with the sick mares. "I must be going," she said. "I'm sure Amma Thruda is wondering where I am."

"Give my regards to Dora," Bjalfur said, attempting a courtly bow. He looked more like a scarecrow taking a bow by falling off its pole.

Jutta made her escape, shuddering in spite of herself. He tried to be nice, but he really was too awful to think about for very long. And imagine, she had been forced to spend the night in his hut, with him gone off his head in some peculiar vegetative state. It was a wonder nobody had chained him up as a madman.

The nearer Jutta got to Bardhol, the heavier her heart settled, near the pit of her stomach. All was quiet, except for the crowing of roosters and the soft moaning of the cows, staring at them over the wall and knowing it was milking time. Then a row of kettir that had hunkered on the wall near the house leapt down at the sight of Jutta and Tova, commencing an excited yowling and trilling chorus of welcome.

The door of the house opened, and Thruda came out to meet them.

"Where have you been? We've been worried half to death!"

"I'm sorry, Amma Thruda," Jutta said. "I had the bright idea to go to Mikillborg for the animal healer, but we didn't get any farther than Bjalfur's."

"And then we were too frightened by noises in the barrows to come back," Tova said. "We should have known better, but it felt good to try to do something for the horses, even though it was something rather stupid."

"I'm just glad nothing happened to you," Thruda said, her

gentle face puckered up with worry and relief. "The barrow field is no place to be on a moonlit night, especially for young girls."

Needing to change the subject before Amma Thruda launched into a lengthy lecture about the dangers of the barrows, Jutta cleared her thoat softly and asked, "And how about the mares? Did any of them make it through the night?"

"Follow me. You'll see."

CHAPTER 17

Only then did Jutta miss the frantic calling of Faelinn for her mother. Worry lent speed to her stride as she followed Thruda to the paddock. In wonderment she beheld all six mares grazing peacefully in the lush pasturage. For a moment she thought it was a vision, too perfect to be real. The grass glowed with an incredible green light, and the glossy hides of the mares radiated health and power as they grazed ravenously, swinging their long plumy tails like black curtains blowing on the breeze. Little Faelinn bounded and bucked exuberantly, her tiny hooves pattering on the soft turf. She halted and looked back at the people, striking a handsome pose with her tail aloft, the light setting her reddish mane and fuzzy tail afire.

"It was the most astonishing thing I have ever seen," Amma Thruda was saying. "One moment they were dying, and the next it was as if they were different horses. They were getting to their feet and shaking themselves, as you know horses do when they are feeling fine. I knew they were going to survive when Bjorgun began nosing around for something to eat in the straw. I could scarcely believe my eyes, I tell you. I fully expected Elska and Birki and Bjartur to die last night, and Eldfjall was just tottering on her legs, and Elding was up and down a hundred times, pacing back and forth in terrible pain. Elderly horses like these can get the bellyache and die in a very short time, and that's what I expected to happen. Not this. Look at them. The very picture of health. It was almost as if— almost as if a spell were lifted off of them."

"Do you suppose it was?" Tova asked in a hushed voice.

"I haven't seen much spell casting for many years," Thruda

said, frowning judiciously. "People have forgotten how to do it. I suppose there may be a few left who can, but who would want to put a spell on our poor old horses? They've done nothing to annoy anyone, and I don't think we have, either."

Bardhol was filled with quiet rejoicing that day. Chores were done with good cheer and lighthearted bantering. The noonday repast was far more extravagant than the parsimonious meal Sigla usually permitted. Ingi in particular glowed with a happy radiance, which, however delightful to behold, seemed to interfere even more with her unclear judgment, so she put the eggs in the milk house and brought the cream to the kitchen and nearly scalded Rugla when she poured out boiling water into the kettir pan instead of the warm milk she had intended.

"I'm just a little twittery today." She laughed gaily when Sigla pointed out to her with great dismay that she was wearing her skirt wrong side out. "I still can't believe not one of our mares died last night. I'm walking on clouds; I feel like singing and dancing." She flapped one hand and knocked over Dora's sewing basket, strewing scraps and balls of thread. Ofsi rushed to the attack, wreaking as much havoc as possible before Jutta snatched him up, with a ball of thread in his mouth, growling at her in defiance.

Jutta and the others looked at Ingi in consternation at the mention of singing and dancing. Ingi's singing was totally tuneless and off-key, and without a trace of abashment Ingi would bellow her songs out as if she were trying to hail down a boat in Mikillborg Firth. For a person who could scarcely cross a room without breaking the furniture, dancing was bound to be a highly destructive and dangerous occupation, especially for the spectators.

"Don't dance, my dear," Margret said. "Last time you tried it, you sprained your ankle."

"It was that little leap I attempted," Ingi said. "If I'd had a partner to catch me, I'd have been fine."

"You might have fallen on him and killed him," Sigla said. "Then we'd be having to pay wergild to his family. I fear you're just not very light on your feet, Ingi."

"Not light on my feet, you say? I beg to differ!" Ingi got up indignantly to demonstrate, but Margret at once commanded her, "Sit down, Ingi, and attend to more important affairs than whether you can dance or not. I don't wish to see any more furniture broken, nor ankles, either."

"There, now, you're getting overexcited," Amma Dora said soothingly. "You mustn't get angry or it will be bad for your heart."

"Don't treat me like a child," Margret snapped. "I'll shout at Ingi if I want to."

At dusk, when the full moon was rising in all its flaming glory over the barrows, Jutta slipped away by herself for a look at it, thinking searing thoughts of Petrus and Einarr down there digging away like moles, looking for her ancestor's cup. Restlessly she paced the length of the wall, passing the place where Margret had been overcome by weakness and pain. She could of course see nothing below her in the barrows. The mist was rising, obscuring everything in clouds tinged with the sinister red tint of the fading sunset. She remembered the four Myrkriddir swirling overhead during that night in the pit in the barrows. Now that the horses were healed, would they ride out again tonight?

She found Dora at the horse paddock, combing Elska's long mane until it hung like silk and crooning softly for only the mare to hear. Elska's ears waggled, and she wobbled her lips in pleasure at Dora's company.

Dora turned, her hair white as wool in the dimness, streaming luxuriantly down to her waist. She always brushed it out at night and rebraided it in a long tail for sleeping.

"Good evening," she said pleasantly. "It's certainly lovely out, isn't it?"

"I wish I had hair like yours," Jutta said. "It looks like skeins of fine thread. Mine looks more like the mane of a wild horse when it's not braided."

"You should have seen it years ago, when I was young. It was the color of ripe wheat, a reddish gold that young suitors wrote scalds about. Now nobody wants to write scalds about a wrinkled old woman's white hair." She laughed gaily and let out a long sigh. "It's a relief, to tell you the truth. No one expects me to be beautiful anymore."

"I believe Bjalfur thinks you're beautiful," Jutta said.

"Him! Well, I'd wear a sack over my head if I thought that he enjoyed looking at me," Dora said.

"Well, he does. He's rather strange, isn't he?"

"Strange as a two-headed calf with frog feet."

"And he did nothing to heal the mares."

"Oh? What did you expect?" Her tone was suddenly guarded, and she darted Jutta a suspicious glance.

"Maybe I'm wrong about that, though," Jutta said. "When we went to his hut last night, we found him sitting like a frozen block in his chair, his eye wide open and staring. It was very peculiar behavior. He didn't talk or seem to hear, but there he was, stiff as a fence post. Then, just as we were leaving, he seemed to wake up, perfectly normal. Do you think he's had some sort of collapse or illness?"

"No, I don't. That's just the way Bjalfur is. Weird."

"And he's got the most horrible old dog you've ever seen. A huge bristly creature covered with scars."

"Yes, I've seen it, and I've threatened to kill it if he allows it to keep following me about. Every time I turn around, I see that revolting hound. I wonder why he doesn't put it out of its misery."

"It doesn't seem miserable."

"Anything that ugly is bound to be miserable." Then, almost as an afterthought, she added, "I wouldn't talk around about finding Bjalfur frozen like that. People might not understand, and he might be thought poorly of if such a thing got spread around and exaggerated, as people will."

"Perhaps you don't think so badly of Bjalfur, after all," Jutta suggested.

"No, indeed I don't," Dora said. "It's just that the notion of being married to him is a bit unsettling. I couldn't bear the thought of leaving Bardhol and my sisters. Does he have a very nice place to live?"

"Oh—ah—it has possibilities." For a cow shed, maybe, but Dora would have to find that out for herself. "Definitely it could use a woman's touch," she added quickly. "A man by himself is rather a pitiful object, if the truth must be known."

"Oh! I can well imagine! And he's lived there for years. No doubt there's a great deal of useless clutter to be thrown away—including that dog. I couldn't abide the sight of it, and I suppose he lets it into the house to smell everything up. Dogs do have numerous ways of producing stenches."

"I'm afraid so," Jutta said.

"Men's dirty boots and their dogs definitely contribute to the shortening of women's lives," Dora said. "Well, I'm for going in. It's getting dark and chilly."

"Are the mares ridable, do you think?" Jutta asked, feeling rather mean about her indefatigable suspicions after such a nice chat with Amma Dora.

"Oh, I wouldn't think so," Dora said. "They've gone through a terrible ordeal. I'd think they ought to have their rest."

It was too good an opportunity to miss, although Tova looked yearningly toward her bed when Jutta suggested it.

"Are you sure we have to?" she asked with a yawn.

"If we don't, Einarr and Petrus will find that cup and we'll be cut out of the deal," Jutta said. "It will be perfect, with no Myrkriddir to worry about."

"What about the wild hunt, though?" Tova asked uneasily. "They could be out again, looking for some poor benighted traveler to snatch up into their midst."

"Forget them. Maybe they're gone now. Probably they were just passing through last night. Nobody has ever seen them around here before. Come on. Let's get ready, and when everyone's asleep, we'll slip out."

On the third night of the full moon it seemed even rounder and brighter than before. Walking from Bardhol into the barrows at early morning or dusk would have been no different. They heard no mysterious winds or noises; the evening was perfectly calm.

At the barrow there was no sign of digging or anyone there. "Halloa!" Jutta called down, and they started down into the excavation.

Someone came scratching out from the portal of the barrow, like a badger backing out of a hole.

"Oh, there you are," Simon said, shaking the sand and earth out of his hair. "We wondered where you were last night. We got quite a lot of digging done, but it was a strange night, with a lot of wind and noises. And you might have guessed—another woman has been killed. A wandering woman called Gunna."

"With a gray cloak?" Jutta's heart leapt up into her throat as she remembered the girl, who had not been much older than she but worlds more ancient in woe and trouble. "I think I met her. She was one of Frida's charity cases."

"She hadn't a cloak about her. All of her clothes were in shreds, and she was scratched and bruised, like Betla."

"I'd say it was the wild hunt that hounded her to death," Tova said. "I know the hunt was out last night. We had a narrow brush with it, Jutta and I."

"Wild hunt? The ghosts are to blame again?" Simon asked. "This looked to me like the work of mortal hands. Ghosts' horses don't leave prints in the ground, do they? In the Scipling realm we'd be looking for the people who did this, not blaming it on magic and ghosts."

"Well, you Sciplings know what a murderous and barbaric race you are, so you have no need to blame your heinous crimes on ghosts," Tova said.

In spite of all their brave talk, Jutta could feel her heart fluttering anxiously, thinking how near she and Tova had been to being victims of the wild hunt—or whoever else had been in the barrows that night. She looked into Simon's earnest and dirty face, trying to imagine him as a killer, but her imagination could not stretch that far.

"You've gone a great ways into the barrow," Jutta said, trying to put Gunna and the wild hunt out of her thoughts. "Have you found anything yet?"

"Not yet, but it's looking very promising," Simon said, lowering his voice and glancing around. Nothing could conceal the spark of excitement in his eyes. "Einarr doesn't think it's been broken into before. This could be it. If it were the barrow of someone important, they would've taken care to bury it and hide it as much as possible, we think."

"We brought our shovels," Tova said stoutly, holding up hers to show. "We shall take our turn digging."

"The earth is as hard as ground that has never been disturbed," Simon said, shaking his head and holding up his blistered hands. "It goes very slowly, and it's very hard. You don't have to dig; we'll do it."

"And claim the treasure for yourselves?" Jutta retorted. "I don't intend to be cut out of this game, my friend. We shall do our share of the digging."

"You don't need to dig to claim a share," Simon said. "No one intends to cheat you out of what is rightfully yours as the nearest representative of the Hesturkonur clan. You can trust us."

"Did you see any Myrkriddir last night?" Juta asked.

"Not a one. But there was something else we didn't much like the sound of. We were hidden here below, so we were safe, but it sounded like a large group of horsemen riding around and searching for something. I have a strong feeling that they were searching for this barrow."

"It was the wild hunt," Tova said, "draugar doomed to ride the face of the earth forever in payment for their crimes or for cursings put upon them by evil wizards. If they touch the earth, they turn to dust. Luckily they didn't find you, or you'd be with them even now, watching your rotting flesh turning into dried leather, wishing you could be freed from the terrible curse of endless riding and hunting for that which you know not."

"We're well hidden in the tunnel of the barrow," Simon said a little nervously. "Nobody can see us. Do you think the wild hunt will return tonight?"

"It seems quiet now," Tova said, glancing around at the barrows, their tops silvered in the moonlight. "Perhaps they were just passing through, or perhaps they're looking for someone who has done something grievous to offend someone who is dead. The dead have ways of getting revenge even from beyond the grave."

"Maybe Sigmund doesn't want that cup dug up," Jutta said. "Maybe he's the one sending the wild hunt to protect his barrow. If that cup had been a good thing, the clan would not have buried it with him. I never thought before that it might have a curse on it, but perhaps digging it up again will be the worst possible thing for the world. Maybe it deserves to stay buried forever, with Sigmund's bones."

"I think it's too late to change our minds now," Simon said. "My father in particular is determined to escape from your realm somehow, and this is the only way he knows. If it proves to cause too much evil, all we have to do is return it to the barrow and wall it up again."

"It's easier to dig up an evil thing than it is ever to get rid of it again," Tova said. "It's not too late to leave that cup where it lies—if indeed we've found the right place."

"We've gone so far and it looks so promising that we can't turn back now," Simon said. "All night long we dug like moles, certain the next shovelful was going to break through. Nothing can stop Einarr now, nor my father."

Einarr and Leckny and Petrus barely acknowledged the arrival of Jutta and Tova except with a grunt or two, and then they went back to their determined digging. Einarr dug away at the standing wall, and Petrus shoveled it backward into the tunnel, where Leckny pushed it farther out of the way. Outside, Simon and Jutta and Tova spread the earth around to conceal the digging site. When Einarr needed a rest, Simon took his place, and so they rotated the hardest digging among them. Jutta and Tova were not allowed to take the foremost position, assured that the earth was far too hard and that it was better to let the stronger arms of the men batter away at it. Reluctantly Jutta and Tova agreed to this arrangement, contenting themselves with shoveling out the loosened dirt so more could replace it.

It was far into the darker part of the night when Simon's shovel suddenly struck a last blow that crumbled the wall into the barrow.

"Back! Back!" Einarr exclaimed, covering his nose and

mouth. "There's poison air in a sealed barrow! Get back until it clears!"

They all backed out of the tunnel and sat in the moonlight, waiting for the poison air to clear, if there was any, and desperately hoping there was, since that would mean that the barrow had not been opened since the burial.

"Whatever we find in there, we've agreed to share equally," Einarr said. "I'm known as a fair chieftain, and I wouldn't be allowed to stay where I am if I weren't. If that cup has all the power that the legends say, then there's enough for all of us to get our fondest wishes."

"Including a war for you?" Jutta asked.

"If a war comes to me, I shall be ready," Einarr said, raising his bristly chin proudly.

When they could wait no longer and the first streaks of dawn were sponging out the darkness in the east, they crept down the tunnel into the barrow slowly and warily, sniffing the air for poison gases. Einarr, as chieftain and defender of Mikillborg, insisted on going first, as he was of warrior predisposition and descent. Jutta suspected that he had never before had the opportunity of risking his life for anything and was enjoying the experience of realizing he could be dead in a few moments. Petrus allowed him this privilege, since he had plenty of experience risking his life and realized that it could be a losing proposition and that certain types of one-time losses were more serious than some people thought.

"I want to be the first to look," Jutta protested furiously, but no one would hear of it.

"One sniff and you could be dead," Einarr said, shaking his head. "And how would I explain that to your grandmothers? Especially to Margret. She'd kill me on the spot with one look from that eye of hers. I'd rather be dead myself from the gases than carry your lifeless little carcass back to Bardhol."

"Then let me," Tova said. "I've got no family and few friends that value me. My life will be a laboring life until I'm too old to work anymore, and there's no one who will take me in beside their fire. I shall die alone beside the road one day, so it matters little now what I do with my life."

"Tova! That's not true," Jutta sputtered indignantly. "I love you more than my own spoiled and silly sisters. You will stay with me forever, and we'll be old crones together, knitting stockings where our old bones find some warmth. I'm the smallest; I can wedge into that hole and take a look around and let the rest of you know what we've found."

"No indeed," Petrus said. "I'll do it. If the cup is not there, then my purpose here is for naught, anyway."

"But if it is, then you'll have wasted your opportunity to get home to your wife and daughters," Einarr said.

"Then you shall send Simon back to take care of his mother and sisters," Petrus said.

"I'll go," Leckny said.

"And break your mother's heart?" Einarr bawled. "She'd have my hide nailed to the side of the house."

"Then let me," Simon said.

"I won't hear of it," Petrus retorted. "No children are going to die here. Leave that business to us old dogs who are just going to be in the way someday anyhow."

"I insist," Einarr said. "As chieftain of Mikillborg, it is my duty, and I order the rest of you to stay well behind me. It makes no difference who sees it first. We are all friends here, are we not?"

So it was that they were delayed by enlarging the hole into the barrow enough so that Einarr could finally fit through. First he put a lantern into the dark interior and looked around. Pressing close behind, the others heard him gasp and begin to chuckle.

"It hasn't been touched!" he exclaimed. "It's perfect, just the way the Hesturkonur left it six hundred years ago, after Sigmund and his five chief retainers were killed by Arni the Coward at Meidslihof!"

Frantically they enlarged the hole so Einarr could crawl through, followed by the others.

It was a large room inside the mound, with a tall-backed seat in the center, drawn up to a table. Instead of lying on biers, the dead in this mound were seated around the table as if they were in the act of merrily feasting and singing. There was no dust, and the sealed atmosphere of the tomb had preserved everything to an amazing extent. The loyal retainers who had perished in battle with Sigmund were propped up, still clad in their burial clothes of fine colors, draped with gold chains and ornaments. Their faces and withered hands had blackened to the color of ancient dried leather, but their withered fingers still bore rings of brilliant gold and flashing jewels.

All eyes turned to the figure seated at the head of the table. He wore the simple russet cloak and coarse gray gown of a common warrior. His armor lay on the ground beside him, and his helmet was hung over his head on the back of the chair, a helmet embossed with gold and silver and formed to depict a snarling bear's face. A plain padded cap sewn in the colors of his clan covered his head; his beard was still gold-hued and neatly combed down over his chest. His expression was peaceful.

"That's him!" Jutta whispered in a strangled voice. "My mother said that the bear was the symbol of the warrior clan he belonged to! It's Sigmund, and that's the cup!"

All eyes fastened on the cup clenched in his right hand. It was not a large and ornate cup like some Einarr possessed, but it appeared to be of the finest workmanship possible, far finer than anything clumsy mortal hands could turn out. It was small enough that his withered hand still nearly engulfed it, small enough that a warrior could easily carry it with him into battle, hung on a string around his neck inside his shirt, perhaps.

"Do we dare take it?" Einarr whispered, still sweating profusely from his frantic digging to get in.

"I think we'd better wait," Tova said. "They almost look like they're alive and waiting for something."

"If we don't take it now, we could lose it," Petrus said. "Someone could come in here and take everything. We're the ones who are meant to have that cup. We've done all the work of finding it."

"We should look for a sign that it is all right to take the cup," Tova said. "The dead can be very sensitive about these things, especially if those who buried them included some curses in their burial rites."

"How do you know all this stuff?" Simon demanded, his voice rather high and squeaky. "Since you've got here, all you do is say terrible things about curses and night riders and the dead. Are you just trying to frighten us?"

"My mother knew a great deal about the old Alfar ways," Tova said. "It's a pity the rest of us don't study them more. Everyone should know that you can't desecrate a grave without offending the dead unless you've got a pretty good reason for doing it."

"I have great respect for the dead," Petrus said, "but I don't intend to leave that cup now that we've found it. I shall stay here and guard it until we think it's safe to take it."

Einarr scowled. "If you stay, then I stay."

"You don't trust me?" Petrus demanded. "Where's all your fine talk of friendship now?"

"It's still there somewhere, but I know well that there's nothing like the sparkle of jewels and gold to kill a friendship deader than anything. And I don't want to lose that cup, either, nor do I want to take my eyes off it. I say we take it now and, if the dead are angry, find a way of dealing with them somehow, after the cup is safe in our possession at Sorengard."

"Sorengard?" Jutta repeated. "It's a Hesturkonur grave, made by Sigmund's wives and daughters and female relatives, and it's a Hesturkonur cup. If it goes anywhere, it goes to Bardhol, into the care of my grandmothers."

"That sounds sensible," Simon said. "Nobody could be more fair than five old women with no more aspirations in life. They're too old to be greedy and too old to want to go anywhere."

"It doesn't matter where it goes!" Einarr snapped. "Let's just get it! I've never seen such a bunch of mincing, puling cowards in all my life!"

Einarr strode forward toward the funeral table, ignoring Tova's exclamation.

"Wait! You can't just steal it! You've got to offer a suitable trade!"

Einarr was still sweating and gasping for air. He wiped the sweat from his brow and leaned over the table. Holding his breath, he grasped the rim of the cup gingerly between thumb and forefinger and tried to remove it from the corpse's grip.

Instantly a shrilling sound filled the barrow with an eardrum-piercing sound, and all the bodies around the table commenced a fearful shaking. Even the ground underfoot quivered, and dust sifted down from the earthy walls.

"It's an earthquake!" Einarr roared. "Get out, quick!"

Somehow they all sorted themselves out and shot through the tunnel opening to the outside, where they stood gasping in the silvery dawn light.

"That was no earthquake," Tova said. "I told you he wanted a trade. Why didn't you listen to me? Something of similar value must be left behind or the draug is going to come after you."

"It was an earthquake," Einarr said, "and I have nothing of similar value to that cup. If I did, I wouldn't need a draug's cup, would I?"

"A cup of some sort, any cup, will probably fool the draug," Tova said. "We'll have to come back tonight. It's almost daylight now."

"My grandmothers are going to think we have some sleeping disease, since we can't stay awake in the daytime," Jutta said, her excitement now replaced by the weariness and despondency inspired by yet another sleepless night.

"We've got to hide what we've done here," Petrus said. "Let's cover it up and choose someone to stand guard over it during the day. We could bury him inside the tunnel even, so anyone who came digging around would have a nasty surprise when they got in."

"I don't fancy being buried with a bunch of draugar," Jutta said.

"Nor could you fight off anyone who came to steal," Einarr said. "We must have someone with a sword and an arm to wield it."

"I shall stay," Simon said. "It would be an easy task, lying in the tunnel and sleeping all day. If someone starts digging,

I'll be sure to wake up. No one can crawl through that tunnel with me on the other side."

The plan was agreed to, and Simon was blocked up with stones inside the tunnel, after first extracting a promise that someone would bring him something to eat later on and pass it through the airhole to him.

"You're sure you're not afraid?" Jutta asked when there was no way to speak to Simon except through a hole about the size of two fists.

"I shall be fine," Simon said. "All I have to fear is another earthquake. That and starving in here."

"I shall bring you something as quickly as I can," Jutta said. "We're baking today, and there's always cheese."

"Don't forget something to drink," Simon said. "It's a bit dusty in here."

Carefully they concealed all signs of their trespassing and went their separate ways, not without misgivings on Jutta's part, thinking of Simon alone in the barrow, walled up with rocks and dirt.

Instead of going into the house, Jutta and Tova planned to begin their morning chores, as if they had arisen earlier, possessed by a fit of unusual diligence. However, a dark figure in a cloak stood waiting at the gate into Bardhol, watching them come up the path from the barrows.

"We've been caught," Jutta whispered. Looking down at herself, she realized there was no way to evade the truth. She was carrying a shovel, and her clothes were covered with dirt. Worse yet, it was Sigla waiting for them, no doubt working up horrible fears and worries to bombard them with.

"Where have you been? What have you been doing?" Amma Sigla gasped. "Don't tell me you were in the barrows all night! And what are you doing with those shovels?"

"Yes, we were in the barrows all night," Jutta said, resigning herself to whatever fate awaited her. "We were digging up Afi Sigmund's barrow."

Sigla laid a hand across her chest and took a step backward. "You were what?" she whispered.

"Digging up Afi Sigmund," Tova said. "But don't worry, we weren't alone. We had four men with us."

"Great gods! You've fallen in with barrow robbers?" Amma Sigla's indignation disintegrated with the shock. "Our own great-granddaughter has come here for the purpose of robbing the barrows of her revered ancestors? Is there no respect in this younger generation?"

Jutta felt her cheeks flaming with embarrassment. "No, I came here because my mother wished it, and she wanted to know more about what she stands to inherit one day when—when the time comes."

"Oh! I can't believe it!" Bitterly Sigla shook her head. "This is truly like a serpent's tooth in our heel. We foolishly thought that Dalla and you were interested in your Hestur heritage. Now it turns out you're interested in nothing but what you stand to get."

"That's not true, Amma Sigla," Jutta protested. "It may have been at the start, but not now."

"No, now you've discovered barrow robbing as a pastime," Sigla said. "This will not be good news for Margret and her weakened heart. It might just kill her, I shouldn't wonder. I wish I didn't have to be the one to tell her this. When I found your beds empty this morning, I feared you'd ended up like Betla and Lina. Instead, this is what I discover, and I can't decide which is worse."

"I'm sorry, Amma Sigla," Jutta said. "But with Sigmund's cup, a lot of good can be done. You won't have to scrape along the way you do on this worn-out old farm. Wouldn't you like a bit of comfort in your old age?"

"Comfort has a way of wearing thin very quickly," Sigla said, her eyes still flashing. "If we'd wanted that cup, we could have had it long ago, but we know it's best left buried where it is. It was a curse to all who lay their eyes upon it. Sigmund never let it be seen, knowing it doomed all who beheld it. Now I shall have to report this sorry business to my sisters and decide what must be done. Finish the milking and we shall tell you what we have decided."

Silently they milked the three cows and poured out the milk in the milk house. Then they trudged to the house for Amma Margret's judgment, for all the world as if they were doomed criminals.

Amma Margret fixed her fierce gaze on Jutta, unflinching, like a hawk contemplating a mouse in its talons.

"This is indeed a sad day," Margret said. "Just when we were getting used to having you around, you have proved to be nothing short of dishonest and devious. I suspected it a few times in your mother, Dalla, but in the next generation the trait is far more in evidence. It is a shameful thing that you have used your family in such a way. We have no choice but to return you to your mother. Nothing will be said of your offense, since it is a high crime for which you could be hanged and we have no wish to be guilty of leading you to your death. For that reason we have decided to remove you from temptation and send you home, where there are no barrows, and hope that you soon forget about robbing barrows again."

"But Amma Margret, I didn't rob a barrow," Jutta said. "I just did a little digging. And truly it wouldn't be a bad thing to have Afi Sigmund's cup back among us again. You know there are evil forces massing in the Dokkalfar realm, and one day we will be under attack."

"Better to die at the hands of the Dokkalfar than to risk the curse of that cup," Amma Margret said. "You must forget it, child. Now pack up your things. You are going home tomorrow."

"But I can't!" Jutta exclaimed with an ill-advised stamp of her foot. "It's Brjaladur eve, and I want to see it!"

"See what?" Amma Margret queried with a narrowing of her eyes. "Was there something you had planned with that awful Frida woman, perhaps? I think not, my dear. Of all the nights of the year, Brjaladur is the one night when you'd better be within doors where it's safe. You shall be far from here, with your mother. Now scat!"

"Perhaps there are things that you have planned," Jutta said, totally carried away by her own wrath and disappointment. "I daresay there are things you think I don't know about, but perhaps I do!"

"Hush, child! Now, do as you're told!"

CHAPTER 18

Sensing something amiss, Ofsi twined around her ankles and climbed up her breeches at every opportunity that day. With an unusual demonstration of affection, he demanded to be held and petted, purring industriously and kneading his barbed little paws.

"What are you going to do?" Tova whispered as they were carrying in peat for the baking. "You can't leave now. What about Simon in the barrow?"

"We'll have to take him something," Jutta said, lifting her chin and scowling stubbornly toward the house. "I can't be banished more than once, can I? So I might as well be hanged for stealing a sheep as for a lamb. I'm not just a thing they can send for or send away when they feel like it. Don't I have dreams and plans of my own? And going back to my mother is not one of them. You don't have to come with me if you don't want to. No one said anything about you being sent away."

"I shall go with you," Tova said. "Let us be sent away together if you have to go. Is there room for me at your mother's house?"

"I don't know what you'd want to go there for when I'm not going to be there," Jutta said.

She went into the house, boldly stuffed some things into a bag for Simon, and strode away toward the barrows without looking back once, Tova at her side. It no longer mattered if she was seen; the worst had happened, and nothing she could do would change Amma Margret's mind—that she knew.

Walled up in the barrow, Simon was very glad to see them when they appeared with his dinner.

"Isn't it fearfully lonely in there?" Tova asked of the muffled voice behind the stones.

"Oh, no, I've got Sigmund and his friends for company," Simon said. "They haven't spoken to me yet, though. I think they're a little too haughty to speak to the likes of a mere Scipling like me. They're all quite stiff and, I suspect, rather dull."

"Don't make jokes about it," Jutta snapped as Ofsi scrambled into the barrow after the food. "If not for you irreverent Sciplings, our problems here would be far less."

"And you'd have less digging done as a result," Simon said. "We're the ones who found the barrow, you recall. Not that we're unwilling to share the powers of the cup, of course; we aren't that type of Scipling at all. What is it that you intend to do with your share once we're gone?"

"I'm going to get as far away from this blighted little pesthole as I can get," Jutta said. "I want to see some fine cities where noble people live, people who think about something else besides milk buckets and bulls and cows and raising enough corn to make it through the winter. I'd like to talk to someone who didn't want to share their lamb-birthing experiences and complain about the weather. It's an endless topic, you know. Either too cold and wet or too hot and dry. No one's ever satisfied."

"I've seen cities," said Simon's voice, muffled by whatever he had stuffed in his mouth. "I've seen these noble people you're talking about. All I can say about them is that at least around country folk you don't have to watch your back at every moment."

"Oh, bah, what do you know?" Jutta snorted. "I'm sick to death of this mucky life. I can't wait to turn my back on it. Tonight we shall have the cup. Who knows where I'll be by tomorrow? It certainly won't be Bardhol. Even if the cup proves to be useless, I shan't stay in Bardhol."

"Where will you go? What about your grandmothers?" Simon asked.

"They've thrown me out for barrow robbing, which is so unfair, because I know they do it themselves." The words popped out before Jutta could stop them. "At least I think they do."

"But they never found the most important barrow," Tova said. "I would have thought they would know which one it was. But time has a way of confusing human memories. Luckily we found it first, and we shall reap the privileges first. Do you still intend to give them the cup when we are done with it?"

"I don't know," Jutta said. "I shall think about it."

"You're thrown out, then?" Simon asked. "Where will you go? You could always come to the Scipling realm with us."

"Maybe I will," Jutta said. "Now, will you please shove Ofsi back out so we can leave? We shall be back here at sundown."

Ofsi emerged from the hole, dusty but satisfied that he had eaten as much of Simon's dinner as possible.

They were on the way back to Bardhol and the rest of the day's chores when Jutta spied a familiar scarf tied in the dead tree at the crossroads.

"Frida's here!" she exclaimed.

Looking around from their high vantage point atop a flat barrow, they saw her and a couple of women resolutely tramping along one of the ley lines with their staffs and pendulums. For a moment Jutta pitied her blind laboring to find that which she herself had already found, and she also experienced a pang of guilt. Perhaps one day she would share the cup with Frida, but not yet, not now, until she was satisfied with what she got from it first. Of course it was Frida who had taught her to dowse, and dowsing had led her to the barrow. For the first time she seriously wondered how Petrus and Simon had found the barrow. With so many to choose from, it was unlikely that it had been just a lucky accident.

"Frida! Halloa, Frida!" Jutta called, waving her arm.

Frida waved back, cried out a greeting, and made her way toward Jutta and Tova.

"Where have you been?" she called out, smiling radiantly.

"Have you been having a lot of fun together, taking care of Bardhol?"

"To be sure," Tova said. "There's been a great deal to take care of, with Margret and the horses falling ill."

"Indeed, I hadn't heard. A good thing you were there to help. And why such a sober face, little one? You look as if a storm cloud had landed on you."

"My grandmothers are angry with me," Jutta said. "They're going to send me back to my mother. I was caught coming out of the barrows."

"Oh, dear. That's my fault; I'm the one that got you started. What a pity. I feel we are getting very close to Sigmund's barrow."

Jutta looked away. "By this time tomorrow I suppose I shall be gone. But I'm not going back to my mother. She'd half kill me anyway. I may be going on a very long journey with some friends."

"Oh, what a pity. I wish you could stay with me, and we'd continue our search."

"With you?" A wave of relief washed over Jutta, thinking of herself ensconced at Thorungard, surrounded by all of Frida's wealth and comforts. "That would be most gracious of you to offer us a home."

"Most gracious indeed," Tova murmured.

"Then it's settled," Frida said. "Bring your things whenever you're ready. Shall I send a cart and a thrall for you both?"

"No, that won't be necessary," Jutta said. "We have very little to carry."

"I'm sorry to hear that your grandmothers are angry with you," Frida said. "Perhaps they will change their minds."

"I don't think so," Jutta said. "They think I'm terribly deceitful and ungrateful. If that's how they think of me, then I no longer wish to be there."

"Then why not come away to Thorungard right now?" Frida said. "If you have nothing to go back for, why return? We can send someone for your things if you wish, but as you know, I enjoy sharing what I've got with the less fortunate."

"We could," Jutta said, glancing at Tova and wondering how

they would explain going off to search the barrows alone. Her heart yearned for Frida's fine white linens and soft new eiders and the thousand other small beauties and comforts that had delighted her starved soul.

"Yes, except that we really ought to help with the evening chores for the last time," Tova said. "It would be better to wait until morning."

"You're being far too responsible," Frida said. "It's your best attribute, but sometimes it makes one a bit too plodding and dull."

"Dull people don't let their own impulses get them into trouble, at least," Tova said.

"Will you be coming into the barrows tonight?" Jutta asked.

"Yes, a group of us are planning to take advantage of the full moon," Frida said. "Just the usual dreamers who fancy a bit of ancient magic in their lives. You met them all once."

"We shall meet you at midnight," Jutta said. "Here, on this spot."

"That will be perfect," Frida said. "Midnight is the gateway hour, neither today, tomorrow, nor yesterday. It is a time when all things happen best. Until then." She saluted in farewell. "I shall leave you to your odious chores of milking and mucking and other terrible things which you shall never have to do again." Then she put a hand on Jutta's arm and spoke in a lower tone. "After what you once told me about them, I am most glad you are getting away from Bardhol. At first I thought you were wrong and fanciful, but things I saw in these barrows convinced me to change my mind. You opened my eyes to something I could scarcely believe myself. I assure you, you can't leave a moment too soon for your own safety."

Tova had wandered away a few steps, so she could not hear what Jutta and Frida were saying.

"Then you believe they are the Myrkriddir, too?"

"Yes, and I urge you to get out of that house as quickly as you can. You can't imagine how frightened I've been for you. My mind was changed just two nights ago, when I was out doing some harmless moonlight dowsing. The Myrkriddir came down upon me and chased me until I thought I would die. Fortunately I found a place to hide and escaped from their clutches. I believe they knew who I was, and they wanted to kill me before I could warn you. If they ever suspected you knew their secret, then yours would be the next shredded body found in the barrows, I fear. Perhaps it is their plan, Jutta. Why else would they suddenly have taken an interest in you and let you stay in their home, if not for some dark purpose of their own? And now they seem to have decided to send you away. No one will know if you truly went home or if something more dreadful has happened to you."

Jutta's thoughts raced around frantically, picking up a great many fragments of thoughts and ideas to prove Frida's words true. "I can scarcely believe it," she stammered, "but what you're speaking must be the truth."

"Then get away immediately, tonight. Now, before it's too late. I wouldn't go back to that house if I were you."

"Not to worry. They won't be doing any Myrkridding for a while. Their horses are still not fit to ride. They nearly all died two nights ago."

"Nearly died? Then they survived?"

"Yes, and I'm not sure why. The only one who came to look at them was old Bjalfur, and I don't know why they even asked him. He looked more like he was wandering in his wits than he ever resembled an animal healer."

"Indeed, he's a fool. Well, we'd have fewer troubles if those Myrkriddir had indeed lost their horses. But never mind, at least you shall be safe at last. Won't you come with me, at once?"

"No, I'm going back to finish my chores and get my things. In the morning I shall start away as if I'm going home, then I'll come here."

"Do be careful how you make your escape. They are dangerous creatures."

On the way back to Bardhol Jutta felt as if she were treading on air. "I can't believe I'm going to live with Frida at last," she said. "I don't know how to hide my joy from my grandmothers. It was far better when I looked like a storm cloud. I hope they don't become suspicious. They really are far more clever than I ever thought."

"Frida, too, is clever," Tova said.

"Good. I despise a fool. I've always greatly admired her intelligence and charm and resourcefulness. One day I hope to be a woman just like her."

Jutta stayed outdoors as long as she possibly could on her last night at Bardhol. When she did come in, it was in time for bedtime and all her grandmothers were already shut away in their cupboard beds—and snoring in some cases. Only Amma Thruda waited up, sitting beside the fire with Mishka curled up in her lap.

"I wanted to tell you farewell," she said. "I've enjoyed having you here, Granddaughter. Bardhol is such a bleak and grim old place, and it was pleasant to hear your young voice and see someone moving without creaking and groaning." She smiled, and her eyes crinkled as if she wanted to laugh.

"It's been good to get acquainted with my ancestors," Jutta said, her words sounding stiff and insincere in her own ears. "I'm sorry I was too disobedient to be allowed to stay with you, but there are things in this life which I feel I must do even though people near to me disapprove and even get angry."

"That's what it means to be young, I suppose," Thruda said. "You must do things which people disapprove of. Well, I'm sorry to see you go. If it had been a smaller sort of disobedience, we might have overlooked it. But digging up the graves of your ancestors is a serious affront."

"It was only one grave," Jutta said in a small voice.

"We simply can't allow you to endanger yourself in those barrows, not with a killer doing his dirty work there."

Jutta looked away, shutting out the dark flapping images swirling overhead with hideous cries. Her own grandmothers, hounding their prey to death, was not what she wanted to think about. Perhaps it was better that she leave and turn her back on her family's dark secret. Her mother had warned her that something was amiss in Bardhol. She would not stay long at Thorungard, not with her grandmothers just over the hill at

Bardhol, still committing their gruesome crimes whenever the moon was full. At least when they perished, which would not be too long, the Myrkriddir curse would be ended.

"Yes. I'll be glad to go," Jutta said. It was still hard to look at Amma Thruda's gentle, withered face and imagine her as a black-cloaked Myrkriddir, wreathed in magic and spell, striding through the night sky on her black mare.

"And Ingi says that you must return for Faelinn after she's weaned," Thruda said. "She wants you to have the last Hestur filly and continue the breeding line."

"No, I couldn't," Jutta said with a thrill of delight.

"Ingi says you must. You'll know how to strengthen the line and bring back the Hestur horse. Her only request is that you try to keep their fetlocks from getting too hairy, like these modern horses. The Hestur horse is clean-limbed, she says, as elegant as a dancer."

Jutta could not sleep. She could scarcely close her eyes on the thoughts racing through her head. Nor did it help that the wind had come up outside, filling the night with mysterious whisperings and creakings. Now and then a fast-moving cloud half blotted the brilliant face of the moon, which shone into her loft window like a great accusing eye. She could not face her grandmothers again and tell them good-bye. She could imagine them all lined up, looking regretful and sweet and worried about her. Even Margret's bluster was merely a front for the tender anxiety she felt about taking charge of a young girl. It was better that she go away than stay and continue worrying them and thereby shorten their lives with distress. Then, on the other hand, she remembered the ghastly attack of the Myrkriddir, filling the air with cold and wind and terrible shriekings calculated to freeze the blood in one's veins. She did not know whether or how much to trust her own convictions or even how to feel about her grandmothers.

Finally she reached over and gave the softly snoring Tova a decisive shake.

"Tova, we've got to go now," she whispered. "I don't want to say good-bye in the morning."

Tova sighed and groaned. "Just when I finally get a bed to sleep in, you're shoving me out?"

"Yes. We must go. You can sleep tomorrow night. You can sleep when you're old. I'll get you a chair and park you in the sunshine with a robe over your knees."

"I'm not that much older than you are," Tova snapped. "Perhaps I'll be the one tucking a robe over your poor old stiff knees. It could happen. I come from a long-lived line. My grandmother was near the century mark when she died. She never had stiff knees, either."

"Frida said she'd be in the barrows tonight," Jutta said. "We'll just visit Einarr and Petrus first, then meet her there and help her dowse or walk ley lines or whatever she's doing tonight. Wouldn't she be astonished to see us with that cup in our hands?"

"I'm sure she would, but I don't think that would be wise," Tova said. "You're far too trusting. You've got to keep back a few secrets once in a while. People want you to trust them, but sometimes they aren't strong enough to bear the burden of being completely truthful with you."

"You think Frida is not completely truthful?" Jutta demanded.

"It's not for me to say one way or the other, since I don't know. All I do know is that it's harder for some people than others."

"So you're saying that you haven't been perfectly truthful with me, when I've told you everything about me?"

"There are things I haven't said, but not many."

"Well, you're a fine one to be warning me about Frida, then. It seems a bit ungrateful on your part, since she has given you so much, like that nice gray cloak you wear."

"Call me ungrateful, then, if it makes you feel better, but I've been out in the world awhile with no one to really care about me, and I've learned that one must protect oneself sometimes. The best way to do that is to keep your mouth shut and think before you speak."

"I'm sorry that I've done something to inspire such distrust in you. I trusted you more than my own sister Asta, who is an idiot."

"And I trust you more than any person living on the face of this land," Tova said. "I doubt there will ever be anyone that I trust as I trust you. And I hope to learn to trust you more in the future, but as for right now, sometimes I want to hide a little bit. If you care about me, you must be patient."

"You are a distrustful person," Jutta said. "So it is that you see your same deceit in other people. What harm could Frida possibly want to do to you by giving you cloaks and gowns and finding you places of employment?"

"I don't know," Tova said. "And that is why I stand myself at a little distance from trusting her completely and wholeheartedly."

"I find that shameful," Jutta said. "That means you don't really trust me, either, if you don't trust me wholeheartedly. I thought you were a better friend than this. I thought I had finally found someone who was completely honest and forthright with me."

"Probably you have, as much as you ever will," Tova said.

"Oh! And what does that mean? That I don't inspire trust in the people I meet?"

"Well, you are rather headstrong, which means that you really don't think much about other people's wishes, as long as you get your own, and everything has to be done your way or it's the wrong way, and all that makes it rather difficult to be fully open with you, since you are likely to trample on my ideas when I speak them."

"Indeed! Well, if your ideas were as good as mine, then we wouldn't have to trample on them, would we?"

"You see how it is? My ideas are simply not as good as yours because they are my ideas. You are you, and I am I, and the difference in our stations in life makes it difficult for us truly to trust one another."

"I have trusted you," Jutta said bitterly. "You cannot imagine how it grieves me to hear what you truly think of me now. You sound as if you don't think I am a very nice person at all."

"We are still friends, no matter what our faults. I will agree to overlook yours, and you will overlook mine. That's how friendship works. No matter how terrible we are, we agree to tolerate each other."

"Terrible? I'm terrible? And all you can do is tolerate me? I don't see how that can be a friendship. I shall do you the great favor of freeing you from any future association with a terrible person you can barely tolerate. I'm sure you can stay here with my grandmothers if you wish, but you'll soon find out how unwise you truly are."

"Jutta, you misunderstand everything. I meant to say only that no one is perfect, and the beauty of friendship is that we don't expect each other's best behavior all the time, and we can relax and be forgiven when we're acting badly. Whatever you do, I shall forgive."

"Well, you'll have to do your forgiving at a distance, because I don't intend to stay here, and if you're wise, you'll just stay in this nice comfortable bed and keep your precious distance from me. If your own distance is what's important to you, then treasure it always, because it will be the only friend you will ever have."

With that, Jutta stuffed the last of her shirts into the sack she was packing everything into, stuffed Ofsi into his kettir pack—scratching and protesting since he hated not being able to see where he was going—and she was finished. Quietly she descended the ladder and let herself out of the house.

She made her way straight to Sigmund's barrow, hurrying a little in case Tova was secretly hastening toward it also to get there ahead of her. She found Einarr, Petrus, and Simon seemingly awaiting her outside the barrow. Leckny was there, too, standing with his back turned to his father. It appeared that they all had been quarreling; there was an unpleasant silence between them, and Einarr was scowling and pacing up and down.

"So there you are at last," Einarr greeted her. "You said you'd be here at sundown. Where's that other female, that Tova who knows so much about magic and dead bodies?"

"We parted company," Jutta said shortly. "I don't know

what made you think she knew so much, anyway. What's the trouble here? Have you got the cup yet?"

"No," Petrus said. "There's a curse or something that keeps anyone from taking it from his hand. We've all tried it, and all those corpses start screaming and shaking whenever we touch that cup. We simply can't take it from him. Something stops us, and it's too terrifying to tolerate. We've got to do something else if we're going to have it."

"At least we don't have to worry about anyone else taking it," Simon said. "I won't need to stay behind to guard it, since it's not going anywhere."

"I told you this was a foolish enterprise," Leckny said, rounding on his father. "You could lose everything: your seat, the respect of your neighbors, your land—even your life—for barrow robbing. I hope you found it worthwhile."

Einarr huffed into his beard and strode up and down. "I wish that Tova woman was here. She might know what to do. Can't you go get her?"

"No, I can't, but you can if you want to. Just tell my grandmothers you need Tova to come and tell you how to rob a barrow, and I'm sure they'd be pleased to let her go."

"That's not true at all," Einarr said. "Your grandmothers would skin us alive if they knew about this. I hope they never find out who we are. What a cursed mess we've gotten into. We can't just bury it again."

"Why not?" Leckny asked. "It's probably happened before. Maybe we'll be as lucky and escape with our lives."

"We need Tova," Petrus said, "or someone with knowledge of the old ways. Isn't there anyone around here who knows about magic? I thought you Alfar were loaded with magic and powers and knowledge."

"We were, until we became more like you," Leckny said. "When Sciplings started coming through the gates in such droves, we abandoned our old ways and turned mercenary. In a few more years we'll be completely indistinguishable from Sciplings."

"Be silent," Einarr snorted. "What an absurd notion. We are

Alfar, a proud race if ever there was one. The powers are still there, mind you."

"What are we to do in the meantime?" Petrus asked. "We can't leave this hole open forever or someone's bound to find it and figure out who dug it. I don't know how we've escaped discovery this long."

"Bury that cup and resign yourselves to living in the Alfar realm for the rest of your lives," Leckny said. "I can think of worse fates, such as being hanged for barrow robbing. Or being tracked by an angry draug forever."

"I'm not giving up!" Einarr snapped. "We'll find a way. That cup is too valuable to let it rot here in a barrow. We need that cup!"

"I suppose I could get Tova," Jutta said. "But I don't think she's half as knowledgeable as she thinks she is."

"Good, good! Go and fetch her!" Einarr exclaimed.

"Well, I can't right now, not without waking up my grandmothers, perhaps," said Jutta, who truthfully did not want to climb back up the steep path to Bardhol that night.

"Tomorrow, then," Petrus said. "Bring her here with you, and we'll see if she can figure out some way to get that cup out of Sigmund's death grip."

"Perhaps it takes a direct descendant," Jutta said. "It only makes sense that a stranger should not have that cup. I shall try it."

"It might not be as easy as you think," Leckny said. "You are no more directly an heir than my father. Not nearly as direct, since you're one generation later. And you're a woman. If anyone owns a warrior's cup, it will be a male descendant, who can carry a sword as well as the cup. I don't think you should go in there."

"Not alone, anyway," Petrus said.

"I'm not going back in there," Einarr said, shaking his head vigorously. "I felt as if I was thrown right out last time."

"So did I," Petrus said reluctantly. "Jutta, you can't go in there. It's a haunted and evil place. You might come to great harm."

"And I might come to great success, which would grieve you even more, wouldn't it?" Jutta replied.

"Well, in that case," Einarr said, "Leckny, you go with her and see she comes to no harm."

Jutta lit a rush lamp and crept through the tunnel, with Leckny following, and into the underground chamber, where Sigmund and his retainers sat around their table.

"They look like rather a jolly company," Jutta whispered.

"Yes, except for that one whose head is beginning to fall off," Leckny said. "He's giving me an ugly look. I've a mind to finish knocking his head off for him, as rude as he's been lately."

Jutta looked at the corpse in question and shuddered. Already the effects of outside air were hastening the disintegration of the corpses and fading the colors of their clothing. Soon they would be nothing but dust if they were not sealed up again.

"You'd better hush," Jutta said. "You're probably somehow related to everyone in this barrow."

"Including you, but it's too far away to even consider it as much of a blood relation," Leckny said. "So you and I could marry without any obstruction."

"Except common sense," Jutta said. "Anyone could tell that I would be forced to kill you before a year was out."

"I don't believe you would. We could have some high old times, annoying our parents and relatives."

"I can't think of anything more annoying than you, that's true," Jutta said. "Perhaps I'll consider it if I decide to choose a life of misery and boredom instead of going away from here and finding something amusing."

"With the gold in this barrow, you'll be able to travel far indeed," Leckny said. "Look at the rings and armbands and neck pieces. And there's boxes of the stuff."

"Don't you dare touch anything, you thief. We came here for one thing only. The rest of this must stay as it is. I'm not a common barrow robber."

Jutta reached out slowly for the cup, feeling the sightless stare of all the corpses resting on her; she had the disquieting sensation that perhaps they weren't entirely dead, after all. Living and undead were very different conditions, she reflected, remembering some of the horrible old spooky stories about draugar she had been told beside the hearth as a child.

"Carefully," Leckny whispered, his eyes gleaming by the light of her rush. They both held their breath in the fetid atmosphere of the barrow as Jutta's fingers closed on the rim of Sigmund's cup.

CHAPTER 19

For a moment she thought it was going to work. The cup actually moved slightly as she lifted it. Then something gripped it like blacksmith's tongs, and a snarling, growling sound commenced from the desiccated throats of the corpses, rising to the pitch of a horrible scream. They jittered in their seats, shaking their heads furiously. The table rocked wildly, and the dishes and cups on it clattered and tipped over, spilling out the hardened remains of the funeral feast. A crashing wave of terror broke over Jutta's head, suddenly making her heart pound until she thought it would burst.

Jutta clapped her hands over her ears and scuttled out the tunnel, with Leckny close behind her.

"Hah," Einarr said, grinning in satisfaction. "I knew a woman couldn't be better than a man, even in a corpse's opinion."

"Well, failing doesn't make me any worse than you," Jutta said, still panting, her heart still racing. "We are pretty much equal right now. None of us can take that cup."

"We need Tova," Petrus said.

"No, we can figure it out ourselves," Einarr returned, and they commenced arguing about it uselessly and showed signs of spending the rest of the night doing so.

"I'm leaving," Jutta said in disgust. "Let me know when you think of something. You can find me at Frida's."

"You're going there now, alone?" Leckny asked.

"Yes, that's what I said, wasn't it?"

"I don't think that's wise, in these barrows alone, on a full moon night."

"Tonight is no different from any other night," Jutta said. "I came here alone, didn't I?"

"I'll walk with you."

"I am fine by myself, thank you. Besides, how do I know you're not the killer? You're always in the barrows here, digging, on the nights someone is killed. It might as well be you as someone we don't know, mightn't it?" Her tone was flippant, but her own words chilled her, and she shivered involuntarily, which was a foolish thing to do. Her grandmothers were the Myrkriddir, chasing and hounding their prey to death, she had decided; but it also made sudden and deadly sense that it could be someone else she had never suspected before—someone seemingly innocent and rather charming in his own demented way.

"Me? You've revealed my secret," he said with a low and evil chuckle. "Now I have no choice but to kill you before you tell the world. Please stand still while I slit your throat, if you don't mind. And please don't bleed on my new pants. It doesn't come out, you know."

"You're horrible," Jutta said furiously. "Stay away from me. I feel safer by myself."

He followed her, however, as she climbed to the top of the barrow. "I really don't want you to go by yourself," he said. "You know it isn't safe."

"You don't know what I know, and as for you, you know nothing," Jutta snapped. "Besides, I happen to know Frida is in the barrows tonight, and perhaps I shall find her. She comes to the barrows all the time at night, and she isn't afraid."

"Haven't you seen those two hulking monsters she takes with her? Those pet ogres she calls thralls? Of course no one is going to bother her, or they'd get their brains bashed out. You haven't got two thralls to guard you. All you've got is me, and I'm going with you. Go ahead and I shall follow, at a distance, if my presence is so odious."

"You're talking nonsense, and yes, you are odious. If you try to follow me, I shall lose you in the barrows and you'll be the one the killer finds."

"Oh, bah, you can't lose me. You can't run fast enough, and

you've got that great heavy bag of clothes and that squalling cat to slow you down."

"Just watch me, then." Jutta turned and fled down the side of the barrow, plunging into the shadows at the bottom. She worked her way into the darkest part of a thicket and sat still, hoping Ofsi wouldn't start yelling and scratching around to betray her. Fortunately he was still as Leckny followed, snooping around ineffectively and standing still to listen.

"Jutta, this isn't a funny game," he finally declared. "You know it's too dangerous out here to be alone."

When he moved away toward the south, which was the logical direction for her to take if she was going to Thorungard, Jutta quietly picked her way westward. She came up out of the thickets and underbrush and hurried across the rocky moonlit domes of the barrows, taking a wide course that would gradually turn southward and put her on the road to Mikillborg, where she would turn and go directly to Frida's house. She hoped Frida would be there instead of out in the barrows, charting ley lines by moonlight. The light wasn't terribly good that night, however, so she had every expectation of a warm welcome when she got to Frida's.

She caught a sudden whiff of smoke and thought she must be nearer to the road than she had thought. It was probably Bjalfur's fire she was smelling. But no, the standing stones in the great circle loomed ahead. Parting a thicket, she could see firelight dancing on the stones, and the shadows of people flickered and vanished, greatly enlarged on the impassive faces of the monoliths. The restless wind brought her ears snatches of voices, which sounded like the weird calls of the wild hunt, but the wild riders never touched earth or they would turn to dust. Someone up there was definitely dancing or doing something peculiar at midnight in the barrows.

Quietly she approached for a better look. The barrows, after all, belonged to her in a way, since they were the graves of her ancestors.

She saw a fire built at the base of the central stone and many people and shadows moving around the circle of the outside stones in a wild dance, with arms flailing, twisting and turning and chanting some sort of nonsensical gibberish. Some of the dancers shook rattles, and a couple had small drums of stretched hide, which made a steady and hypnotic pattering rhythm. The only person not dancing stood in the center by the great heel stone, painting symbols with something black and rather runny. For some reason, from the way that person moved, Jutta knew it was Frida, and Frida was doing something Jutta did not understand. Whatever it was, it did not seem to be Frida's usual harmless ley walking and pendulum dowsing.

Jutta advanced to the next black thicket for a closer look. Something lighter on the ground attracted her attention, something with a cloak tossed carelessly over it. Somehow the moonlight lured her eyes into seeing the tossed form of a human being lying there.

Jutta stared, and Ofsi growled, which made the hairs of Jutta's scalp rise stiffly in no uncertain warning. With her knees suddenly feeling weak, she crept backward.

Suddenly a rough hand grabbed her, gripping her mouth so she could not scream. Her attacker flung her down on the ground and tore off her hood to get a look at her face.

"It's that wench from Bardhol!" a deep voice rumbled.

"What are we to do with her?" whispered another shadow looming over her and smelling of peat and fried onions. "She'll tell everyone she knows!"

"Not if we just give her skinny neck a twist here and now, before the mistress finds out."

"Better ask the mistress first. She might have some use for this girl."

After a brief argument deciding which of the thralls was going to interrupt the ceremonies, one of them slunk into the stone circle and called to Frida from a safe distance. Frida flung down the rush she was painting with and strode out of the circle. When she recognized Jutta, her angry scowl vanished in astonishment.

"Jutta! This must be a sign," she said.

"What are you doing here?" Jutta asked, struggling against a betraying quaver in her voice.

"Oh, that?" Frida waved one hand toward the dancing circle, who had not ceased their feverish tempo. "We're just behaving barbarically, that's all, in a rather pallid reenactment of what must have gone on here a long time ago. It does the heart good to act heathenish once in a while."

"What—what's that on the ground?" Jutta made bold to inquire, nodding toward the bloody bundle behind the thicket.

"What? Oh, that? It's just a sheep. We had to have a little blood for our ceremony, and no one was kind enough to donate it voluntarily." Frida smiled at her own joke. "We'll have mutton stew when we all return to Thorungard. Now, my dear, won't you tell me what you're doing out in the barrows in the middle of the night, and all alone, I suppose."

"I ran away. I don't want to be sent home to my mother. Since I was leaving in the morning anyway, I thought I'd just get an earlier start. I was coming to your house when I saw the fire and decided to see who it was. I was hoping it might be you."

"Early start, indeed. And what became of Tova?"

"We quarreled. I left her at Bardhol." Suddenly the drums and the rattles made Jutta feel weary and ready for sleep. "I hope you don't mind if I join you sooner than we planned. I just couldn't stay any longer where nobody wants me around."

"I assure you, you are much needed at Thorungard," Frida said. "Why don't you join in our dance? It's great fun when the power of this place seizes you like a leaf and tosses you around helplessly until it decides to let you go. Some of us dance until we drop."

"I think I'll just sit down and wait until you're finished," Jutta said. "I'm feeling rather sleepy."

"Good. Just curl up here on the ground and go to sleep until we're finished. It won't be long. Dawn isn't too far off. How long have you been here, just watching?"

"Only a few moments. I heard the drums and saw the fire and came to look, and I saw the sheep, and then your thralls grabbed me as if I were the barrow field killer."

Jutta alternately dozed and awakened for the short remainder of the night, dreaming occasionally, and when she opened her eyes, she could scarcely tell if she was awake or still dreaming. The dancing figures and incessant drumming and rattling spun through her head like a feverish nightmare. Finally, the easten sky blushed with shades of lavender, and the scene began to lose its startling clarity of light and shadow and melted away into the gray mist of an early morning mizzle. Too fine to be rain, the moisture settled on every twig and blade and jeweled every boulder. Where Jutta had lain, the ground was pale and dry beneath her.

The dancers straggled away one by one and disappeared rather furtively, covering their heads against the mist, so Jutta had no idea who any of them were. There were no merry farewells and last moment conversations. They simply vanished into the gray atmosphere of the barrows.

"Come along," Frida said with a weary smile. "It's time we went home and had some breakfast. I can't wait to get a proper sleep in a proper bed, between clean sheets with a little bit of lace on them. Thver, let Jutta ride on your horse. You may carry her bundle. How did you enjoy our little revel, my dear?"

"I slept through most of it, but it looked most interesting, what parts I saw."

Jutta took a surreptitious look around for the slaughtered sheep. Nothing of it remained, divided up perhaps among Frida's fellow barbarians and carried away and used to the last piece. The heavy mist showed signs of deepening into a light rain, which was washing away the last streaks of sheep's blood from the central stone. In a few moments all traces of the revel would be gone.

"I'm glad you enjoyed it. We're doing it again tonight. The moon is at perigee—at its very closest and largest presence possible this summer. In the olden times it was known as Brjaladur, the night of terror, when all order ceases and chaos returns. Surely tonight of all nights we should be able to discover some clues in the search for the cup."

A tall dark figure suddenly loomed out of the fog.

"Bjalfur!" Frida cried, recovering from her fright quickly. "Whatever are you doing out so early?"

"Not early," Bjalfur's calm voice said. "If you've been out all night, it's late, not early."

"We were having one of our barbaric evenings. A pity I can't interest you in attending."

"All a bunch of womanish nonsense," Bjalfur said. "You're just pretending, all of you, to know something that you don't. It's a waste of time and sleep dancing around and chanting a lot of rot, just to look like you know about the old ways."

"Maybe by pretending, one day we will actually stumble onto something," Frida said with her pleasant smile.

"And you might shoot a sheath of arrows into the air blindfolded, hoping to kill something," Bjalfur said with a contemptuous snort.

"Where's that hound of yours?" Jutta asked, looking around. "That great shabby creature with the scars?"

"Oh, he's about somewhere," Bjalfur retorted. "As useless a beast as I've ever seen. I'll be glad when he's dead and gone." He stalked away, shaking his head and making rather daft flapping motions with his hand, as if shooing Frida and Jutta's association out of his memory.

"What an old curmudgeon," Frida said with an indulgent laugh. "He spies on our rituals and hangs around long enough to make fun of them, but I've seen him doing some peculiar things of his own. He pretends to sneer at magic, but I've seen him doing some pretty strange things."

"Like what?" Jutta asked a little too sharply.

Frida shrugged. "Nothing of consequence. Throwing bones and carving sticks. Just superstitious things that old people tend to do. My, I'm about starved, aren't you? I hope Gunna's got something nice fixed for breakfast."

Jutta was sure it would be nice as long as she didn't have to fix it. At home in Bardhol she had to get up first to light the fire and shove the big old blackened oatmeal pot over the coals. Her grandmothers believed in a good thick gluey gruel to start the day, nothing that would shock the stomach and something sticky enough to enable one to retain one's food longer and get the most out of the full feeling oatmeal engendered. She supposed they were well into their breakfast by then and planning out the day's chores as if they didn't miss her at all.

"I'm worried about Tova," Jutta said as they rode along. "If my grandmothers are what we think, I fear Tova's life is in danger."

"Yes, we must do something about Tova," Frida said, frowning slightly under the beak of her hood.

Breakfast was as wonderful as Jutta could have dreamed. Gunna must have risen early indeed to have made fried bread already, little blobs of dough with bits of sausage rolled up inside and dropped into a kettle of grease. Small sausages fried up crisp and brown were accompanied by eggs cooked in grease instead of insipidly boiled, as her grandmothers always cooked them. The grandmothers held that sausages were a luxury, saved for great occasions, not to be wasted by daily usage. One could get accustomed to the finer things with shocking ease and become dissatisfied with struggling and scraping along, and that would be a shameful thing indeed, to want to be comfortable. It implied a certain lack of mettle or even moral fiber to want more than the grim, bare minimum to eke out one's life.

After a long and luxurious steaming in the bathhouse Jutta was ready for the final and most evil indulgence of all—taking a nap before midday. Even Ofsi was ready to be quiet. He hadn't liked the noise of the drums and rattles, and he didn't at all care for the water and steam in the bathhouse, and he, too, was stuffed to the gullet with sausages and eggs and fried bread.

When Jutta awakened, she put on the clean clothes Frida had provided, an embroidered blue gown with a matching cape pinned around the shoulders with a flashing jeweled broach shaped like a shield. This was more womanly attire than Jutta was accustomed to ever since leaving Thorgestrstead. She was accustomed to wearing rough clothes and working like a thrall all day.

While Frida slept, Jutta explored the house and hall once more, reveling in the bright colors of the painted beams, the fine workmanship of the furniture and chests and shelves and tapestries. It was all purchased or hired work; none of it had been done by Frida's hands. That was the way a fine lady should live, Jutta thought, with plenty of servants to use their hands instead of hers.

Ofsi did not stray far from her except to upset and disembowel Frida's sewing basket when Jutta was not looking and to climb up the tapestries covering the walls. He had a maniacal gleam in his eyes, as if he didn't have enough to keep him busy. He provoked Frida's hounds into barking at him so he could climb up a beam and hiss down at them, and he finished up his performance by jumping on a dead chicken waiting to be plucked on the kitchen table.

It was all Jutta could do to resist grabbing the chicken and plucking it herself, although Frida had three kitchen maids for such chores. Work was a dreadful habit to get into, she reflected. It destroyed one's ability to enjoy doing nothing important. She could scarcely believe her great luck in finally landing in the position of luxury and ease to which she had always aspired.

The head cook, Gunna, was a great red-faced woman who had spent most of her life searing her face and arms over fires and in ovens until she had the appearance of being almost half-cooked herself. Though she was not tall, her girth made her impressive, and unpleasant mistresses had etched a scowl between her bristling black eyebrows that warned the world to tread carefully. Even Frida, Jutta had noticed, always spoke to her almost deferentially. A definite telltale sign was the demeanor of the three kitchen maids, who were as quiet and meek as if it were a house of death, almost tiptoeing their way around, glancing behind themselves frequently with large and apprehensive eyes.

So it was that Jutta presented herself cautiously in the kitchen to inquire if there was a scrap of bread to be obtained, if it wasn't too much trouble.

"No trouble," the cook replied shortly, resoundingly slapping down a lump of fresh dough on the dough trough. "Have one of those useless girls fix you something."

Jutta sat down at the table, which had been mercilessly

scrubbed and sanded to perfect whiteness. Ofsi climbed onto the table and sat down expectantly, waiting to attack Jutta's food the moment it was placed before her. To his delight, he was given a nice bit of herring all his own, which he devoured with the usual haste and wicked little snarling sounds at every bite.

"I haven't seen Asgerda and Hallgrima," Jutta said by way of making friendly conversation.

The cook slammed down the lump of bread dough again. "You aren't likely to, either," she replied in a low voice.

"Why, where are they?" Jutta asked.

"No one knows for certain," the cook muttered, kneading away furiously on the bread dough, as if she had a personal grudge against it.

"Frida must have found them positions somewhere," Jutta said. "She's so good that way, to care about the lot of people poorer than herself."

The cook crinked one black and bushy eyebrow slightly higher; otherwise her expression was unaltered. "Yes, very good," she mumbled. "Amazingly good."

"Asgerda and Hallgrima must realize how lucky they are," Jutta chattered on in spite of the cook's obvious discouragement; Jutta was determined to show that she wasn't afraid of a cook's temper or too proud to sit down in the kitchen and chat with the help. "If only there were more people like Frida to watch out for those who are less fortunate, then we'd have a lot less homeless wanderers traveling about, trying to find enough to stay alive."

"A lot less," the woman agreed, her scowl deepening.

"I daresay I can do some good someday," Jutta said, "now that I'll be staying with Frida for a while. Not that I'm homeless and kinless, of course. I stand to inherit some degree of independence from my parents."

The cook looked at her squarely for the first time and ceased her pummeling of the bread. "So that explains why you seem a little stupider than the rest," she said. "Frida's girls usually aren't from your station in life, and scrambling up has made them a little more canny. If you had any eyes in your head,

you'd run right out that back door and never stop running until
you were a good long ways from these barrows."

She terminated the discussion with a particularly violent
slamming of the bread dough and turned her back to do something else, while Jutta sat there with her mouth hanging open.

Cooks, she reflected, were permitted all sorts of eccentrici-
ties in the name of keeping the peace. The better the cook, the
more vagaries were tolerated, as long as the food on the table
was passably fit to eat.

Jutta was nearly done with her morning fare anyway, so she
hastened a bit so she could leave. Ofsi was washing himself industriously, and the three kitchen maids were smothering
snickers behind their hands to see a cat taking a bath in the
middle of the sacred kitchen table.

"Well, we shall have to talk again," Jutta said.

"If that's possible," the cook replied, with a black-browed
scowl of dismissal over one round shoulder.

Later Jutta wondered if the cook's churlishness could have
been attributable to Ofsi's arrogant presence on her table. She
might be the sort of overfinicky person who thought that cats
carried the plague or something. It was a very clean kitchen,
she recalled, with no chickens running about with their usual
mess and loose feathers. Some cooks even permitted their favorite pig to warm herself on the hearth, not to mention the oc-
casional half-dead newborn lamb or calf or goat.

She decided not to complain about the cook's rudeness to
Frida, and she also decided to attempt to teach Ofsi some manners. He might sit in her lap at the table, but he was no longer
going to be allowed free run of the tabletop.

She found Frida poring over her books in her room, casually
dressed in a plain white gown.

"Tonight is the third night of our ritual," Frida said, "and the
second night of Brjaladur. For the last two nights we awakened
the sleeping powers of the earth with an offering of blood, and
tonight we shall do the ceremonial beating of the bounds. It
was a very old and charming ritual, with the elders of the clan
walking the young children around the perimeters of their land,
teaching them the boundaries between what was theirs and

what was nature's. It was always done at a significant moment in the cycle of the planets or a changing of season. I've invited several of the young girls from hereabouts to attend, and you of course must be there."

"Thank you, it will be an honor," Jutta said.

They assembled at dusk, all the women of Frida's ley-walking group, and they set out as soon as the stars began to appear in the sky. It was warm and pleasant, and everyone seemed to be in a festive humor as they rode along. The full moon made it almost like morning.

"We shall go to the top of that hill," Frida said, pointing to a stone cairn standing on the crown of the hill. "That is the northwest corner of Thorungard. By the time we're finished, I promise you'll all have worked up an appetite."

From the crest of the hill the boundary went down into a wide meadow and toward a deep ravine that gouged a huge black scar across the silvery velvet of the meadow.

"From here," Frida said, reining in her horse, "we go north toward the barrows."

"But the barrows aren't part of Thorungard," Jutta said. Ofsi was struggling around in his sack, scratching to get out. Frida had almost talked her into leaving him behind, and now she wished she had.

"Boundaries are not always established by mere men," Frida said. "Asgerda, light down from your horse. For this part of the ritual it is more like playing hare and hounds. We are the hounds; you are the hare. We shall give you a head start, and you are to run as fast as you can straight north along that old fallen wall you see there. You may start whenever you are ready. Leave your cloak."

"I shall do my best," Asgerda said. She dismounted and removed her cloak so she could run better and tied up her laces. Then she took off at a light-footed run, her white blouse a white spot in the gloom. Frida had just given it to her to wear to the ritual that night, and she had been most proud of it.

Frida gave the signal, and they started after her at a slow trot, gradually increasing to a canter as they closed the distance between themselves and the white patch that was Asgerda.

Asgerda's white face flashed as she glanced over her shoulder at the galloping horses. Jutta started to pull up, but the others flailed right on past her, urging their horses onward.

"Run, run!" Frida screamed, and the others echoed her.

The first rider to overtake Asgerda dealt her a solid whack on the shoulder with her stick. Before Jutta's astonished eyes, several other women also aimed vicious blows at the fleeing Asgerda. The girl screamed and ran, trying to twist and dodge. The riders drew back to let her get ahead.

"Run, run, run!" Frida shouted in a frenzied shriek. "If you can make it to Sigmund's barrow, you will be safe!"

Jutta spurred her horse alongside Frida's in the short interim and forced her to a halt, while the others went screaming on, pursuing their prey. "What are you doing? Are you mad?" she exclaimed. "She doesn't know where Sigmund's barrow is! Nobody does!"

"Perhaps if she is lucky, she will find it!" Frida cried. "It's the power of the earth and the standing stones! One day that power will guide my rabbit to Sigmund's lair!"

"You're going to kill her!" Jutta gasped.

"Yes! The blood is an offering to the earth! It's a very thirsty earth, and these barrows are full of nothing but dust. It's been too long since it was enriched with a feast of fresh blood. So I have promised, and so I will be rewarded with the secret of Sigmund's cup. Don't tell me you're going to be squeamish. I thought you had enough steel in you to know that sacrifices must be made for immense power."

For a moment their eyes locked, dark pools in the silvery moonlight, as Jutta struggled against the undeniable waves of revelation crashing down over her.

"Then you killed all those others!" Jutta gasped.

"Yes. But they were nobody, nothing anyone cared about. Poor working trash, all of them, doomed to die soon enough anyway from poor food and overwork. Better to let them rest than keep on struggling." Frida added a throaty chuckle, which sounded a little strained.

"And last night? That was no sheep, was it? It was Hallgrima, wasn't it?"

"Hallgrima it was, and she was glad to be sacrificed for the cause."

"Frida, you must stop. You mustn't kill any more women."

"But I must if I am to have that cup. Don't be foolish, Jutta. I thought you and I were cut from the same cloth. I thought you were strong and sensible like me and the rest of my friends."

"I am, I am, but you must stop this killing. What if you are caught someday? You'll be hanged!"

"I shan't get caught, and if I did, no one would be angry at me for merely ridding the world of its scrofulous scum. I have killed no one of importance; therefore, I have killed no one."

She spurred her horse then, leading the charge after the fleeing white spot that was Asgerda. Jutta charged after Frida, recklessly cutting off several other riders and forcing them to rein in sharply to avoid a collision. Angry at her, they raced ahead of her, brandishing their sticks and shrieking like witches.

Asgerda fell down under a merciless barrage of blows, struggling to get to her feet, attempting to shield her head with her arm. Gasping, begging for pity, she stumbled away from her tormentors, who again waited to let her get ahead.

"Run, run, little hare, and find Sigmund's barrow!" Frida cried. "Let the earth spirits lead you to safety! Now do you smell blood, my foxhounds? The earth wants to smell her blood, also!"

"Frida!" Jutta called, riding up alongside her. "Let her go! She doesn't know where the barrow is!"

"Don't be foolish, Jutta," Frida snapped. "I'm beginning to regret bringing you here tonight."

"Frida, if you'll let her escape, I'll take you to Sigmund's barrow," Jutta said. "I know where it is. I found it a few days ago. Please let her go. There's no need to kill her."

CHAPTER 20

"And you didn't tell me?"

"I didn't want to tell you like this." Jutta snarled, her heart pounding, and not just from the breakneck race across the uneven ground. "Not with these others swarming around. I thought that just you and I would share it, not a crowd of other people."

"I see. You're pretty smart, after all. Maybe these vultures are the ones I should have been getting rid of all these years instead of innocent girls." Frida laughed, a cold and heartless sound. "I had a feeling you would be the one to lead me to the cup. From the moment we met in the barrows that day I felt that you knew more than you cared to tell me. How did you come to find the barrow?"

"You know who my grandmothers are," Jutta said, "and what. I wanted to tell you, but my grandmothers forbade me to come to you."

"Yes, your grandmothers, of course. I've had a feeling about them for a long time, even before we knew they were Myrkriddir. We shall have to fix them, won't we? Now, then, you shall take me to the barrow."

"Not tonight. Wait until these others are not here. Tomorrow night. Otherwise, you'll have to share it so much, there might not be anything left for you."

Frida hesitated, while Jutta's heart pounded so hard that she was afraid it was audible.

"Very well, tomorrow night, although it's a bitter thing to have to wait," Frida said. She whistled to the others, riding ahead, and they stopped to look back at her in surprise. "I do hate to deprive them of their fun. They've gotten to look forward to our little game of hare and hounds."

"They must get used to being disappointed," Jutta said in a low, rapid tone. "I for one don't intend to share that cup with everyone. It wouldn't be fair. You've done so much of the work to find out the secrets of the earth, and what have they done? Eat your food and drink your ale and chase around on the barrows at night. You owe them nothing."

"Jutta, you've read my mind exactly. That's what I liked about you from the start. You know the truth, and you aren't afraid to say it. Tomorrow night, then, we shall receive our prize."

Frida again whistled sharply to her companions, who had resumed following Asgerda. They turned around to look at her again in amazement.

"We're going home," she said. "Let this hare escape."

The women made disgruntled and puzzled mutterings as they rode back to Thorungard, keeping well behind Frida and Jutta.

"They're talking back there," Frida said. "I hope they don't think they're plotting an insurrection. Surely they remember that I can hang them, every single one, for their involvement in eleven barrow field murders."

"Murder is a strong word," Jutta murmured, realizing that she, too, had just involved herself as deeply with the killings as any of the others.

"I prefer to think of them as ritual sacrifices," Frida said. "A murder is usually for gain of some sort. No one can say we've gained anything from our ceremonies—at least, not until now." She smiled conspiratorially at Jutta and gave her arm a sharp little dig with her fingers as they rode stirrup to stirrup. "Whatever is that furry little fiend doing, scratching around like that?"

Ofsi struggled furiously to get out of his kettir sack.

"I don't know," Jutta said. "He's been very restless tonight. Usually he enjoys riding along on a horse. He seemed very happy last time we were at Thorungard."

"Perhaps you should have left him at Bardhol."

The troop of women returned to Thorungard and had a rather disgruntled very early morning breakfast. No one seemed very talkative, and Jutta felt suspicious eyes turned in her direction. Rather to everyone's astonishment, Asgerda came creeping in at the back door, with the dried blood still in her hair and streaking down her cheek. With huge frightened eyes she crept into the kitchen and curled up in her usual place on the sleeping platform near the old and ancient hearth from the original hall, which most of the house had been added on to over the years. She pulled up her eider and soon appeared to be asleep.

"What about Asgerda?" Jutta whispered under the cover of the women's chat. "Won't she tell someone what almost happened to her tonight?"

"Oh, no one would believe it," Frida said with a careless wave of one hand and a weary yawn. "No one from her station in life had better speak out against someone like us. What's she going to do, bring a lawsuit? Has she got nine neighbors that would stand up against me? I think she would be hard pressed to find nine neighbors who are not already present in this kitchen."

Jutta looked around unwillingly and shuddered at the faces she recognized, all powerful women of substance, land, and wealth, married to men of the same ilk, most of them, unless they were widowed. They were exactly the kind of women who would associate with her mother and whom she had once dreamed of associating with herself. Now they looked like nothing more than a flock of black-cloaked vultures grouped around the table, cackling and squawking as they fed on rotting flesh.

"I believe I'll go to bed," Jutta said, not having to feign great exhaustion.

"And tomorrow we shall come to the end of our hunt," Frida said with a covert little smile. "Sleep well. I expect tomorrow night may be quite taxing."

When Jutta had the door to her room safely shut, Ofsi leapt out of his sack and raced around in a state of wrath. If she attempted to pick him up, he bit and kicked at her until she had to drop him. He investigated every dark corner, uttering hoarse, determined little yowls. Finally Jutta gathered him up in spite of himself and took him outside, thinking he wanted to dig a hole. Once out of the house, he frolicked around in the lush soft grass, leaping at her and scuttling away in an invitation to chase.

"Ofsi, what am I going to do?" she murmured, picking him up for a moment to hear his busy purring and pattering heartbeat.

Ofsi struggled frantically to get down and bounced away, yowling back at her imperiously. She observed that the sky was beginning to light up faintly in the east. The lights had gone out in the kitchen, and Frida's house of day-sleeping nightfarers was dark. Ofsi yowled demandingly, and when she continued to ignore him, he sprinted up to her and bit her ankle. Then he dashed away, glancing back to see if she followed. It wasn't lost on her that he was heading in the direction of Bardhol.

Jutta impulsively scooped him up and hugged him to her cheek, wondering what would become of him if something happened to her. Would he die because he was made of and especially for her, or would he heartlessly attach himself to the next human who came by and wanted him? Would he remember her, if kettir were capable of remembering anything? Would he go back to Bardhol with the other kettir and wait for a more suitable and intelligent owner? Was a secondhand kettir any good for anything?

When she sat down cross-legged in the tall summer grass, Ofsi sprang into her lap, purring loud and hard. He stood up and pawed at her face, fascinated by the tears rolling down her cheeks. His golden, unblinking eyes stared into her face with unusual intensity, even for a kitten who never shut his wide eyes except when he was asleep. He had huge round eyes, and he often stared into her face as if he wanted to talk. Suddenly resolved, Jutta stood up, pointed herself in the direction of Bardhol, and started walking. Ofsi scampered at her heels, clearly delighted, as if this were what he had intended all along.

Very soon Ofsi was tired of racing and playing and attempted to climb up Jutta's pantaloons into his kettir sack. She scarcely hesitated long enough to shove him inside, glad that this would make it easier to tell him good-bye.

She found Tova at the edge of the meadow, calling in the cows for milking and waving a long switch to encourage them in their leisurely ambling toward the barn. They smelled of milk and sweet grass breath, strolling along and taking time for grazing as they walked.

"Tova!" Jutta called, and Tova looked around eagerly.

"Jutta! Are you back?" she called in delight.

"Just for a moment," Jutta said. "I've got to return before Frida misses me. How are my grandmothers?"

"Dismayed," Tova said. "I told them where you had gone. Margret got that grim look, when she knows she's right and the rest of the world is wrong, and said that you'd live to rue the day you ever saw that woman. Why do you have to go back in such a hurry?"

"Frida doesn't know I'm here. Listen, I must give you Ofsi. He's a terrible little nuisance where I am, and I don't want him to get—" Hurt, she had meant to say, but she didn't want to upset Tova, who would probably tell her grandmothers she had gotten herself into some sort of trouble. "—in the way," she finished a bit lamely.

"You can't give me Ofsi," Tova said. "He belongs with you forever."

"Well, perhaps I'll be back for him," Jutta said. "Another thing you must do: Go to Einarr and Petrus and tell them to meet me at the barrow tonight around midnight. Tell them I learned something from Frida and her rituals. Tell them that I am bringing them something they've wanted to find for a long time."

"Jutta! This all sounds very strange," Tova said.

"It is strange, but it will be all right. Just do exactly as I tell you, if you value my life. Now here, take Ofsi. I've got to go."

She thrust the kettir sack into Tova's hands and turned away to hide the tears in her eyes. Ofsi knew that he had been abandoned and set up an indignant caterwauling.

"Jutta! Jutta! Wait! Can't you explain?" Tova called after her, hindered by the cows and a furious little kettir.

"No, I can't," Jutta replied, hurrying away as fast as she could go.

When she got back to Thorungard, she slipped into the kitchen, where she found Frida waiting impatiently for her.

"And where have you been so early?" Frida demanded.

"I took Ofsi back to Bardhol," Jutta said. "He was only going to be in the way here."

"That's certainly true enough," Frida said, still boring her eyes into Jutta, detecting every falsehood and attempted deceit. "Why didn't you tell me you were going?"

"Everyone was in bed. The idea came to me just before dawn. I found Tova bringing in the cows, so I didn't have to go to the house to speak directly with my grandmothers."

"That's good," Frida said. "I'm sure they could have seen straight through you, although you are a rather good liar. You don't even turn pale or red or appear nervous."

"I'm sorry you think I'm lying," Jutta said quite truthfully. "But I said I would take you to the cup, and that's exactly what I intend to do. I knew from the very beginning that if you and I had that cup, then I would realize all my dreams of the fine life which I hope awaits me. I lay in wait for my grandmothers, I snooped in their trunks and boxes, I spied on them, and I sneaked out at night. Isn't this enough to prove to you that I am completely committed to our cause and trustworthy?"

Frida sighed and released her arm, which she had been digging into with her fingers. "Perhaps I am overtired. Distrust is a curse which blights my brain. So many of these cackling women would stab me in the back at the slightest excuse, and I know it well. If I didn't have them by their throats, then I would be worried. So you are still loyal to me and none other?"

"That's why I gave them back their cat. I wanted to be free of all reminders of Bardhol. I have completely washed my hands of them. From now on you are the only one I will honor."

"That's good," Frida said with a small and rather contemptuous smile. "I am glad I could never accuse you of ingratitude, at least."

Jutta had no trouble thinking up something else stupid to say. "They did their best, I must say, but I must also say that five old women on a worn-out farm are simply not up to my mark. Even if they are Myrkriddir, and I'm beginning to think that may have been a trick."

"My dear, I assure you it's no trick. Your grandmothers are the ghastly, harrowing hags of the barrows. I meant to tell you before, but in all cases we actually let our rabbit escape before she was killed."

Jutta stared for a moment, astonished. "You do? But I saw you hitting Asgerda with sticks. She was bleeding. Eleven women have been killed or not found. You yourself said you held the ax of eleven killings over the others to keep them silent."

"You must have misunderstood me," Frida said with a scowl. "I killed no one. We always released the rabbit when she couldn't run anymore. Then the Myrkriddir finished her off when we were gone. But to anyone from the outside looking in, it would look as if we were responsible, wouldn't it?"

"Yes, I suppose it would," Jutta said.

"And you saw us release the rabbit with your own eyes, didn't you? Didn't you?"

"Yes, I did—"

"And that's how it always is. Oh, we must make her think she's about to be killed. That's the emotion that we require in order to find the barrow. That absolute terror and the knowledge that death is near releases all manner of fascinating powers that we can capture if we know how. You saw Asgerda coming back into the kitchen. She wasn't harmed in any way, luckily. A fortunate thing I made those horses too sick to be of any use for a while."

"What? You made the horses sick?"

"Oh, it was just a little herb I sprinkled around on some tempting clover."

"They nearly died."

"I do feel rather remorseful about that. I think I shall send a little gift to Bardhol to compensate—a nice joint of meat, perhaps. I shall prepare it myself. In fact, since I'm feeling so generous, I believe I shall send one to Einarr Sorenson, also."

Jutta drew a deep breath, trying to convince herself that she felt better. "Well, no harm has been done."

"Small loss indeed, since they are Myrkriddir horses. I had the best of intentions for everyone. If the horses had died, that would have been the end of the Myrkriddir of Mikillborg. A pity that meddling fool Bjalfur interfered."

"Bjalfur interfered? How? I didn't see him do anything," Jutta said. "He's just an old hermit with a very messy house and an extremely ugly old dog."

Frida tossed her head back and laughed. "Yes, and he is an extremely ugly old dog himself, isn't he? My dear, you are simply too precious for words. Now tell me exactly how it was you found the cup."

"I followed my grandmothers one night when they went out. They tried to drug me with something in the warm milk they like to take every night at bedtime. They made a great fuss about being tired and how a nice warm drink always put them right to sleep, and since I don't much like warm milk, I put mine in the kettir pan. Before long, all the cats were unconscious, and I knew they had tried to drug me. So I lay awake and listened and followed them when they went out. They went straight to a certain barrow, one quite far from the stone circle and nothing remarkable at all to look at, because most of it is underground and it's nearly buried by brush. They went inside for a long time, getting power from Sigmund's cup, I suppose. When they were gone, I went inside, too, and I saw it."

"Why didn't you take it then and bring it to me?" Frida demanded, a fierce light in her eyes.

"Because it's held tight in Sigmund's fist," Jutta said. "Whenever anyone tries to take it, he refuses to let it go and the other corpses sitting around the table start shaking and screaming and the ground shakes."

"This sounds like something your grandmothers would do," Frida muttered. "Or maybe old Bjalfur."

"He's there," Jutta said. "I've seen him lurking around the barrows and trying to frighten everyone off."

"Everyone?" Frida pounced. "There are others? Who else knows about this?"

"No one important," Jutta said with a slight and telling stammer. "Just—just a couple of friends of mine and Tova."

"Oh, hardly anyone at all," Frida snapped. "Who are these friends of yours?"

"Just—Simon, the Scipling. And Leckny."

"Leckny? Isn't the chieftain's son named Leckny?"

"Yes. That's him, I suppose."

"Ha! The chieftain's son. A Scipling we can do away with and no one would care, but Einarr isn't going to sit still for someone killing his son."

"Killing his son? Why do you have to kill anyone?"

"If they know about it, they'll be after it. This is a worse mess than I thought. How careless of you, Jutta, to tell everyone you know about Sigmund's cup. How do we know they haven't stolen it by now?"

"The barrow is a very frightening place," Jutta said. "No one who tries to take that cup once will want to repeat the experience. Leckny and Simon are not as determined about getting it, either. As long as it looked like simple barrow robbing, they were interested, but now that it's become so difficult, they don't know what to do. They are waiting for me to do something. I don't believe they'll get in the way, and if they do, they're easily frightened."

"Nothing shall stand in the way of my getting that cup," Frida said. "It is the reason I took this house. I didn't inherit it, as you've been told, although no one is around any longer to contest my ownership, if you know what I mean."

Jutta felt a chill at the marrow of her bones that spread to goose bumps all over her from scalp to heels. All her instincts for self-preservation were wide-eyed with alarm and shouting warnings to her. She had done well to get Ofsi out of this place. Still she managed a small smile and a vague nod of her head.

"I think I'd like to get some sleep now," she said, stretching her arms and offering a convincing yawn.

Frida escorted her to her room, chatting pleasantly the whole way, and the moment Jutta was inside, she heard the soft sound of a key turning in the lock outside. Holding her breath, she listened a long moment before she heard Frida's soft shoes go padding away down the rush matting of the corridor.

Sinking down onto the comfortable feather bed, Jutta looked around at all the comforts and beauties and felt sick to her stomach with loathing for herself. She also missed Ofsi terribly, with all his comical antics, savage kittenish attacks, and sleepy cuddling and purring. Never had she felt so utterly and miserably alone, but she sternly refused to permit herself the luxury of a good bawling spree. It was time to do some fast thinking.

She looked around with what she hoped was a practical eye. The walls were several feet thick with stone and turf, but if she had two days she probably could dig a hole through them. The windows were mere slits for shooting arrows from, far too narrow to get through.

When she was sufficiently wearied from worry and lack of sleep, she curled up on the bed and fell asleep, still shedding a few lonely tears onto the soft pillow. A soft pillow in an enemy's house was scant comfort, she decided. Better to sleep on stones with someone you could trust. And never again, if she got out of this alive, would she ever go anywhere without Ofsi.

Considerably later she became aware of a comforting warmth in the hollow of her back and a soothing rumbling sound emanating from it. All her fears seemed like inconsequential things that would soon go away. As she came closer to the surface of sleep, she identified the rumbling lump as a cat, far too large to be Ofsi. Sitting up, she recognized a great furry black heap as Svartur. He opened one eye slyly and smiled at her, with his whiskers bushing out with gladness to see her.

"Svartur! What are you doing here?" she whispered, suddenly smitten with a powerful yearning for Bardhol and everything in it. She also wondered why the grandmothers had invented such a creature without giving it the power of human speech. She desperately wanted to know if all was well at Bardhol, if they missed her or talked about her.

Purring, Svartur gazed at her through half-shut eyes and kneaded his large paws affectionately, as if to reassure her that all was well. She astonished him with a breathtaking hug, from which he politely detached himself after a few moments, hastily licking down a ruffled spot of fur.

"Svartur, what am I going to do?" Jutta whispered.

Svartur blinked sleepily. He stood up on his toes, arched his back, and yawned until his head seemed to come in half, then he sat down and licked his belly fur.

The key turned softly in the lock. Lightly as a feather Svartur leapt to the window slit and vanished as the door opened. It was only one of the serving girls with a tray of food, and Frida stood barring the doorway, smiling in a friendly way, but her eyes were cold as steel.

"Why am I being held here like a prisoner?" Jutta demanded, moving forward.

"Because you are too precious to me to risk losing," Frida said soothingly. "You are not a prisoner. I am only protecting you. When the cup is in my possession, there will be no need for locks and doors. You may come and go as you wish. Did it never occur to you what danger you're in from the Myrkriddir? I shudder to think what might happen to you if they suddenly became suspicious. This is only for your own protection, and be assured that Thver and Thjodmar are guarding Thorungard carefully so that no one can come in. You are perfectly safe here."

Jutta looked out the arrow slit and saw that it was nearly sundown. She had slept long and well. She also saw a number of horses that weren't Frida's grazing in the paddock.

"I thought you would send those vultures home," Jutta said. "You're not going to show them the cup, are you?"

"No indeed, but they have their uses," Frida said. "Look, sit down to eat. I fetched enough for the two of us, so we'll have a cosy little chat while we eat."

"What's going to happen tonight?" Jutta asked. She sat down, but the sight of the food was repulsive to her.

"That all depends on you, my dear. I hope you'll lead me straight to the barrow and Sigmund's cup."

"And then?" Jutta asked.

"And then we'll do whatever we please," Frida said as she began to eat. "With that much power, we shall be free of all constraints."

Jutta was glad when Frida finally left. Svartur returned almost immediately, and she gathered him up in her arms, wishing that she could talk to Amma Margret, whose sensible advice and conduct would surely have prevented her from making such a mess. It was comforting just having Svartur there, who was a part of her great-grandmother, and the ragged wrack of fear gradually ceased racing through her brain. She sat down on the bed, still holding Svartur in her arms as she thought of a plan. Svartur put his forearms around her neck and rested his chin on her shoulder, heaving a contented purring sigh as if warning her that he was too comfortable to stay awake much longer. Then he jumped into the middle of the bed, curled up, and went straight to sleep.

When the sun was down, just barely, Svartur awakened suddenly, ears pricking and whiskers bristling alertly. Stretching and yawning, he walked over to Jutta to bump his head against her and rub around her, purring furiously. Then, with a wave of his thick black tail, he vanished through the arrow slit and did not return.

The next time she heard the key in the lock, it was nearly midnight.

"Are you ready?" Frida asked, her eyes flashing with an almost feral excitement.

"I am," Jutta said with a last glance toward the arrow slit as she followed Frida from the room.

Outside, the group of women waited on horseback, just the same as the night before: a flock of seven black vultures who feasted on death, and they were waiting for her. No one talked or laughed; it was a grimly silent company that stood there. They also carried their bounds-beating sticks like lances.

"We shall forgo the northwest boundary," Frida announced, swinging astride her horse. "We shall ride directly to the barrows tonight and resume where we left off last night, riding the far eastern ley line into the barrows. It might not specifically be my boundary, but it is a boundary of a more ancient kind and far more profitable to trace."

"Now, then, Jutta," she said when they were well past Hrokr and the crossroads cairn, "you will show us the direction of Sigmund's barrow."

"I believe this is the way," Jutta said, pointing into the oldest part of the barrows.

"This is far enough," Frida announced, after riding up and down the sides of barrows for a time. The horses puffed and blew, stumbling in the dark over mossy stones and crashing through clumps of brush. "Jutta, you will light down and lead the way on foot. The ancient traditions must be continued, and we must have our symbolic pursuit of the hare by the hounds. I think you'll have a decided advantage over the horses in this rough terrain."

Jutta knew there was no choice. As she dismounted, her legs felt weak and shaky. She took her time unfastening her cloak and tying it to the saddle. Fortunately she was wearing thick stout boots and sturdy breeches to protect her against the rocks and thorns.

"Then catch me if you can!" Jutta said, and set off toward Sigmund's barrow before anyone could deal her a whack.

Sigmund's barrow was probably a mile away, she guessed, across some of the roughest and rockiest terrain in the barrow field. With any luck, a few of the hags pursuing her would get spilled off and maybe break their necks.

They caught her twice, however, as she tired, and someone gave her a stunning thwack on the head that staggered her to the knees. It might have been finished then and there, since she was too breathless and dazed to get to her feet.

"This is not the place to kill her, you fools," Frida snapped sharply, holding back the rest of the pack with her outstretched stick. "Blood must be shed for the sacrifice, it is true, but tonight I feel in my bones that we are finally being led in the right direction. Leave her alone until I say you can have at her. Jutta, my pet, are you all right?"

Jutta wiped away the persistent trickle of blood that was soaking her hair and glared at Frida in fury and terror.

"So you are going to kill me once you get the cup?" she demanded.

"I have no choice in the matter," Frida said. "When something is taken from the realm of death and power, something else must be given in exchange. There is nothing so valued, no gift so powerful as that of a life. You should be honored that you are so chosen. Only the best will be sacrificed, the brightest life, the dearest child."

"And Lina and Betla and all those others were also the best and dearest and brightest?" Jutta demanded, getting to her feet.

"Ah, that was my mistake," Frida said. "I chose the unwanted and the poor and the dross, so no wonder I failed. Now I have the last flower of the Hesturkonur clan to offer up, and I know I shall succeed. Are you ready to resume now? I shall give you to the edge of that barrow there, where the tree is growing, before we start."

Jutta took a few more gasping breaths and started for the tree. It was not much farther, she knew, to the barrow, where Simon and Petrus and Einarr and Leckny would be waiting. She only hoped she could recognize the way in the dark. The moon shone out at intervals, then the clouds engulfed the light in strangling darkness. Luckily, when it was too dark to see, Frida and her band halted to wait for the moonlight and let their horses recover. Jutta also stopped to catch her breath and regain her strength.

Finally, after a long stretch of moonlight, she saw Sigmund's barrow looming ahead. Its top was as flat as an anvil, rising out of a crown of scrubby plum and thorn, and no bushes grew on it. Her legs were trembling, threatening to refuse even one more mad rush to get away from the trampling, cackling, stick-swinging hags who pursued her.

"This is it," she called back, panting, while a part of her wondered if they would decide to dispatch her now as part of their grisly ritual. She hoped she would have enough energy to scream loud and long for help, and she hoped that Einarr and the rest would hear instead of having their heads stuck inside the barrow, trying to figure out what to do with the cup and the screeching draugar.

Jutta pressed on, looking back over her shoulder. Frida spurred her tired horse forward eagerly, cresting the top of the barrow in a shower of rocks and sparks.

"The opening is concealed beneath a heap of brush," Jutta said between gasps. "Let me show you."

"There's no need for that," Frida said. "I shall find it by myself. Your part in this is done. Grimlaug! Jora! You may finish it now in whatever way you choose."

The ravening pack uttered a chilling cry and plunged forward, sticks waving aloft, with cries of "Run, rabbit! Save yourself if you can! Get the rabbit!"

"You're nothing but a filthy murderer!" Jutta screamed at Frida. "All that blood is upon your hands! And now you want mine, too? I'm so sorry to disappoint you!"

Jutta plunged down the slope toward the pit, crashing through the brush, heedless of the scratches and pokes it was inflicting on her.

"Leckny! Simon!" she gasped as she tumbled into the open area before the entrance.

In the moonlight she could see that no one was there and that the careful camouflage of the entrance was still untouched. They had not come, and she was alone with the black figures charging over the top of the barrow, brandishing their sticks aloft in bloodthirsty anticipation.

CHAPTER 21

Jutta's exhausted knees gave out, and she sank into the sand, gasping for breath. Frida's cold laughter floated down to her pounding ears.

"This is as good a place as any," she said as she rode down the sloping side of the barrow. "Very good, Jutta. I shall remember you often in the years to come. And to think, I shall really owe it all to you. A pity you won't be with me to enjoy it."

"I'd rather be dead," Jutta gasped, "than to live with a creature such as you!"

Frida's only answer was a laugh.

Something moved in the shadows of the underbrush and clustering stones. A small shadow darted across a patch of moonlight, straight toward Jutta, and something warm leapt right into her face. Disbelieving, she clutched at it with her numb hands, recognizing fur, claws, and a mighty purring from a tiny throat.

"Ofsi!" she whispered, knowing it could not be possible. Surely it was only a trick of her mind in the face of impending death, conjuring up comforting images to soothe her last moments.

Ofsi trilled and twittered, flinging himself against her in a glad frenzy of greeting. Other trills floated from the underbrush and the opening of the barrow as eight kettir materialized from the shadows.

Jutta crouched, clutching Ofsi in her arms; then she scuttled into the opening of the barrow with all the speed she could muster, which was astonishing, considering her condition. The tunnel was only the size of a crawling man. Surely she could stand them off from there. All she needed was a weapon, even if it was nothing but a stick.

Completely blind, she charged into the musty open feeling that was the interior of the barrow. Hands outspread, she groped around until she encountered the nearest leathery corpse. Seizing it with a shudder at the brittle boniness of the thing, she felt around for a sword, encountering at last the sheath and hilt. The corpse began to disintegrate at such rough handling. Ofsi sneezed loudly in the ensuing cloud of horrible musty dust. Jutta sneezed, too, and after a brief struggle to the death, she managed to smash and mangle the corpse into rubble before extracting the sword from its owner's sheath.

Throwing herself again to the earth, she sought out the tunnel and crawled back toward the opening, with Ofsi jumping on the calves of her legs and biting her for encouragement. She bumped softly into the other kettir in the tunnel, where they were gathering just inside the entrance. They purred greetings and whipped their tails across her face and bumped heads with her, but most of their attention was fixed on what was happening outside.

The killers had dismounted and tied their horses and were approaching the mouth of the tunnel, chattering in great excitement.

Frida stepped to the forefront without a word, and they all shrank back in sudden respectful silence. Kneeling at the entrance, Frida held up a lantern, which shone a yellow glow into the tunnel, making Jutta and the kettir all squint in its unaccustomed glare.

"Why, what on earth are you doing in here with a bunch of cats?" Frida demanded with an incredulous laugh.

"They're not cats," Jutta snapped. "They're kettir, and my grandmother created them out of precious things, and they are the most wonderful creatures on earth. Do not call them cats, for it is a woeful underestimation of their talents."

"Jutta, it's time you came out," Frida said. "We really can't begin this without you."

"I'm so sorry," Jutta said, "but you can tell those other murdering hags that I'm indisposed."

Frida crept forward a kneeling pace, and all the kettir drew back their lips, showed their teeth and curling tongues, and hissed like a nest of snakes. A singing chorus of siren wails and threatening growling filled the tunnel. In astonishment, Frida drew back.

"Nasty little brutes!" she spat, as virulent as the kettir. "They can't save you, you know."

"Try coming in after me, then, and see what happens," Jutta said. "You'll get your eyes scratched out."

"We'll see about that!" Frida brandished her stick, and the kettir all flattened their ears, growling and glaring, but they did not retreat. When she flailed at them rather ineffectually in the low tunnel, they easily dodged her clumsy swats, spitting and hissing. Jutta menaced her with the sword, wishing it were not such a great long clumsy thing. Truly it was a weapon for making huge scything motions in a large area of space. A pitchfork would have been more welcome in Jutta's situation.

Frida gave up and backed away, calling out imperiously, "Grimlaug! Come here!"

For a long moment Jutta and the kettir waited. In the meantime Jutta pulled a stub of tallow candle from her belt pouch, lit it with her tinder kit, and wedged it in a crack between two rocks. The kettir settled down their bristling fur, and the dainty little Asa sat down to wash her immaculate paws. Asa with her long silky fur resembled nothing more fearsome than a huge ball of milkweed fluff, but when she became angry, she looked four times as large and her facial expression was truly ferocious. Svartur and Mishka came over to Jutta to rub against her reassuringly, with Ofsi prancing and leaping on their backs as if it were the greatest lark of his life instead of a battle to the death.

Jutta rubbed their ears and scratched their backs, smiling through the tears running down her cheeks.

"I can scarcely believe you're all here to help me," she said to them all earnestly. "My faithful kettir friends. I only hope we make it out of this barrow alive."

They purred back at her and waved their tails. Loki kept his eyes on the tunnel, switching his red-ringed tail back and forth like a bushy warning flag.

Someone came crawling into the tunnel, face swaddled in a cloak except for an eye slit. To the rear of her Frida's voice called, "Jutta, you know you can't win against me. I wish you'd be sensible about this and realize that this is your fate and you can't deny it."

"My fate has nothing to do with being murdered by you," Jutta said, thrusting at the attacker with her sword.

The kettir backed away from the strange muffled face, hissing in alarm. "I've got you now," the woman snarled at Jutta, reaching out a wrapped hand and grabbing the sword blade.

Then Rugla sank her teeth into the woman's arm, penetrating the wrapping to the flesh below. With a shriek the woman jerked her arm around, with Rugla hanging on grimly, unmindful of the battering she was getting. The other kettir leapt to the attack also, biting and scratching furiously until the woman's cursing and shrieking from kettir bites reached an intolerable pitch.

Backing away, the wounded woman ignored Frida's furious shouting. "You try crawling in there with a dozen mad cats," Grimlaug retorted, for it was she. "I'm covered with puncture wounds and scratches. They almost got to my eyes!"

"They're nothing but cats!" Frida spewed wrathfully.

"And cats have sharp teeth and claws," Grimlaug snapped. "And they may be diseased, for all I know."

"You're a fool!" Frida spat.

Jutta laughed and hugged every kettir she could get her hands on, except Ofsi, who was too excited for anything except racing around with his tail hooked and bushy.

After quite a stretch of silence Frida poked her head inside the tunnel once again. "This is your last chance," she called. "Come out now, Jutta, and don't force me to do something unpleasant."

"I don't know how you could avoid that," Jutta said.

"You're a very unpleasant person. My mother would say you were just plain evil. I don't believe you actually came from the well-bred background you pretend to. I think you are worse than common. At least common people are not killers."

"Indeed. And common people never get anywhere with their lives. Well bred and wealthy or common as dirt and manure, it makes no difference. What really matters is what you manage to get. And I shall have Sigmund's cup, never you fear. I am so uncommon that I never rest until I have the thing that I want. Woe betide the person who stands in my way, and right now, Jutta, you are standing in my way to a fearful extent."

"And I shall continue to do so," Jutta said.

"Very well. There's no reasoning with a fool. You're as foolish as your grandmothers."

"And you tried to kill Amma Margret, too, didn't you? I suspect that business with her heart was something that you did. She might have died. And that insulting pole was your invention, wasn't it?"

"Nasty meddling old hags. The world would be better off without them and their Myrkridding. If the people of Mikillborg knew they were still dabbling in ancient magic, they would hang them instantly."

"But then you'd have nobody to take the blame for your killings. And the wild hunt over the barrows. That wasn't my grandmothers; that was you, harrying one of your victims to death."

"My dear, we must all use the means best suited to us for getting the things that we want. Your accusations are beginning to annoy me exceedingly. Why can't you stop being such a nuisance? Can't you see that there's no use in resisting your inevitable fate?"

"I shall determine my own fate, thank you."

Frida withdrew, muttering something horrible under her breath. After a few moments a wisp of smoke came curling into the tunnel. Frida was building a fire at the entrance, and the smoke was being fanned into the barrow.

The kettir flattened their ears and backed away. Jutta took

her candle stub and retreated to the center of the barrow, where she placed the candle on the table and looked around at the festive party disintegrating around the board. Heads were askew, and clothing was falling away in shreds. Jutta looked regretfully at the corpse she had flung so heedlessly away, seeing only a heap of bones and rags, with a jewel or bit of gold sparkling here and there.

"I'm sorry," Jutta said to the silent company. "But you must surely understand that when the time for battle comes, sensibilities tend to fall by the wayside. You're part of this battle now, too, you know, and I expect all of you to help in whatever way you can."

They didn't seem to hear much of her speech. Jutta watched the smoke oozing into the barrow. Already the kettir were squinting and shaking their paws in disgust, prowling restlessly, looking for a way out. Svartur uttered a hoarse and desolate yowl. One could not sink teeth and claws into smoke.

It smelled as if they were piling on green branches to make the fire more smoky and acrid. Jutta rubbed her burning eyes and looked around for a way to plug the opening. The best she could do was to drag one of the funeral chests across it and plug up as many of the holes as possible with bits of flags and tapestries. But the smoke oozed in relentlessly, like misty snakes. Jutta sat down on the floor beside Sigmund's seat, where the air was slightly less thick with smoke, and covered her mouth with a handful of her shirt. The kettir staggered around, still hopelessly searching. They were panting, their eyes huge with fright. Looking at them, Jutta knew she could not bear to watch them die before her eyes. If she gave herself up, it would be a better death than slowly suffocating in a barrow.

Her only regret was the cup. Struggling to her knees, she leaned on the table, staring at it clutched in Sigmund's blackened fist. Something must be done while she still had the strength.

"We mustn't let her have it," she said. "She'll only do more evil with it. I hope you'll forgive me, my dear ancestor, but this is war, and even in death you are not safe from its outrages."

Cringing, she seized the arm that clutched the cup and, with surprising ease, broke it off at the wrist like a rotten branch from a dead tree. Shuddering at her own temerity, she waited for the horrible shrieking and shaking to commence. Sigmund and the others sat there moldering away as if nothing had happened.

Trembling, Jutta dared to look at the object in her hands. Sigmund's fingers were still clutched around the cup as firmly as stone. Tenatively she picked at one finger to see if the dessicated claw could be pried away, but it seemed as if the cup and the hand were made of one piece. It was still a manageable thing to carry around, so she relinquished her idea of getting rid of the hand that held the cup.

"All right, ancestor, if your cup truly possesses any powers, put them to work for me now," Jutta said with a ragged breath. The smoke was almost too much to bear.

Hopefully she looked into the shiny interior of the cup, bright gold as luminous as if it had just been polished. She saw her face, curiously distorted in the metal. Then other figures swam before her eyes, and she recognized her grandmothers. Their faces were ghastly pale, and they were lying against pillows. For a moment Jutta thought she was seeing a vision of their deaths and they were lying on their funeral biers. Then she realized somehow that they were not dead but were very sick. Somehow she was present at Bardhol, and everything in the room was as perfectly clear to her as if she were standing there.

"Tainted meat," Amma Margret whispered, her papery eyelids fluttering open. "Jutta! Is that you?"

"Yes, Amma Margret, it is Jutta. I fear I'm in trouble. I'm in Sigmund's barrow."

"Thruda! Sigla!" Margret sat up unsteadily and threw off her eider. "We must go to Jutta. She needs our help. Ingi, Dora, stir yourselves. It's not that bad."

"Oh, yes, it is," Sigla groaned. "I'm dying. That woman Frida has poisoned us."

"If Bjalfur were here," Dora said in a tremulous voice, "he would heal us."

"I'll get him," Jutta said.

"Jutta? Are you here?" Thruda called. "Oh, Mother, I felt as if she blew through here like a cool breeze. What do you think it means? Is she dead?"

"I don't know," Margret muttered, tottering to her feet and clutching at the doorposts for support, "but we've got to get to that barrow somehow. She needs our help."

"Barrow? I can't even get out of bed," Sigla whimpered.

"Courage." Ingi grunted, hoisting herself up on one elbow. "Once the vomitting is done with, there's nothing much worse that can happen."

"Perhaps I can make it as far as Bjalfur's," Margret said.

"With your heart fluttering like a sick bird?" Sigla asked. "I think you'll fall down and perish before you get to the crossroads."

"The crossroads," Margret said. "Hrokr will be there. If we could get that far, he could get to Bjalfur."

"Don't go, Amma Margret," Jutta said. "I can find him much quicker."

As she spoke, Margret seemed to listen intently. "Jutta, is that you?" she said.

"Don't talk like that, Margret," Dora said with a shudder. "It makes me think you're dying."

"Jutta is here," Thruda said. "She'll help us."

The vision faded. Jutta found herself back in the barrow, coughing and clutching the cup. Focusing her thoughts on Hrokr and the crossroads cairn, she saw his image at once, tiny in the bottom of the cup and growing larger as she gazed at it. He was crouched beside the cairn with his knees drawn up to his chest, asleep and looking more like a hairy beast clad in dirty rags than the respectable and industrious farmer he once had been.

"Hrokr," she called, and his shaggy head snapped up from dozing on his chest. "You must help the Hesturkonur. Fetch Bjalfur."

"Fetch Bjalfur?" Hrokr craned his neck around warily to see if someone was speaking to him.

"Yes, to Bardhol. Hurry as fast as you can."

"Betla? Is that you? Have you come back?" he whispered.

"No, it is Jutta. If you want revenge for Betla, tell Bjalfur to hurry to Bardhol."

Hrokr got to his feet, still looking around for the person speaking to him. "Betla will be avenged," he said grimly, and set off in the direction of Bjalfur's hut as fast as he could go.

When Jutta returned to the barrow, she found the kettir lying around her feet, puffing desperately with their jaws hanging open.

"Einarr, where are you?" Jutta whispered, gazing once more into the bottom of the cup. "Leckny, have you forgotten me?"

She saw their images and saw that they, too, were almost too sick to stand, as were Petrus and Simon. They were all saddling their horses slowly and weakly, but they were as grimly determined as wounded warriors struggling back into the fray.

"We must hurry," Leckny muttered, his face positively green as he hoisted himself into his saddle. He swayed and nearly went off the other side.

"I think it was that meat from Thorungard," Simon said, clutching his stomach convulsively. "I thought at the time it was a little too aged. It had that strange smell to it."

"Let's not talk about food," Einarr said with a horrible grimace. "I'm going to become a skinny man after this. Meat is like a treacherous friend. You never know when it will turn against you."

"I don't think I've got much left to do me any harm," Petrus said, pale as a corpse. "I've nearly puked up my bootlaces."

"I've eaten bad meat before," Simon said, "but it was nothing like this. We might all be dead if I hadn't brought along my own mother's emetic from the Scipling realm. She was worried about the food here and insisted I take it along. I guess Modir was right."

"I think your Scipling emetic was worse than the poison meat," Leckny growled.

"I remember once when a group of us were out hunting Arni the outlaw," Petrus went on. "We'd gotten lost and ran out of food, and we found this beast frozen in a glacier. Some of us thought it was just a cow, some of us thought it was something enchanted, but we all ended up eating it. Talk about puking and retching—"

"Let's not, please," Einarr whimpered, mopping his perspiring brow.

"Just hurry, hurry!" Jutta gasped, and this rather discouraging vision also vanished.

She could stand it no longer. The kettir were limp, their eyes glazed, gasping faintly.

"All right, Frida! You win! I'm coming out!" Jutta called, choking, her throat burning and raw.

"How sensible of you," Frida said.

Jutta wrapped the cup and hand in a fragment of cloth and stuffed it inside her shirt. She gathered up the kettir and pushed them ahead of her. They were too limp to resist much, staggering weakly down the tunnel.

"Watch out, there's those cats!" Grimlaug cried.

A few breaths of fresh air restored the kettir, and Jutta was relieved to see them perk up almost immediately and bound away into the brush. Svartur's voice commenced a husky crooning call, eerie in the dark.

They seized her, dragging her away from the barrow, and flung her down, standing around her in a dark circle of menace.

"Watch her," Frida commanded. "Don't let her escape. We're not finished with her yet."

"Yes, you think you've won." Jutta leaned against a rock and drew in deep breaths, her head pounding and her throat burning. "But you haven't got the cup yet."

"The cup is mine!" Frida exclaimed with an excited laugh, her eyes on the barrow. "When the smoke clears, it is mine!"

Grimlaug cleared her throat. "Some of us are a little tired of hearing all this talk of mine, mine, mine. We've all worked hard to find this barrow, and the rest of us think that you had better plan on sharing that cup equally among us, Frida."

"I was only speaking in the loosest sense of 'mine,' " Frida said. "I really meant that it was yours and mine, of course. A great chieftain tends to think of all the victories of his warriors as his own victories, and it is only because he loves them so much, as I truly love all of you, my sisters. We've been searching far too long and gone through far too much together to begin to distrust each other now that we have the cup almost in our hands."

"Don't believe her," Jutta said. "She told me that she and I would be the sole sharers of the cup and that the lot of you were nothing but old vultures, and she wished she'd been killing you off instead of innocent young girls."

Grimlaug and the others made an unpleasant muttering sound among themselves as Frida protested. "What nonsense! Why should you believe her? She's doomed and she knows it, and she's saying anything to save her neck! We might just as well kill her now, so we don't have to listen to this vile nonsense she's spewing out. Look how long we've known each other—four entire years—and you're going to take her word against mine?"

"She is the great-granddaughter of Hesturkona Margret," Grimlaug said, "and you are an outsider, and we know you are a killer. I know who I'd consider the more honest."

"Oh! This perfidy strikes me to the quick!" Frida snapped. "After all I've done for you! I was willing even to kill for you, to obtain the wonderful things that you covet. I was willing to take all the risks for you, to search out a sacrifice, to find a place, to watch out for that wretched Hrokr and Einarr and those filthy, meddling Myrkriddir. Do you think I did it all for nothing but fun? I had to bear Einarr and his men always searching around, always coming to my house to ask if I'd seen or heard anything. It was I who had to worry if my servants knew something or if some of you would talk. I suffered the most for you!"

"But you are mad, and we are only greedy," Grimlaug said.

"We knew that you would one day go too far and destroy yourself. Perhaps that day has arrived."

"Oh, I don't think so," Frida retorted. "And it is true you are greedy fools, hanging about me like the vultures you are, hoping for tidbits of power once I get that cup. I warn you, once it is in my possession, I shall remember any offense you may have given me."

"'And we shall remember all the killing that has been done," Grimlaug said. "It sounds to me as if we are thoroughly married for the remainders of our lives, Frida. You'll never be rid of us. You owe us far too much just to maintain our silence."

Frida smiled. "Well, and that door swings both ways. What if I were to blame all these killings on you and say that I had nothing to do with it?"

"There's too much blood spilled for none of it to splash on your robes," Grimlaug said. "You can't taint us and not expect to be tainted, also. Now, why don't we stop quarreling and do the sensible thing and decide to get along. If we are fighting, none of us will enjoy the powers and benefits of the cup. There's plenty to go around, so why don't we just agree to milk it for all it's worth and keep our secret? We are none of us worse than the other, and certainly no better."

"That was fairly spoken, Grimlaug," Frida said. "I apologize for such a rude outburst. If I am mad, it is only because I have thought about nothing but Sigmund's cup for many more years than you have known me. And now it is within our grasp." She looked back at the barrow. "We must offer the earth powers a gift if we are to take something so valuable from it. A gift of life force and warm blood. Grimlaug, it is time for our ritual. Get your rabbit-chasing sticks, everyone. I don't think this chase will take long. We shall pursue it on foot."

The women picked up their sticks. Jutta edged away, not daring to turn her back lest they attack with a flurry of vicious blows.

"You are fools to listen to a word she says," she said. "Once a liar, always a liar. She won't ever tell you the truth. The truth of the matter is, the cup is not in that barrow. If you go in there, you'll see that Sigmund's hand has been torn off and the cup is taken away. All your killing and hoaxing have come to naught, Frida. The cup is not there."

Frida's vulpine smile froze and slowly faded. "But you told me it was there," she said.

"I lied," Jutta said. "I only wanted to save poor Asgerda. You yourself were suspicious of me or you would not have locked my door. I confess, it was all just a ploy to gain myself a little more time to escape."

"I don't believe you," Frida said, furiously clenching her fists.

"Then go into the barrow and look," Jutta said. "It is just as I told you, but the cup is gone. You should know by now that all these barrows were robbed long ago of every last valuable nail and penny."

Frida glared at her a moment, then she swiftly stooped and crawled into the barrow. When she reemerged after a few moments, her eyes were blazing. She snatched up her rabbit stick in a fury and screamed, "After her!"

Jutta's throat burned in agony as she ran, and she could scarcely draw a breath after inhaling the smoke for so long. The women and their sticks closed in rapidly. Jutta picked a place to stage her defense, with her back against a big rock, and pulled the cup and hand out of her belt pouch, wishing she knew how to unleash all those legendary powers and wonders.

"Sigmund," she whispered, "if you can do anything at all in this situation, you'd better hurry and do it."

Jutta held the cup before her and called out, "Halt! Do you see what I've got here?"

"The cup!" Frida gasped. "You liar! You said it was already gone!"

"Yes, but I didn't tell you I had taken it. But you see I've got it now, and you'd better not come any closer or there's no telling what it might do to you."

Confident again, Frida leaned on her stick. "Jutta, you clever thing. You're determined to escape from this somehow, aren't you? I don't believe you know how to make that cup work for you. I can walk right up to you and take it, which is just what I shall do. A pity you aren't going to live to get even more clever. You could have been as fearsome as Margret one day."

"Thank you," Jutta said, "but compliments are not going to take you anywhere. I've got the cup, and you dare not approach me."

"I do dare," Frida said, demonstrating her courage by walking straight toward Jutta. Extending her hand, she commanded, "Now give me that cup."

Jutta had only a moment to think about her wretched situation. Her chances of survival were extremely thin and getting thinner as her hopes of keeping the cup from Frida dwindled away.

"Then go fetch it," Jutta said, and threw the cup into the darkness as hard as she could.

Frida uttered a cry, but it turned to a nasty laugh. "Never mind. I can find it easily," she said, raising her stick. "Now let's finish what we've begun."

Jutta cringed and flung up her arms as the women swarmed toward her with ugly snarling sounds. Pebbles rained down on her head, and the snarling burst into her ears and the women shrieked. The confusion of sounds was probably a herald of death, Jutta thought, not opening her eyes as she cowered, waiting for the inescapable hail of blows. Instead, something landed on her shoulders, flattening her to the ground and knocking the wind out of her completely. Gasping, she opened her eyes and beheld the moonlit figure of a great hairy snarling dog bounding after the fleeing attackers. Nimbly it dodged a few wild swings from their sticks, and once Frida dealt him a mighty whack that scarcely slowed him down. He grabbed her stick in his huge jaws and shook her and the stick like a rat, jerking the stick out of her hands. Then he was after her, grabbing a mouthful of her cloak and bringing her down.

"Good dog! Hold fast!" Jutta called, scrambling up and grabbing Frida's stick.

"Get this beast off me!" Frida gasped, flailing at the dog with her fists and feet.

"Get her! Sic 'em!" Jutta shouted, thrusting at Frida with the stick and tripping her up as she struggled to rise.

The dog chivied Frida all the way back to the barrow as if she were an ill-tempered cow kicking at him so viciously.

Jutta expected the rest of the women to be astride their horses and gone, but they were still there, in a very silent group as they confronted Einarr and Petrus and the rest of the chieftain's queasy company.

"Einarr!" Jutta shouted hoarsely, deliriously glad to see his blocky frame clumped uncomfortably on his horse. "I want to swear a complaint of murder against these women! They tried to kill me, as they killed eleven other women in these barrows over the past few years."

"Don't be a fool, Einarr," Grimlaug said. "Do you know who I am? The wife of one of your own retainers cannot be accused of murder unless you want to lose the support of my husband, as well as the husbands of these others. Without men, you'll no longer be a chieftain over Mikillborg."

"A good point," Einarr answered, blinking in surprise.

"But these women are killers," Jutta said fiercely. "You can't just let them go! Where's your sense of justice? You can't be a true leader if you have no justice in Mikillborg!"

"There's no need for all this," Frida said loftily. "The killings will cease. Their purpose is finished. It will do Mikillborg no good to hang us and anger the husbands of these women into rebellion against Einarr."

"Silence, all of you," Einarr said, his brow corrugated in a mighty scowl. "Killings I can forgive. Barrow robbing I can also forgive. But there's one thing I cannot forgive, nor will I ever forget, and that's the crime of sending that poisoned meat to my house. You might as well have sent a dozen men with swords. I don't care if the husbands of these women come to my house with torches. They can form armies and attack me if they wish. But no one poisons my table with impunity, no one. I intend to see every one of you punished for your crimes. Never in all my days have I seen such a pack of deliberate and coldhearted killers, and never did I ever expect that the worst that I would encounter would be women."

Frida tossed her head. "I shall take that as a compliment. But the pity of it is you are a great fool, Einarr Sorenson, and I don't intend to accept your compliments or your justice, either one."

Frida spun away from the watchful teeth of Bjalfur's great ugly hound and leapt into the saddle of her horse. Spurring and shouting, she was away like lightning and disappeared into the darkness.

CHAPTER 22

"After her!" Einarr bellowed.

With a groan, Simon and Leckny set off at a rather feeble trot. Bjalfur's hound threw his head in the air with a mournful howl and charged after her.

"They'll never catch her," Grimlaug said with an unpleasant laugh. "That horse of hers is faster than anything else in this settlement. And she's got those two great ugly thralls of hers lurking about somewhere. If you value the lives of those lads, you'd better forget about us and go after them. Thver and Thjodmar wouldn't hesitate to cut their throats."

Einarr muttered some colorful curses and gathered up his reins. "There'll be no escape for you hags," he warned. "We'll track you down eventually. Come along, Petrus, Jutta; there's no sense in having any more bloodshed in these cursed barrows. Even if we do lose a few of these creatures, we'll still have them outlawed at Thingvellir come spring when the chieftains meet."

"No, wait," Jutta said, holding up her hand for silence. "Do you hear anything?"

What they heard was a singing of the wind and the thunder of hooves approaching. A bundle of mist and cloud gathered before the face of the moon, tinting its pale white rays with shimmers of rainbow. A shrill "Hallooa!" rang out over the barrows.

"Myrkriddir!" Grimlaug gasped.

"I daresay Frida's nag isn't faster than Myrkriddir horses," Jutta said pridefully. "Let them catch her. I wish they'd put her head on a stake, but knowing them, they won't. I hope they at least chase her awhile and give her a taste of the torment she dealt out to her victims."

"Not to mention that tainted meat," Einarr added, his temper kindling anew. "You know, I've been thinking she might have intended to kill us all with it. You can bet your britches I intend to mention that at the Thing, also."

"At least the cup is safe, isn't it, Jutta?" Petrus inquired anxiously. "No one could have touched it."

"The cup is no longer in the barrow," Jutta said. "I was able to remove it without too much complaint from Sigmund. The only problem is that we shall have to search for it as soon as it's light enough to see. I gave it a fling into the bushes when Frida tried to take it from me."

"No matter," Einarr said. "It's almost light."

Frida returned, riding between Simon and Leckny, with six black-cloaked figures surrounding them—Jutta's grandmothers riding respectably behind, their black cloaks muffling them to the eyes, and, to Jutta's surprise and considerable envy, Tova was the sixth Myrkriddir.

"Greetings, Margret," Einarr boomed. "This is quite a secret you've kept all these years. I should think you could have told me."

"A blowhard like you?" Margret retorted. "I should certainly think not, unless I wanted everyone to know."

"Myrkridding is a crime," Frida snarled. "You should all be hanged. I shall make a complaint of it, and I won't have any trouble raising nine neighbors against you."

"See here, you little wretch," Margret said, "we'll have none of your impertinent chatter. If not for your killings, we would not have been forced to put on these costumes again. We had to commence defending the graves of our ancestors, which were getting a bad reputation, thanks to you."

"I have no little influence at Thingvellir," Frida retorted haughtily. "I shall see to it you're punished for your crime. Plenty of people will stand witness for me."

"Barrow robbing is a worse crime," Margret said as they all dismounted, "and eleven murders and another attempted is worse yet. Whatever possessed you to think you had the right to dig up Sigmund's grave and steal his most cherished prize?"

"I didn't do it," Frida declared. "You owe this handiwork to your dear chieftain and this outlaw Scipling. Not to mention your own great-granddaughter. It was they who intended to steal from you."

Margret turned her stern glare on Einarr. "Einarr! Is this true? I've known you since you were born. Truly I am ashamed of you. At least you might have come to me and presented your idea, if you had one behind this astonishing scheme."

"I am sorry," Einarr said. "I've never had a gift for thinking things out from one end to the other before acting upon them. I was worried about the things old Bjalfur was saying about Dokkalfar and barbarians attacking Mikillborg, and everyone has heard the legends of Sigmund's powers, so I thought it was the best way to protect us all."

"And speaking of barbarians," Petrus said, "as a barbarian myself, I intend to take full blame for digging up the barrow. We barbarians tend to think it's easier to gain forgiveness than permission, so we dug into the barrow almost entirely before Einarr even knew what we were about. I'm sorry to have offended such a fine host and a good friend, but what I want most is to go home. I miss my wife and my other children, and I can't bear to think that I'll never see them again. I consulted all manner of wizards and charlatans and wasted a great deal of time and money, until one happened to tell me about Sigmund's cup. I knew it was the only way I would ever see home again."

"And I have nothing to say for myself," Jutta said. "It was pure arrogance and greed on my part. I am truly ashamed and sorry, but at least my interference has led to the capture of the killers. I hope that's good for something."

"Most certainly it is," Einarr declared. "And since I was there, I can truthfully say you never did any actual digging, since I did that mostly myself. Not that digging up a barrow is a particular crime if nothing's in it, anyway. And nothing was really stolen, since Sigmund is your ancestor and he might just as well have left that cup to you."

While he talked, Bjalfur's old hound was crashing around in the brush and loudly sniffing and snorting. Then he came trotting sedately out with something held in his jaws.

"It's the cup!" Frida gasped.

The hound approached and laid it gently at the feet of Margret, then sat down, wagging his disreputable tail.

"Good dog," Margret said, venturing to scratch his bristly head with a rasping sound, as if she were scraping muddy boots. She picked up the cup and held it aloft in the gray morning light. Even in the dimness the gold rim gleamed invitingly. She looked into it and seemed transfixed by what she saw.

"Well, we have it now, whether we want it or not," Margret said gruffly after a long moment of silence. "It's up to us to do as much good with it as we can. First of all, Einarr, I suggest you banish these women from Mikillborg until we meet again at Thingvellir in the spring to settle this matter. By then the families of these dead women will have their lawsuits prepared and know how much wevegild they want. We know all of you—Grimlaug, Brigldis, Katrina—I've known all of you most of your lives. You would all do well, I believe, to think of someplace else to stay until your trials. Certain people may be feeling vengeful. And if you do not appear at Thingvellir next spring, you'll spend the rest of your lives alone and hunted like the vermin you are. By standing trial, at least you may have a chance at pardon or banishment to some other part of Skarpsey. Personally, I would hang you all, but that is up to the mercy of the judges at the Thing. Now begone, all of you, and don't show your faces around Mikillborg. Some people may not be inclined to wait until your trials to mete out their justice."

They wasted no time in departing, riding in the opposite direction from Frida, who haughtily ignored them all, setting off at a gallop toward Thorungard.

"You're just going to let them go?" Simon demanded incredulously. "Just like that?"

"It's the Alfar way," Einarr said. "Either they come to trial or they become outlaws. If they refuse to appear before the judges at Thingvellir, they will be homeless outcasts, outlawed, with a price on their heads. We will all know what they do. If they choose to become outlaws and dare to come back here, we will hang them then."

"Sciplings wouldn't do it that way," Simon said, shaking his head. "We'd lock them up until their trials. Otherwise they might get away completely."

"Oh, they could, but Skarpsey is not a large place," Einarr said. "And no one can escape from their roots forever, even if they leave Skarpsey and go to the great continents over the sea. Something will draw them back. It is almost impossible for an Alfar to die without settling up his old debts. Let them go. Their worst punishment is living with themselves."

Tova edged forward, leading her horse, to give Jutta a breathless hug. "Jutta! I was terrified they were going to kill you!" she exclaimed. "Why did you go back?"

"I wasn't about to let her escape with the cup," Jutta explained. "Besides, I was afraid of what she might do to everyone else. She's mad, you know. But tell me, what is it like to be a Myrkriddir?"

"Very thrilling," Tova said with a laugh.

"It was the quickest way to find you once Bjalfur had cured us of that poisoned meat," Amma Thruda said. "And there was no time for discretion, so we just snatched up Tova to show us the way."

She stole an apprehensive glance toward Amma Margret, who scowled back at her, still holding the cup in her hands.

"Well," Margret said as if she had just arrived at a decision, "no further harm has been done, and we are rid of a plague of killings. But I am still shocked at you, Jutta, and disappointed that you would fall prey to such nasty feelings of greed and selfishness. That woman had you completely swayed out of your senses. Fortunately you woke up in time to save your own life and who knows how many others."

"I'm sorry I was so stupid," Jutta said. "It seems so trivial and embarrassing now. All I wanted was to be away from here, with cartloads of wealth and surrounded by other stupid, greedy people. While I was being smoked out of that barrow, I would have given all the gold in the world for just the privilege of breathing fresh air. Take that miserable cup and put it back. Seal up the barrow forever and forget where it is, for all I care. But first—" Her eye lit on Simon and Petrus. "—can't we send Simon and Petrus home?"

Margret smiled her rare wintry smile. "I believe we can do that. With the help of one of the best wizards of the realm."

She turned to look at Bjalfur's old hound, which was sitting on the ground beside Dora's horse and looking up at her worshipfully.

"You mean Bjalfur?" Jutta said, hoping the others wouldn't burst into laughter.

The hound gave her a reproachful look. He got to his feet and trotted away into the thickets, as if his feelings had been very much hurt.

"Bjalfur is not what you think," Margret said. "He came here long ago to hide from some old enemies and to put some distance between himself and the problems of the realm. He came here to retire."

"And I did a good job of it, too," Bjalfur's voice said, and he came to the edge of the pit, "until that woman commenced her killings and this Scipling came to pester me. My retirement was ruined. I had thought only to settle down in a pleasant little house somewhere with a pleasant little wife and live the life of a simple man."

Dora snorted and simpered. "Well, don't look at me!" she said, glancing around anxiously to make sure he was.

"But you said you could send us back if we had the cup," Petrus said. "Now can you do it?"

"Only if Margret will lend it to me," Bjalfur said.

Margret scowled, shaking her head with a resentful sigh. Then Svartur commenced rubbing around her ankles, bumping his head on her knees. He sharpened his claws on the toe of her boot in his endearing way of begging to be picked up and held. She gathered him up, and he sniffed inquisitively at the cup and the dead hand fastened to it.

"I suppose I shall be forced to," Margret said. "We don't want a couple of homesick Sciplings moping around here, although I'm still angry about this hole in Sigmund's barrow. The dead have been disturbed in their rest, and I have no idea what sort of consequences there might be."

"Sigmund was a good and generous man," Bjalfur said, knotting his weathered hands on the top of his walking staff. "There was no evil in him while he was alive, and you'll find no evil in him now. I believe he would prefer to see his cup and his influence used for good. It's too late to try to put everything back the way it was. Forces that bound that grave have been loosed. We must act upon them or face the consequences."

"This cup has been buried for six centuries," Margret said. "You may use it once, but then it's going back to the barrow."

Bjalfur turned to her. "Margret, you've had your head buried in the sand long enough. If you wish the clan Hesturkona to survive, look to Jutta and listen to her. Young girls are not supposed to wither away like thirsty and forgotten flowers on a rocky old mountaintop."

"I'm a rocky old mountaintop?" Margret snapped.

"Only when you're being foolish," Bjalfur said. "And if you let her go back to her father's house, the clan will sputter away to extinction."

"Don't let her go, Margret," Ingi declared. "Bardhol is so dull and boring without her. I don't care how much she misbehaves. Besides, I want to give Faelinn to her. I'm too old and brittle to break a filly."

"And I'm too old and brittle to train a young Hesturkona," Margret said, shaking her head.

"Then don't worry about it, Modir," Thruda said. "The old ways don't fit on Jutta. You won't perish if the ways of the Hesturkona are changed."

"We have no more use for warriors," Sigla said, "but we could make money on horses and ale. And look at Thruda's fine weaving and Dora's wonderful jackets and shirts and pantaloons. People like to buy fine things now instead of making war. We could take in apprentices to teach them our skills."

"Ah! You want to turn us into merchants?" Margret cried. "I wish I'd died that day I beat Tova at wall building!"

"Think of the fame we could restore to the clan with our fine horses," Ingi said, rubbing her hands together excitedly. "Jutta and Tova can train them. We need new blood—and the horses do, too."

"We shan't quarrel about it in front of strangers," Margret said with freezing dignity, casting her eye in the direction of Einarr and Petrus. "It's time we went home. We shall talk, of course, about sending the Sciplings home. This other matter— well, Jutta needn't go anywhere until it is decided. Bardhol will always be her home as long as she wants to come there."

"There's no time for idle chitchat," Bjalfur said, rapping his staff on the ground. "We have one more night of this full moon before it begins to wane, and we must send the Sciplings back through the gateway into their realm. Tomorrow at midnight, Margret, we must meet in the stone circle—with the cup."

"I never thought I'd live to see the day an old hermit living in a hut would be ordering me about," Margret growled. "All right, I'll be there, with the cup. No one had better be late. And you, young Einarr, I shall have to talk with you later and remind you of your manners. Your lovely mother has been dead too long, and it seems your wife is far too kind to you. I shall have to give her some instructions on the proper treatment of husbands. Come along, Jutta, Tova, don't dawdle."

"It's high time we were home, too," Einarr said with an uncouth yawning and stretching. "I hope this will be the end of this nightlife. I'm getting too old to fool around all night and work all day, too."

"We shall walk home, Amma Margret," Jutta said. "Please?"

Margret bristled, opening her mouth for a sharp retort.

"It will be all right, Modir," Thruda said. "Let them come along as they wish, and they will come; try to drag them, and they will surely resist all that you try to tell them."

"Very well," Margret said. "But I don't have to like this new way, do I?"

"No, Modir, you may complain all you wish."

"Good. Complaining makes me feel good."

Dora cleared her throat. "I believe we should invite Bjalfur to Bardhol for breakfast. I did make that prune pudding just yesterday, and we've such a lot of blueberries and fresh cream."

"Oh, do as you wish," Margret said with an exasperated flap of her hand. "It seems to be the new way things are done now. Whatever you wish, instead of whatever it was we thought we did to please the clan."

"There's only six of us left now," Ingi said, "so why not suit ourselves for a change?"

"There are seven," Tova said, "if your clan does adoptions."

"I guess we do," Margret said. "Don't we, Thruda?"

"Of course," Thruda said. "Tova, you are welcome, and from now on you are a Hesturkona."

"But not a Myrkriddir," Margret said firmly. "I'm going to burn those cloaks, and we're going to forget those old spells. No more Myrkridding."

Jutta and Tova lingered, and Simon and Leckny let their fathers go on without them.

"So you'll be leaving us," Jutta said to Simon. "Good luck to you wherever it is you're going."

"I've already been very lucky to see your realm," Simon said. "I'll be sorry to go but glad to get home. I shall think of all of you often and miss your company."

"Perhaps you can come back," Leckny said. "Or since we have the cup, perhaps we can go find you."

"That would be splendid," Simon said. "The Scipling realm is not so different sometimes, except that warfare is much more encouraged than peace. Einarr would like it, I'm sure."

"I would like to see far realms and strange people one day," Tova said in a wistful tone.

"With that cup, who knows what may be possible?" Leckny said in a rather gruff tone. He kept his shoulders hunched a little and glared at the ground around his feet. "Listen, I'm sorry I was such a nasty-tempered old snipe. We could've had a great deal more fun. I guess I was more jealous than anything else. I'm not great at hunting and fighting, the way my father wants me to be."

"You don't need to be," Simon said. "You're a good talker and longer on brains than most of us. Those are two weapons that will serve you better and longer than a sword and a shield. Look at Jutta. She didn't capture these killers with a great bloodbath."

"It wouldn't have done her any good to try fighting," Leckny said. "She's too scrawny. By default, she's been forced to develop her brains."

"And you, on the other hand, were sitting at home stuffing yourselves with poisoned meat," Jutta snapped. "It was a very near thing, thanks to you."

"You'd have thought of something," Leckny said with an odious grin. "The fearless Hesturkona, ever resourceful, triumphs again. I can scarcely wait to see what you'll do next. Bardhol is going to become famous for horses, shirts, beer, and cats." Ofsi, Bensi, and the other kettir were twining around all their ankles, purring and trilling with approval.

"Don't call them cats," Jutta said, picking Ofsi off her breeches as if he were a large and demanding cocklebur. "They're far more than just cats; they're kettir. My grandmother Thruda brews a very fine kettle of kettir, indeed. I think we must be going now, Tova. The kettir are asking for their breakfasts."

"Can't they eat mice?" Leckny demanded.

"Only for recreation," Tova replied, elevating her chin haughtily. "Come along, Bensi dear."

Jutta marched away smartly with a procession of kettir following, waving the tips of their tails pleasurably, as if they thoroughly enjoyed being taken for a nice walk at dawn. Looking back and counting, Jutta perceived that Rugla and Asa had wandered off somewhere, perhaps tempted by the aroma of a field mouse.

"Kettirkettirkettirkettir!" Jutta trilled in a thrilling rendition of Amma Thruda's kettir call.

Amma Margret spent most of the day stalking around muttering darkly, "I don't know what's going to become of us," or sitting at the table with the cup before her and grumbling, "Nothing good can come of this."

"I don't believe that hand is very sanitary," Sigla observed with a shudder. "Must you put it on the table?"

"It's the hand of your own forefather," Ingi said indignantly. "Have a little respect!"

In the end Margret sent Leckny to fetch Dalla for a calling of the clan. "She's got a right to know," Margret said. "After all, she is my own daughter, no matter which way she has gone with her life, and we must tell her that the ways of the clan are changing. I wonder if she's still got that old stallion."

Jutta cleared her throat. "It's time for some new blood, Amma Margret. There are some wonderful stallions over Threlkeld way which I intend to go look at."

"Crossbreeding?" Margret gasped. "They won't be Hesturkona horses anymore!"

"Of course they will," Jutta said. "If we are Hesturkonur, then our horses are Hesturkona horses. What I'd like to see," she continued, turning to Ingi, "is a little more bone in our horses, and heavier substance."

"But these cart horses nowdays can look like such great cloddy horses sometimes," Ingi protested. "It has taken almost forever to refine the Hesturkona horse to what it is today."

"We may have to sacrifice some of the refinement if we want more size," Jutta went on with a frown. "A larger horse is needed if it is to be truly useful."

Amma Margret flapped one hand in disgust and strode away, leaving them to argue endlessly about the future of the Hesturkona horse.

At midnight everyone gathered at the stone circle, where a fire was built at the base of the central stone. The grandmothers, Jutta and Tova, Einarr and Leckny, the Sciplings, and the kettir all arranged themselves in a respectful half circle with Bjalfur at the center. Margret reluctantly passed the cup into old Bjalfur's weathered hands as they stood inside the stone circle.

"Don't make a fool of yourself, now," she warned.

"I'm far too old to care if I'm a fool or not," Bjalfur said.

"Dora knows what a fool I am. I shan't hide it. Now, then, my friend Sigmund, what do you and your cup require to send these travelers home? I hope I won't be expected to perform too many gymnastics. At my age it's getting rather difficult."

He tapped the earth with his blackened old staff, closed his eyes, and cleared his throat. What followed sounded like a rather meandering and seemingly interminable song, sung mostly through his nose, and a few vague symbols sketched in the air. Jutta met Leckny's questioning stare and had to smother a laugh when he hoisted one eyebrow to an incredulous position.

"Well, all right, that's done," Bjalfur said abruptly, his eye snapping open as if he had just awakened from a good nap. He shook hands with the two Sciplings. "Good-bye, good-bye. It's been pleasant meeting you. Enjoy your journey."

"Farewell, then." The Sciplings hoisted their bulging packs to their shoulders, laden with all manner of gifts and food. "Until we meet again, wherever that might be."

Simon whispered, "Are you sure we're going anywhere? I don't see anything different."

"Just walk over there, between those two stones," Bjalfur directed. "The two that look like a gateway, with the arch over the top."

The Sciplings stepped through rather hesitantly and turned to look back. As Simon raised one hand in farewell, their images misted over and disappeared, leaving the half circle of Alfar and kettir staring at nothing.

"Well, that looked easy," Einarr exclaimed, blinking in astonishment. "Bjalfur, I must talk to you. I think we can do a great deal of business. I've got this horse that's been lame for over a year, and my barn has a corner settling into soft earth—"

"Of course, my friend, we can solve all your problems," Bjalfur said. "But you realize, for every time I've gone into the realms of power and spirit to ask for an exchange, a price has been exacted. The elements and fate became more jealous and reluctant with the increase of petitions from an inceasing number of wizards. Do you see this hollow eye socket? For my eye, I ransomed a king from death. Usually we have no idea what price is going to be extorted. What is it worth to you to cure your horse or fix your barn? An eye? Your right hand, perhaps? Your son?"

"Never mind," Einarr said hastily. "A lame horse and a sagging barn are evils I can easily live with. Life is uncertain enough without messing with powers."

"Exactly, my friend. And if you are attacked by your enemies?"

"I can raise up an army," Einarr said. "We can defend Mikillborg by natural means."

"Or better yet," Leckny said, "we can try to talk them out of their grudge against us. Perhaps their claims are legitimate. We may need to negotiate."

Bjalfur returned the cup to Margret, who put it quickly into a bag, drew up the strings, and knotted them decisively. "I don't want to see this cup used again," she said. "It's far too dangerous when you have no idea what sort of trade you've just made. Something unpleasant is sure to come of this." She sniffed the freshening wind, as if testing it for evil vapors.

"I'm sure we can find a way to offset it, Modir," Thruda said, putting her arm through her mother's. "A great good deed, perhaps. Something that would benefit all mankind."

"And what might that be?" Margret queried suspiciously.

"I have a plan for the kettir," Thruda said. "Think how many more we could make if we had the power of that cup. Think what additional gifts we could give them."

"No. Never," Margret said, trying to walk away, but Thruda remained fastened to her arm.

"Now, Modir. You've often told me yourself you'd like to know what Svartur was trying to tell you. Think what a blessing it would be if kettir could speak."

"And what a cursing. They're yelling for something almost every minute." Indeed, the kettir were all getting under her feet, peering up into her face intently and setting up a chorus of yowling and purring and trilling.

"It's only because we're too stupid to understand. Come now, Modir. We've got the ability to do it now."

"Talking kettir? Never!"

"Now, Thruda," Sigla fussed, "remember how ill your mother has been. All this badgering is going to affect her heart if you're not careful. What I would like to see is a nice little house in the settlement, away from that rocky old mountain."

"With nice barns for the horses," Ingi said. "And paddocks with good walls that aren't always falling down."

"Impossible!" Margret snapped. "We aren't rich, even if we do have that cup!"

Einarr rode after them on his horse, calling out as an afterthought, "Halloa, Hesturkonur! You can't go off without your reward for capturing the killers. Since Thorungard is now standing empty and Frida's properties have all been seized by the chieftain of the settlement, which is me, I hereby award all her properties to the clan Hesturkonur, with only the stipulation that you will do something to help the orphans some of these women have left behind."

"Orphans!" Margret repeated in horror.

"Of low birth, at that," Dora muttered.

Ingi clapped her hands. "Children! How delightful! It's the quickest way we're going to bring this clan back to life. We shall adopt them all and teach them our skills."

Bjalfur nodded his head in agreement. "You are a wiser chieftain than you know, Einarr. I was getting tired of walking up that hill to Bardhol."

"Well!" Margret threw up her hands. "You may turn us into a merchant clan of beer brewers and horse breeders, and you may inundate us with orphans. But never will you force me into making talking kettir. I refuse! Now scat, all of you!" She stamped her foot at the encircling kettir, but they were not in the least frightened or even respectful. Svartur stood on his hind legs and batted at the bag holding the cup, and they all yelled demandingly.

"It's that hand grasping the cup," Jutta said to Tova and Leckny. "I think they like the smell of it."

"She doesn't have a chance," Leckny said, shaking his head. "She's doomed, and she doesn't even know it. Before long we shall know exactly what the cats are saying."

"Never!" Margret declared, but her tone was not quite as forceful as before.

In a short while the move was completed to Thorungard, with Amma Margret grumbling all the while about the soft beds and fine tapestries and elegant furniture. It was all going to be endless work to take care of and a nuisance to get accustomed to after a lifetime of deprivation at Bardhol. And servants weren't the blessing everyone supposed them to be, what with the general insolence of the serving class these days.

Dalla arrived for the moving and the settling in at Thorungard. By common consent, Jutta and her grandmothers swore a pact not to tell her anything about the cup and the Myrkridding and the Sciplings and Bjalfur. She was told a watered-down version of the truth, but she wasn't terribly content with it.

"Didn't I tell you they were up to something?" she needled at Jutta at least once a day, sensing large holes in the story somewhere. "And I still don't see how it was they came to be awarded this nice house and property. Tell me, how was it again that five creaky old ladies put a halt to the killings?"

"I told you, Modir. Their cats all meowed and woke them up, and they saw who it was, and Einarr banished them. You see, cats are good for something."

"Well, I never thought I'd hear you say so. I don't suppose you're ready to come home now the ammas have got servants to care for them."

"No. I'm part of the clan now. I'm staying here."

"But what if you marry?"

"Then he'll have to join the clan, too. Amma Margret tells me that long ago, before warfare became stylish, the clan was simply Hestur, and it was a male clan. The women took over only after the men all perished. I believe our clan should go back to the old name—clan Hestur."

"I still don't quite understand how this is all possible," Dalla went on with a perturbed frown, watching a troop of young orphans happily guiding Thruda's fine white sheep out to the meadows to graze. "I thought the old clan was almost dead, and now it is full to bursting with youth and hope and life.

Whatever have you been up to, Jutta? I feel you're keeping something from me, just like your grandmothers. And you've even turned to liking cats. It's most unforgivable."

Dalla drove away to Thorgestrstead, feeling quite left out of things and wondering if she had done the right thing in sending her daughter to live with five potty old cat keepers. There was something about those cats . . . She couldn't put her finger on it, but somehow she suspected they were the cause of all this trouble.

The kettir—as yet—had nothing to say about it.

ABOUT THE AUTHOR

Elizabeth Boyer began planning her writing career during junior high school in her rural Idaho hometown. She read almost anything the bookmobile brought and learned a great love for nature and wilderness. Science fiction in large quantities led her to Tolkien's writings, which inspired in her a great curiosity about Scandinavian folklore. Ms. Boyer is Scandinavian by descent and hopes to visit the homeland of her ancestors. She has a B.A. from Brigham Young University at Provo, Utah, in English literature.

After spending several years in the Rocky Mountain wilderness of central Utah, she and her husband now live in Utah's Oquirrh Mountains. Sharing their home are two daughters and an assortment of animals. Ms. Boyer enjoys horseback riding, cross-country skiing, and classical music.